Dare to
Be Dirty

Dare to Be Dirty

SAVANNA FOX

HEAT | NEW YORK

THE BERKLEY PUBLISHING GROUP
Published by the Penguin Group
Penguin Group (USA) Inc.
375 Hudson Street, New York, New York 10014, USA

USA I Canada I UK I Ireland I Australia I New Zealand I India I South Africa I China

Penguin Books Ltd., Registered Offices: 80 Strand, London WC2R 0RL, England
For more information about the Penguin Group, visit penguin.com.

This book is an original publication of The Berkley Publishing Group.

Library of Congress Cataloging-in-Publication Data

Fox, Savanna.
Dare to be dirty / Savanna Fox.—Heat trade paperback edition.
pages   cm   (Dirty Girls Book Club)
ISBN 978-0-425-26297-9 (pbk.)
I. Title
PS3606.O95653D37   2013
813'6—dc23   2012048948

PUBLISHING HISTORY
Heat trade paperback edition / July 2013

PRINTED IN THE UNITED STATES OF AMERICA

10 9 8 7 6 5 4 3 2 1

Cover image of leather background © Shutterstock; cover image of belt © Shutterstock.
Cover design by Danielle Abbiate.
Text design by Laura K. Corless.

AUTHOR'S NOTE

When I conceived of the Dirty Girls Book Club, I hoped that each member would have a chance to enjoy her own sexy literary inspiration and her own erotic romance. In *The Dirty Girls Book Club*, when the club read historical erotica, marketing executive Georgia Malone found her unlikely soul mate in hockey star Woody Hanrahan. Now, in *Dare to Be Dirty*, it's Kim Chang's turn. The artist and confirmed city girl doesn't believe that the words "cowboy" and "erotic" could possibly belong in the same sentence. She's about to learn differently from the book club's next selection—and the field trip to the rodeo where she sets eyes on sexy rodeo star Ty Ronan.

Thanks to my editors at Berkley, Katherine Pelz and Wendy McCurdy, for helping me bring Kim and Ty's story to life. Thanks also to my agent, Emily Sylvan Kim of Prospect Agency, for her belief in me and for always being there when I need her.

Thanks to my critique partners, the members of my own book club, and others who've offered insight, information, and support: Nazima Ali, Elizabeth Allan, Doug Arnold, Kate Austin, Kate Denby, Nick Franson, Michelle Hancock, and Alaura Ross. Couldn't have done it without you!

If you enjoy *Dare to Be Dirty*, I hope you'll check out my other titles at www.savannafox.com, where you'll find excerpts, behind-the-scenes notes, recipes, a monthly contest, my newsletter, and other goodies.

I love hearing from readers. You can contact me through my website at www.savannafox.com.

One

Kim Chang flung open the door of the Davie Street restaurant, juggling her backpack, the big bag from Opus, and a wet umbrella that refused to stay closed. Despite being what her cousin Peter referred to disparagingly as a flaky artist, she believed in traditional values like being on time. It was inconsiderate to keep the other book club members waiting. She should have known better than to go to Opus Art Supplies, where she always lost track of time.

As the hostess led her to the back of the small room, Kim glanced around. When Georgia—called George by everyone except her fiancé—had said Laziza was Mediterranean, Kim hadn't expected modern décor. Her artist's eye approved of the blue lights and deep blue ceiling, but she'd add cloth napkins in another blue, rather than those plain white paper ones.

George, Lily, and Marielle, an attractive bouquet of redhead, blonde, and brunette, had been there long enough to order drinks. Their usual white wine, martini, and fruity cocktail sat on the table.

"Sorry I'm late." Her unmanageable umbrella flipped open, showering all of them. "And now I'm totally humiliated. I could go out and start over?"

Laughing, Marielle took the umbrella and battled it into submission. She looked vibrant as always, her curly dark hair and coffee-colored skin set off by a teal-colored tee over black jeans. "Why do we live in a place where it rains in August?"

"But I love Vancouver," Kim said. "The air's so fresh." Though she adored her hometown, Hong Kong, she didn't miss its pollution. Since childhood she'd been in Vancouver a lot, and each time she arrived she sucked in huge, blissful gulps of air scented by deep blue ocean and white-capped green mountains. She felt a moment's guilt for dissing Hong Kong, the beloved city she'd return to in a couple of months when she finished up the assignments that would complete her two years of art school.

Man, she had a talent for guilt! Being late, the wet umbrella, now Hong Kong's smog—she shoved all those things aside. "I need a beer."

"Of course you do." George passed the drink menu. The marketing account manager was stunning, with her wavy red hair, creamy skin, and amber eyes, though her softly tailored suit and olive green silk blouse could have used a vibrant scarf or necklace for accent.

Kim scanned the menu. Perhaps due to her tiny size, she had a low tolerance for alcohol and generally stuck to having a single beer. British Columbia had incredible designer ales, lagers, and beers and she loved experimenting. She ordered a Hophead India Pale Ale from Kelowna.

Lily, the fourth member of their group, a married family practice doctor in her early thirties, put down her martini glass. Her khaki suit and white shirt were classy, but with her short, wheat-colored hair and light blue eyes she should be wearing blue and gold, peach and pink.

"Kim, I love that top," Lily said. "It's one of your own designs?"

"Yes, thanks." She beamed and touched her light purple silk tee with its abstract silk-screened pattern in orange, deep purple, and black. The orange was echoed on her fingernails and in the streaks in her short, spiky black hair. "It's based on the wings of the Question Mark butterfly." Wings fascinated her: butterflies, dragonflies, birds.

"You're talented," George said. "You could sell those."

"Oh, it's just a tee." Humility was ingrained, which was tough for an artist who had to learn to self-promote.

"I'd buy," Marielle agreed. "And that one with the purple butterflies you wore two weeks ago."

"You're sweet. But clothing's a hobby." At the Emily Carr University of Art + Design, students worked with a variety of media, which Kim loved. Designing and making clothes for herself—picking fabric, sewing, adding paint or silk-screening—was fun, but it didn't click as being her special thing.

Still—a shiver of panic rippled through her—she had to stop playing and get serious. She had only two months to settle on one endeavor, one that *was* her special thing, and create a business plan for making a living from her art. A plan that would wow her parents. The alternative was to join Chang Property Management, the company her mom and dad had founded. Bringing her into CPM had been their goal since before she'd even been conceived.

Kim had worked part-time there all her life. It wasn't awful, just tedious. She couldn't face a lifetime of it. Her passion was art, but, despite what her cousin said, she wasn't flaky. She had a business brain and the degree to back it up. She was determined to create a career that excited her.

Her parents didn't understand passion. They were all about security and family solidarity. She knew they were humoring her with the art thing, confident that she'd realize it should only be a hobby. That she'd return home to do her duty, to honor not only her parents but her ancestors. Oh yeah, her folks were experts when it came to laying down a guilt trip.

She brushed away the troubling thoughts. "It's our night to choose a new book. The last one was good, but man, it took so

much concentration to get through it. I could use another sexy one."
Since she'd broken up with Henry, the only sex she'd be getting in
the foreseeable future would come from fiction.

"I'm always up for sex." Marielle gave a wicked grin. She was the
one who'd suggested spicing up their selections with an occasional
dirty book, and recommended an erotic historical novel, *The Sexual
Education of Lady Emma Whitehead*.

The sex scenes were arousing, and the book stimulated discussions about sex and relationships. Ones that made Kim reexamine
her love life.

Henry was from Hong Kong too, and their parents knew each
other. When Kim came to Vancouver, the parents set up a meeting.
Henry'd already been here a few months, working in his family company's Vancouver office. Her parents had hoped that he, a few years
older than Kim, would take care of her since they weren't around
to do it. His had wanted him to date someone from a respectable
Chinese family, a girl who'd also be returning to Hong Kong. Honestly, their parents seemed to think the two of them might go wild
if left to their own devices, but neither was that kind of person. They
were both practical, responsible.

Henry was a great guy and shared the same history and values. Kim had thought she loved him and imagined them returning
home together and thrilling both sets of parents by getting married.
But, gradually, she realized something was lacking. Still, fondness,
loyalty—and habit, to be honest—had kept her with Henry.

Then the book club read the erotic novel and George had a
passionate romance with a sexy hockey star—and Kim realized her
feelings for Henry weren't strong enough for a happy marriage.
There was something missing: that spark of passion.

"I wouldn't say no to sex." George's voice broke Kim out of
her thoughts. The redhead was grinning. She sure didn't need to rely
on books for sexual stimulation, not since she'd hooked up with

Woody, the man who'd put that topaz-and-diamond engagement ring on her finger.

Kim turned to Lily. "I know you didn't want to read erotica, but you ended up enjoying Lady Emma. How about a vampire book? Vampires are *so* erotic." You could go with the fantasy, never worrying about how you'd actually get along with the guy day to day. Never finding out that what you'd taken for love would become ho-hum, and likewise for the sex.

Lily's fair brows arched. "Vampires? Kim, they're dead. How can that possibly be sexy?"

"Read, and you'll find out." But Kim wasn't pushy, so she quickly added, "But I'm open to anything else the rest of you want."

"Cowboys," Marielle said. "Those dudes are really, really hot."

"Cowboys?" the other three echoed questioningly.

Then George's lips curved again. "Okay, I can see it. An incredibly fit man on the back of a beautiful horse, shirt open at the neck, tanned skin."

"Faded jeans," Marielle put in. "Leather chaps framing an excellent package."

Lily let out an amused snort.

"Body moving in synch with the horse," Marielle went on, "with a natural rhythm, so you can just imagine him in bed with you." She winked. "Making you wet and riding you hard."

They all chuckled, then Lily said, "I admit, that's a fun sexual fantasy." She turned to Kim. "What do you think?"

Honestly? That the words "cowboy" and "erotic" didn't belong in the same sentence. A dusty, sweaty cowboy? Wearing boots with— God forbid—horse shit ingrained in them? She had only a vague notion of what cowboys did, based on a couple of Westerns she'd seen on dates, but none of it appealed to her. Herding smelly cows? Riding bucking broncs? *Oh, please.* She was a city girl. Always had been, always would be. She loved the cosmopolitan world where a woman could experiment with fashion, drink designer ale, study with incredible artists. Cowboy erotica was so *not* what she'd had in mind when she suggested reading another sexy book.

But she'd been raised to be polite, and she'd joined the club to expand her literary horizons. If she could find dead guys sexy, maybe the same would hold true for dusty, sweaty, horsey ones. "If that's what you all want, count me in."

Marielle pulled out her iPad. "I'll look for books."

Kim sipped her beer, savoring the hoppy, slightly burnt sugar taste, until Marielle said, "How about this?" A white grin split her summer-tanned Jamaican skin. "It's called *Ride Her, Cowboy*. A photojournalist is writing an article titled 'The Modern-Day Heroes of the West,' and goes along on a cattle drive where she falls madly in lust with the sexy head honcho. Look at the cover." She turned her iPad toward them, so they could see the half-naked cowboy.

"Sounds like fun," George said.

Lily rolled her eyes—she was the club member with the most highbrow taste—then said, "All right. I could handle some light entertainment."

"Fine," Kim agreed. It was only a few hours out of her life. Besides, maybe the sex scenes would be so hot, she'd forget the guy was a cowboy and get some vicarious satisfaction. She sipped her lager. "Did you order appies?"

"A Lebanese platter," George affirmed. "Falafel, hummus, stuffed grape leaves, things like that." She glanced at Marielle. "What are you doing?"

The brunette was clicking away. "Aha, I found it." She looked up. "This is why I had cowboys on the brain. On the radio this morning, I heard about a country fair and rodeo in the Fraser Valley this weekend." Eyes dancing, she said, "Ladies, let's go on a field trip."

Lily tilted her head. "You're not serious."

Kim hoped the doctor was right. She had absolutely no desire to watch a bunch of big sweaty beasts—the horses, bulls, *and* the macho idiot cowboys.

"George, take my side," Marielle pleaded.

"Well . . ." The redhead deliberated. "I condemned hockey without knowing anything about it, and I was proven wrong."

"Yeah, falling for Canada's Mr. Hockey can have that effect on a girl," Kim teased. "But you and Woody are engaged. You're not going to hook up with some cowboy."

"I might," Marielle said.

Big surprise. Marielle was all about fun; she switched jobs and men as readily as Kim changed the color of her hair streaks. For Marielle, variety was the spice of life. For Kim, variety was great in art and fashion, but when it came to relationships she believed in loyalty, commitment, and the long term.

George shot an amused glance at Marielle, then said to Kim, "No, I'm not going to hook up with a cowboy. I'm *very* happy with my fiancé."

Lucky her. Kim sensed that what George and Woody shared would really last.

George said to Lily, "I'm just saying, it's good to open yourself to new opportunities."

"Right," Marielle affirmed. "You may be—what, thirty-two?—Doc Lily, but you're way too young to be stuck in a rut."

Kim nodded. That was how she'd felt with Henry.

Lily took a sip of her usual martini, frowning a little. When they'd formed the club early in the year, the blonde had tried to take charge. She was the oldest and had an established family practice, but more than that, she just had that kind of personality. The same as Kim's parents: "I know best, so fall in line." Lily had eased up lately, though, and was more willing to listen to others' opinions. "You're right," she said. "Being open to new things is good. So, fine, if everyone wants to go to the rodeo, I'm in too."

"Woo-hoo!" Marielle lifted her girly cocktail and took a slug. Then she eyed Kim. "You're in, right? It'll be so much fun."

Sitting in the blazing sun in some outdoor arena way to hell and gone out in the country, smelling horses, sweat, and—to put it bluntly—shit? Her nose wrinkled. *Oh yeah, heaps of fun.*

She could be making art, going out with friends—or getting her butt in gear and turning her mind to that business plan. But she liked to please others. Her only rebellions to date had related to her art. First, she'd persuaded her parents to let her study art for two years in Vancouver rather than going to work full time at CPM when she got her degree in business admin. Then, she'd got them to agree that, if she came up with a business plan, they'd seriously consider letting her pursue it. Of course, she didn't think they actually believed she'd produce a reasonable plan. So far she'd proved them right.

"Kim?" Marielle's voice broke into her thoughts. "Don't let me down, girlfriend."

Kim refocused, and the conciliatory smile she'd learned as a toddler curved her lips. "Sure. It'll be a whole new experience."

"Maybe you'll start silk-screening horses onto your tees," George said.

"Go with cowboys," Marielle advised. "You'll make a fortune."

Kim barely suppressed a shudder.

Two

After book club, Kim stopped at Chapters to pick up *Ride Her, Cowboy*. The other club members usually bought the selections in e-book format, but—maybe it was the artist in her—Kim preferred the look and feel of print books. She had to admit, the semi-naked guy on the cover of this one did look better in glossy, hands-on color than on Marielle's screen. Still, the cowboy hat and the coiled rope slung over his bare, muscled shoulder weren't her thing. She was more into the suave cosmopolitan, or long-haired artistic type of man.

Laden with bags and umbrella, she returned to her Yaletown condo. She loved this building, an old brick warehouse that had been converted to apartments. Her studio was perfect, with lots of light, a hardwood floor and high ceiling, and a wall that cranked up like a garage door to reveal a tiny balcony. She'd chosen it from the options available in the two Vancouver properties owned and managed by Chang Property Management.

In the flush of Asian investment after Vancouver's Expo 86, Kim and her mom had lived in Vancouver for four years—kindergarten through third grade for Kim—as her mom checked out opportunities for CPM. Her dad visited often, and Kim's parents bought the two buildings. After her mom trained property managers, she and Kim returned to Hong Kong, but one or more of the family visited

Vancouver at least a couple of times a year to check on things. Kim had come as often as she could, maintaining friendships with kids she'd gone to school with.

Humming, she put a noodle and veggie dish in the microwave to heat while she unpacked today's purchases. When she placed the new book on the table, her gaze caught on that half-naked hottie. She'd never been with a man who had a body like that. That kind of musculature came from hard physical labor or too many self-absorbed hours at the gym, and she wasn't attracted to either kind of guy.

Henry had a slender build like her. But, while she walked everywhere and did yoga every day, the most physical labor he ever did was change a lightbulb, and he said he had no time for exercise. Still, he never gained weight, and he did have a nice body. He'd been a good lover too. Just not an exciting one. They'd been comfortable together, almost like they were already family. Was she crazy to want passion, fun, a man who'd go to galleries with her and support her in her desire to pursue her art?

She would make her parents so happy if she joined CPM and married Henry. But surely life had to be about more than duty, living up to expectations, and making others happy.

Sighing, Kim dished her dinner onto a plate painted with a Chinese design, something she'd found in a thrift shop. She settled at her two-seater table and opened *Ride Her, Cowboy*.

Speeding along the highway, Marty Westerbrook spotted a wooden sign for Lazy Z Ranch, and slowed her rental car to make the sharp turn. She had accepted hundreds of assignments in the last ten years. A photojournalist went where the story was. Sometimes that meant a resort on a tropical island; sometimes it meant a war zone.

This week's assignment fell in between. She expected heat, dust, and discomfort, but on the bright side, no one would be shooting at her. She might step in a cow pie, but that was a zillion times better than a land mine.

A cow pie? Kim prided herself on her mastery of Canadian and American slang, but she didn't know the term. Still, she could guess what it meant, and made a mental note not to wear good shoes to the rodeo.

Marty might not know much about ranches, but her research had told her this was a professional operation. The split-rail fenced fields and well-maintained outbuildings supported that.

She respected professionalism. It annoyed her that a delayed flight had made her two hours late for her appointment with Dirk Zamora, the owner of this ranch and the subject of her article.

Kim smiled. She and Marty had something in common: hating to be late.

Squinting against the blaze of afternoon sun—she should have taken her sunglasses from her duffel before tossing it in the trunk—she whipped into the parking area, searching for a sign indicating the office. There it was, on a small building attached to a large barn.

Intent on her goal, she stomped on the brake, flicked open the seat belt, flung open the door of the car, and jumped out—

Straight into the path of a huge horse, stomping its feet and blowing hay-scented gusts in her face.

She jerked backward, feeling a sting of pain as her butt whacked the edge of the open car door. Where had that horse come from? She'd ridden enough times that horses didn't scare her, but that didn't mean she wanted a giant one in her face.

Rubbing her sore butt cheek, she squinted again and peered up-ward at the rider. The sun was behind him, dazzling her, so she saw only the outline of a broad-shouldered man wearing a cowboy hat.

"Whoa there," a husky male voice drawled.

The horse, invading her space, tossed its head and puffed smelly breath.

"Yes," she said, "would you please keep your horse away from me?"

"Not speakin' to the horse. Speakin' to you. Where you off to in such a blistering hurry?"

"To the office. I'm late."

"Late's no excuse for speeding when there's animals about."

There hadn't been any animals in the parking area when she turned in. "Your horse looks like he can take care of himself."

The man gave a quick snort that might have been laughter, but all trace of humor was gone when he said, "What's your business? We're getting ready for a cattle drive."

She stepped to the side, hoping to see his features, but the horse parried her move, so Marty still couldn't see the man's face clearly.

He was trying to intimidate her, all high and mighty on his giant horse. Many men had tried, and failed. She countered with, "Would you get down here so I can see you?"

For a moment, she didn't think he'd comply. Then, with a creak of leather, he swung his powerful body across the horse's back and, quicker than she'd have believed possible, was standing in front of her. "I'm Dirk Zamora. Who are you and what do you want?"

What did she want? How could she even think, now that she could see him clearly? He was one hot, hard hunk of man. She was athletically built and stood five eight, but he loomed over her. Had to be six two or six three. Every inch muscled, solid, powerful—showcased to perfection by faded jeans, chaps, and a denim shirt, open at the neck and rolled up his forearms. The shirt revealed firm, tanned skin; the chaps framed a well-packed fly.

Lust rippled through her in a hot, shivery wave. When had she last had sex?

His Stetson shaded his face, but he took it off, saying, "Ma'am?"

She saw glossy black hair, chiseled features, and dramatic indigo eyes. The article she'd been assigned to write was titled "The Modern-Day Heroes of the West," and this man was her subject. "Well, at least you look like a hero." Damn, she hadn't meant to say that out loud.

His wingy eyebrows rose. "Hero?" And then, "Oh hell, you've got something to do with that journalist who wants to do the story."

"No, I am that journalist." She thrust out her hand. "Marty Westerbrook."

He didn't take her hand; he was too busy frowning at her. "I thought you were a man."

It had happened before: confusion due to her gender-neutral name. "How flattering." She aimed for a joking tone, hoping to soften him up since the article depended on his cooperation.

"Flattery's a waste of time," he said absentmindedly. Those near-black eyes made a slow, thorough survey: from the curly red hair she'd pulled back with a scrunchie, to her jade green eyes and unpainted lips, to the old, comfy, figure-hugging tee and jeans she'd worn for travel, to the battered walking shoes that had taken her around the world. His piercing indigo eyes warmed and sparked with something she'd have taken for attraction if they hadn't gone cold the next instant.

"No woman's coming on the cattle drive," he stated flatly. He jammed his Stetson back on his head, put his booted foot in the stirrup, and swung up into the saddle.

Male chauvinist asshole! *As he turned the horse away from her, Marty instinctively grabbed the reins. "Oh, yes, I am."*

And there she was, hanging on to God knows how many pounds of horseflesh that was snorting and stamping its feet, while a very annoyed cowboy glared down at her. "Let go or you'll get hurt."

"*No horse—or cowboy—scares me.*" *She did her best to sound believable.* "*I'm coming. You already agreed.*"

"*Hell, no, I didn't. Josie did.*"

"*Who's Josie?*" *His wife? He had to be in his mid-thirties; of course he'd be married.*

"*My ranch manager.*"

Marty knew he could rip the reins out of her grasp, but he didn't.

"*You have a female ranch manager.*" *Maybe he wasn't a total chauvinist.* "*So you can have a woman on a cattle drive.*"

There was a long pause. "*Josie's my sister.*"

Okay, a chauvinist except when it came to family. This probably wasn't the time to point out that women's lib had happened forty years ago. Better to make nice, in the interests of getting her story. A story that might well question whether an old-fashioned macho chauvinist could truly be considered a hero.

"*I won't slow you down,*" *she said.* "*I won't be any trouble.*"

He snorted again. "*Believe that when I see it.*"

Between Dirk Zamora and his horse, she was tired of being snorted at. The man might make her hormones buzz, but he was annoying as hell. She fisted her hands on her hips and stared at him, letting body language do the talking.

After another long pause, he gave a terse nod. "*We move out at dawn.*"

The horse wheeled quickly and the reins slid through her hands, leaving a tingly burn. At least that burn, unlike the one between her thighs, had a sensible explanation.

The next thing she knew, she was staring at the horse's rump, its switching tail, and the silhouette of a tall broad-shouldered back topped by a Stetson. Another shiver of heat rippled through her, a shiver of purely female awareness.

She'd said she wouldn't be any trouble, and she'd do her best to honor that promise. As for Dirk Zamora, she had a feeling "trouble" was the man's middle name.

The chapter ended and Kim looked at the time, stuck a bookmark in the book, and closed it. She ought to think seriously about developing a plan for a clothing design business, and might as well do yoga at the same time.

She pulled out her mat and changed into stretchy shorts and an exercise bra, then began her routine. As her body moved easily from position to position, she cleared her mind. Then she tried to visualize herself launching a clothing line. The images wouldn't come, and instead her thoughts wandered to the book.

Marty was crazy to be attracted to a dusty, sweaty cowboy. Yes, he was a bad boy, and bad boys were sexy. But when it came to bad boys and sexual fantasies, Kim's pick would be a man like the worldly Comte de Vergennes who'd seduced Lady Emma in the first dirty book the club had read. A bad boy did *not* have to be sweaty.

Kim had easily related to how the naïve Lady Emma had fallen for the charming Comte. Marty Westerbrook was anything but naïve, Dirk Zamora was anything but charming, and yet Marty felt an animal attraction. That was harder for Kim to relate to, but women's tastes were different.

Did Dirk Zamora feel the attraction too? He'd tried to get rid of Marty, not seduce her. It could be interesting to see how the male chauvinist cowboy and the feminist journalist were going to hook up. Okay, maybe the book wasn't as bad as Kim had expected.

She could only hope the same applied to Saturday's rodeo.

Fish out of water," Kim muttered. She passed a crazily spinning amusement park ride with people shrieking at the top of their lungs, and walked down an alley where hawkers urged her to shoot at targets or toss balls to win stuffed animals. Where was the rodeo arena?

Lily and George had decided to drive out together. Marielle said she'd bring her own car. "Keeping my options open," she'd e-mailed, "in case I find me a cowboy to go home with." Kim had chosen to go on her own too. *Not* because she hoped to pick up a cowboy, but because she might want to bail early.

City girl to her core, she didn't own a car, but belonged to the iCar car sharing program. In the cute red smart car, the drive had taken little more than an hour, but she'd entered a whole different world.

Around her, kids munched on pink cotton candy, teens in shorts stole kisses, and seniors sheltered under sun hats. The air smelled of hot dogs and popcorn, sunscreen and sweat, and sunshine baking into dusty ground.

Dressed for comfort, Kim wore cheap ballet flats, a long black cotton skirt, and a cerulean blue tank top covered by a floaty blouse she'd made herself. The silk-screened pattern, based on the Pipevine Swallowtail butterfly, was in vivid shades of blue and turquoise, with accents of black, white, and orange. She'd echoed the cerulean blue in her nail polish and the streaks in her spiky hair. The fabrics of the skirt and blouse were so light, they'd catch the slightest hint of breeze.

Except there wasn't even the rumor of a hint of a breeze.

How could so many people bear to wear jeans, boots, shirts, and cowboy hats? As the number of western types increased, she realized she'd found the arena.

There was Marielle, decked out like a cowgirl, waving a beige cowboy hat that contrasted dramatically with her dark, curly hair and coffee-colored skin.

"You look authentic," Kim greeted her, "but aren't you broiling?"

"I was born in Jamaica. Things can't get too hot for me." She winked, letting Kim know she intended a double meaning. "Here come the others." Again she waved her hat.

Kim turned to see George and Lily, both clad in capris and summer tops, Lily wearing a sun visor. "A cowboy hat?" Lily asked Marielle.

"Just bought it," she said proudly. "It's woven straw, like the rodeo cowboys wear." She settled it back on her head. "Half an hour until the first event. Let's get cold drinks and find good seats." She took a rolled magazine from under her arm. "I bought a program. The first event is calf roping, then there's saddle bronc. The one I'm really dying to see is bareback bronc riding."

"Riding a bucking horse bareback," Kim said as they walked over to a refreshment stand. "They must be insane."

"Don't they wrestle steers too?" George asked.

"Yes," Marielle said, bright-eyed. "And ride bulls."

"Insane," Kim repeated under her breath. Then, remembering something she'd noticed when she drove into the parking lot, "I saw animal rights picketers outside. Are rodeos inhumane to the horses and bulls? That would be terrible."

"I'm sure they're not," Marielle said. "Cowboys are heroes, right?"

"Right," Lily said dryly. "But seriously, I wondered about that too, so I did a little research. Rodeos are well regulated. They depend on having healthy livestock. One person said the animals are healthier than the cowboys."

"If it's anything like hockey," George said, "I'd believe that. Athletes take a beating."

Reassured, Kim joined the others in buying sodas, then they went into the arena. Wooden bleachers rose maybe ten rows high on the long sides of the oval. Excited, chattering spectators were quickly filling them.

Marielle led the group toward a section near the top with space for four. She peeled off her western shirt to reveal a pink tank that clung to her curvy breasts. She was the most generously endowed of the four of them, and played up her assets.

"I brought sunscreen." Lily took a plastic bottle from her tote.

As they passed it around, Kim studied the setup of the arena. There were pens of different sorts at the short ends, along with a section of covered stands and an announcer's booth with three men sitting in it.

One of the guys tapped the microphone, then his voice boomed out, welcoming everyone. The audience quieted, then horses and riders entered the arena, at least two dozen of them, some riders carrying banners with a variety of logos.

Kim had hardly ever seen a real live horse before. Now the ring was full of them, their legs moving powerfully and rhythmically, their coats—all shades and patterns of brown, black, and gray—gleaming, their manes and tales flying. Wow, they were really beautiful.

The riders were clad in jeans, boots, and colorful long-sleeved shirts with sponsor logos. They all wore cowboy hats, a few dark but most in shades of beige like Marielle's.

Last night, reading another couple of chapters of *Ride Her, Cowboy*, Kim had, to her surprise, developed a crush on Dirk Zamora. Not only was he incredibly handsome, but also strong, fearless, capable, and commanding. A real man, for sure.

That first night, Marty, feeling grubby and achy after a long day in the saddle, had climbed out of her bedroll and snuck off to the river to bathe. There, she found Dirk, naked and wet. Despite the fact that they didn't exactly like each other, passion flared. Sex under the stars. Not romantic, but fierce and primitive, very different from the Comte's smooth and sensual seduction of Lady Emma. It had worked for Marty, and for Kim as well.

Okay, maybe a cowboy could be hot—at least in fiction. And

maybe Kim secretly hoped for some Dirk clones. The riders moved too quickly to afford a clear picture of any individuals, but she could see they were a mixed bag in terms of age and build. There were even, she realized, a couple of women.

"Women compete?" she asked Marielle, who sat on her left.

"Only in barrel racing."

Women raced barrels? What was that all about?

Watching, Kim stretched, the sun warm on her head and shoulders. The air was hot and dusty with an unfamiliar earthy note that must come from the horses.

This was actually kind of interesting. Not to mention visually very different from her normal experience as the horses, riders, and waving banners wove around each other making ever-changing patterns. Creativity fed on a variety of stimuli. She nudged Marielle with her shoulder. "I'm glad you suggested this."

Marielle's eyes danced. "And you haven't even laid eyes on Blake Longfeather yet."

"Who?"

"Here." The other woman opened her program. "He was last year's bareback bronc champion. Isn't he incredible?"

Kim glanced over. *Oh my.* This was the stuff of fantasies!

The top of the page featured a cowboy on a golden-colored horse that had its front hooves on the ground and its back hooves so high in the air it was almost vertical. One of the cowboy's hands gripped something attached to the horse, his other hand was raised in the air, and his hat was flying off. Insane, yes, but hot.

So was the head shot below. "Yummy." Blake Longfeather had bronzed skin, black hair, carved features, and a half smile. "This is how I imagine Dirk Zamora looking."

"I know, right? And Blake's riding today!"

The afternoon was definitely looking up.

In the ring, the horses and riders lined up down the middle

while the announcer talked about rodeo sponsors. Kim gazed from rider to rider, looking for Blake Longfeather, then stopped abruptly.

Here was another cowboy worth looking at. Tall and lean in the saddle, he wore a sage green shirt with a Wrangler logo, and a beige hat rested rakishly atop streaky blondish brown hair. His skin was tanned, his features strong, his smile captivating. His horse was attractive too, sand-colored with a darker face and a black mane and tail. The pair made a pretty picture.

She couldn't wait to see this guy compete.

Three

The first event was called tie-down roping. The announcer was explaining how it worked, but the sound system wasn't great and Kim didn't catch it all.

"Here." Marielle opened the program to a new page. "There's a summary of each event."

Kim and George, seated on either side of her, leaned in to read. The basic idea was clear: the cowboy had to rope the calf then jump off his horse, run down the rope, throw the calf to the ground, and tie three of its legs together—and the horse had to hold the rope taut while the cowboy did it. There were other rules, like the calf couldn't already be down on the ground, and the tie around the legs had to hold for six seconds.

When Kim passed the program to Lily, the blonde waved it away. "I read it online."

"And memorized it?" Kim teased.

"I like to be prepared."

"The first rider's ready." George's voice turned everyone's attention back to the arena.

When the brown calf ran out of its chute, a rider in hot pursuit, Kim saw the rules in action. The cowboy could have been demonstrating how it should be done.

The announcer said that the contestant had set things off to a great start with a score of 9.5 seconds.

"Look." Lily pointed to a display screen at the other end of the arena. "There's the rider's name and his score."

Kim noted that it said the rider was from Alberta. "He's come a long way."

Marielle flipped through her program again, to a black-and-white insert.

Kim now saw that the glossy program was generic, while the insert related to this weekend's rodeo. It listed all the events, the contestants, and where they were from. For the bronc and bull riding events, it even gave the names of the animals—or stock, as she realized they were referred to.

There were lots of Alberta riders, several from BC, a few from other parts of Canada, and a bunch from the States. A number of riders had come all the way from Texas, and there were even a couple from Australia. "Wow, this is a big deal."

"I think it's a way of life," Marielle said. "I guess especially in Alberta and Texas. Blake Longfeather is from Texas."

The next contestant's rope missed the calf's head, and the third guy had trouble throwing the calf and getting it tied, so his time wasn't very good.

The next rider came into the arena—and it was the handsome cowboy on the sand-colored horse. Kim glanced at the display board. Ty Ronan, and he was from the Fraser Valley. Virtually a hometown boy.

She'd noticed that before the contestants competed, they rode around swinging their ropes, warming up, and that's what Ty was doing. He looked so easy and agile in the saddle. As he removed his hat to run a hand through sun-streaked light brown hair, a grin that looked like pure pleasure crossed his strong, tanned features.

Oh my! Kim smiled approvingly and nudged Marielle. "I'd match him against your Blake." Maybe it was because every Chinese guy had black hair like her own, but there was something about a man with sunlit hair she found very attractive.

"Mmm, he's nice, but I'll stick with Blake. You can have that one, girl," Marielle teased.

"Yeah, like that's going to happen." Though, if she fantasized about sex under the stars tonight, it might be with this guy.

Hat back on his head, the cowboy entered his chute.

Knowing it was silly, she crossed her fingers and held her breath.

Ty Ronan, a ring of rope in his mouth, nodded, the signal to release the calf. The brown and white animal shot out of the chute, horse and rider on its heels. A quick whip of the rope, and the loop settled neatly over the calf's neck. In the same instant—maybe even before—Ty was on the ground as his tan horse backed away from the calf, tightening the rope. In a quick movement, the cowboy pitted his weight against the calf's and tossed it deftly, almost gently, then he whipped the rope around its legs. His hand shot up, and he was on his feet again.

Kim cheered along with the rest of the crowd, her whole body heating the same way it had when she read that sex scene by the river. Okay, fine, Dirk Zamora and Ty Ronan had convinced her, "erotic" and "cowboy" could go together very nicely indeed. If cowboy Ty wanted to take her to bed right now, she wouldn't toss him out for being dusty and sweaty.

She suppressed a giggle. No, she was being silly. Of course she wouldn't sleep with a stranger. But, mmm, what a delicious fantasy to explore later tonight, home in her bed.

The riders who would untie the calf held back. Kim knew everyone was counting the six seconds. Then the cowboys moved forward and released the calf, which hopped to its feet and trotted in a beeline toward the exit gate, clearly knowing its role. The announcer called a number: 8.4. The crowd cheered louder, clapping vigorously. This was a timed event where the quicker you were, the better.

Ty removed his hat again and waved it in acknowledgment, giving an even wider smile. Kim couldn't tear her gaze off that handsome smiling face, that rangy body, but she heard Marielle say, "Hey, 8.4 sounds really good."

"Like you know anything about this," George teased from her other side. "But I will say, you and Kim have good taste in men. Almost as good as mine."

The next rider, red-haired and red-shirted, warmed up, but Kim's eyes followed Ty. He joined other contestants in a waiting area, taking a back slap and an arm punch from a couple of guys.

Her gaze still on the attractive cowboy as he stroked his horse and chatted with the other riders, her body throbbing with lust, she was barely aware of the next contestant's ride until cheers drew her attention. Yes, this man had successfully roped his calf. His score— 8.9—made her grin smugly.

There were a few more competitors, and only two were successful. Sadly, one—a stocky blond guy who looked a few years younger than Ty—got an 8.3.

No one could top Ty in the looks department, though. She watched him as all the contestants rode back along the side of the ring to the exit. His body moved so easily in the saddle, and he and his pretty horse made a great picture. Marielle had teased her about silk-screening cowboys on T-shirts. Now she could almost imagine doing it.

She could imagine lots more than art. Marielle was right. Watching a cowboy's body in natural synch with his horse could make you imagine his body moving with yours during sex. Making you wet and riding you hard, the brunette joked. And yeah, the wet part was true, even just from watching Ty.

As for riding her hard—well, she'd never had that kind of sex. Making love had always been . . . pleasant. Not hard, not visceral. If she'd had sex like that with Henry, she might not have broken up.

When Ty's back disappeared, she sighed and refocused on the ring. A miked clown bantered with the announcer up in the booth, filling time during setup of the next event.

Kim borrowed the program and leafed through it. Ty Ronan wasn't listed in the glossy generic program where she'd seen Blake Longfeather, which meant he hadn't been last year's Canadian champion in any of the events. Too bad: no photo. Next she turned to the event schedule, searching for his name then sighing in disappointment that he wasn't in any other afternoon events. She wouldn't have minded more fuel for her cowboy fantasies.

She flipped to the evening schedule and there he was, listed for bareback bronc riding along with Blake Longfeather. Maybe she wouldn't bail early after all.

Marielle said, "I wish they'd hurry up. Blake Longfeather's in the next event, saddle bronc riding." She gave an impatient wriggle. "He's really versatile. Tonight he's in bareback bronc riding, and tomorrow he's bull riding."

"I can see it already," George teased. "You're coming back tomorrow, right?"

Marielle chuckled. "You're assuming I'm not going to hook up with him tonight and stay over?"

And there was the difference between the two of them. Though Kim occasionally envied Marielle's spontaneity and fun attitude, she could never be like her. Kim might stay to watch Ty tonight, get wet over him again, and fantasize about hooking up with him, but she'd never act on it. She looked at men in terms of the future, which meant a Hong Kong guy who got along with her parents.

"Oh, look!" Marielle screeched.

A black horse leaped out of the chute, bucking and spinning, doing its best to unseat the rider. The horse won. The rider went flying, to roll in the dust and quickly rise, apparently uninjured, as a couple of other riders chased after the still-bucking horse.

"Insane, and tough," Kim commented. Why would someone risk being tossed through the air to land any which way, then possibly be hit by a flying hoof? "What a crazy way to make a living."

If they even did make a living. A lot of the ropers had missed their calves, and she guessed a fair number of bronc riders got tossed. How could you make money like this? What a precarious career.

Was that how her parents viewed her own desire for an art career? If so, she'd prove them wrong.

The next bronc and cowboy burst out of a chute. Her breath caught as she willed the rider to stay on. And when he did, she cheered.

Next up was Marielle's crush, Blake Longfeather. He rode a madly bucking chestnut horse, stayed on, and scored 80.5, better than the rider before him.

Kim studied him closely. Yeah, he was a strong, striking guy, but for her he wasn't the stuff of fantasies. That honor went to the rangy guy with sunlit hair and an infectious smile.

A couple of hours later, Kim was on overload. She'd seen skills and thrills, from team ropers to female barrel racers, from steer wrestlers to men who rode bulls bareback.

Even if she didn't understand the fine points of rodeo, it was exciting. Primitive and raw. Utterly physical. Full of drama. Scary too.

And sexy, when her own cowboy crush appeared in the ring again on his tan horse, in the steer wrestling event. He didn't compete, but acted as what the announcer called a hazer. It was his job to keep the steer running in a straight line for the contestant who had to jump off his horse onto it and topple it to the ground.

Kim had watched Ty, not the contestant. It reminded her of how, in *Ride Her, Cowboy*, photojournalist Marty'd kept her gaze and her camera trained on Dirk. She'd had the excuse that he was the subject of her story. Kim had no excuse, and didn't care. She was having fun, she was turned on, and she was building a store of images that her vivid imagination could draw on for erotic fantasies.

After the last afternoon event, the four women climbed down the bleachers. Marielle asked, "Who else is staying for tonight's rodeo?"

"I'm in," Kim said, and George and Lily agreed.

The scent of the food stalls drew them, and they decided the day called for hot dogs and mini donuts. They took a ride on the Ferris wheel, and Kim and Marielle, both boasting strong stomachs, also went on the Tilt-a-Whirl. They poked their heads into 4-H tents with every kind of animal imaginable, and salivated over fruit pies, jams, and other goodies entered in the cooking competition.

In the arcade, Marielle tossed balls to whack down a row of ducks. When she won a big stuffed panda, she gave it to a cute brown-haired girl who had tossed balls beside her and only hit one duck.

"That's nice of you," Kim commented.

"I have my eye on the bigger prize. I'm out to bag a cowboy."

"Just how do you plan to do that?" Lily asked dryly.

Kim expected a joking response, but Marielle laid out an actual plan. Turned out, she'd chatted in the ladies' room with a barrel racer, who said most of the competitors didn't go to the dance on the fairgrounds after the competition ended. Lots headed back to their own RVs or trailers, or to motel rooms, and some went out for a beer together.

"I told her about my crush," Marielle said cheerfully. "Guess she liked me, or she thought Blake Longfeather might like me. She said he's at the Wagon Wheel Motel, same as her and her husband, who's a bull rider. She also said he'd probably be shooting pool in the closest country and western bar."

"Where's the Wagon Wheel Motel?" Kim asked.

"Found it on my smartphone, and I Yelped the nearest pubs. There's one across the street, so I'll start there. Coming with me?"

"I'll see how I feel after the rodeo," Kim said. Ty Ronan wasn't likely to be at the bar. He was local, so would just go home.

George and Lily agreed, and they all headed back to find seats in the stands.

As they watched the first evening events, dusk began to fall and big lights came on, illuminating the arena. The lighting changed the atmosphere, making it a little less real, more glamorous and Hollywoodish.

But it was real. Those winces were real, when contestants who'd been thrown dragged themselves to their feet and tottered to the exit. Why did they do it? Some looked no more than eighteen; others had to be forty or older. Did they see this as a sport, or was it a performance? Did they do it for the physical challenge or the money?

Finally, it was time for the fourth event, the one she'd been waiting for: bareback bronc riding. The schedule showed Blake Longfeather as the fifth of twelve riders, and Ty Ronan as the eighth.

Eight seconds, she mused, as the third rider took an inglorious tumble. To travel from Texas, as this cowboy had, just to hit the dirt after a few seconds—or to survive the full eight, if he was lucky.

The fourth rider managed to stay aboard a wildly twisting, bucking horse, and got the top score so far, an 82. Then Blake rode, his horse a dark brown one. It bucked pretty much in a straight line, and the cowboy rode dramatically and stuck on until the end, then with the assistance of one of the pickup riders, slipped off and to the ground.

His score was posted as an 80.5, which put him in second place. Marielle hissed. "That's not fair."

Anticipation building, Kim sat impatiently through the next two rides—one a fall, and one a score lower than Blake's—then the announcer said that the next rider, in chute two, was Ty Ronan. Though Kim couldn't catch all the words, she did hear that he'd been champion at the Calgary Stampede, and top all-around cowboy at some other event. He was not only handsome, but a winner.

"Hey," Marielle said, "isn't that the guy you're hot for?"

"Is it?" she asked innocently, peering toward the chute. She saw Ty's beige cowboy hat and a slice of green shirt as he leaned down, doing something with the horse he'd be riding. The horse's name, she noted, was Dirt Devil.

The man responsible for opening the gate got ready, and a second later the horse burst out. Kim crossed her fingers, staring intently. The horse was pretty, gray and white with a white mane and tail, but—ouch!—it bucked and whirled like crazy. Ty's hat sailed off, but somehow he hung on, raking the horse's shoulders as she'd read that riders were supposed to do.

From the row above her in the stands, a woman said to her husband, "Lord, that horse is rank."

The couple had exchanged comments during the previous events, and seemed to know what they were talking about. She crossed her fingers even tighter for Ty. Why did he have to draw the nasty horse?

It seemed like forever until the eight seconds buzzer went off, but the horse wasn't listening. It kept on bucking fiercely, moving across the arena as pickup riders tried to approach. Still Ty clung to it, for what had to be at least another eight seconds, and now Kim clenched her fingernails into her palms, hoping he made it off safely. Finally, one of the pickup riders got close enough and Ty freed his hand from the grip and slid off, resting briefly against the other horse then dropping to the ground.

She joined the rest of the audience in cheering and clapping.

He looked so great, bending that athletic body to pick up his hat, which he dusted off then waved toward the crowd. God, he had the sexiest smile. The sexiest, strongest body. What would it be like to make love with a man like that, for just once in her life? Damn it, the closest she would ever come was reading *Ride Her, Cowboy*, and imagining Ty Ronan in the place of Dirk Zamora, riding *her*, not Marty Westerbrook.

When Ty's score of 83 went up, he was the leader.

He held that position until the final rider came out and nailed an 83.5, and Kim sighed with disappointment. It would have been the perfect end to the day if Ty'd come out on top.

K im had visited her share of bars, but she'd never been in one like this. That wasn't surprising given that it was called The Rusty Spur. Yes, she, along with George and Lily, had decided to join Marielle and complete their day of cowboy research with a trip to a country and western bar. Kim was curious whether Marielle's bold plan would work. She'd seen her friend in action before, and was a little in awe of her vivaciousness and confidence. Sometimes a girl had to live vicariously.

They were definitely not in downtown Vancouver. The décor featured rustic wooden tables, barstools modeled after saddles, and western photos on every inch of wall space that wasn't occupied by posters, slogans, T-shirts, leather horsey stuff, and a couple of broken guitars.

And yes, there was music. At one end of the room, two guys and two girls clad in western wear played a twangy country number with one of the women crooning the lyrics. Kim had never been into country music, but this was kind of catchy.

The floor in front of the stage was crowded with smiling, laughing dancers, most in jeans and boots, many of them hoisting beer bottles as they moved in time to the beat. The crowd ranged from late teen through to white hair, and everyone mixed together like age didn't matter.

The music finished and the female singer announced, "We're dry and we need us a beer. Y'all hang around and we'll be back onstage soon."

As the dancers cleared the floor, Kim saw that there were a couple of pool tables across the room. A man bent over one, his back to her. Well, his butt to her. That was one pretty amazing butt, firm and strong as it stretched against washed-out blue denim. He shifted his weight, apparently studying the lay of the balls on the table. She hoped he took his time deciding what kind of shot he wanted to make. "The scenery's not bad in here."

"Seriously?" Lily said. "It looks like something out of a bad Western."

"You're not looking in the right direction," Marielle said. "Oh yeah, Kim, that scenery is very fine."

"What are you—" George started, and then, "I see what you mean."

Four

Ty Ronan's back felt prickly, which threw off his concentration. When he aimed for a tough bank shot, the ball was a good inch short of the pocket, nicely set up for his opponent to sink it. "Oh hell," he said good-naturedly as he straightened.

Blake Longfeather said, "Hah," and bent to the table. Blake was a rodeo buddy from way back, still a full-time pro, unlike Ty, who'd cut way down on rodeo since he bought the new Ronan Ranch three years ago. Now, whenever they competed at the same rodeo, they got together for a couple of beers and a game or two of pool.

Blake slid Ty's ball neatly into the pocket, then moved around the table, figuring how best to sink the one remaining ball. It was a tough shot, but he was a good player.

Guessing this game was over, Ty stretched his back, achy from the bone-jarring ride on Dirt Devil. Luck of the draw had been with him. He'd pulled a truly rank mare and he was happy with his ride. He'd make it into the finals tomorrow, for both events he'd competed in.

He still felt that prickly sensation, like someone was watching him. Lifting his beer bottle, he turned. Four women clustered by the door staring at him and Blake.

One, a lush, dark-skinned babe in figure-hugging western clothing, looked almost like she belonged in The Rusty Spur. Almost. Her hat was brand-new and perched at the wrong angle atop masses of wavy dark brown hair. A wannabe cowgirl or a buckle bunny, one of those rodeo groupies who wanted to get it on with a cowboy?

Two others, a pretty blonde and a striking redhead in tailored capris and pretty tops, looked like professional women from the city who'd strayed off course and ended up in the wrong place.

As for the fourth . . . He didn't have a clue what to think about her, except that she took his breath away. Like when Dirt Devil jammed her forefeet into the ground and corkscrewed her hindquarters toward the sky.

The woman was sexy; the arousal tugging at his groin told him that. Sexier than the one with all the curves, even though this one was tiny and less curvy. She was Asian, probably Chinese, and she looked—he shook his head, baffled and turned on—well, she defied labels, that was for sure. She was kind of exotic and kind of punky, in a cute way, with short, spiky black hair streaked in the same turquoise as the stone in one of his favorite rodeo buckle belts.

The streaks matched one of the colors in the unusual top she wore over a skinny black skirt. The top looked silky and floaty; the design, as well as the blue pattern made him think of wings. She reminded him of a dragonfly, like she might lift off and fly around the room.

Sexy and intriguing, but not his type of woman. No way. None of the four were. He wanted a woman who'd fit in at the ranch, get along with his parents, enjoy raising kids and animals, and help him heal horses. His mom was right when she said it was time he got serious about a woman. He just hadn't found the right one.

Hell, he hadn't had much time to look in the three years since he'd quit the full-time rodeo circuit and bought Ronan Ranch. There'd been so much work in getting the ranch on its feet, with his dad's purebred Angus cattle, his mom's llamas, alpacas, and angora goats, his own horse training business.

And why was he thinking about a wife now, looking at these four attractive but out of place females, and particularly the sexy dragon-fly one who was the most out of place of all?

Behind him, he heard the snick of Blake's cue against a ball, the smooth slide of the ball, a resonant *clunk* as it fell into the pocket, and a satisfied, "My game. Pay up." Then, "What are you starin' at, man?" And then, as Blake came up beside him, "Ah now, would you look at them. Figure someone's GPS sent them on a wild-goose chase?"

"I would, except for the one in the hat. Buckle bunny?"

"Bunnies usually know how to wear a hat."

"True." In their younger days, he and Blake used to welcome the female attention, but that lifestyle got old. That was why Ty, who lived not too far away, had suggested this bar, a haunt for locals. A cowboy could have a few beers with a buddy, undisturbed, then walk across the road to the Wagon Wheel Motel.

The gal in the hat herded the other three toward the pool table and flashed a vivid smile. "We saw you ride this afternoon. You were awesome." She focused on Blake. "Blake Longfeather, right?"

Oh yeah, she was a bunny, and she'd set her sights on Ty's buddy.

"At your service, ladies." Blake made a kind of bow. "And this is my pal—"

Before he could introduce Ty, the dragonfly one blurted, "Ty Ronan."

"You were at the rodeo?" Ty stared at her in disbelief. "You don't look like the rodeo type." And man, she was even cuter and sexier up close, with those pixie features and big, sparkly dark eyes fringed with black lashes. Behind his fly, his cock pulsed and thickened.

"Oh, I'm not." A sudden grin flashed, lighting her face. "Or I wasn't, until this afternoon. I had no idea how exciting it could be."

When she said the word "exciting," something zinged in his blood. Yeah, lust, but something more. It was like that adrenaline-rush moment in the chute when he perched atop a thousand pounds of unpredictable, energy-charged horseflesh, locked his hand in the handhold, then took a steadying breath, leaned back, and nodded to open the gate. Anticipation, challenge, joy, a touch of fear.

"Can we buy you a drink?" the one in the hat asked. "A celebratory drink?"

"Neither of us ranked first, ma'am," Blake drawled in his low, husky voice, a touch of humor threading it. The fact that he hadn't just said, "No thanks," told Ty he was interested in the brunette.

As Ty was in the Asian woman. She knew his name. Today she'd watched him; tonight she'd recognized him. She had to be into him too. *Right?*

"No, but we met you, and that's cause for celebration," the ringleader responded cheekily. "Besides, you both rode really well."

"At least we stayed on our broncs." Blake turned to Ty. "Though I still say I should've scored higher than you." The tiny lift of his brows asked Ty if he was into having a drink with these women.

Tonight, Ty wasn't looking for a wife, so why not spend some time with a sexy female? He'd burned out on buckle bunnies long ago, but dragonfly girl was different. It had been a while since he'd felt that tug of attraction, and he had a feeling it might be mutual. Giving his friend the slightest of nods, he told him, "You were on a carousel horse. Pathetic thing couldn't buck its way out of a paper bag." Blake had given the best ride he could, but his horse was having an off day.

"Yeah, you got the luck today," Blake said. "Dirt Devil's rank."

"Rank is good?" the dragonfly one asked.

Ty gave her his best smile, and her eyes widened slightly. "Rank's what we hope for. The score's made up of two parts, one for the horse and one for the rider. Best rider in the world—not that Longfeather's anywhere near that," he added with a teasing glance at his friend, "can't score high if his horse doesn't do its part."

Her eyes were dark, almost black, and sparkled with interest. He hoped that interest had to do with him. "The horse gets a higher score if it bucks a lot, and twists around?"

"Yeah, and—"

"Why don't we have this conversation over a drink?" the ringleader said impatiently.

The blonde spoke for the first time, a slight smile touching the corners of her mouth. "We would be delighted to buy you a drink, gentlemen, but feel free to say no if you have other plans."

The redhead nodded. "And congratulations on how well you both rode. It was really impressive."

"Flattery," Ty said, slanting a glance at Blake.

"Way to a man's heart," Blake responded.

"You've been friends for a while," dragonfly woman said, and it wasn't a question.

"Friends?" Ty gazed at the other man. "Me and him? What's your name again, cowboy?"

They all laughed, then Ty noticed a group leaving a big table. "There." He strode over to claim it and they all followed. Ty made sure, when he took one end of the table, that dragonfly girl was beside him. The blonde sat on his other side. Blake, at the opposite end of the table, had cowboy hat girl and the redhead on either side.

A pretty young waitress in jeans, red cowboy boots, and a tight red tee with the bar's logo came over. "Hey there, I'm Judy. What can I get y'all?"

"Beers all around?" Blake asked.

Ty was going to suggest they get a pitcher, but dragonfly girl asked Judy, "What kind of lagers and ales do you have?"

The waitress started to list them, and dragonfly girl said, "Dead Frog? Cool name. And does honey lager mean it's made with honey?"

"You got it. It's good."

"I'll try it."

So she liked to experiment. Was he—a rodeo cowboy—an experiment? Did he care? He was more curious whether her mouth would taste like honey after drinking the beer—and whether he'd find out. The thought had him shifting to ease the pressure behind his fly.

"Granville Island amber ale," the redhead said.

"George, I didn't know you drank beer," the blonde said.

"Woody introduced me to it."

George and Woody? Unusual names. He guessed the guy was her fiancé. She had a ring on her engagement finger: little diamonds surrounding a big, sparkly goldish-colored stone. The blonde had a wedding ring that was a band of small diamonds. The two brunettes both wore rings, but not on the "I'm taken" finger.

Dragonfly girl had small, slender hands, delicate and feminine. Her short fingernails were the same color as the streaks in her hair. He tried to imagine one of those blue-tipped hands gripping reins, and stifled a grin. Then he imagined one of them stroking across his thigh, heading upward, fanning out over the front of his rapidly swelling fly. This time, it was a sound of arousal he held back.

The blonde ordered a martini. He would've predicted beer for the one in the hat, but she said, "Something fruity. Sweet, but not too sweet. Any suggestions?"

"You like strawberries?" Judy asked. "The little wild ones?"

"I don't know the wild ones, but I like strawberries."

Ty knew the wild ones. They were one of the best things in the world, coming close behind horses and sex. Though maybe horses and sex should rank in the other order. No, that depended on the sex. Some was spectacular; some just mediocre. It had been a while—maybe six months?—since he'd had either kind. That was way too long a dry spell. What would sex be like with dragonfly girl? Would he find out tonight?

He realized the waitress had turned to him and was asking what he wanted. And she didn't mean sex. Or maybe she did, from the glint in her blue eyes. She was pretty, curvy, might be his type. But he didn't feel that tug of sexual chemistry like he did with the woman sitting beside him. He gave Judy an easy smile. "Can I have a Moosehead?"

"Sugar," she drawled, "you can have any little thing you want."

Yup, she meant sex.

When the waitress left, they all stared at each other for an awkward moment. "You have the advantage, ladies," Ty said. "You know our names."

"I'm Marielle," the hat girl said, "and she's George." She pointed to the redhead. "Georgia, really, but everyone calls her George. She's Lily"—she indicated the blonde—"and that's Kim."

Kim. It suited her.

"You go to the rodeo often?" Ty asked, figuring it would be rude to say he took them for rodeo virgins.

Kim chuckled, perfect white teeth flashing in a lightly tanned face. "Do we look like it?"

What she looked like was kissable. He smiled at her. "I was being polite. Did you enjoy it?"

"Way more than I expected to. I'm not a country girl—"

"Could've fooled me," he drawled, tongue in cheek, winning another laugh.

"And I can't ever imagine being one, I'm a city girl to the core, but—" She broke off as Judy arrived with a tray of drinks.

The waitress served them expertly then asked Marielle how she liked her drink. The brunette raved, then the waitress turned to Kim. "What do you think of your Dead Frog?"

She lifted her beer, the glass looking like it didn't belong in a delicate, turquoise-tipped hand. Unlike his cock, which was quite willing to feel her grip. She inhaled, then sipped, her lips moving like she was rolling the beer around in her mouth.

He wanted to part those lips with his tongue, steal a kiss.

"Nice," she said approvingly. "Balanced. Not too bitter, not too sweet. I can taste that hint of honey."

Lager with honey, flavored by her own sweet mouth. Oh yeah, he could go for that. He'd kiss her deep and long, and show her that he tasted as good as lager and could make her a hell of a lot happier.

Testing, he moved his leg under the table, so his knee touched hers.

She jerked and her long lashes flicked down then up—God, she had big, pretty, sparkly eyes—but she didn't move her leg away.

Judy spoke to Ty. "Y'all let me know if you want something more than beer."

"No, that'll do me just fine. Thanks anyhow, Judy."

"Can't blame a girl for trying," she said cheerfully, and headed over to the next table.

Marielle said, "Have to admire a girl who goes after what she wants."

"Ty has some experience with those," Blake said.

"Like you don't," he rejoined.

Across the room, the band trooped back onstage and took up their instruments, launching into a Taylor Swift number.

"Where were we?" Ty nudged Kim's leg under the table. "You can't imagine being a country girl, but you enjoyed the rodeo?"

"Right." Her eyes went slightly out of focus, like she was seeing images inside her head. "There was something so physical and . . . raw about it. It's exciting and dramatic. And scary." A shiver twitched her shoulders, and her wingy top fluttered.

So she liked physical and raw. He could give her that. He ached to give her that.

"It's all of that," Lily said. "I'm a doctor, and I'm trying to understand why a—pardon me for phrasing it this way, Ty and Blake—why a reasonably sane man would do it."

Kim nodded vigorously. "I wondered that too."

Ty exchanged glances with his buddy, who shrugged. How could you explain rodeo to women from a totally different world?

He was still pondering that when George—a crazy nickname for a feminine woman with sweet curves, curly red hair, and amber eyes that matched her engagement ring—spoke up. "I thought people were crazy to play hockey until my fiancé enlightened me."

Ty put her fiancé's unusual name together with the mention of hockey, and there was only one conclusion. "Woody Hanrahan? The Vancouver Beavers' captain?"

She gave a proud smile. "Yes. You watch hockey?"

"Mostly just the finals." That sparked a memory. "Hell, you were the one on the JumboTron when the Beavers took the Stanley Cup." She and Hanrahan had yelled "I love you" to each other, and the giant screen had captured it.

"Wasn't that fantastic?" Marielle gushed.

Ty wasn't a romantic, but the moment had made him smile. "It was nice." He took a long swallow of Moosehead. "Anyhow, nothing against hockey, but I'm not much on spectator sports." He liked to do rather than watch—and *doing* was exactly what he wanted with Kim.

He felt the warmth of her skin through the thin fabric of her long skirt. Though he generally liked women in jeans or short skirts, the skimpy cotton made him think dirty thoughts. What lay beneath it?

"Anyhow," George said, "if you two are like Woody, I'm guessing you've been riding for a long time."

Her words distracted him from imagining running his hand up the inside of Kim's naked thigh, and he focused on the redhead.

"And it's not just a challenge and exciting," she went on, "but it's in your blood. It's a place where things feel right, like you're where you're supposed to be."

His mouth fell open. He'd thought only another cowboy would get that.

"Yeah," Blake said, "that's it," and Ty nodded.

"It's a passion," Kim said with a tone of revelation. "It's the thing you were born to do."

When he turned to her, the glow on her face told him she knew what she was talking about. In a minute, he'd ask what she'd been born to do.

But first, for some reason he wanted her to understand his passion. "Yeah, it is. For me, it's not just rodeo, but horses, the country, ranching. That's what I was born to do. Mostly, it's a lot of hard work, but rodeo spices it up. Rodeo's demanding, challenging, exciting." He grinned. "An adrenaline high. Addictive. So yeah, maybe folks like Blake and me are a little insane."

"Insane to follow your passion?" She shook her head, those streaky spikes of hair flicking. "No way."

Marielle asked Blake how he got into rodeo, but Ty's gaze stayed on Kim's expressive face. From the moment he'd laid eyes on her, she'd fascinated and gut-level attracted him more than any woman he'd met in a very long time. He wanted her. Bad. Did she feel the same?

"You talk like you know about *passion*, Kim." He put deliberate emphasis on that word, letting her know he intended a double meaning.

Five

Color tinted Kim's cheeks. "I know about passion." Her flush deepened. He couldn't tell if she was flirting back or was just embarrassed. "Though mine's about as different from yours as you could imagine. It's art."

"Oh, yeah?" Yeah, that sure as hell was different. "That's pretty cool. I don't know any artists."

"Well, now you do." It was the blond doctor, Lily. He'd forgotten she and the others were there. "Kim's very talented. Her blouse is one of her creations."

He smiled. "It's pretty. Makes me think of a dragonfly."

Kim's face lit. "Thanks. It's actually based on the Pipevine Swallowtail butterfly, but I'm glad the idea came across."

"When I saw you, I thought you might lift off and fly around the room." He hoped she didn't. He wanted her right here beside him, their knees rubbing. And then, before long, he wanted more. A slow dance, vertical to start with, then with any luck a horizontal one.

She beamed. "Perfect!"

He gulped. No, she hadn't read his thoughts and agreed, she was responding to what he'd said. "So that's what you do? Design clothes?"

"No, though I'm thinking about it. I'm a student right now."

"An art student?"

"Yes, at Emily Carr in Vancouver. Before that, I got a business degree in Hong Kong."

Vaguely, he was aware of the others talking, but he was interested only in Kim. "You went away to school in Hong Kong, or you're from there?"

"From there."

"You sure are a city girl. Vancouver and Hong Kong?"

"Oh, yes! I love cities. All the bustle, color, excitement. The stimulation, the galleries, the restaurants, the—" She broke off. "Sorry, I'm gushing."

"It's okay. I mean, I don't get it, the whole city thing, but whatever turns your crank."

Odd that someone so different from him would turn his sexual crank, but she did. "So you came to Vancouver to study art?"

"Yes, I persuaded my parents to let me do it for two years."

Let her? "Uh, sorry if this is rude, but how old are you?"

"Twenty-four. You?"

"Twenty-nine." And he'd made his own decisions and supported himself since he graduated high school. But he shouldn't judge; people had different family stories. His grandparents and parents had raised him to pull his weight around the ranch from the time he was a toddler. Now, the original Ronan Ranch in Alberta had fallen victim to social change, a poor economy, and the Mad Cow scare—things that, he always reminded himself, would have done it in even if he'd been around to help, rather than at college and getting his kicks on the rodeo circuit. And in the end, despite him and his dad butting heads all those years ago about Ty hitting the circuit, rodeo had provided the money to buy the new ranch in the Fraser Valley where he and his parents lived.

Judy came to ask if they'd like another round. Ty said, "Sure, thanks." He glanced at Kim, but she'd turned to answer a question from Marielle. "For her too," he told Judy.

The waitress said, good-naturedly, "Lucky girl," and headed off.

Kim giggled at something Marielle said, then turned back to Ty. "Have you been riding in rodeos all your life?"

"I was up on a horse before I could walk. My dad's a rancher but my grandpa was a pro rider for more than fifteen years, and my grandma too, a barrel racer, before they settled down and had my dad and his younger sister. My grandparents saved their rodeo winnings and bought a ranch. My aunt was never into ranching, but Dad loved it. When he grew up, he built a house for himself on the property and worked with them. That's where I grew up."

"Your grandparents got you interested in rodeo?" She leaned her elbows on the table and rested her chin on her clasped hands, staring at him like she was fascinated by his life story. Or, he hoped, like she was fascinated by *him*.

Judy put fresh drinks down, and he reached for his Moosehead, his hand brushing Kim's arm accidentally on purpose. Her skin was soft, warm, and that one simple touch fired his blood. "You bet. Grandma's name was Tammy Tyson, and I'm Tyson Ronan, named for the two of them. The house was full of pictures of them in action, belt buckles, trophies. Some kids grew up on fairy tales but for me it was rodeo stories. True ones, that got me hungry to do it myself." To his dad's chagrin. His dad and grandpa had butted heads just as much as Ty and his father used to. Let's face it; Ronan males had strong opinions and didn't bend easily.

"Belt buckles?" Kim cocked her head, sipped her beer. "What do you mean?"

"Winners get these big belt buckles."

"Seems like a strange prize. Do you have any?"

He bit back a smile. "One or two." As in, one or two trunkfuls. He was wearing an old favorite right now, the World Rodeo Champion buckle he'd earned for bareback riding when he was twenty-three. Some of the other special ones sat in a glass case in the office at Ronan Ranch, to impress clients.

He'd been turned to face Kim, keeping the pressure of his leg against hers. Now he realized that Lily, seated on his other side, was rising.

George stood too. "Time for us to head home."

Damn. He wanted more time with Kim. She was into him. He wanted to dance with her, seduce her slow and easy, take her back to his cabin at the Wagon Wheel across the street.

"I'm going to hang out awhile longer," Marielle said. "I brought my own car. Kim, how about you?"

She made an indecisive sound and absentmindedly took a long swallow of beer.

Marielle winked. "It's book club research."

Huh?

Kim's lips twitched. "I suppose it is." She flicked a glance at Ty from under partially lowered lashes. "What do you think, Tyson Ronan? Should I stay?"

"Please."

His prompt reply turned her lip-twitch into a smile. "Then I will."

After a chorus of good-byes, Marielle stripped off her shirt to reveal a pink tank top that hugged impressive curves. She rested her hand on Blake's forearm. "I feel like dancing, but I've never danced to this kind of music. Want to be my teacher?" She put a sexy emphasis on the last word.

"Texas two-step," he said, "and I'd be happy to teach you anything and everything, Marielle."

"Bet there's a thing or two I could teach you, cowboy," she joked back.

Laughing, the two of them rose.

Seizing the opportunity, Ty turned to Kim. "Bet you don't know the two-step."

Her eyes sparkled. "Bet you can teach me."

He rose and held out his right hand.

She took it, murmuring something under her breath that sounded like, "Bet that's not all you can teach me."

He must've been too eager, or underestimated his own strength when he pulled her to her feet, because she lost her balance. Quickly he caught her arm, steadying her. She was so tiny, a foot shorter than his six foot one, couldn't weigh more than a hundred pounds. More careful now, he linked his fingers gently with her small, feminine ones.

Kim didn't have Marielle's abundant curves, but he found her even sexier. Marielle was vivacious and fun, but, like the waitress Judy, she was right in a guy's face. Kim was more subtle, more fascinating. How could a guy feel both protective and aroused at the same time? He'd better work on that arousal thing, or dancing the two-step would be tough.

Ty led Kim to the edge of the dance floor. "Two-step's a lot like fox-trot."

"I don't know any of those dances. I just go to clubs and, you know . . ." She gave a sexy shimmy that sent her top and skirt flying, making her look even more like she could fly.

He swallowed hard, imagining that slim, lithe body caught up in the rhythm of the music. "No one's gonna care if we get it right." All he wanted was to hold her close. With any luck, the band would play a slow number next. "Basic thing to remember with the two-step is quick, quick, slow, slow." He flashed her a teasing grin. "And the guy leads. Always."

She wrinkled her cute little nose. "How old-fashioned. But then, what else would I expect from a hero of the Wild West?"

"A what?" Had he heard right?

She shook her head. "It's a book club thing."

He was starting to catch on. "Your club's reading about rodeo?"

Her eyes danced. "Not exactly."

Kim couldn't help grinning. She wasn't on a cattle drive, but the whole day—the rodeo, the western bar, talking to cowboys, learning the Texas two-step—it could be called book club research.

It could also be called a major turn-on. Watching Ty in the rodeo ring had been arousing, and she'd happily anticipated him starring in her erotic fantasies. Now she was with the actual man, and could hardly believe it. He was a hundred times more potent in person. So potent, her head swam, her heart raced, and her panties were damp with arousal.

She couldn't take her eyes off Ty, broad-shouldered, lean-hipped, and rock solid in worn jeans and a shirt with rolled sleeves and an open neck. Tonight his shirt was the creamy brown of a latte after you'd stirred the milk into the coffee. It was a perfect accent for his bronzed skin, hazel eyes that sometimes looked greenish and other times golden brown, and the sun-streaked hair she found so attractive. That hair, which she'd bet had never seen a stylist, was a million shades of blond and brown, mostly straight but with a few wayward strands curling around his ears and down his nape. His brows, his nose, his jaw, they all made a statement: pure man. His lips, though . . . They were softer, a touch sensual, and they easily quirked with humor.

His jeans were belted with leather and, now that he'd enlightened her, she realized the elaborate oversized buckle might well be a rodeo trophy. Cool that he was a winner, but she was more intrigued by the way the denim gently hugged his slim hips, muscled thighs, and long legs, and was strategically faded around what appeared to be an excellent package.

He wore cowboy boots, of course. Did he wear those things to bed?

She stifled a giggle at the thought.

A woman walking past jostled her and Kim lost her balance, almost tumbling headfirst into Ty's powerful chest. The room swayed, and this time she did giggle. A big hand caught her shoulder. Ty no doubt intended to steady her but his touch instead made her pulse jerk, just the way the press of his knee under the table had.

He was rough and ready, not the least bit smooth or cosmopolitan, much less arty. Not her type, but oh man, he oozed good stuff: testosterone, pheromones, whatever all those yummy things were called. Oh man, the man was hot.

She held back another giggle. Oh *man,* the *man* was hot? That was cute.

And what was up with her? She wasn't usually a giggler. Had the sexy cowboy and the unusual situation made her a little crazy? Or was that honey lager especially potent? Her friends teased that she was a cheap drunk, quick to lose her inhibitions. Like the night she'd had two appletinis at a karaoke bar and belted out "I Will Always Love You," even though her singing voice was terrible. This was why she stuck to one drink—and tonight she was driving.

She *was* driving, wasn't she?

No, she was dancing. Ty had guided her hands into position. Gripping one easily, his other arm circling her back, he steered her around the dance floor. Or tried to, because she was stumbling in her black ballet-style flats, cheap shoes she'd chosen because she didn't care if they got ruined at the rodeo. "Wait, Ty. Tell me again how it goes."

"You let me lead rather than thinking for yourself."

She fluttered her eyelashes. "Yes, sir." And how could a girl think when Ty Ronan had his hands on her? She was overwhelmed by his sheer physical presence, by the fact that they'd talked and shared their passions, and by the realization that, of all the women in this room, including that flirtatious waitress with the big boobs, he'd chosen Kim to be with.

He rolled his eyes. "Like this, Kim." Firm hands guided her as he moved, saying, "Quick, quick, slow, slow. Quick, quick, slow, slow."

She concentrated through a few repetitions of the pattern. Hey, it was easy, the rhythm matched the music. "Now I get it." Now she could relax and enjoy the smooth way his powerful body moved, the heat he gave off, his fresh, woodsy scent. He was like a magnet, making her want to move closer and snug her body tight against his. Tight and intimate. Intimate and sexy.

Man, he was hot, and it wasn't just his looks. He rode his tan horse like they were one being—was that called a centaur? She'd watched him rope a calf and toss it easily, yet not roughly. She'd white-knuckled it as he clung to the back of that *rank* Dirt Devil. He really had been a kind of hero out there in the arena, definitely larger than life.

"You're a natural." His grin flashed. "When you let me lead."

"Yeah, yeah, cowboy. You couldn't get that bronc to behave, so you're picking on me."

He chuckled. "Weren't you listening when I said they're supposed to buck? Spirit's a good thing." The hand that held hers tightened. "I'm not picking on you. I'm dancing with you."

Next thing she knew, he'd swung her away so they were side by side, stepping forward together, then he reeled her back in. Her head spun again—was it the alcohol or Ty?—but she managed to follow.

"I think you've got it," he said.

"This is fun." Especially the part about being in the arms of a handsome rodeo star who made her whole body buzz. "I'm even getting used to country music."

"Horses and women and heartache. That's what life's all about." He winked.

"*Your* life, maybe." Horses and women, she'd bet on. Heartache? That seemed a stretch. Ty Ronan struck her as a guy who got what he wanted. He had the looks and easy confidence.

What would it be like to be with a man like him? She'd never even known one before.

She knew what Marielle would do. What Marielle was probably doing right now with Blake Longfeather. Seduce him, or let him seduce her. But Kim wasn't into flings.

She hadn't slept with Henry until they'd dated for six months. She'd thought she was in love with him, that they were heading toward a future together.

The band finished the number and the dancers stopped to clap and cheer.

Separated from Ty now, Kim felt off balance again. What was she doing? She glanced around, searching for Marielle. There she was, back at their table, laughing with Blake, their heads close together like nothing else in the world existed.

Feeling as if she was intruding, Kim looked away, back to the stage.

The singer took the mike off its stand and raised it to her lips. "Bet y'all are ready for a slow one, am I right?"

More cheers were her answer.

Ty took Kim's hand, almost swallowing it up. His hand was so hard, with ridges of callus. What would it feel like on her body? Caressing her breasts, sweeping down her stomach, parting her thighs?

Rough. It had to feel rough. Even if he tried to be gentle—and would he?—those calluses would abrade, but in a good way. In a sexy way. She trembled, imagining it.

The singer said, "I'm gonna do my female version of a little number made famous by the great Garth Brooks. Y'all get ready to be a little . . . shameless."

More cheers. When the audience settled down, Kim asked, "Shameless?"

"Name of the song." Ty's greenish gold eyes gleamed. "Good song." Without asking if she wanted to keep dancing, he gathered her into his arms.

Without thinking whether this was a good idea, she went. And . . . *Oh my God.* Had anything ever felt this close to heaven?

He was so big, so physical, so totally male, yet she didn't feel overwhelmed. Just . . . surrounded by wonderful sensations. The press of his firm thighs, the gentle strength of his hands, the heat rising through his clothing, the scent of warm, freshly showered man. Nothing exotic or complex, just a soap or shaving lotion that smelled deliciously like the great outdoors.

Her head was only a couple of inches from his chest. If she leaned forward, she could rest her cheek against the firm pecs that pressed against his well-washed shirt. But she wouldn't. She didn't even know this man. But she was in his arms, snuggled up against his wonderful body. She wasn't used to slow dancing. Wasn't used to being held like this on a dance floor.

This night was incredible. She might still be a fish out of water, yet she felt better than she could ever remember feeling. The man was magic. Even the music sounded great as the woman singer crooned in a low, husky voice. Sexy voice.

Sexy man holding her like she belonged in his arms. And she felt like she did. They were such different sizes and builds, she and Ty, yet they fit as if they were made for each other.

Against her belly, behind his fly, an erection was growing. He wasn't the only one who was turned on. Until today, she'd only experienced arousal during sex or at least heavy foreplay. But ever since she'd first laid eyes on Ty, her body had been flushed and tingly. Now, she felt moisture on her inner thighs and had a bizarre craving to climb his strong frame and grind her sex against him, seeking relief.

How much of this was because of *Ride Her, Cowboy*? Was she channeling the journalist Marty's attraction to Dirk Zamora? Kim had been aroused when she'd read the Lady Emma book too, but that feeling hadn't carried over when she was with Henry.

So maybe it wasn't the book; it was Ty. Ty, and a day in the sun watching tough, strong guys and tough, strong animals. Ty, and that supremely male body of his. Ty, and the firm hard-on pressing against—

"Kim?" Ty's voice broke into her thoughts.

She tilted her head up, knowing her cheeks were pink. "Yes?"

"Your friend's trying to get your attention."

Kim glanced over to their table, to see Marielle and Blake with their arms around each other. Marielle waved and winked.

Kim waved back, and watched the pair head for the door. It wasn't the first time she'd been at a bar with Marielle and her friend had gone off with a guy she'd just met.

It made Kim aware of the time. The drive home was lengthy, it was past midnight, and she wasn't even sure where she was. She'd driven here following Lily, who followed Marielle, who used the GPS on her phone.

Kim didn't want to leave. This was a blissful kind of torture, dancing with Ty. Feeling turned on, special, completely unlike her normal self. She'd never had a moment like this, and she wanted it to go on forever. Reluctantly, she murmured, "I should go too."

"Aw," he said, giving her a seductive smile, "don't do that. I don't want you to go."

"I don't want to either," she admitted, "but it's late."

"You're okay to drive?"

"Sure, I only had one beer." Even if it had packed a wallop. She gave in to temptation and leaned her cheek against his chest, that hot, hard vee at the open neck of his shirt.

He shook his head. "Two."

"What?" Mmm, he smelled so good. If she licked him, would he taste woodsy too?

"Two beers. We got refills."

"We did? I wasn't paying attention." She'd been so wrapped up in talking to him, in savoring the sexy way he made her feel. Two beers? No wonder she felt so strange: giggly, dreamy, lustful, off balance. "I should drink coffee, have something to eat." The hot dog and mini donuts had been hours and hours ago.

If she had coffee and food, she'd be okay to drive, wouldn't she? She socialized a fair bit, but always in the city where she could walk or take public transit. Drinking and driving had never been an issue.

"Or you could stay," he said softly, his hips teasing hers.

Six

tay? Kim's breath caught. They'd danced, their bodies had flirted, but . . . Did he think she was like Marielle, carefree and shameless, like the title of that song?

She wasn't. Was she? He did turn her on more than she'd ever been before . . .

Maybe that wasn't what he'd meant anyway. She shouldn't jump to conclusions. "Stay?" she echoed. "You mean, find a room somewhere?"

"Somewhere." His hips and hard-on pressed seductively against her. "Like with me."

Oh, yes! But . . . no, she couldn't.

When she didn't reply, he went on. "Or get yourself a room at the motel across the street. Wouldn't even have to move your car, much less drive home."

Okay, he was being a gentleman. That was good. Really, it was good. She didn't want him pressuring her. The arousal that quickened her body was already doing a fine job of that.

Swaying with him to the slow music, she tried to think. If she got a room, she wouldn't have to worry about driving. In fact, she could even have another drink if she wanted one. No, then she might go really crazy. Climb up on the bar and sing, or jump the cowboy's bones. She bit back a giggle.

If she kept dancing with Ty, she could keep her hottest erotic fantasy going until . . . Until? Until she wanted it to end, she supposed.

Though, right now, it was hard to imagine ever wanting this bliss to end. How far dare she take it?

The gal in Ty's arms hadn't said she was staying, much less sharing his room. But actions spoke. She pressed close, her cheek against his chest, which was bared by the open neck of his shirt. Had she really not made up her mind? Was she playing hard to get? Did she want him to seduce her? Kim was harder to read than a buckle bunny, but he was up for the challenge. In more ways than one.

He didn't want to settle for easing the ache in his groin with a quick jack-off. He hadn't had sex, real live sex, in way too long, and he wanted it—with dragonfly girl.

Ty still wasn't sure why. She was pretty, fun, smart, but so were lots of women. Maybe it was the differences that made her intriguing: a cowboy rancher and an artist city girl. Maybe it was what they had in common, like both understanding passion. Passion for very different things—but also passion for each other. Would she give in to it?

He eased her even closer, the friction of his hard-on against her lithe body driving him crazy. "I've never danced with an artist before."

She giggled, her breath whispering against his chest. "I've never danced with a cowboy."

"I like it." He reached a big hand down to cup her tight little butt. One thing he knew from the horse world: you couldn't judge the quality of the animal by its size. Sometimes the smallest ones had the finest bodies, were the smartest, had the most courage and fire. Was Kim one of those?

"I like it too." She tilted her head, those bright, long-lashed eyes gazing up at him. "I've never been in a place like this, never danced to music like this. Never met anyone like you."

"It's good to broaden your experience." Like by going to bed with him.

"That's what I was telling myself earlier. It's good for my creativity."

Her creativity? Was she creative in bed? His cock surged. "Yeah, I like creativity." He dipped his head, taking all the time in the world to let her know he was coming in for a kiss.

Her eyes widened, her lips parted slightly, then she came up on her toes and met him.

Her kiss was hesitant, and God, her lips were soft. Yes, she did taste of honey. Lust slammed through him. It took all Ty's willpower to keep his grip on her body loose and easy, and keep the kiss gentle and teasing. He wasn't riding a bronc. This wasn't eight seconds of crazy intensity and a struggle of wills. It was more like gentling a wild horse, persuading it that letting him ride it would be a good thing for both of them.

She wanted him. And shit, he wanted her. He wanted her bad. And soon.

Grateful to the band for keeping the slow numbers coming, he swayed to the music, his hips and groin teasing Kim's while his lips and tongue explored her small, perfect lips. He stroked the crease between them, felt her breath sigh out.

She parted her lips wider in invitation.

He swept his tongue inside to explore, his body tightening with urgency. Would her pussy taste as sweet as her mouth? Would it be as warm and wet?

Her tongue mated shyly with his at first. Then suddenly it thrust boldly and her body surged against him like she'd been hit by a bolt of the same lust that blazed through his veins.

Finally, he eased off on the kiss to croon, "Oh yeah, Kim, that's so good." He could barely speak. She'd stolen his breath.

"So good," she echoed, looking dazed. "I can't believe the way you make me feel."

Forcing himself not to rush her, Ty danced a couple more numbers with her. Slow dancing, kissing, fondling as much of her body as he could in public.

She gave back as good as she got, her hands on his ass, her tongue licking a seductive trail on his bare chest.

When he was sure she'd stopped giving off mixed signals, he said, "I want to be alone with you, Kim."

Her eyes were so big, so beautiful, in that delicate face. "Yes," she breathed.

Hallelujah!

In less than a minute, he'd led her back to their table, left bills to pay for their drinks, and helped her find the yellow bag she'd tucked under the table. Semicold bottles of Moosehead and Dead Frog lager sat on the table—from Blake and Marielle?—so he snagged them by the necks with one hand.

He headed Kim toward the door, his arm around her waist, holding her tight against his side. He wasn't sure whether he was afraid she'd get away or just didn't want to let go of her, but it sure as hell felt fine.

Outside, the air was fresh against his overheated skin. A string of flashing red and white lights lit up the sign that read THE RUSTY SPUR. He tugged her away from them. Slowing his long-legged stride to accommodate her shorter legs, he led her across the quiet road to the motel.

The Wagon Wheel had small log cabins scattered among cottonwood trees. His truck with the Ronan Ranch name and double R logo—the name and logo founded by his grandparents—was parked outside his unit.

When he'd decided to stay here rather than drive home, he'd figured he and Blake would be having a few drinks. He sure hadn't expected to take a woman back to his room.

Kim gazed around at the log cabins, the trees. "I've never been in a motel."

"Seriously?" But then, he guessed a city girl would have no reason to. "I couldn't count the number I've stayed in over the years, on the circuit."

She tipped her head back, then lost her balance and stumbled.

"Watch it." He wrapped an arm around her waist. She'd tripped a couple of times before too. Was she tipsy? No, she hadn't even finished two beers. Must just be a touch clumsy. He studied her rapt face as she stared upward. "What are you doing?"

"Looking at the stars! They're so beautiful. I've never seen so many stars."

He glanced up. It was a nice night, but the stars were nothing special. Of course she wouldn't see them all clear and shiny like that in Vancouver or Hong Kong.

When she straightened, he handed her a bottle of beer.

Her arched brows lifted. "Alcohol outside? That's illegal, isn't it?"

He clicked his bottle to hers and took a long swallow. Could've been colder, but it still tasted damned good after the heat inside, and the dancing. "You into following the rules?"

"Pretty much." She cocked her head. "That makes me sound awfully boring." She tipped the bottle to her mouth and took an equally long swallow.

He chuckled. "You're definitely not boring, Kim."

"I'm not?"

"You're the most intriguing woman I've met in a hell of a long time."

Her lips quirked. "That's quite the line, cowboy."

Another swallow of beer. "Something you should know about me: I say what I mean. If I can't do that, I keep my mouth shut."

"Oh." She drank some more beer. "Well, then, thanks." Staring up at him, her dark eyes reflected the stars. "Okay, Ty Ronan, I'll tell you the truth too. You're the most intriguing man I've met in a hell of a long time. I don't meet guys like you." A giggle escaped. "Except in books. This really is like something out of a book."

He didn't have time to do much reading that wasn't ranch-related, but made a guess. "An attraction of opposites thing?"

"Kind of. Yeah." She giggled again.

"Hey, as long as there's an *attraction*." He put his beer bottle on the hood of his truck, then took hers from her and did the same with it.

When she looked questioningly at him, he cradled her fine-boned head between his hands. That spiky hair was soft, like the breast feathers of a bird. He tilted her face up, and leaned down to kiss her slowly. Very slowly, deliberately, and gently, though his body urged him to just take her, hard and fast.

Her lips opened to him on a honeyed sigh, and her tongue met his. It didn't take much coaxing before she was kissing him eagerly again, reaching her arms around to stroke down his back and squeeze his ass.

Her eyes were shut, her lashes silky and long against the upper curves of her cheeks. Then her lashes fluttered, her eyes drifted open. She gazed into his eyes, then past his face, and her eyes widened. "Oh," she breathed. "The stars. We're kissing under the stars. That's so cool."

Kissing her was cool. He didn't much care where they did it.

He took her mouth again, felt her eager response. No, "cool" was the wrong word. Her body, her mouth, the woman was *hot*. And he was hot for her. Lust sparked between them and the kiss went deeper, wilder. He hooked his hands under her butt and hoisted her up into his arms. His sore back gave a twinge, but he quickly forgot the pain as Kim wrapped her legs around him and clung. Still kissing, he ground his erection against her center, and she pressed back.

"Oh God," she breathed when he broke the kiss.

"Yeah." Need consumed him, drove him. He lowered her onto the hood of the truck, hurriedly put the bottles on the ground, then raised the hem of her skirt.

Oh God, oh God, she'd had sex before, but Kim had never felt like this, never experienced anything like this.

A starry, starry night, tall trees all around, air as pure as water from a mountain spring. Her body soft and mellow but on fire at the same time, her sex pulsing with need, hot moisture seeping from her. The man—this tough, hard-bodied cowboy, this smooth dancer, this incredibly sexy kisser—his big hands brushing her legs as he lifted her skirt.

She'd never wanted anything as much as she wanted this man, this moment, under the stars.

Ty found the side straps of her thong, his roughened skin a sensual caress against the tender skin of her hips. He peeled her underwear off and fresh air brushed her damp pussy. Then he rolled her skirt to her waist, baring her to the air, the stars, and his gaze.

Shameless. Like the song. She should protest, but she couldn't. She needed him. Here, now.

"Jesus, Kim, you're pretty," he said in a rough-edged croon. "So pretty."

He stood back, deftly undid his fancy belt buckle, and unzipped his fly.

She watched, captivated. This was all so foreign. Sex was about taking off clothes and neatly folding them, sliding under covers, hugging and stroking until arousal glowed.

But not now. This was so raw, such a weird mix of elements. The most romantic starry sky she'd ever seen. The elaborate buckle that proclaimed this man the toughest of the tough. Under her thighs, the chilled metal of a truck with a ranch logo. The visceral need that had her clenching her thighs against the ache. So unreal, all of it. Exactly like something out of an erotic novel.

She was living an erotic novel and felt sexier than she'd ever have believed possible. She leaned back, straight armed, to rest her hands against the hood, flaunting her body.

Ty groaned and grabbed his wallet from a jeans pocket. He found a condom, unwrapped it, then shoved down his jeans and underwear in one rough sweep.

His cock sprang free, and she stifled a gasp. It was full and bold, bigger than she'd ever seen, more arousing than she'd have believed possible. She wanted to hold it, stroke it, suck it. But later. Right now, as more moisture slipped down her thighs, she wanted him inside her. Needed him inside her, to satisfy the ache he'd created.

"Ty," she moaned, "I need you."

"Jesus, yeah." He sheathed himself. Were those strong, capable hands actually shaking?

The hood of the truck was high enough that she was at his chest level. He grasped her thighs firmly, separated them, and leaned forward to bury his face between them.

Startled, she let out a squeak, but it turned to a groan of pleasure as he lapped at her. Henry had done this, but he'd been almost . . . polite about it. Her body had never peaked, much less shattered, under his tongue.

Ty definitely wasn't polite. Nor was he slow, gentle, or teasing.

Instead, his tongue and lips were rough, demanding. To her surprise, that was exactly what her body wanted. Had anything ever felt this good? She arched back, thrusting her sex against that hungry mouth, and gave herself up to the sensations he created.

Delicious tension raced through her with each lick against her pussy lips, each stab of his tongue between them, each suck and swirl around her clit. Helplessly, she moaned and twisted against him, not sure she could take any more of these intense, exquisite sensations without breaking.

And then she did break, in a swift surge of release that was so sharp and powerful it verged on pain.

Ty held her together with strong fingers circling her hips. Then, as trembling waves still coursed through her, he lifted her toward him, off the hood of the truck and into his arms.

Her legs, more jelly than muscle, somehow managed to wrap around him.

He kissed her fiercely, and tension raced through her again, a hair-trigger return to arousal. Now her legs tightened, the years of yoga paying off, and she clung to him as the head of his cock probed between her legs, blunt and hungry.

She wriggled against him, her body opening, shifting, accommodating his size as he pushed slowly, relentlessly upward. He filled her, stretched her, in a brand-new way. A way that didn't allow her to hold still but made her lift upward, using her thigh muscles and the arms she'd braced on his shoulders for leverage. Up, sliding up his shaft, his flesh already slick with her juices, then down again, creating friction against her inner walls, pressure against her clit.

It was irresistible, addictive. Like scratching an itch, when it feels so good that you just have to keep doing it. And so she did it again, again, as he supported her, one big hand fanned out under her butt, the other around her back. He supported her hundred pounds as if she were as light as a butterfly.

"Shit, Kim." Ty's voice was ragged; his grip tightened.

He shifted position, bracing himself against the truck, then he pumped his hips, taking control of the action, plunging faster, compulsively, into her.

His thrusts were so forceful they almost hurt, but they also stroked every tingling, throbbing nerve ending with a pressure more delicious than anything she'd ever known. Gasping for breath, she arched, flinging her head back.

Head swimming, she managed to focus. And there they were: the stars. She gazed in wonder at the canopy of midnight velvet scattered with stars as brilliant as twinkling diamonds. Sex under the stars, with a man who possessed her body and gave her the kind of bliss she'd only read about.

Ty bent his head, touched his lips to her shoulder, then his teeth in an almost bite. A groan wrenched through him and he said roughly, "Come with me. Fly for me, dragonfly girl."

He pumped even harder, so fast she was powerless to do anything but cling, whimper with pleasure, and climb to a tight, coiled peak of sensation.

His body tensed for a moment and she tensed too, then he climaxed with a hoarse shout and a series of jerky thrusts that took her over the top. Her eyes glazed and above her, the stars were a cascade of fireworks while inside her, her body exploded in its own fireworks display.

Panting, face heated and damp, she struggled to hang on, to not let her muscles loosen and melt like hot wax.

His arms held her securely, though his chest heaved as he struggled to catch his breath.

Then he tensed again. "Hell. Keep quiet."

"What—?"

"*Shh.*" He pressed the back of her head so her face was buried in his neck.

Now she heard what he must have. Voices approaching. Male and female, laughing, singing off-key under their breath.

Getting caught would be so embarrassing. But on the other hand, she felt delightfully naughty. Good girl Kim would never do anything so daring. Good girl Kim would be shocked. She smothered a giggle against Ty's neck. Tonight, with Ty, she'd created dirty girl Kim.

The voices veered off, and a moment later a door closed with a *clunk*.

"That was close," Ty's voice rumbled close to her ear. Gently, he let her down until her shoes touched the ground. "Sorry, I got carried away. This was crazy."

She grinned, feeling her skirt drift down to cover her legs. "Crazy isn't always bad. I'd just as soon no one else came along though."

His hand cupped her shoulder. "I'm with you on that. Let's go inside."

Seven

T y pulled up his jeans and boxer briefs, which were tangled around his lower legs. Man, when Kim made up her mind, she sure got into it. He'd broken his six-month drought with a bang. He picked up the two bottles of beer, which they'd somehow managed not to knock over, and found the room key in his pocket. He unlocked the door of the log cabin and clicked on a lamp. "Sorry, it's nothing fancy."

Kim walked in and put her yellow bag and her discarded thong on a table by the door.

He handed her the bottle of beer, and she glanced around the room. He hoped the place wasn't a mood-buster. It sure wasn't city-sophisticated and it definitely wasn't artsy, but it was clean and cozy, with wood furniture and red and brown plaid upholstery. His rigging bag rested on a chair, his open duffel was on another, and his straw Resistol hat sat on the bedside table. On the road, he rarely bothered to unpack.

She tilted the bottle to her mouth and took a long swallow. "Nice hat, cowboy."

"If you're good, I'll let you try it on."

Mischief lit her dark eyes. "Didn't I already prove that I'm good?"

He chuckled. "Yeah, you got a point. Okay, you can wear my hat, but before you start putting on clothes, let's take some off."

He guided her toward the four-poster bed and put both bottles on the side table. Hoping his rough hands wouldn't damage the delicate fabric, he tugged the floaty blouse up over her head and tossed it onto the bed. Under it, she wore a skimpy body-hugging top in vivid turquoise. No bra; he could tell from the way her nipples poked through the thin cotton.

He undid the fastenings of her skirt and she caught it as it dropped, stepping out of it and laying it over the back of a chair.

The top was cropped, not quite reaching her waist. What a picture she made, all slim and sexy and, somehow, kind of elegant: tousled black hair with turquoise streaks, fine-featured face, sleek torso clad in turquoise, and all the rest of her naked and golden in the lamplight. Gently curved, nicely toned arms and legs, flat belly, and a tiny, enticing vee of black hair, an arrow pointing to treasure.

He didn't get much chance to admire because she was fumbling with the top snap on his shirt, clearly expecting a button.

"Lie down and let me do this," he told her.

"As long as I can watch." She pulled down the bedspread and slipped between the sheets, sitting up against pillows. Picking up her beer bottle, she ran her tongue around the rim, then took a swallow.

His cock promptly imagined that tongue circling it, and, despite having climaxed explosively only a few minutes ago, stirred to life again. He tugged the front of the shirt so the snap-style buttons popped open one by one. A couple shrugs of his shoulders and the shirt slid off. He sat on the edge of the bed to take off his boots, his back registering a protest as he bent down.

She giggled. "You don't wear them to bed."

"Not if I want to get my jeans off." He stood, peeled off his jeans and boxer briefs, and left his clothes on the floor.

She stared, wide-eyed. "You have an amazing body."

"You stole my line." He dropped to the side of the bed and touched her cheek. "You do, Kim. Such a sexy body. But you're so small I'm scared I might hurt you."

"I'm small but I'm strong and flexible." She gave a flirty smile. "Bet I can hold my own."

"Promise to tell me if anything hurts."

She tapped the bottle playfully against his shoulder. "Just what are you planning to do to me, Ty Ronan?"

"All the good things," he answered promptly.

"Hmm." The tip of her pink tongue came out and touched her upper lip, then retreated, making him want to chase it. "*All* of them, you say? That sounds promising."

"And I'm a man of my word." He took her bottle and put it on the table.

Ty started by kissing her, slowly and thoroughly, sinking deep into the kiss until they were both breathless. He kissed her small ear, the sleek line of her neck, wrung a moan from her when he sucked a sensitive spot where her neck met her shoulder. Licked the dip between her collarbones where her pulse thrummed wildly.

Her head twisted from side to side as he worked his way down, slipping the skinny straps from her shoulders as he went. She drove her fingers through his hair to grip his head. Yes, she was surprisingly strong as she guided him to her breast, her nipple hard beneath the thin cotton.

He breathed warm air then licked her through the fabric until she freed one hand from his head and impatiently jerked her top down, releasing her soft breasts.

Such pretty breasts, pale and smooth with those rosy brown buds like cherries on top. He licked circles around her nipple, then sucked it into his mouth. She tasted delicious, a little salty from a day in the heat. The kind of salty that made a guy want to keep on nibbling.

He switched to her other small, perfect breast, so soft and

female, so responsive. Some guys were breast guys; some went for
butts; some were into legs. He'd always gone for the whole package,
and Kim was just about the prettiest package he'd ever unwrapped.
Pretty, sexy, responsive. The breathy whimpers, the way she arched
and pushed into his mouth, the needy writhing of her hips, they
were almost more than he could take.

Her top had bunched below her breasts, so he hooked his hands
into it and peeled it over her head. Then he worked his way down
her smooth, taut body. Her skin was softer than silk, but underneath
he felt a tensile strength.

The sweet curve of her waist, the gentle plane of her belly, the
subtle flare of her hips. A thoroughbred, all the way. As he fondled
and kissed, he scented the sweet musk of her arousal. It drew him,
like a bee to her honey. Her knees bent and came up, her legs parting
for him. Her inner thighs were damp, her pussy lips swollen and
slick. *So beautiful.*

So inviting. He wanted to bury himself deep inside her.

But her hips were lifting, twisting, and she whimpered, "Ty. Ty,
please."

He licked the swollen folds, slid his tongue between them, found
the engorged pearl of her clit. Gently he flicked the tip of his tongue
against it.

She shuddered and thrust up against his mouth, almost grinding
against him.

He licked faster, more firmly, and she moaned, twisted, then
froze, cried out, and her climax pulsed against his mouth.

A little later, her legs relaxed and settled to the bed. "Oh my
gosh," she murmured huskily.

Ty walked to the bathroom and took a couple of condoms from
his travel kit. When he returned, Kim was flopped out on the bed
like she was boneless, but her eyes were open and her gaze followed
him. He held up a condom. "Ready?"

She nodded. "Oh, yes. You warmed me up nicely."

He was pretty hot himself. He sheathed himself and lay down beside her, his body taut with need. He ran his hand down her arm, up again, across her shoulder, down to her breast, that small, perfect handful. "You take top."

"Me? Why?"

"So I won't squash you." He could see she was about to protest—probably to again say how strong she was—but he kept talking. "And you'll have more control."

"Control? Hmm." Her eyes lit with that sexy sparkle. "You mean you want me to ride you"—she paused, then slowly drawled, "cowboy?"

"Damn right. Let's see if you can last more than eight seconds." He stretched out on his back, his sore muscles clenching a moment then beginning to relax.

"You're going to try to buck me off?" She sat up, laughing. The quick motion must have thrown her off balance because she swayed, put a hand to her head.

"Not if I can help it."

"That's good to know." She swung over to sit astride his thighs and grasped his cock, the warm pressure making him jerk with the need to thrust, to pump, to drive to orgasm.

She didn't make him wait, thank God. Holding him firmly, she lifted up on her knees. He felt the hot slickness of her center, and then he was sliding inside with a groan. Kim was so small, the tight grip of her channel so erotic. Not wanting to hurt her, he held still, letting her move at her own pace.

Slowly, she slid down on his shaft, her moisture easing his way, until she'd taken him in.

He rested his hands on her smooth thighs as he fought for self-control. "Shit, Kim, you feel good." Her body was a glove, clinging to him, heating him.

"You too. So good."

She was lovely, slim and exotic. Delicate skin, dusky nipples, the black vee of silky hair between her legs, the punky haircut with turquoise streaks.

Under his hands, her thigh muscles flexed and she began to rise and fall. Riding him, like she'd said.

The thought gave him an idea. Stretching one arm, he hooked his Resistol hat from the bedside table. "You wanted to try this on? Now's a good time, cowgirl." He reached up to plunk it on her head, tipping it back so it didn't fall down over her eyes.

She laughed again and began to move faster, really getting into it now.

He pumped his hips, not taking over, just meeting her halfway. Fighting to hold on to control while the friction, the heat, the sight of her, conspired to make him lose it.

The vigorous motion made the hat tip forward on her small head. She put up a hand to adjust it, then clamped down on the crown to hold it in place.

"Great ride," he managed to gasp.

Grinning, she raised her other arm the way bronc riders did, and waved her hand triumphantly in the air.

That did it. She was so fucking hot. He let go, plunged deep and fast. Saw color bloom on her chest, her cheeks. Heard, "Oh, yes!" And then he was coming, pumping and filling her as her body rippled and pulsed around him, demanding everything he had to give.

Kim woke in the darkness, curled up in bed. Her head pounded, her mouth tasted as if a rodeo bull had stampeded through it, and her stomach was queasy. *Ooh, nasty.* Was she sick, or had she had too much to drink?

Wait a minute. Where was she? In her apartment, the mini blinds always let in a little light, but this room was pitch-dark. And . . . wait a minute. *Rodeo bull?* Where had that thought come from?

She tensed, suddenly aware of the sound of slow, steady breathing and the hardness of something—a male hip?—pressing into her butt.

In a flash, everything came back to her. Oh my God, she'd tied one on with a cowboy named Ty. What had she been thinking?

What had she been drinking? Whatever it was, she was never having it again. And certainly not two bottles, or had it been three? On top of how many hours outside? How many hours of blazing sun?

She was dehydrated, hungover, maybe she had sunstroke. She was insane. She'd lost her mind and had totally meaningless sex with a man she'd just met. A rodeo rider!

It was like the night of the two appletinis, only worse. Public embarrassment at karaoke was nothing compared to this. When she dropped her inhibitions, she did it with a vengeance.

Her heart raced. What was she going to do? She couldn't stay, couldn't wake up with this man, couldn't deal with . . . whatever would happen in a "morning after." She wasn't this person. She was a good, responsible girl, one who took relationships seriously.

And now she felt like a slut.

Gingerly, she eased her naked body away from that warm hip and, inch by inch, toward the edge of the bed, then slipped out. Where was the bathroom? Could she find it in the dark? Sliding her feet slowly along the floor, she headed in what she thought was the right direction, careful not to stumble over anything. Yes, now she felt the frame of the bathroom door.

She whipped inside, eased the door closed, and turned on the light.

Promptly, she slammed her eyes shut against the assault of that light. Then, as cautiously as she'd eased out of bed, she opened them.

Shit. Her hair was a disaster, the touch of eye makeup she'd worn was smeared around bloodshot eyes, and patches of red beard-burn dotted her chest and face. What would her mother say if she saw Kim now? She looked . . . She searched for the word. Dissolute. Exactly as bad as she felt.

Greedily, she drank down a glass of cold water, feeling it soak into every pore of her parched body. Marginally refreshed, she scrubbed off the old makeup with a damp washcloth, then for good measure ran the cloth over the rest of her body. She wouldn't risk turning on the shower and waking Ty.

Her clothes were somewhere out there in the pitch-black room where he slept. The motel room. She'd had sex in a motel room. And outside, under the stars, on the hood of a truck. No, that had to have been a dream. Didn't it?

That honey lager must have something odd in it, like an aphrodisiac. For a moment, she toyed with the idea that Ty had slipped a drug into her drink. Then she shook her pounding head. No way. A guy like him could have pretty much any woman he wanted—including her, apparently. He didn't need drugs to help him out.

He *was* the drug. Him, the booze, and that stupid book giving her ideas about cowboys. Cowboys and starlight.

This was what alcohol did to her. It loosened her inhibitions, turned her crazy. She did stupid things. And most of the time, she didn't even act like she was drunk, so no one knew her actions were booze talking, not brains. Probably, Ty hadn't had a clue she was drunk. After all, how many women got loopy on two or three beers?

Silently she eased open the bathroom door a slit and surveyed the room in the small amount of light the open door provided. The bed loomed large. A four-poster, with the hump of Ty's body on one side. On one of the wooden posts, set at a rakish angle, was his beige cowboy hat.

That hat . . . She put a hand to her mouth to stifle a groan. Had she really sat atop Ty's body, that hat on her head, and ridden him like he was a bucking bronc?

No, she couldn't have. Could she?

God, she hoped he didn't wake up.

Creeping as silently as a ghost, she moved into the room, locating her clothing piece by piece and avoiding looking at the bed. Her thong, thank God. She pulled on the skimpy bit of fabric as if it was a security blanket. Skirt, tank, ballet flats—she added layers, feeling more herself with each one. The canary yellow bag she loved. But where was the butterfly top?

She glided closer to the bed, having to look now, to find her blouse.

The tangle of sheets was down past Ty's waist, leaving his torso naked, a sculpted work of art in the dim light. And there—she pressed her fist against her mouth to stifle a groan—there was her top, under his head, anchored against the pillow. No way could she possibly slide it out.

Fine. It would only be a reminder, and she wanted to forget that this night had happened.

She hurried toward the cabin door. Hand on the knob, something made her pause. Had he awakened? Would he try to stop her? She turned slowly, feeling like a fugitive ready to flee.

But he slept, oblivious. He wouldn't be stopping her.

Even if he had woken up, he likely wouldn't try to stop her. He'd gotten what he wanted.

* * *

When she woke for the second time Sunday morning, this time safely in her own bed, Kim's hangover had pretty much gone. Now she just felt stupid and embarrassed and slutty.

She put coffee on to brew, and took her cell out of her yellow bag. She'd had it turned off all day yesterday. There were texts from friends, which she'd respond to later. One from Marielle too.

Guess what, I'm still in the Valley! Hot, hot night!!! Coming to the rodeo? Let's meet up.

Kim ground her teeth and texted, Not coming. Have fun. And Marielle would. How damned easy things were for her.

There was a voice mail from Henry, calling from the office yesterday afternoon to ask if she wanted to go for dinner.

He'd been a good boyfriend, attentive and considerate. Smart and ambitious. Good-looking, in the cosmopolitan way she liked— or at least, had liked until yesterday—with his great haircut and beautifully styled clothes. He was a city boy just as much as she was a city girl, though his taste was conventional and hers was anything but. They shared common values, and their only real disagreement had been over her art. He had taken her parents' side, saying she must be loyal to her family and could still pursue art as a hobby.

He'd taken their breakup with his usual lack of visible emotion, saying he hoped they could remain friends. She did care for him and was glad not to lose him.

She poured herself a cup of coffee and sipped gratefully. What time was it? Eleven. She should call Henry, apologize for not e-mailing him back. Tell him they'd have dinner soon. Not tonight. She couldn't face him yet. Not that she'd tell him about Ty. Yes, she and Henry were free to date other people, but what she'd done was over the top. He'd think she was a slut.

Which she was, kind of.

Why did it seem fun when Marielle hooked up with Blake Long-feather, but slutty when Kim had sex with Ty?

She settled at the table with her coffee and checked e-mail. There was a message from her mom, which immediately sent a twinge of guilt through her. If her parents had the slightest idea what Kim had done last night . . .

Eight

B ut her parents didn't know. And they wouldn't. It was done, over, would never happen again. She would put it out of her mind. If she'd been home with them in Hong Kong, she'd never have gone crazy like that.

She and her parents had flown back and forth a few times since she'd moved to Vancouver, but it was four months since she'd seen either of them. Despite their occasional differences, she missed them like crazy. She read her mom's message, smiling nostalgically. Her mother was completely fluent in English, but had a staccato style of writing that reminded Kim of the dazzling pace of life back home, the bustle, the energy, the vibrant colors, the constant noise.

Her mom filled her in on what was going on with the company and with various family members, a gush of news and commentary that made Kim feel lonely.

Not as lonely as almost two years ago, when she'd moved here at the age of twenty-two. Now she not only had her old childhood friends but new ones at school, she had book club, she had Henry. She'd explored Vancouver as an adult, and loved her second home. Yet, as the treasured only child of forty-something parents who'd given up hope of a baby, she'd never lived alone until now. It still took getting used to.

Her parents felt the same. They never failed to remind her that they'd much prefer she had stayed home, joining the company and working with them, living at home until she found the right man and married. Preferably, a man they chose for her. Which, at the moment, didn't sound like all that bad an idea.

Now, her mother wrote:

Your time in Vancouver is almost up. You must now realize that your proper place is with the company. Just say the word, and we'll buy you a ticket home. Your father and I want only what's best for you: a good career in the family business, and a good marriage. Art is fine as a hobby, but now it is time to take your place with us in CPM.

A shiver of anxiety rippled across Kim's shoulders. Yes, her time had almost run out. It had taken all her persuasive skills to convince her parents to allow her this time to study art, but finally they had agreed to support her for two years and not a moment longer. They'd said it was a waste of time, that an artist couldn't make a living. She told them she'd find a way, and return to Hong Kong with a viable business plan. She wasn't flaky; she was businesslike and wanted financial security, but she also wanted to pursue her passion.

Her parents loved her. They had agreed that, if she convinced them she could make a living from her art, they would let her do it. She'd die if she was stifled in an office all day, managing the ever-growing number of commercial and residential properties her parents kept amassing, some as owner-managers and some as managers. Her mom and dad had come from the country; they'd been entrepreneurs and built their empire. How could they and those ancestors they kept invoking fail to be proud if she displayed her own entrepreneurial spirit and started her own business?

She should think seriously about designing clothing. She had a flair for it and enjoyed it. And yet, so many other people did that. She wanted something more uniquely her own—and she had to find it soon.

Frowning, she turned back to the e-mail, and promptly groaned. Her mom had moved from one guilt trip to another.

On the subject of marriage, Peter and his girlfriend Lin have announced their engagement. As I've told you, she's a clever, charming young woman who is studying engineering.

She couldn't be all that clever if she didn't see that Kim's cousin was an arrogant, not terribly bright, bore.

How is Henry? I saw his parents on the weekend. We hope the two of you will have an announcement of your own before long.

No, no, no. Kim shook her head, feeling her spiky hair flick back and forth.

When her mom was in Vancouver four months ago, Henry'd had dinner with them. As far as both sets of parents knew, Kim and Henry were still a couple. "Henry and I are cowards," she muttered. But they both hated disappointing their parents. Easier to let their folks assume they were still dating, then reveal the breakup when they returned to Hong Kong.

She really did have to call Henry.

When he picked up, she tried to banish all thoughts of Ty. "I'm sorry I didn't return your call," she said. "I was out with my book club friends and had my cell turned off."

"I understand. I stayed at the office until late."

"You work so hard." His family's company was hi-tech. He was getting international experience, then would return to Hong Kong and ascend the corporate ladder. Henry was a diligent guy and put in long hours, learning everything he could.

"Of course. I will work this afternoon as well." His English was excellent, but not as informal and colloquial as her own. "How are you today, Kim?"

She swallowed. "Oh, I'm fine." As fine as a hungover slut could be. Quickly, she changed the subject. "Mom e-mailed. My cousin Peter's engaged."

"Now she puts more pressure on you?"

She knew he'd understand. "You bet. There'd be even more if she knew we broke up."

"She would perhaps look for someone else in Vancouver to match you with." His tone was neutral, so she couldn't tell if that idea upset him.

"Not likely, with me heading home so soon. That's when the matchmaking will start. The same with your parents, right?"

"I have no interest in that," he said softly.

What did that mean? That he didn't want to be matchmade, or did he perhaps hope she'd change her mind? She and Henry had both been raised to be reserved about sharing their feelings, and to respect other people's privacy. So, curious as she was, she didn't push. "You still plan to go back to Hong Kong in two months too?"

"Of course. I look forward to this."

"You won't miss Vancouver?" Much as she loved Hong Kong, it was going to be hard to leave this city.

"No. Why would I?"

Because it was an incredible, vibrant, cosmopolitan place. But then, Henry hadn't seen much of that. Kim had explored, on her own and with old and new friends, making the city her own. Henry spent most of his time at work, only coming out for business dinners or meals with her. He wasn't interested in long walks, sightseeing, visiting galleries or museums, clubbing, or any of the other activities she so enjoyed. In fact, now that she thought about it, his entire time in Vancouver—both his work and dating her—had been oriented toward his return to Hong Kong. Toward meeting his parents' expectations.

Home. Parental expectations. She'd be home herself in less than two months. If she didn't want to join CPM, she had to get serious. Pouring a second cup of coffee, Kim vowed to forget about last night and concentrate her energy on a business plan for a clothing design business. Perhaps she could turn it into something she'd be excited about.

As for Ty Ronan, he was the past. Done, gone, never to be thought of again.

Kim trudged down Burrard Street toward Cactus Club, this Monday's meeting place. The club members had such busy lives, they'd quickly realized they could never find one whole evening when they were all free. Instead, they met late every Monday afternoon for an hour. They had set a rule: to read only one-third of the book each week, and not go further. But they were supposed to read that third, and for the first time Kim hadn't done her homework. Last night, she picked up *Ride Her, Cowboy*, and the stupid book reminded her of Ty. She didn't even open it.

She probably wouldn't open it again. Bad enough that Sunday night's sleep had been plagued by erotic dreams about Ty. Reading about Marty's affair with Dirk Zamora would only fuel those stupid fantasies. How ironic and frustrating that, at the rodeo, she'd reveled in imagining sexy fantasies featuring cowboy Ty. Now, the last thing she wanted was a reminder of what she'd done Saturday night.

If she wasn't going to read the book or attend meetings, maybe she should drop out of the club. Except, she liked Marielle, George, and Lily. The women, the books they read, the discussions, all made her think.

If it wasn't for the club, she'd still be with Henry, stuck in a rut that could have turned into a lifetime sentence to mediocrity. On the other hand, the club was the reason she'd met Ty. It was their fault. Marielle's, mostly. Maybe Kim should go to the meeting and vent.

Not that she ever vented. She wasn't the type. But then, she wasn't the type to go at it on the hood of a truck either.

She eyed Cactus Club, across the street. Marielle had picked a place where they could sit outside. Too bad. Normally Kim loved being outside in Vancouver's fresh air, but today it reminded her of those hours in the sun at the rodeo. If it had been her turn to choose, she'd have picked the darkest bar in town; she could lurk in a hidden corner and nurse her shame and guilt. The dark corner would match up with her plain old jeans and navy tee, and the black hair she hadn't felt like color-streaking.

She trudged across the street. Though the Ty thing made her feel shitty, it wasn't the only thing that had her depressed. She'd spent hours working on a business plan and didn't feel the slightest spark of enthusiasm. Maybe she should skip book club and get back to work on it.

But no, she owed it to the others to show up, then she'd decide whether she would stay with the club.

Lily and George were already there, seated at high chairs around a tall table for four, with the typical martini and glass of white wine. Kim hoisted herself up into a chair—trying not to remember Ty lifting her onto the hood of his truck. When the stylish black-clad waitress asked what she'd like to drink, she said grimly, "Cranberry and soda."

Lily, her fair skin complemented by a thin rose-colored sweater, raised her delicate blond eyebrows. "Are you feeling all right?"

"Sure. I don't always have to drink booze, you know."

Lily and George, who wore a gold-colored jersey that made her hair look especially fiery, exchanged glances.

Kim pretended not to notice.

"How did . . ." George started cautiously, then broke off as Marielle, in white capris and a vivid orange top, rushed in. A quick scan of the drink list, and she ordered something called a Brazilian. It sounded like a wax job, but must be one of the colorful, boozy drinks she loved.

The brunette looked as happy as Kim felt miserable. The moment the waiter left, Marielle leaned forward, eyes flashing. "Wasn't Saturday the best day ever?"

George said, "It was fun, but I'm dying of curiosity. What happened with you and Blake?"

"What didn't happen?" She gave a burbly, smirky laugh. "That man is amazing! Believe me, that Dirk dude in our book doesn't hold a candle to Blake." Elbows on the table, she leaned forward eagerly. "And yes, I stayed over, and went to the rodeo Sunday too. They had afternoon events, then the finals in the evening. Blake was amazing in the bull riding, and he won saddle bronc with a score of 89. He got fifteen thousand dollars! I think I inspired him. And last night, oh man, he took me for one wild ride."

She turned to Kim. "I thought you'd come see Ty compete. He was in the finals too, and he—"

"Stop!" Kim almost yelled. "I don't want to hear about it."

Oops. Was that an overreaction? Three faces stared at her curiously.

"The two of you seemed to be hitting it off," Lily said. "Was it okay that George and I left? If we'd thought there was any problem—"

"No!" Kim rarely interrupted people, but now did it for the second time in twenty seconds. "There was no problem. I'm perfectly capable of looking after myself in a bar."

"You had to look after yourself?" George's eyes narrowed. "Did Ty Ronan try something?"

Kim stifled a moan. What hadn't he tried? Sex this way, that way, every fabulous way she could imagine. Well, not quite every way; they'd fallen asleep before they could— She dragged her mind away. "He was fine. We danced."

She'd been raised to be honest, which she interpreted as not straight-out lying. Omitting an occasional detail wasn't a lie. Like the way she and Henry hadn't told their parents they were just friends now. Let their parents be happy—and not bug her and Henry—for a little while longer.

"And I drove home," she added. "And I really have no desire to hear about him again. Are we going to eat? Has anyone ordered appies?"

After a moment's silence, everyone picked up a menu. They decided on tuna tataki, crispy dry ribs, and edamame.

"All right then," Lily said crisply. "Let's talk about the book." She turned to Kim. "Did you like it?"

"Actually, I didn't manage to finish the first part," she confessed. At their surprised looks, she said, "I was busy. I'm sorry."

"Are you sure you're all right?" Lily said with concern. "It's not like you to not finish."

"Stop playing mom," Kim snapped. "I'm fine."

The wounded look on Lily's face gave Kim an immediate case of the guilts. "I'm sorry." She grabbed her friend's hand. "So sorry. I'm a bitch. It's PMS or something." *Something* being Ty Ronan.

"It's all right," Lily said quietly. She squeezed Kim's hand then released it and picked up her martini. "Maybe we shouldn't talk about the book. There'd be spoilers for Kim."

"How far did you get, Kim?" George asked. "We could discuss it to that point."

Kim deliberated. Maybe she was a little curious about how the others saw Marty's fling with Dirk. She waited until their server had put platters of appetizers on the table, then said, "The last part I read was the sex scene at the river."

"Under the canopy of stars?" George took a dry rib. "Wasn't that incredible? Can you imagine sex outside, under the stars?"

Yeah. It'd be like fireworks. Kim took an edamame pod, though she didn't have much appetite.

"George, George," Marielle chided. "You haven't done that? Woody's slipping."

"No, he's not," George returned, a satisfied gleam in her eye. "But it's a good idea. Where, though? We don't want to get arrested."

"Spanish Banks, Queen Elizabeth Park, Second Beach," Marielle said promptly. "There are loads of places." She glanced around. "Kim, Lily, do you have any suggestions?"

Lily shook her head. So did Kim, not about to suggest the hood of a truck in a parking lot.

"I loved how the passion overcame them," George said. "Woody and I've had times like that, where you're so hot for each other you lose your minds."

Lose your mind. Exactly.

"But they barely know each other and she's not even sure if she likes him," Lily objected. "Can a woman really get so carried away that she has sex in those circumstances?"

Yes. Kim swallowed. Though, actually, she had kind of liked Ty.

"Yes," George said with a private smile.

Marielle nodded vigorously. "Sex is a great way of getting to know someone."

"Look," the blond doctor said, "you know I think consensual, safe sex is healthy. But a woman needs to look after herself. It can be dangerous, having sex with someone you don't know."

Kim, who'd been halfheartedly squeezing edamame beans out of the pod and munching them one by one, almost choked on a bean.

"Says the woman who's only had sex with one man for . . . How many years has it been?" Marielle asked Lily.

Lily's jaw tightened. "Fifteen."

The doctor rarely said much about her personal life, beyond that she was married and didn't have kids. Still, Kim had picked up on an occasional hint that Lily wasn't thrilled about her marriage. She was curious, but didn't want to pry.

"Man, that's forever." Marielle shook her head, her wavy dark hair tossing. "Sounds awful to me."

"Sounds great to me," George said. "If you're with the right man, why would you want someone else? Right, Lily?"

"Right." She sounded less than ecstatic.

"Well," Marielle said cheerfully, "you know me. There's no one man, job, or drink that's going to keep me happy for the rest of my life. As for being safe, I happen to be a great judge of character." She turned to Kim. "You're being quiet. What do you think?"

"That the ideal is what George says," she answered slowly. "It is for me, anyhow."

"Yeah, but you thought you had that with your boyfriend," Marielle said, "and found out you were wrong. So now, why not have some fun? Like you seemed to be having with Ty."

Only the most fun she'd ever had. Maybe Marielle was right, and it wasn't such a bad thing to have some harmless fun. Thoughtfully, Kim sipped her boring cranberry drink. Maybe she wasn't a total slut.

"There's a difference between dancing and having sex," Lily said.

Nine

Kim swallowed. *Right*. That was the bottom line for her too. Slowly she said, "Yes. Dancing, socializing, that's great. But sex . . . It should be special." Sex under the stars, sex in a cowboy hat, that had been pretty special. She frowned. "I mean, uh, emotional. Intimate. With someone you know and care about, where you think maybe there's a future for the two of you."

Marielle, who'd been lifting a forkful of tuna tataki toward her mouth, paused. "Why?" she asked bluntly.

"I guess . . . because otherwise you're wasting your time."

"Having fun isn't a waste of time," the other woman said. "You go drinking with friends. Isn't that as much a waste of time as having sex with a hot guy?"

Kim frowned again. "Okay, then maybe it's about valuing yourself. Not giving yourself to anyone who comes along."

"Hey, not just anyone. Did you hear me say 'hot guy'?" Marielle tilted her head. "You think Marty Westerbrook disrespected herself by having sex with Dirk?"

"I'm not sure."

"You think I'm disrespecting myself by having sex with Blake? Or you'd be disrespecting yourself if you'd done more than just dance with Ty?"

That was how she'd felt when she studied her debauched reflection in the motel room mirror. But, hmm . . . She took a long drink of cranberry and soda. It was complicated, sorting this stuff out. "I don't think you're disrespecting yourself, Marielle. You have such a strong sense of yourself and so much confidence, and you know what you want. But what you want is temporary, and what I want is permanent." And that was why she felt so much shame and guilt.

"How about Marty?" George asked. "Do you think she was wrong to have sex with Dirk, given that—" She broke off. "Sorry, I forgot you haven't read past the sex scene."

"Right," Lily said. "We can carry on the discussion next week, when we've all read the next section." She raised her eyebrows in Kim's direction. "That's not going to be a problem for you, is it?"

Of course it would. It would make her think of Ty. But, to be realistic, she'd think of him anyhow. And she didn't want to drop out of book club. This afternoon had reinforced how much she liked these women, and the way they challenged her. "No problem."

Alone in his bedroom at Ronan Ranch on Thursday night, Ty gingerly touched the silky winged top with one rough finger. He'd done that a lot since he'd woken Sunday morning to find that Kim had gone. No note, no phone number. She hadn't even told him her last name. But she'd left the top. Intentionally, as some message that he was too stupid to get? Or had he been lying on it, and she couldn't pull it free?

Why had she left? They'd had incredible sex. She'd been into it; she'd liked it.

Could she be married? She hadn't worn a ring, but he'd known women to take off their wedding rings and hook up with a rodeo cowboy.

He shouldn't waste time thinking about Kim. She'd been a one-nighter, great sex to break his dry spell. He should find a woman with long-term potential. He was nearing thirty. Ronan Ranch was getting established. This was the right time to marry, and then think about a family.

He needed a ranch wife, a woman like his grandma and his mom. An equal partner who'd share in the hard work and love the country lifestyle. No point wasting his time with a dragonfly art student from Hong Kong.

But man, Kim was something. She was different, unpredictable, exciting. Passionate. Oh hell, he wanted to see her again. Or at least find out why she'd skipped out and ended one damned fantastic night.

Kim from Hong Kong, an art student at Emily Carr who designed clothes and was into butterflies. How hard could it be to track her down?

He sat in front of his computer, and in less than a minute, he was looking at her Facebook page. The art was a vibrant abstract design that looked like wings. In her picture, she had orange streaks in her black hair. That hair looked kind of spiky, but when he touched it, it had been soft as silk. Soft as feathers.

Maybe she really did have wings. Maybe she'd flown away, not driven.

Ty wasn't a fast typist—his hands were too big—but he clicked out the letters deliberately.

Why the hell did you run and when the hell am I going to see you again?

He studied the blunt words. Yup, that pretty much said what needed to be said. He added his e-mail address and phone number, and sent the message off to her.

And now it was bedtime. If the past nights were any example, his sleep would be filled with sex dreams of Kim, and he'd wake with a hard-on as rigid as a fence post.

* * *

Thursday night, after working on more ideas for a clothing design business, Kim turned off her computer with a frustrated sigh. This just didn't feel right, and agonizing over it wasn't helping. Inspiration and creativity didn't feed on angst.

She curled on top of her double bed in a nest of pillows and opened *Ride Her, Cowboy*.

It was now the second day of the cattle drive. Marty's muscles had loosened up, and she found she enjoyed riding along with nothing to do but take photographs and record notes.

Despite the dust and noise of the sizable herd of cattle, the occasional shouts of the cowboys, and the barking of their dogs, there was something surprisingly peaceful about the experience. The country was so vast. Awe-inspiring. It made her and her companions seem small and insignificant, yet, oddly, that thought was almost comforting.

She did know that what she did mattered. She brought information and enlightenment to people. What Dirk and the cowboys did mattered too. Their cattle fed hungry people, and the work supported them and their own families.

Important, yes, but only a blink of time in the grand scheme of the centuries these mountains and plains had been here.

Last night—the wild sex under the stars at the river—had been less than a blink, yet the memory of it throbbed pleasurably in her body. Would they do it again?

She'd had sex when she was on assignment before. Three years ago, she'd even fallen in love. She'd been in Afghanistan, death waiting around each corner. Sex and love were so intense, an affirmation of life and hope. Hope that there'd be a future.

Her soldier had stepped around that corner and death, in the form of a teenage suicide bomber, had taken him and half a dozen others.

*She was alone again, the way she'd been since her parents both died in
a car crash when she was eighteen.*

*Now she was happy to have sex, but love was something to avoid.
When she thought of the future, it was in terms of her work. More
assignments, more travel. It kept her busy.*

Kim nodded, guessing what George had been about to say
on Monday, before she remembered Kim hadn't read this section.
No, Marty wasn't disrespecting herself in having sex with Dirk.
Like Marielle, she chose sex and rejected love, though in Marielle's
case it was about fun and variety, and in Marty's it was because of a
broken heart. How sad. Kim read on.

*Maybe she'd felt a little worn-out lately, but that was because she'd
been working too hard. This assignment was timely. Long days in the
saddle, inspiring scenery, interesting chats with the cowboys as they
took turns riding alongside her, and—with luck and privacy—more
blazing sex with Dirk Zamora.*

*It might take luck, because he was avoiding her today, though
she'd caught him watching her more than once. Maybe he regretted the
passion that had flared between them. She figured he still resented her
being here—both as a woman on a cattle drive and as a journalist
writing a story he'd rather not have written. He'd told her he only
agreed because his sister had insisted, saying they needed the good
publicity. Marty figured she'd be giving that to him too, because the
more she saw of him, his cowboys, and his operation, the more she respected him.*

*They'd barely exchanged two words by the end of the day, but
there he was, sitting across the circle from her as everyone gathered
around a crackling fire under that same canopy of stars she'd seen over
his shoulder when they had sex last night.*

Tonight, she was a little achy from the long ride, but less so than last night. She felt pleasantly tired, and grateful to be drinking chilled beer and eating perfectly grilled filet mignon, potatoes fried with onions, and sautéed greens.

"I'm not surprised to be eating beef," she said, "but I hadn't expected gourmet fare."

"Been watchin' them old cowboy movies?" a graying man called Len, who did most of the cooking, asked. "Figured I'd serve you up a mess o' beans on a tin plate?"

She grinned at him. "Pretty much. And I've eaten lots worse."

"Yeah, sure." It was Dirk, a touch of disbelieving snark in his voice. "Gotta say, I'm surprised you're still with us. Bet you're feeling crippled after all the riding."

"Nope. I'm in pretty good shape"—she paused, then added deliberately—"in case you haven't noticed." He certainly should have noticed the strength in her thighs when she'd tightened them around his hips as he pounded into her last night.

He snorted and, not giving an inch, said, "Yeah, sure, you're a tough girl."

She cocked an eyebrow, fed up with his attitude. "You think this is tough? Wait until you've been in Afghanistan, where you can't walk an inch without being afraid you'll trip an IED, or that"—she swallowed—"some kid on a bike or woman in a burka will turn out to be a suicide bomber and blow you up." She fought to hold her voice steady. "If I can handle that, cowboy"—she said the word disparagingly—"I can handle your little cattle drive."

"You were in Afghanistan?" The snark was gone now.

"Twice." The first time, she'd loved and lost. The second time, she'd gone back to prove to herself she could handle it. Now that, she figured, was tough. Not that she'd share that bit of personal history with Dirk Zamora.

"Okay," he said slowly and almost grudgingly. "I'm impressed. I figured you'd covered . . ." He shrugged.

"Fluff pieces? The latest styles in fake fingernails? Yes, I've written about beauty pageants and breast implants, though I'd hardly call those fluff subjects. I've also covered civil war in Syria, the drug war in Mexico, and . . . well you get the picture."

"That's one hell of a life you live, girl," one of the cowboys said. "Can't say as I'd want to do it."

"Each to their own," she said.

Across the circle, Dirk remained silent, but his gaze didn't leave her face.

"Well," Les said, "better clean up and hit the sack. Dawn'll be here before you know."

The men rose and went about chores, each clearly knowing his role. Dirk headed toward the horses, and she followed.

Though she walked quietly, he must have heard her because as soon as they were out of sight of the fire, he turned. "Glad you came. There's something I need to say."

"Go ahead."

"I misjudged you. Sorry."

She hadn't liked the way he'd made assumptions, but she respected a person who'd admit he was wrong and apologize. "Apology accepted." She held out her hand. If he touched her, he'd feel that spark between them. She curved her lips as he reached out to take her hand. "Does this mean you like me a little?"

He grasped her hand firmly, but didn't shake. Instead, he gave a quick, firm tug.

Surprised, she stumbled forward.

He released her hand, caught her by the waist to steady her, then next thing she knew the front of his body met hers.

"Maybe a little," his voice rumbled close to her ear. He caught her

jean-clad butt, pulling her tighter against him so she felt the hardness of his dick through his fly.

She ground against him, damp for him, craving him. "We can't do this now. I don't want your men to know."

He shook his head. "Me either. It's got nothing to do with them."

Nothing to do with his real life, he meant. For the first time, it occurred to her to ask, "Why aren't you married? Shouldn't you have a ranch wife and a passel of kids?"

He chuckled. "Don't tell me you're volunteering?"

"God, no. Just curious."

"Been busy, I guess. But yeah, I gotta do me some looking, one of these days before too long." One hand left her butt to slip under the front of her shirt and tease her nipple through her bra. "How come you're not married? Too busy traveling all over the world, writing about breasts and civil wars?"

Three years ago, she'd thought about settling down in one place, with one man. But that was a romantic dream fueled by being in a war zone. "That's right. My lifestyle's nomadic. I follow the story. That's what I always wanted to do."

"We're 'bout as different as two people can get. Funny how there's this physical thing between us."

"Funny," she echoed. "So what're we going to do about it?"

"The hands will be asleep in ten minutes. Make like you're going to bed, then when they're all snoring, come meet me right here."

So, they'd be having sex again. No surprise, and Kim liked how Marty and Dirk had come to respect each other. She decided to go through her bedtime ritual and climb under the covers, so she could really get into the sex scene. With any luck, she'd click off the light with fantasies of Dirk Zamora—not Ty Ronan—filling her mind and heating her body.

One final check of e-mail, and a quick glance at Facebook—and her jaw dropped when she saw a message from Ty Ronan.

Why the hell did you run and when the hell am I going to see you again?

He wanted to see her again?

He didn't say anything about the top she'd left behind, so it wasn't that he felt obligated to return it. And he'd tracked her down on Facebook.

The possibility of seeing him again had never—except in sexy dreams—crossed her mind. It was a sleazy one-nighter; it wasn't a date. It wasn't a relationship. It had definitely been great sex, though. Did he agree, and want more of it?

Why her? There was nothing so special about her. Or, at least, the things that made her special, like her quirky creativity, couldn't really appeal to a cowboy, right? And why was she fussing over why *he* wanted to see *her*? The important fact was that she hadn't the slightest desire to see him again. She wasn't like Marty in the book, nor like Marielle, who was all about fun. Saturday night had been an aberration, a onetime thing. The real Kim wasn't into casual flings.

The real Kim didn't have fun.

No, wait. Where had that thought come from? Of course she did. Making art was fun, hanging out with friends was fun, book club was fun. She'd had fun with Henry when they'd been a couple. Okay, the sex hadn't been as phenomenal as with Ty, but it had been fun believing they loved each other and had a future.

A future that she'd ended. No, it wasn't as dramatic as having her man torn apart by a suicide bomb, and it hadn't made her swear off men. She'd meet someone else once she was home in Hong Kong, and they'd have loads of fun, in and out of bed.

Ty Ronan had no place in her life.

She stared at his message again. Blunt; the opposite of romantic. She didn't owe him an explanation. Her fingers rested on the keyboard. Probably, she should just delete this. Instead, she slowly tapped out:

Why?

She sent the message to his e-mail address, turned off her computer, and got ready for bed. When she picked up *Ride Her, Cowboy*, she knew that, no matter how hot the scene between Marty and Dirk, there'd be a different cowboy in her erotic dreams tonight. Just because a guy wasn't a marriage prospect didn't mean a girl couldn't fantasize about him.

Did it mean she'd be disrespecting herself if she did more than fantasize?

Ten

Ty got up before dawn and found Kim's e-mail. *Huh.* So she could be brief too. He figured the "why?" referred to why he wanted to see her again. He responded:

Had fun. Thought you did too.

Then he headed out to do some chores.
When he came in to make breakfast, he found her response:

Life's about more than just fun.

That sent his eyebrows jumping. He responded:

You're talking to a guy who's put in more than 3 hrs
hard work before 8 am. A working man needs some
fun too. So does a gal.

He shook out his large hands, cramped from this bit of typing. Thank heavens his mom handled most of Ronan Ranch's e-mail. Frustrated, he typed:

Why are we talking this way? Give me a call.

A minute later his cell rang. "Hey, Kim."

"What do you want?" She sounded jittery, a nervous dragonfly ready to take flight.

"Just to see you."

"I don't think that's a good idea."

"We both had fun. We could have fun again. How's that a bad idea?"

A long pause. Then, "If I'm going to see you, we need to talk." Her voice was higher pitched than on Saturday,; still, it sounded good to his ears.

"We are talking."

"I mean, uh, I'm not like that. Not like I was Saturday night. I don't just, you know. With any guy who comes along."

They'd talked, they'd danced. She'd known his name before she met him. He wasn't just any guy. But he guessed she was feeling sleazy for having had sex on a first—well, it hadn't even been a date. "Let's get together again. We can talk. Talk's good." She was interesting, smart. "How about I come into town and take you for dinner tonight?" If they hit it off like before, they'd end up in bed again. If not, then it was just one wasted evening.

"You'd drive into Vancouver? It's a long way."

He laughed. "After years on the rodeo circuit, an hour or two's drive is nothing."

There was a long pause. "Dinner. Just dinner. And talk."

He wouldn't make that promise. "Dinner and talk, then we'll see what we feel like. I'll pick you up."

"No, I'll meet you."

She didn't trust him. That pissed him off, but then why should she trust a rodeo rider she'd hooked up with in a bar? "Where?"

"Um, do you like Mediterranean food?"

Mediterranean food? Did that involve olives, pizza, feta cheese? Sounded good to him. "Sure." It occurred to him, because they were

talking about the big city, to ask, "This place fancy?" God forbid
he had to put on a tie.

"No, it's just a nice neighborhood restaurant." She told him
the name was Laziza and where to find it, and said she'd make a
reservation under his name.

A reservation. He was used to casual places where, if the place
was full, people hung out at the door waiting and talking. "Thanks.
See you then."

As he cooked up scrambled eggs, sausages, and toast, he wondered what the evening would bring. Kim wasn't his typical date.
She was unpredictable, which made things interesting. His blood
quickened with that adrenaline rush of anticipation, and he whis-
tled Garth Brooks' "Shameless."

After a hearty meal, Ty had a busy day, barely finding time to
grab lunch. Late in the afternoon, he took a quick shower, shaved,
and changed into black jeans and a white snap-button western shirt.
Just a plain leather belt; he figured a rodeo buckle wouldn't go over
so well downtown. He bundled Kim's winged blouse into a paper
bag, then headed out.

The weather was hot, the skies clear. Driving with the window
open and his arm resting on the sill, he figured that tonight would
turn out or it wouldn't. Either way, his life would go on more or less
the same. With the brim of his hat shading his eyes from the sun as
he headed west, he cranked up the radio and sang along with Tim
McGraw.

As he neared the coast, darkish clouds mounted in the sky and
by the time he drove into the West End of Vancouver, a brisk breeze
was slinging raindrops. He rolled up his window. It wasn't exactly
cold, just a lot of degrees lower than where he'd started from.

He found the restaurant, decided not to squeeze the truck into
street parking designed for cars and SUVs, and located a parking lot.
Tucking the paper bag under his arm to protect it from the rain, he

sauntered down the block, checking out the various businesses: a gay bar, a KFC, a produce store, an Asian restaurant. Yup, he was in the city.

When he reached Laziza, he glanced through the front window. No sign of Kim, but he was a few minutes early. He turned away from the window and saw, coming down the sidewalk, the circle of a purple and blue umbrella, held like a shield to block the wind and rain from the invisible person carrying it. The design looked familiar, like a painting of water lilies by some famous European painter whose name he didn't recall.

An art-style umbrella, held at a height that told him the owner was short.

He stepped into the path of the umbrella, hoping she wouldn't run him down.

She pulled up short. From behind the umbrella came, "Cowboy boots." Then the umbrella tilted, revealing black calf-length leggings and a long-sleeved white tee with a flock of stylized butterflies in black, turquoise, and red, and finally Kim's face. Tonight her black hair was streaked with red.

"And a cowboy hat," she added. A grin tipped her pretty lips. "Lost your way, cowboy?"

"Sure hope not." He grinned back at her. God, she was cute, and she packed one hell of a lot of sex appeal in such a tiny package. He remembered her naked, wearing his hat, and wondered what she'd do if he kissed her.

She shifted uneasily. "You're looking at me funny."

"Appreciatively," he corrected. Would she be flattered or upset if she knew what he was thinking? "You look great." Best not to try the kiss and risk scaring her off. "I like that tee."

"Thanks. It's based on the Red Spotted Admiral butterfly. You look"—she surveyed him, something gleaming deep in her dark eyes—"like you."

"Is that a good thing?" Should he have left the hat behind, swapped the boots for loafers? He owned loafers, but it was second nature to slip into comfy boots.

"It's a good thing," she said almost reluctantly.

A gust of wind caught her umbrella, and he put his hand over hers, steadying her grip. "Crazy gizmos. Don't fly away, dragonfly girl." Her skin was cool, yet somehow sent a zip of heat through his palm.

She stepped away, as if she felt that strange zip too. In the shelter under an awning, she struggled to close the umbrella. Sounding nervous, she said, "They never work properly, but they beat getting wet."

He took it and did it for her. "Don't need an umbrella if you have a Resistol." He secured the Velcro fastening, and handed the umbrella back to her.

"Resistol?"

"Name of the hat."

"I thought they were Stetsons."

"That's another brand. Most rodeo riders wear Resistol because they're a sponsor. Same with Wrangler jeans."

"Interesting. But I don't think I'm the Resistol type." Then her eyes widened, meeting his for a moment before her lashes fluttered down. Color tinted her cheeks.

He thought about her wearing his hat, riding him. Was she remembering too?

"Are you hungry?" she asked, without meeting his eyes.

He was, for her. Seeing her had whetted his appetite. But that wasn't what she was asking. "Yeah, it's been a long day."

They went in, him taking off his hat while Kim told the hostess they had a reservation. The sleek, smiling dark-skinned woman led them to a table near the small bar at the back.

The restaurant didn't fit his image of Mediterranean. It wasn't unattractive, but kind of plain. Modern, he figured. Kim fit in just fine, he thought as the hostess gushed over her tee.

This was her world. She wasn't the Resistol type, not anywhere outside of bed. She'd be as unsuited to life at Ronan Ranch—even his updated version in the Valley—as his biological mom had been to the original ranch.

Ty had no memories of the woman named Miranda. She left when he was a baby. The only mom he knew, the only one he wanted, was Betty, the woman his dad married when Ty was three. She was the perfect mom, the perfect wife, and Ty's model for the kind of woman he was looking for.

But that was for the long term. Tonight was about tonight. Him and Kim. Just following her slim back across the restaurant and gazing at her animated face as she talked to the hostess had made his body stir.

When the hostess left them to study the menus, he took the bag from under his arm and handed it across the table. "Here's your top."

Kim stared down at the bag, color mounting to her cheeks again. "Thanks," she mumbled as she stowed it inside a large blue purse she'd slung over the back of the chair.

He wanted to ask why she'd run out on him in the middle of the night, but she was already nervous, so he instead said, "How about a drink?"

Her lashes flicked down then up and she stared at him. "Only one."

"Uh, okay. Why?"

Her eyes narrowed. "That's what got me into trouble on Saturday."

Slowly, he processed those words. "You're saying you were drunk? But you only had two or three beers, over a couple hours." Maybe she'd swayed a little, lost her balance, giggled a lot, but she was young, female, and, he'd thought, having fun. Girls did that stuff. A horrible thought struck him. Keeping his voice low, he asked, "Did I take advantage of you?"

"It did cross my mind you might have slipped a drug into my beer."

"God, no! I'd never—"

"I know." She stopped him. "I realized that. The truth is, alcohol affects me, so I almost always stop at one." She pressed her lips together. "I wanted to blame my behavior on the booze, but it only relaxes my inhibitions and maybe I wanted an excuse to let loose. After the book I'd been reading—" She broke off as if she'd said more than she intended to.

"The one your book club's reading? The research one?"

"Research." Her mouth twisted wryly and she reached into her blue bag.

She passed a book across the table.

When he saw the cover, he almost dropped the thing. Warily, he placed it on the table and stared at a picture of a cowboy, naked to the waist. *Ride Her, Cowboy.* "Huh. So you *are* a buckle bunny. Just the most unconventional one I've ever met." The words left a sour taste in his mouth. A taste like disappointment. But why should he care why this crazy dragonfly girl had sex with him?

"A what?"

"Buckle bunny. A groupie who hangs around rodeos hoping to meet the guys and hook up."

"Like puck bunnies in hockey. George told me about them." She shook her head. "No, really, I—" She broke off as the smiling waitress returned.

"Have you decided what you'd like to—" She caught sight of the book. "Oh my, very nice." Her gaze skimmed Ty. "You're a cover model?"

He gave a snort of outrage.

Kim laughed. "No, but he could be if he wanted to."

"Jesus," he said. "Can we order drinks?"

The waitress straightened twitching lips. "Of course. What would you like?"

"Haven't looked yet," he had to admit, flipping open the drink list.

Kim did the same, then asked the waitress, "Is the Stanley Park Amber fairly light?"

"Light, clean, and nuanced."

Whatever that meant. Usually, he drank plain old beer, but why not try something more interesting? "I'll have the oatmeal stout."

When the waitress left, he and Kim looked at each other across the table. She bent to the menu, saying in a rush, "Let's see what looks good. I've only had appetizers here, and never had a chance to study the menu."

Yes, she was unpredictable. The evening was unpredictable. Ty reminded himself that he'd wanted that. So why should it be so disconcerting not knowing—anything? Not knowing why she'd hooked up with him Saturday, why she'd left, why she was here with him now, how this evening would end, or why he was so damned attracted to her that his blood thickened with lust whenever he looked at her?

He couldn't see her now, hidden behind her menu.

Ty studied his own menu, noting with approval that Laziza featured free-range and hormone-free meat. They had lots of lamb, and they also had AAA beef. The beef came from Alberta, which to his mind was insane. If he hadn't been on a date, he'd have spoken to the manager and made a sales pitch for Ronan Ranch's purebred Angus, and maybe for adding ostrich to the menu. He'd give them a call next week.

Kim was still behind the menu. Was she memorizing the damned thing, being really indecisive, or avoiding meeting his eyes?

"I'm going to have the prawn appetizer," he said, "then the lamb chops with saffron rice and grilled vegetables. How about you?" The moment he spoke, he wondered if by chance she was vegetarian, or had a thing about not eating lamb.

But she said, "I looked at the lamb too. But I think I'll go with the saffron prawns. Or maybe the Bedouin chicken, or . . . Hmm, it all looks so good." She finally lowered the menu enough that he could see her eyes, just as the waitress came back with their drinks.

"Have you decided?" the brunette asked.

"I have," he said. "Prawns, then lamb chops. Kim?"

"Uh . . . Okay. The saffron prawns entrée. No appetizer, but I might have dessert."

"Great choices." The waitress collected the menus and left.

Ty lifted his glass of stout in Kim's direction. "It's good to see you again."

"Uh, yes." She lifted her own glass and tapped it quickly against his.

He took a swallow of the dark stout, tasting barley and oatmeal. "This is nice."

She sipped her own drink, then her tongue darted out to capture a stray drop on her top lip. "So's this."

He wanted that tongue. His body quickened at the thought of that tongue licking his hardening cock.

It was time to get a thing or two clear. "So, Saturday night had something to do with this book. You'd never been to a rodeo before, but this book made you and your friend Marielle want to hook up with a rodeo cowboy?"

She shook her head, the red strands in her hair flicking. "Not really. Well, I can't speak for Marielle." She sipped at her ale, frowning a little. "At first I only agreed to go to the rodeo because the others wanted to. I couldn't relate to the whole cowboy thing. But the book"—she touched the cover, then grabbed it and shoved it back in her purse—"it was kind of interesting. It made me curious."

From the cover, he wondered exactly what it had made her curious about. If it was sex with a cowboy, he'd be happy to satisfy her curiosity, over and over again.

"And like I said Saturday, I really did enjoy the rodeo." Her long lashes fluttered down, then back up. "And when I saw you . . ." Her cheeks were pink. "I liked what I saw. I liked how you rode, how you treated your horse, how gentle you were when you tossed that calf down. I liked how you related to the other riders. And you looked incredible riding that bucking bronc."

"Huh." Behind his fly, his cock swelled further. She'd noticed things like how he treated his horse and threw a calf. "How did you know I'd be at The Rusty Spur?"

"I didn't. Someone told Marielle that Blake might be there. I had no idea you two were friends."

"So you weren't stalking me?" He wasn't sure whether to be pleased or disappointed.

Another head shake. She tilted her glass to her mouth and took a small sip.

The waitress arrived with his prawn appetizer, and when she left, Kim said, "But I wasn't sorry you were there."

She baffled him. A lot of women did, but her most of all. He tasted a prawn. It was cooked with lemon, garlic, tomatoes, chilies, and Sambuca. Normally, he ate pretty plain food, but this was intriguing. Complicated, like Kim. "Try one," he offered.

She transferred one to her side plate. "Thanks."

"You liked me at the rodeo," he said. "You were glad I was at the bar. But you ran out on me in the middle of the night. I don't get it."

"I woke up and realized what I'd done. It was so unlike me and I felt . . ." She shrugged then lifted the prawn to her mouth and nibbled.

The sight of her pink lips sucking on that prawn sent a jolt of lust straight to his groin. He had to get things clear in his head. "You're sorry we had sex?"

"I, uh . . ." She went pinker. "It was great. Amazing. Memorable. But I shouldn't have done it." She finished off the prawn.

"Why not?" He scowled suddenly. "You aren't married?"

"No!" She glared at him. "No, of course not. And I'm not dating anyone." Her eyes narrowed. "Are you?"

"No. I wouldn't do that. I mean, there were times on the road, one-nighters. But if I'm dating someone, I don't screw around on them." He worked his way through the tasty prawns as they talked.

"Me either."

"Okay, so why shouldn't you have had sex with me? What's wrong with having a little fun?" *And doing it again tonight*.

Eleven

"You sound like Marielle," Kim told him.

"And that's bad?"

She plunked her elbows on the table and rested her head in her hands, peering at him. "I've never done anything like that before. My last boyfriend, we dated for six months before we had sex."

"That sounds rough."

Her mouth twisted. "I guess it depends on the couple. But we thought we might have a future together, and we wanted to take the time to make sure."

"Huh. I figure it's best to find out right up front if you get along together in bed. If you don't, how's the relationship going to go anywhere?"

Her smooth brow creased, and remained creased when the waitress came to remove his empty appetizer plate and serve their dinners.

"If you love someone," Kim ventured, "then when you finally do have sex, won't it always be good?" Her tone said she wasn't arguing, but asking a genuine question.

He didn't have an answer. He'd never been in love, never even come close. "I don't know. It'd be nice if it worked out that way."

He cocked his head, thinking that she looked as cute and sexy when she was all serious and puzzled as when she'd flirted on

Saturday. What was it about this woman that got to him? "You and the guy broke up, though."

"Hmm?"

"Even after you took that time to try and be sure about your relationship."

She sighed. "It felt right for a while, but it just kind of . . . Well, in the end it wasn't right. I couldn't imagine spending the rest of my life with him."

A horrible thought struck Ty, and he gulped. "Look, uh, I'm not sure how to put this, but . . . I told you I don't lie, right?"

"I remember you said that."

"It's true. And I don't lead women on. When I said I wanted to see you again, I wasn't talking about the rest of our lives."

Kim gaped at the handsome cowboy sitting across from her, a pained expression on his strong-featured face. "Oh jeez, you thought that I thought that . . . No, of course not! You and me? I'm going home to Hong Kong in less than two months. I'm a city girl to the core. And you're all about rodeos and country life, right?"

"Yeah, right." He lifted his glass and took a very long swallow, no doubt relieved.

"You see, that's what I'm trying to say," she went on. "I shouldn't have had sex with you because it was only casual sex, and I don't do that." Even though her hormones were putting in a strong vote to try it just one more time. Ty really was so sexy, so different from every other man she'd met.

He put his glass down. "I still don't get what's wrong with it. I thought we had a great time." He cut a slice off a lamb chop and lifted it to his mouth.

So he'd had a great time too. The rodeo star who had buckle bunnies throwing themselves at him had had a great time with *her*.

"What's wrong with it?" she echoed, trying to remember what she'd said to Marielle. "Well, it's kind of a waste of time, if what you're really looking for is a life mate. Which I am."

"Guess I kind of am myself, but—"

"You are?" Yes, it was rude to interrupt, but he'd stunned her. She didn't see him as a one-woman man, at least not for long.

"Yeah, it's time. But anyhow, if the right person hasn't come along, what's wrong with a little fun while you're waiting?"

Her body tingled with the memory of his arms around her, his tongue mating with hers, his hard penis pumping inside her. It wasn't like she was going to find the right man until she was back in Hong Kong, so seeing Ty wouldn't interfere with her future.

Munching absently on a saffron prawn, she struggled to remember the other thing she'd said to Marielle. "Isn't casual sex kind of, like, not valuing yourself? Just hooking up with whoever comes along?"

He scratched his jaw. "Guess it could be, if that's what you were doing."

Mesmerized, she remembered how that finger had felt on her sensitive skin. Gentle but callused. Oddly, that bit of roughness was more erotic than the touch of a smooth finger.

"But you liked me, right?" he went on. "Me, not just any cowboy at the rodeo or at the bar. And you were the woman I noticed. The one I wanted to talk to, dance with, leave with."

"Why?"

"Uh . . ."

"I told you what appealed to me about you. Now it's your turn."

Ty's hazel eyes danced, the green in them particularly noticeable tonight. "Guys suck at this, you know?"

She had to smile. "Man up, cowboy. Answer the question and I'll give you a prawn."

He gave a mock groan. "You're harsh. Okay, here goes. You're cute, sexy, distinctive. You have your own style. You're interesting, different than anyone else I've known. And did I mention, you're hot?"

"Hot?" Henry had never told her that. No guy had.

It could just be a line, yet Ty had said he didn't lie, and she actually believed him. Maybe, with him, she *was* hot. "Thanks," she said, pleased and embarrassed. "You earned your prawn." She transferred one to his plate and watched as he ate it. "What do you think?"

"Good, but I liked mine better. The flavor's more complex."

"You like complex?"

He shook his head, looking a little baffled. "Not usually. Maybe I'm changing my mind."

Did he mean she was complex? Probably so, compared to buckle bunnies who jumped into sex, all hot and uncomplicated.

Which really did sound awfully appealing.

To distract herself from his dancing eyes and sexy grin, and from the way they made her body hum, she asked, "Could I taste the lamb?"

"Sure." He cut a generous slice, but didn't pass it over. "If you pay the price. I get to ask you a question."

"Seems to me you've been asking a lot of them." In fact, he was proving to be more complex himself than she'd first assumed.

"I kind of asked this one before, but you still haven't given me a straight answer."

She frowned. "I thought I answered everything you asked."

"I asked what was wrong with having a little fun in bed. You said that stuff about not valuing yourself if you hook up with just anyone. And I said, you and me, Saturday night, we weren't just anyone."

She swallowed. Was he going to ask if she'd sleep with him again? How would she answer? She wanted to, but it was so unlike her. "That's not a question."

"I'm building up."

Despite her nervousness, he made her smile. "I didn't take you for the subtle type."

"Ask the horses I train. I can be subtle."

"You're a horse trainer? I thought you were a rodeo rider."

"Sidetrack. Now, here's the question. If you and me had sex tonight"—his eyes gleamed and his sensual lips pronounced the words slowly and seductively—"would you feel like either one of us doesn't value you?"

Heat flooded through her, centering in a needy pulse between her legs. She blinked, trying to focus on his question.

"How badly d'you want to taste my lamb?" he teased.

"I'm thinking." She waved a hand quickly. "Not about the lamb; I know I want to taste it. I'm thinking about your question."

He groaned. "You know you want the lamb. You don't know if you want me. I'm screwed." But his eyes still danced.

He was totally adorable and totally sexy, and she really had to put that aside and be analytical rather than tease back that he *wanted* to be screwed.

Okay, an analysis. Marielle advocated having fun. Lily said sex with a stranger could be dangerous. Marielle trusted her judgment when it came to men. Marielle had loads of experience. Kim had very little experience. Did she have good judgment?

Ty had been polite, nice, a gentleman in a rough-around-the-edges way, both Saturday and tonight. He saw her as an individual, thought she was special. Thought she was hot. On Saturday, he could've taken advantage of her but he'd treated her nicely and been a generous lover. A sexy lover. An unbelievably sexy lover. A shiver of remembered pleasure rippled through her.

"Man," he said wryly, "that's a lot of thinking."

"All right. I guess I wouldn't think that either one of us didn't value me."

A smile flashed, happy and victorious. He slid the lamb onto her plate, then gave her a forkful of the saffron rice that accompanied it.

She ate slowly, appreciatively. "That's really good." Then she took another sip of her Stanley Park Amber. Ty was so gorgeous, so sexy, and he had her whole body buzzing with desire. If she had another bottle of ale, it would be an excuse to get over her inhibitions and give into the attraction she felt. She didn't honestly believe it would be dangerous having sex with him. And she knew the sex would be terrific.

"What's wrong?" he asked in a resigned tone.

"Wrong?" she stalled.

"You didn't do this much thinking on Saturday."

"I had more alcohol on Saturday." She put down her glass. "Ty, I'm not really the person I seemed to be on Saturday. I'm just not the kind of girl who leaps into bed with a stranger."

"I'm not a stranger."

"Kind of. We don't know much about each other."

He studied her. "Tell me you're not saying we'd have to date six months before you'd go to bed with me again."

"N-no. I'll be long gone in six months." And she really did want more sex with him. She scratched her head, trying to work it out. "I need to know more about you than that you're a hot cowboy. And I want you to know more about me than that I'm an artist from Hong Kong."

He didn't answer, just kept looking at her.

"Okay," she said, feeling a pang of loss. "I'm too old-fashioned, too boring. Not worth taking the time over." If that was the truth, better to know now.

He shook his head, looking exasperated. "I drove into town to take you for dinner. We're talking, getting to know each other. You're not boring, Kim. Don't say crap like that." He reached across the table and took both her hands in his. "Yeah, you're hot and I want you. In bed. But that doesn't mean I'm not interested in you. You're not like the people I usually meet."

It was hard to concentrate on his words when his hands felt so warm and strong, reassuring and sexy all at the same time.

"So, talk," he said. "Tell me something about you. Ask me something about me."

Tell him something about her? Like what? As for what she wanted to know about him . . . How many lovers had he had? What was his favorite position in bed? How many erections could he have in a night? No, those weren't things a good girl like her should want to know.

The waitress came to clear their empty plates, and Ty released Kim's hands.

"Another drink?" the waitress asked. "Or dessert?"

"I'm not much of a dessert guy," he said, "but I'll have another stout."

No, Kim absolutely wasn't having more alcohol. "What do you have for dessert?"

The waitress recited the options, ending with, "And flourless chocolate cake, which is my personal favorite."

"Okay, I'll try it. And a coffee, please."

A moment later, the waitress returned with their orders.

Kim tasted the cake and moaned. "Oh, this is good. So rich and fudgy. Want to taste?"

He shook his head, eyes gleaming. "Yeah, but not the cake. D'you have any idea what you do to me when you moan like that?"

"Oh!" Was it sexy? She filed that bit of information away.

"If you want me to think about something other than sex, then talk, woman," he said, humor in his voice.

All right. What did she want to know about him other than sexy things? Lots, actually. "You told me a bit about your grandparents and parents, and the family ranch. Your truck . . ." She flushed, remembering what they'd done on that truck. "Your truck says Ronan Ranch and I noticed at the rodeo that you're from the Fraser Valley. That's your family ranch?"

"It is now. The original ranch was in Alberta. Grandpa was from Alberta, Grandma was from Texas. They met on the rodeo circuit, got married, saved their winnings. When they were ready to settle down—this was the early 1950s—they bought a chunk of range land and raised cattle."

"That's about as different from Hong Kong as I can imagine." It didn't sound the least bit appealing, but she wouldn't be rude and say that.

"Yeah, I'm sure. Anyhow, Grandpa was around forty and Grandma was in her late thirties when they quit rodeo. They had two kids. My aunt didn't like ranch life, but Dad loved it. He worked alongside them over the years, facing all the challenges that came along. Mom too, when she married Dad."

"And you?"

He swallowed, looking uncomfortable. "Sure, as a kid. But from the time I was seventeen I was away at college and rodeoing. Back home, well, I guess things just got harder and harder."

"Harder?"

"When they started out, beef was in demand. There were no worries about cholesterol, global warming, stuff like that. But times changed."

Her parents, with their property management and investments, had hit exactly the right timing. Ty's family had the opposite experience. "That must have been rough."

"Yeah." He took a long swallow of stout. "Maybe I should've stuck around and worked with them. That's what Dad wanted. Mom too. But from the time I competed in my first Little Britches rodeo, Grandma and Grandpa encouraged me to follow in their footsteps."

Kim thought about the pressure her parents exerted on her, and how they believed that all the deceased ancestors wanted exactly the same thing they did. "That must have been strange, having your parents want one thing and your grandparents want something else. How did you decide?"

He gave a wry grin. "Hell, I was a kid, and I loved rodeo. Sure, I loved the ranch too, but it was steady, not exciting. I told myself there'd be time for all of that later. And it wasn't like I was just rodeoing. I was in college too, on a rodeo scholarship—"

"There are scholarships for rodeo?"

"You bet. Anyhow, I studied agribusiness and animal sciences, learning things I planned to bring back to the ranch eventually. Except the ranch went under."

"That must have been devastating for your family." She tried to imagine her parents losing CPM, the company they'd built from the ground up and took so much pride in.

"Yeah," he said grimly. "They fought hard. Adapted to the times, went grass-fed, hormone-free, but they were fighting a losing battle. My parents said things were bound to pick up, but then the scare over Mad Cow disease hit."

He took another long drink. "My grandparents were fighters, but they were worn out. And old. He died of a heart attack when he was out riding. Grandma died in her sleep a couple weeks later. The next year, my parents surrendered. The only way to dig themselves out from under the mountain of debt was to sell off."

She heard guilt in Ty's voice and knew he must beat himself up over not having tried to help. Not that he'd likely have been able to save the ranch, but he could have been there. Her parents would blame him, but she didn't. It was hard to balance your family's needs and your own desires. "How sad. What did they do then?"

"Got jobs in town. She did bookkeeping and he worked in the feedstore. They hated it. I came home and saw that. Guess that's when I grew up."

Sipping coffee, she studied his expressive face. "What d'you mean?"

"I was in my early twenties. I'd been having fun at college, traveling around to rodeos, hanging out with guys like Blake, enjoying the buckle bunnies—"

She wrinkled her nose.

He grinned and went on. "Building a name for myself. Don't get me wrong; rodeo's hard work. But I love it, and I'd been working hard since I was a toddler, so that part didn't bother me one bit. Anyhow, I got to thinking about the future, and how long I'd keep rodeoing."

"And?" Kim took another small bite of cake, savoring the chocolaty richness.

"I saw my folks, aging and unhappy. And I remembered how great it had been, growing up at Ronan Ranch, the whole family working together. I thought maybe that would be a better way to live than traveling from rodeo to rodeo, motel to motel. So I started saving money. I made a fair bit, those years. When I traveled I checked out the opportunities for ranching, thought about where I'd like to live. Where my folks might be happy as well."

Now she realized where this was heading. "Are you saying *you* bought the ranch in the Valley?"

A satisfied smile spread across his face. "Three years ago. Saw land for sale, halfway to Hope—"

"Hope? Is that a town?"

"Yeah. Cool, eh? Called it Ronan Ranch, of course. Mom and Dad moved out and we've got us a nice little spread."

Her heart warmed. Ty was a lot more than the admittedly gorgeous picture that met the eye. What woman could resist a man like this? "That name, Hope, it was symbolic."

Twelve

G uess so," Ty said. "A second chance for Ronan Ranch. For my family."

A chance to heal, she figured. "How wonderful." His parents probably felt abandoned when he chose rodeo over the ranch, then like failures when they lost the ranch. And Ty felt guilty, partly responsible. She doubted he would come out and say any of that, or if he even totally realized it. Yes, she was learning a lot about this man tonight. He was human, flawed, and incredibly appealing.

"The new place is way different from the Alberta one, but times change."

"Different?" She nodded. "I guess it would have to be, if the old one couldn't survive."

"Yeah. I put my education to use, did more research, a lot of thinking. Talked to my folks." He made a face. "That was a challenge. Dad and I butt heads; Mom tries to mediate. A traditionalist would say the new place isn't really a ranch, but we hung on to the name. Dad's a cattle guy, and we've got purebred Angus. That's his baby. Mom handles the other specialty stock: ostrich for meat; llamas, alpacas, and angora goats for wool."

Fascinated, Kim leaned forward, elbows on the table. "And you rodeo and train horses?"

"Yeah, and a lot of my time goes to management, with input from Mom and Dad and our workers. I only hit a few rodeos now, mostly in BC where the travel time's shorter. Don't see myself giving up rodeo for a while yet. Besides, it's promotion for the ranch." He gave a boyish grin. "That's my story and I'm sticking to it."

That grin gave her a hint of the kid he'd been: hardworking yes, but with a touch of the devil. The little girls had no doubt been as crazy about him as adult women were.

"I've always been a horse guy," he went on. "I have a way with them, so I've set up a training business."

"You break broncs?"

His laugh rang out, rich and infections. "Hell, no. I gentle them rather than break them."

"Gentle them? You mean like horse whispering?"

"That's what some folks call it."

"But . . ." She tilted her head, puzzled. "How do those go together? Bronc riding and horse whispering? They seem like opposites."

"In the old days, yeah. Back when rodeo had its roots, cowboys who needed horses would capture wild ones, climb aboard, and stay on until the horse gave up. They called it breaking, which, you're right, is the opposite approach to gentling. But the bronc riding you see in rodeos now, that's a different thing. Those horses are bred and trained to buck. It's their job. The ones that do it well—"

"The rank ones?"

"Yeah, the rank ones. They're worth a lot and they're treated great. Bronc riding's not about trying to break a horse's spirit and make it submit. The horse would be worthless then. It's more like— have you ever gone surfing?"

"Surfing?" She gave a startled laugh. "No. Have you, cowboy?"

"Matter of fact, yes. It's not like the big wave's your enemy; it's a challenge. It'll do what it does, it's a force of nature, and you have to read it, feel it, go with it. And when you connect with it that way, when you ride it all the way, man is it a thrill."

Spellbound, she read all of that on his face. She could also imagine him, bronzed body almost naked, powerful and graceful as he rode a board along a curling wave. "You, Ty Ronan, are a man of surprises."

He shrugged. "I'm a straightforward guy. But hey, enough about me. Tell me about you. How does a Hong Kong girl with a business degree decide to study art in Vancouver?"

Flattered that he remembered what she'd told him Saturday, she said, "I've been coming to Vancouver since I was a kid. I've always wanted to study art, and I didn't want to do it in Hong Kong. I wanted fresh influences."

"You've enjoyed your studies and living in Vancouver?"

"Oh, yes, so much! I almost hate to go home."

"Then don't."

She shook her head. "You don't know my parents."

"Meaning?"

How could she possibly explain her parents and their expectations? With Henry, she hadn't even had to try; he understood because his parents were the same. Searching for common ground, she said, "Your grandparents started a ranch? Well, my parents came to Hong Kong and started a business. Theirs is property management. They do it very well and keep expanding the properties they manage and also the ones they own. Chang Property Management is the family business, like Ronan Ranch. And when I say *family*, even the ancestors get dragged into it, though they'd never even been to Hong Kong. But the business is a matter of family pride, honor, and, according to my parents, destiny. If they had their way, there'd be no escape."

"Escape? You mean they want you to go into the business?"

Why had she raised this subject? It always brought her down. "I'm an only child. It's not *want*, it's expect and demand."

He frowned. "I'm an only too, but parents don't own their kids."

"Try telling them that." How to explain this? "Your family has rodeo and ranching in their blood. What if you'd said you wanted to be—oh, I don't know—a surfer?"

He gave a startled laugh. "A surfer?"

"You know. Something completely different. Something they don't think is a serious way to make a living. It's an okay hobby, but not a job. But, even more important, it means rejecting the family business. Rejecting the family, destroying their honor, shaming your ancestors."

"Jesus." He stared at her disbelievingly. "Really?"

"Culture shock, right? I know Western people have trouble relating to it."

"You have to live your own life," he said firmly.

Sadly, she shook her head. "That's the last thing you're supposed to do. It's not your life. It's your family's."

"Family's important and you should respect them, but that's crazy."

When she didn't answer, he reached across to take her hand. "Kim, do you believe all of that?"

His hand, the hand of a near-stranger, felt like the only steady, secure thing she knew. She intertwined her fingers with his, wishing for a moment that she never had to let go. "Yes and no," she answered softly. "It's what I grew up with. Most of my friends from Hong Kong have the same kind of pressure. And yes, I believe in respect, loyalty, and honor. I love my parents. They're wonderful and they've always been so good to me. And yet . . ." She glanced down, biting her lip.

"Yet?" He squeezed her hand.

She studied their linked hands, his so brown, so big and strong, hers so delicate. How could they fit together so perfectly and the bond feel so real? "Saturday night, we talked about how some people feel as if they're born to do something. It's in their blood, it's the one right thing. Hockey, for George's fiancé. Horses for you. For me, it's art."

He frowned. "They want to take that away from you?"

"No, but they treat it as a hobby. They want me to join the company, work the same long hours they do, invest all my energy in CPM. Mom's sixty-four and Dad's almost seventy. They want me to take over the company one day. There'd be no spare time for art. More than that, I think it'd kill the creative part of me."

"Like caging a butterfly."

Surprised at his insight, she lifted her gaze from their clasped hands to his face. "Yes."

"That would be a real pity."

Somehow, those words meant even more than when he'd called her sexy and fascinating. "Thank you."

"So what're you going to do? How are you going to keep the butterfly flying?"

She straightened her shoulders. "Make a living from my art."

"Good for you."

"You don't think I'm crazy?"

"You're talking to a guy who rides in rodeos. What's wrong with a little crazy?"

"Not a damn thing. So you don't think it's impossible?"

He shrugged. "Some people must make a living from art. Like with rodeo. It's tough and not everyone's going to do it, but if you have talent, determination, a pinch of luck, why not?"

"Exactly!" She beamed at him. "And I shouldn't whine so much about my parents. I got them to agree—probably mostly because they don't think I'll ever actually do it—that if I come up with a solid business plan for how to make a living from my art, they won't make me join CPM."

He frowned slightly, maybe because she'd used the word "make," then said, "A business plan. For designing clothes like those tops of yours?"

She sighed. "I guess. That's what I've been working on."

"I don't get it. You don't sound enthusiastic."

"I enjoy designing clothes, but so many people do it."

"You're afraid of the competition?"

"It's not that as much as it's just not quite, you know, the thing. The thing that really excites me."

A slow smile curved his sensual lips. "It's like raising cattle."

"Uh . . ." It was pretty much the opposite, in her opinion.

"I mean, for me. Raising cattle's okay. It's outdoors, on the land, working with my family. All good stuff that's important to me."

Now grasping his point, she nodded eagerly. "But you want to work with horses."

"That's it. So, Kim"—his hazel eyes, looking almost gold in the restaurant's dim lighting, studied her intently—"what's it for you? What's your thing?"

"That's just it." She shook her head, frustrated with herself. "I don't know. It's like there's something I'm reaching for, but it's just out of sight. It's nothing that my fellow students are doing, it's something that's mine. Just specially mine." Then she shook her head quickly. What an ego. "But really, who am I to think I deserve something unique? That's not how I was brought up—to be self-centered."

"It's not self-centered to want your own special thing. You're a special person, Kim." He said those words as if he really meant them.

Gazing across the table at Ty Ronan, she realized something. In almost two years of dating Henry, he had never understood or supported her dreams the way this cowboy did. No, Ty couldn't possibly relate to her family issues and how difficult it was to go against her parents, but he saw her, Kim, as someone special who was entitled to follow her passion.

Her small hand felt so good wrapped up in his big callused one. That same strong hand had clung to the grip on Dirt Devil's bare back; it had deftly flung a rope over the head of a calf. It had caressed her cheek, her breasts, her most intimate spots.

She wanted him to do it again.

He made her feel tingly and moist and sexy and needy. She wanted to run her own small, soft hands over his hard body, to touch and taste and tease. Saturday night she'd done that, and he'd caressed her inner thighs, circled her clit with his tongue, thrust deep inside her. But she didn't remember all the details; she'd been tipsy from too much lager. Now, if she was intoxicated, it was by him, not alcohol. This time she'd savor every exquisite detail.

If she was entitled to follow her passion, why shouldn't she have another night with Ty? Or at least be alone with him, kiss and explore, decide how far she wanted things to go.

"Jesus," he said roughly, "I told you not to do that."

"What?"

"Moan like that."

Had she moaned?

"You give me dirty thoughts, dragonfly girl." His eyes glittered and she read in them the same need, the same passion she felt.

Kim made up her mind. "That's because I'm thinking dirty thoughts. I think it's time we got out of here, cowboy."

His eyes widened and so did the grin that took over his face. "Hell, yeah."

He turned to locate their waitress and asked for the bill.

The waitress glanced at Kim's half-eaten dessert. "Oh, you didn't like the cake?"

"I did." A mischievous imp made Kim say, "I just got a better offer for dessert."

The waitress winked. "The one thing that's better than chocolate."

Sex. The waitress assumed they'd be having sex. Probably so did Ty. And maybe—okay, probably—they would, but Kim didn't want him taking that for granted.

Ty paid the bill, stood, and held his hand out to Kim.

She took it and came to her feet, hooking her purse off the back of her chair.

He bent and retrieved her umbrella. "Don't forget this." He handed it to her then collected his hat.

"I've lost a lot of umbrellas in Vancouver. I come in with one, then it's sunny when I leave and I forget it. But I'd hate to lose this one. It's the nicest I've found."

"It suits you." He guided her toward the door, his hand on her lower back, a tantalizing hint of what was to come when they were both naked. "When I saw that umbrella coming down the street, I knew it was you."

Body humming with anticipation, finding it hard to think of anything except sex with this man, she said absentmindedly, "Umbrellas are so boring. Most are black, and the others are plain solid colors. If you have to carry an umbrella on a gray, drizzly day, I like something more cheerful." An idea teased at the back of her mind. What had Ty said when he'd seen her? *Don't fly away, dragonfly girl.*

Umbrellas were kind of like wings. Clumsy, boring wings. But did they have to be?

"When I first saw you tonight," he said, and her attention refocused on him, "I wanted to kiss you. But I figured you might not like it."

They were on the sidewalk outside the restaurant. All signs of rain had disappeared, and it was a warm, almost balmy, evening. "I'd have liked it, but I wasn't ready."

* * *

No, Kim hadn't been ready for a kiss when they'd first met tonight. But now . . . Yeah, dinner had been fun. Talking to her, feeling like they connected, getting turned on by her. Seeing her get turned on too—and tonight it wasn't booze talking.

Ty put on his hat so both hands were free, then he used those hands to capture her head. That soft, spiky hair tickled his palms as he tilted her face up toward him. When he bent down, she came up on her toes to meet him, her dark eyes sparkly and welcoming.

Pent-up need surged through him, but this wasn't the place for a down and dirty kiss. He fought to restrain himself. A brush of his lips against hers, the same with his hips. He could be patient. Especially when he was pretty sure where all of this was leading.

"Oh," she sighed, a warm chocolate breath against his lips.

He might not be a dessert guy, but her mouth could get him addicted. "I want to be alone with you, Kim. To kiss you properly."

"Kiss?" A smile flickered then she studied him intently. "I'm sober."

"I hope that's not a bad thing."

"It means . . ." She bit her lip. "I'm not sure where I want tonight to go. I do want to kiss you . . ." That smile flickered again. "Properly? Hmm, improperly sounds more fun."

"You bet it does."

"But I'm not promising we'll . . . you know. Is that okay?"

She was going to test his patience. But he sure as hell didn't want to have sex with her unless she was ready. He took her hand and squeezed gently. "It'll be up to you. I'm not the kind of guy who'd try to force a woman."

Her intent expression relaxed. "No, I don't think you are. Okay, let's go to my studio."

"Great. Where is it?"

"In Yaletown. It's five or six blocks. Where's your truck?"

"In a lot down the block."

He hung on to her hand and they strolled along the sidewalk. Ty was aware of people glancing at them with curiosity. Was it his hat, her unusual top, or the unlikely couple they made? When he opened the passenger door of the ranch truck and helped her up, he thought how out of place he was. Just as out of place as she would be at Ronan Ranch. Two different worlds, two different futures. Weird, how attracted he was to her and how much he enjoyed her company.

She directed him on the short drive to Yaletown, then pointed to a nicely converted old brick warehouse five or six stories high. "That's my building. There's guest parking under it." After using a fob to open the gate, she directed him to a narrow spot that hadn't been designed with a ranch truck in mind.

He went around to open her door, caught her by the waist, and lifted her down. The front of her body slid along the front of his in a long, tantalizing caress that instantly made him hard.

She wriggled her pelvis against him like she couldn't help herself, then pulled away.

The elevator picked up other people at ground level, so he kept his hands to himself. And, when Kim unlocked the door to her place and clicked on a light, curiosity kept him from tugging her straight into his arms. He glanced around.

When she'd said studio, he'd assumed artist's studio. It did have an easel, a drafting table, and art supplies, but it was also her living space. There was a tiny kitchen, a table with a couple of chairs, and a semipartitioned area with a wardrobe and a double mattress on the floor. The duvet on the bed had an abstract design in yellow, orange, purple, and black, clearly Kim's art. She'd fastened sketches and photographs to the brick walls, probably her own work as well. "Nice place."

"I love it. I'd never had my own place before." Sounding nervous, she went on. "See that big wall of windows? It lifts up like a garage door. I'll crank it up; it's a beautiful evening." She'd slipped off her shoes and hurried away from him, barefooted.

He bent to take off his boots and socks, and tossed his hat on the kitchen counter.

Kim tugged on a lever. The windowed wall on the studio side of the apartment slid up to hang below the ceiling, revealing a balcony with a wrought-iron railing and a pot of vivid mixed geraniums.

"That's cool." He walked over. "I've never seen anything like it." Her unit was on the alley side, facing the blank brick wall of another warehouse-type building. No windows over there, so no one could see into her place.

"I like things that are distinctive."

"Ah," he teased, "that's why I'm here. A cowboy in Yaletown is pretty distinctive."

"You, Ty, are pretty distinctive wherever you are. Even at a rodeo, you stand out."

He stepped closer, and she didn't move away. Testing, he rested his hands on her shoulders and leaned in for a kiss.

Thirteen

Ty got his answer when Kim went up on her toes and wrapped her arms around his neck.

He clasped her firm butt in his big palms and tugged her into him until their bodies pressed together. And then he kissed her. Teasing her lips, savoring her slowly. As she warmed and loosened, he dipped inside to taste her chocolaty sweetness. The curves of her butt were taut under his grip. His heart raced and, behind his fly, his swollen cock demanded to be released.

Her response heated, so he stopped holding back. He let all the wanting, the buildup of the past hours—of the days and nights since Saturday—pour into that kiss.

She answered eagerly, showing that she wanted him just as badly. What could possibly be wrong with two people on fire for each other, just wanting some fun together?

"I'm glad I tracked you down," he told her.

Huge dark eyes gazed up at him. "Why did you?"

"Couldn't get you out of my mind."

"Me either. I've been dreaming about you."

"Me too. Sexy dreams."

She nodded. "Yes, that kind." Her gaze darted across the room, then back. "I dreamed about you in my bed."

"Dreams do come true." *Thank God.*

He was about to haul her toward the bed when she stepped out onto the little balcony. Okay, she needed more seduction before they made it to bed.

Gazing up, she said, "You can hardly see the stars here."

She really had a thing about stars.

He joined her. The air smelled pretty good for a city, but it didn't carry the scents of hay and forest he enjoyed. The sky was murky. "You want stars? You should live on a ranch."

Her cute nose wrinkled and she laughed. "Yeah, right. Not gonna happen, even if there are stars." Quickly, she said, "I'm sorry, I don't mean to be rude. It's just not my thing. I'd bet Hong Kong isn't yours."

He gave an involuntary shudder. "People, buildings, traffic all crowded into a tiny space? You got that right. Vancouver's all the 'city' I can handle, then only in small, infrequent doses."

"And I love it." She rested her forearms on the balcony railing, angling her body so her curvy backside was aimed toward him. She had a graceful way of moving, like a dancer or athlete, and her body was so hot. "We sure are different," she said.

Ty stepped up behind her and leaned forward, his hands on the railing on either side of her arms. "I know one way we're compatible."

She made an *mmm* sound and wriggled her butt against his erection.

He kissed her nape, trailing damp nibbles from her hairline to the neckline of her top.

She shivered, gave a sexy moan, and twisted her neck to give him better access.

Still kissing and nipping her exposed nape, he slid a hand under the bottom of her shirt, brushed the smooth skin of her rib cage, and moved up to cup her breast. She wore a bra, thin and lacy, and through it he felt the small, full curve of her breast. He teased her nipple until it tightened to a hard bud.

Her body arched so her backside thrust more firmly against him.

Bed would be great, but he had a better idea. He glanced around, confirming there were no windows across the way. On her own building, other small balconies jutted out but no one was on them. The alley below had a few parked cars, and another driving into the underground lot. He and Kim stood in the middle of a big city, but they were alone.

He slid his hand inside the front of her skintight leggings, caressing the silky skin of her stomach, toying with the side straps of what had to be a thong.

She drew in a quivery breath but didn't object.

With the other hand, he tugged the leggings down until they pooled at her ankles.

She tensed. "Ty," she whispered, "we should go inside."

"Be daring," he murmured against her ear. "No one can see us."

He reached between their bodies to undo his leather belt and unfasten his black jeans, then they too fell. He peeled his underwear off, stepped out of his clothing, and kicked it aside.

"What are you doing?"

"Looking at the view." He hiked her tee up to her waist. A hot, candy pink thong framed the sweet curves of her butt. He wanted to lick down the center strap, all the way between her legs. But later, when they were in bed. Right now, the idea of having sex on her balcony was an incredible turn-on.

He stroked across the front of the thong, feeling firm flesh and soft curls underneath. Two fingers followed the fabric down, between her legs, where she was hot and damp.

She moaned and shifted position, trying to spread her legs but hobbled by her leggings.

He steadied her as she freed herself from them. Now he could stroke her through the crotch of her thong, sliding his hand back and forth as she pressed against him. He eased the fabric aside, needing to touch her sensitive flesh, the full folds, the steamy slit.

She was slick with arousal, yet small and tight when he eased one finger inside her. Her muscles caught it, then relaxed. He slid in farther, slowly and gently. Another finger, opening her, widening her. He pumped slowly in and out with both fingers as her head dropped forward, her breath coming in soft pants.

"Jesus, you're sexy, Kim." Bending to kiss her neck, he let his erection ride the pink line of her thong as it bisected her butt. He was big, and she was a tiny woman. He had to make sure she was ready, so he didn't hurt her.

But patience was killing him. His cock ached with the need to thrust, his balls with the need to come. He nipped her neck and, still pumping his fingers in and out, caressed her clit with his thumb.

"Oh!" she gasped. "Oh, yes." Her body pressed and wriggled, telegraphing the way she wanted to be touched.

He gave it to her until she clenched, moaned, and spasmed against his hand.

Bit by bit, her body relaxed and he held her steady, one arm around her waist, until she got her feet under her again. Head still bowed, she murmured, "I can't believe we did that."

"And now we'll do this." Body throbbing with urgency, he bent to find a condom in his jeans pocket, and rolled it on. She was short for what he had in mind, but he'd make this work. "Lean farther forward."

When she did, he took her by the hips, tugging her back toward him so her backside was tilted up in invitation. He looped an arm around her waist, holding her steady, then slid the strip of thong aside. Gently, he opened her so the blunt head of his cock could nudge inside.

A tremor rippled through her and she lifted up on the balls of her feet, raising her butt higher, changing the angle so he could more easily slide into her moist channel.

He filled her, inch by inch, slow and steady even though his body urged him to thrust hard and deep. She softened around him, taking him in. When he finally let himself pump, her body hugged him with such a snug caress, the sensations were almost unbearably intense. Unbearably good and arousing. "Does this feel good?" he asked.

"So good."

He pulled back a little so he could see the flex of muscles in her curvy butt, and watch his cock as it slipped out of her body then back in. His balls slapped gently against her with each thrust, and the need to come tightened them.

He wasn't going to last long, and she couldn't balance on the balls of her feet for long either. He reached around her and slid his hand between her thighs again. He tapped her clit gently with his finger, circled it, then, as she whimpered with need, caught it between his thumb and finger and teased it.

"Oh God, oh God, oh God," she panted, writhing against him.

He couldn't hold back. The orgasm raced through him, poured out of him, and as it did he heard Kim's sharp cry of pleasure mingle with his own groan of relief.

Through the blissful haze of release, he was dimly aware they were being too noisy. Kim would be embarrassed if someone caught them. He slid out of her, reached down to collect her discarded leggings, and tugged her away from the balcony rail.

As they moved back into the apartment, she stared at him, eyes wide and stunned. Slowly, her lips curved and her eyes sparkled. She let out a giggle, then another.

Relieved that she wasn't upset, he laughed too. "That was pretty wild."

"Crazy," she said. "Wow. You bring out a side of me I didn't even know I had."

"What side's that?"

"My inner dirty girl." She sounded smug, and she had a right to be.

"I like that side." He studied her: flushed face; T-shirt smoothed back down over her hips; bare, shapely legs. He'd told her she was special, and it was true. "I like all sides of you."

Talk about liking all sides of someone. When Ty tossed off his shirt and walked to the bathroom to dispose of the condom, Kim stared in fascination at his naked back. She'd been with Henry and two other lovers; she'd painted nude males in life drawing; but she'd never seen a man who was so big, so muscled, so utterly male. So sexy.

With him, she lost her mind. That was the only explanation for what they'd done on her balcony. It was, hands down, the most outrageous thing she'd ever done.

He returned, strolling toward her with an easy, athletic gait, his body rock solid and mouthwatering. Fascinated, she focused on his genitals, another part of his body that was definitely bigger than she'd seen before.

"I said I dreamed of you in my bed," she commented, "not on my balcony. But I'll be dreaming of that too, from now on." And she'd draw him. From memory. Or . . . was there any possibility a rugged guy like him would agree to sit for her?

"Beds are good too." He went to collect his jeans, took another condom from the pocket, and tossed it on the bedside table. He flicked the duvet aside to reveal yellow sheets she'd painted in a pattern that complimented the one on the duvet. "Cool. You made these?"

"Yes, thanks. Common Buckeye."

"That's a butterfly?"

She nodded, then dared to ask, "I'd like to paint you. Would you let me?"

He glanced at the bed again and said disbelievingly, "Paint butterflies all over me?"

A giggle spluttered out at the image that brought to mind. No, applying paint to his body wasn't what she'd had in mind, but now that he mentioned it . . . Ooh, that could be so much fun! "Not butterflies. Nothing girly. Abstract, I think."

"You're serious."

She could point out that he'd given her the idea, but decided to take credit for it. "You bet. Be daring, Ty." She quoted his words back to him. "Lie down and get comfortable."

"Won't the paint ruin your sheets?" he asked hopefully, stretching out on the bed.

"I'll use something that will wash out." And that was nontoxic. Pity she didn't have flavored body paint. Hmm. There was an idea for the future.

That thought gave her pause. What future? A future with Ty? Would she see him again? Would he want to? Would she? This kind of relationship—or casual sex, or whatever you'd call it—was so out of her experience.

She pulled out a box of children's paints she'd used for a fun project with preschoolers. "What are your favorite colors?"

Stretched out, looking less comfortable and natural than usual, he said, "Blues and greens, I guess."

"Outdoorsy colors."

She'd focus on those, but also use fire-engine red and sunshine yellow for accent. No brush. If a dirty girl was going to play, she'd coat her bare fingers in paint and stroke them over his body. Adult finger painting. She's soon loosen Ty up—and turn him on.

"If I let you do this," he said, "there's a condition."

"What's that?"

"You have to be naked too."

The naked human form didn't embarrass her, and she liked her body. Even though she didn't have the generous curves a lot of men ogled, she knew Ty found her attractive. "I thought you'd never ask." She collected rags to wipe her fingers between applications, sauntered over to the bed, and dropped her supplies on the sheet beside him. In one smooth motion, she pulled the tee over her head, then shed her bra and thong.

"Now there's something that should be painted. Jesus, Kim, you're beautiful." His penis stirred and grew.

Her pussy gave a needy throb, tempting her to climb aboard and ride him the way she had on Saturday. But no, playing with paint and playing with Ty would ramp up their desire, their anticipation. How long would they last, and who would be the first to beg? Oh, yes, she liked her inner dirty girl.

Studying Ty's strong, perfect body, she decided it called for boldness. She'd dive right in and leave her mark. The most basic mark, the one used by prehistoric cave painters and by kids with their first set of finger paints.

She applied red paint to her fingers and palms and kneeled with one leg on either side of his waist, for the moment avoiding touching his growing erection. Applying her hands to his upper chest, she pressed steadily, evenly. When she lifted her hands, he was decorated with two prints, adhering not just to his bronzed skin but to the scattering of light brown curls.

After wiping her hands on a rag, she smeared green paint onto two fingers and stroked double lines along his collarbone, then did the same to his ribs, tracing the firm bones.

He squirmed, his swollen penis pressing against her leg. "I like how you touch me."

"I like touching you." Using paint made her even more aware, more appreciative, of how beautifully he was put together. Appreciative as an artist, and as an aroused woman who wanted to press the sweet ache between her legs against his hard flesh. She resisted, wanting to prolong this intriguing foreplay.

Next, she chose vivid blue, sweeping paint on the bottom curve of his rock-hard pecs. Blending blue and green to make turquoise, she circled his nipples, making rings, until the hard peak of each nipple was a bull's-eye.

He shivered. "Can I touch the artist?"

She gazed up, saw the hungry glow in his eyes, and summoned willpower. "Not yet. You'll disturb my concentration."

She chose yellow to blob onto his nipples and accent the green lines that highlighted his bones. "Now, I think it's time to move below the waist."

"Oh yeah."

She slid down his body, letting the damp folds of her sex press against his penis—no, a dirty girl would call it his cock—for one long, tantalizing moment. She shuddered as need rippled through her.

Before she could move, Ty caught her hips and held her there. "Put the condom on me."

Though she was tempted to give in, she pulled away to straddle his thigh. "I haven't got to the good part yet."

"I'll give you the good part."

She gazed down at his cock jutting up in invitation. Another perfect part of him, shaped for a woman's pleasure. She itched to stroke him, to taste him, and mostly to feel him thrust between her legs. But later, after she played some more.

Unless he was tired of her game. This dirty girl stuff was new; she didn't know how she was doing. Tentatively, she asked, "Are you hating this?"

"Jesus, no. It's a turn-on. You're driving me crazy, Kim."

She gave a satisfied grin. "Me too. So let me turn us on awhile longer. You're a tough guy, cowboy. You can hold out."

"Guess I can if you can." His thigh flexed under her, and she resisted the urge to squirm against him and stroke her own sexy itch. "Besides," he said, "you're giving me a new appreciation of art. Maybe I'll do some painting myself one day. If you're the canvas."

A shiver tingled through her. "We could buy edible body paints."

"Or we could improvise." His hazel eyes glinted with mischief. "I have some blackberry syrup that tastes great on pancakes. I'm guessing it'd taste better on you."

She squirmed at the notion. She was such an artist, it had never occurred to her to paint him with food. But now that he mentioned it . . . "I love whipped cream with a dash of vanilla."

"Orange marmalade," he countered.

Her eyebrows rose. "Seriously?"

"Mmm. Between your legs, all sweet and tart and sticky."

She gave an involuntary whimper. "Oh God, Ty."

"Yeah, I'm getting into the idea of painting. Got any whipping cream?"

"No. And stop distracting me. There's a masterpiece in progress here." She got busy again, swirling paint in strokes that were part art and part pure sensual appreciation of his fine body as she painted from his knees to his waist. She applied paint to every part of him except his genitals; applying a condom over paint might not be the wisest idea. If she had whipped cream, though, you bet she'd be slathering it on—and licking it off.

The heat in her body, the moisture between her legs, built with each stroke of paint.

Ty twitched, writhed, and let out occasional groans and soft curses, but didn't stop her.

Finally, she figured they'd both had enough sweet torture. With classic black—the first time she'd used black—she wrote the Chinese symbols for her name to the left of his thick erection. Didn't ranchers brand animals to show who owned them? For this moment, Ty Ronan was hers, and she was putting her mark on him.

"We should have colored condoms," she said, reaching for the package he'd tossed on her bedside table. "That would be the finishing touch."

"We can come up with a different finishing touch."

She knew what he meant, and it was exactly what she had in mind. Except, his words gave her a flash of inspiration. She tossed the condom down, unopened.

"What now?" he groaned.

Fourteen

S he gave Ty a wicked grin. "I want to take my work of art and . . ." She slid down to lie on top of him, and wriggled her body against his, side to side and up and down.

"What the—" he started, clearly taken by surprise.

She sat up to straddle his hips and studied first his body, now a glorious abstract swirl of colors, and then her own. The two of them looked primitive. If she did this onstage, as performance art, people would pay to see it. They'd pay, and go home turned on.

But this was personal. She could only imagine indulging in this kind of sexual, artistic play with Ty.

His face had an expression of wonder. "Kim, you look incredible. I've never seen anything so wild. You're . . . a tropical bird." Then a golden spark lit in his eyes. "When we have sex, every move will create a new painting."

Oh, yes! "I'm turning you into an artist," she teased. A fair trade, because he'd turned her into a creative lover, a more sexy, kinky woman than she'd ever guessed she could be. The idea of combining her passion for art and her newfound passion for sex was a total turn-on.

"Then come here, painter girl, and let's make beautiful art together," he said. Then, chuckling, "Sorry, hokey line."

"Great idea, though." Quickly, she wiped smears of paint from his cock with the already stained sheet, then sheathed him. She rose up, guided him between her legs, felt him press firmly against her sensitive clit, then shifted so he could slide into her.

His hands caught her by the hips and held her steady, then he thrust up, hard, like he couldn't wait a moment longer to be buried deep inside her.

He pumped a few strokes, then pulled her down so their paint-slick bodies rubbed against each other, slippery and sensual. Wrapping his arms around her, he rolled them so they were side by side, and separated their upper bodies to study the new colored patterns.

"You're crazy," he muttered, voice raw, "but I like it."

"You make me crazy. You give me ideas."

He swirled his fingers around her painted breast, making patterns, the sweat from their bodies keeping the paint from drying. He dabbed up some red and stroked lines along her cheekbones, then he pulled her close again and they kissed hungrily while he rolled their bodies until he was on top.

She wanted him so badly, the need inside her coiled tight. He gave her exactly what she wanted, pumping into her fast and deep as if he could no longer hold back. Seeing him above her, his body a work of multicolored primitive art, a painting they'd created together, was the most erotic sight she'd ever seen. Everything inside her tensed and gathered and waited. She ached from that waiting.

He thrust deep, and it shattered, all the tension and waiting. It burst in sensations as vivid as the colors on their bodies and she cried, "Ty!" as she spasmed around him.

He lost it then too, giving a hoarse cry and jerking with his own climax.

Slowly, both of their bodies loosened and he collapsed down on her, then pulled himself off to lie beside her. His chest heaved as he drew in quick breaths, but he got out, "Oh, man."

"Yeah." She struggled for breath too.

After a few long, silent minutes, he lifted his head and gazed down at their bodies. "Jesus, would you look at us."

She forced her head upright and did the same. The paints were all smeared, blending together. "We created colors that didn't exist before."

He chuckled. "Finger painting on steroids."

"No, on hallucinogenic drugs. It was mind-blowing."

They laughed together, then he put his arm around her shoulders and pulled her up against him. She snuggled a painted cheek against his painted chest.

Smiling at Kim's comment, Ty realized something. "You speak English like a native." Then, realizing his comment might sound condescending or even racist, he said, "Sorry, did that come out wrong?"

Her soft hair brushed him as she shook her head. "No, I know what you mean. Lots of people from Asia who came here as adults and are totally bilingual still have a bit of an accent, slightly different speech patterns. They don't get the colloquialisms. But I'm the next best thing to a native speaker."

Intrigued, he shifted so their heads were on separate pillows, facing each other. He looped his arm over her slim waist. "How d'you mean?"

"I lived here for four years as a little kid. Kindergarten through third grade."

"Oh, yeah? How did that happen?"

"My parents had me late in life. By then they'd built CPM. They not only managed property, they'd bought some. Apartment buildings in Hong Kong. Anyhow, in 1986, there was a big world's fair in Vancouver. Expo 86."

She sounded so businesslike, yet looked like a tropical bird. The woman was so damned fascinating. "I've heard of it."

"The world discovered Vancouver. Asian businesses opened branches there, Asian kids were sent to English-language schools, Asian restaurants sprang up. My parents wanted to check out the investment opportunities. In the early nineties, we all came for a visit. Now, my parents never do anything impulsively—"

Ty laughed. "Yeah, I can relate to that." He stroked the curve of her hip, trying to be gentle, aware of his rough, callused skin against her smooth flesh.

She grinned. "Investment is different than risk, right? Anyhow, they wanted to invest in property in Vancouver, but only after thorough on-site research. Dad would run the business in Hong Kong and Mom, whose English was better, would stay here. Aside from flying back and forth a few times a year, Mom and I lived in Vancouver."

Her dark eyes softened with memories. "It was so much fun. I already spoke English, but those four years as a kid made me fluent. After that, I was back often, with my parents when they came here on business. I stayed friends with some kids from those early school days and we e-mailed all the time. Add in American TV, books, Facebook . . ." She shrugged.

"You're at home in two worlds, Hong Kong and Vancouver. That's pretty impressive." Compared to him, a country boy through and through.

She cocked her head. "You think I'm impressive?"

"Damn right."

"Hmm." Her lips curved in a self-satisfied smile. "Cool. The rodeo star thinks I'm impressive."

Her words pumped his male ego and he gathered her in again, snuggling her against the base of his throat, one of the few places where his body was paint-free. Damn, but she felt good there.

She must have felt the same, because she sighed softly and planted a warm kiss against his chest.

At the ranch, Ty slept with the window cracked open for most of the year. There, the nights were quiet but for the sounds of nature: stirrings of wildlife, the patter of rain, occasional thunder and lightning. Here, the noise of traffic through Kim's open window-wall was a constant hum accented by the occasional roar of a motorcycle starting up or the shrill whine of a siren. She didn't seem to notice.

Despite the noise—and even after what was, hands down, the craziest sexual experience of his life—it was peaceful. He stretched out contentedly with his arm around her as she curled into him, warm and naked, her head on his chest.

It would be easy to drift into sleep, but then he'd have to get up at a ridiculous hour. He squeezed her shoulder. "I should get going."

She stirred. "You don't have to."

It was nice, her inviting him to stay. Sex was one thing, but trusting a guy enough to let him sleep over was another. Wanting to sleep over was another too. So he let her know. "Thanks. I'd like to stay, but I have to be at the ranch doing chores by five."

She shuddered. "I'm a morning person, but that's crazy early. Especially on a Saturday."

He gave a slow, lazy laugh. "Ranches don't sleep on weekends. Neither do ranchers."

"I guess not. I don't really have a picture of your life. What do you do, Ty?"

"Business stuff, help Dad with the cattle, train horses, exercise, do my rodeo practice."

She ran a finger across the now-dry paint on his chest. "No rodeo this weekend?"

"Nope. Used to be at rodeos two hundred days of the year, but those times are long gone. Now it's more like a dozen. I have another in three weeks, in the interior."

"But you still practice?"

"If you're out of shape, it's easy to get hurt. 'Sides, when you've been champ, it bruises a guy's ego to drop too far in the standings."

"How did you end up doing last weekend? I'm sorry, I never asked."

"Came second in bareback bronc and fourth in tie-down roping. Took home a nice chunk of change."

"Wonderful. Congratulations." Now she wished she'd gone back on Sunday. She lifted her head and peeled her body away from his. Eyeing him, she giggled. "Better take a shower. You don't want to put your clothes on over"—she gestured—"that."

He pushed himself up to a sitting position and studied the abstract swirls and smears of color, duller now that the paint had dried, then laughed.

She sat up, chuckling too, and he said, "Oh man, look at you. Lord, I wish I had a camera. And your hair, you gotta see your hair. It's terrific."

He rose, reached down a hand, and pulled her to her feet. She had a full-length mirror on one wall of the room and they studied their reflections.

Yes, they looked funny, but there was something oddly attractive about their painted bodies and her messed-up black hair. One side sported only the red streaks she'd applied intentionally; the other side, where she'd rested her head on his chest, was a crazy mix of red, yellow, and green.

She tilted her head. "I'm a parrot. I kind of like it."

"Me too. I kind of like all of you, in fact."

She turned away from their reflections to smile at him. "I kind of like all of you too, Ty."

"Join me in the shower?"

"Don't I wish, but have you seen my shower? There's barely room for one."

"Too bad." His own shower and his Jacuzzi tub were sizable, with pulsing jets to ease the aches and pains caused by rodeo and hard work on the ranch. Impulsively, he said, "You should come out to Ronan Ranch. What are you doing this weekend?"

Wait a minute. What was he doing? He didn't take women to the ranch. Not the women he dated casually. Only someone he was serious about belonged at Ronan Ranch. And Kim had already made her thoughts about ranches very clear.

So, it wasn't a surprise when she shook her head. "Me at a ranch? I don't think so."

He should be relieved rather than disappointed and ticked off. He definitely shouldn't say, "You didn't see yourself at a rodeo either, but you had fun." All the same, that's what came out of his mouth. He followed it up with, "I promise I won't tie you up and make you live there. It's just one visit."

She bit her pretty bottom lip, which already looked swollen from his kisses. "It would be interesting to see a ranch before I go home."

If she came, he'd try to keep her out of his mom's way. Betty Ronan was bound to read more into it than he and Kim intended. Or would she? He took another look at his Asian lover, her petite body smeared with paint, her hair even punkier than usual. It was pretty unlikely his mom would think he saw Kim as wife material. "Come out Saturday afternoon and stay the night," he suggested. "If you're worried about finding the place, I could pick you up and drive you back."

"You figure I'll get lost in the wilds of the Fraser Valley, halfway to Hope? I'm sure I can find my way. But I thought you had all that work to do."

"I'll get up extra early. Besides, the ranch'll survive if I goof off a little." He headed for the shower. Was this a stupid idea? Kim might be bored out of her mind, hate the ranch, decide he was a country hick—which he pretty much was—and dump him flat. But it was done now. No point in second thoughts.

He washed quickly, dried off on a towel that was more the size of her body than his, and went to get dressed.

She was in bed, the top sheet tucked across her breasts. A demure pose, but the wild hair and colored streaks across her cheeks sent the opposite message.

"The shower's yours."

"I'm going to stay like this for the night." Her dark eyes gleamed with humor. "I like being a dirty girl."

He chuckled. "Dirty girl, painted woman—yeah, the look suits you. But maybe you should wash before you come out to the ranch, or you might scare the horses."

She flung a pillow at him and he ducked.

Scare the horses, Kim mused as she headed the iCar smart car out of the city. Hopefully, they wouldn't run for their lives when they saw her.

She refused to follow Marielle's example and dress all cowgirl, pretending to be something she had no desire to be. But she had toned things down a little. She wore her most casual jeans—no rhinestones or embroidery. Her silk-screened tee was fairly conservative—shades of purplish blue with subtle orange and black highlights, based on the Eastern Tailed Blue butterfly. She'd debated leaving her hair unstreaked, but black hair was so boring. Ever since she'd come to Vancouver, she'd been adding whimsical color to her hair. When she moved back in with her parents, she'd have to be more conservative with her appearance, but not a moment earlier. In fact, she'd taken inspiration from last night's unplanned color job and now sported both blue and mauve streaks. Still, they were more subtle than usual, and she'd chosen delicate violet on her nails rather than the more flashy cerulean blue that decorated her toes inside her sneakers.

As she drove under a clear blue sky, she wondered for the millionth time why Ty had invited her and why she'd accepted. They had great sex. Incredible sex. He was her sexual muse, awakening her curiosity and creativity. She could handle lots more of that, if he was interested, in the weeks before she went back to Hong Kong.

But inviting her to the ranch . . . It was like inviting her into his life.

Hmm. At dinner yesterday, she'd made it clear that a sober Kim wouldn't leap into bed with a stranger. She'd wanted to talk, wanted them to get to know each other, and they had. Maybe today was something similar, his way of reassuring her that he was a decent, trustworthy guy as well as being a sex god.

She'd pretty much reached that conclusion herself, but she appreciated the gesture. And yes, she was curious. About the ranch, about what a horse whisperer did, about his house.

Oh-oh. A thought occurred to her. Did he live with his parents, the way she did in Hong Kong? She couldn't have sex with him if his parents were nearby.

Kim was so engrossed in thought, automatically following the flow of traffic in the slow lane of the highway, that she almost missed her exit. Now, as she headed onto a smaller road that cut through farmland, butterflies took up residence in her stomach. Normally, she loved butterflies. These ones, not so much.

She tried to ignore them as, slowing periodically to consult the straightforward map Ty had e-mailed her, she headed toward spectacular mountains. The few white clouds clustered around the peaks were the only break in the vivid blue sky. For the first time, she really took in the scenery: flat fields planted with crops she didn't recognize, then fencing, and now cows. Black cows. Odd; she thought of cows as brown and white. These were healthy looking, their coats glossy under the sun, the same color as her hair. They could use color streaks to liven them up.

A carved wooden sign said RONAN RANCH. The logo was the two Rs she'd seen on Ty's truck, the first one backward with its spine resting against the second, normal R. The sign looked old, probably a memento his parents had saved from their Alberta ranch. Under it hung newer wooden slats attached to heavy chains: PUREBRED ANGUS one read, the next was HORSE TRAINING, and the third read OSTRICHES, LLAMAS, ALPACAS, ANGORA GOATS.

She stopped in front of a gate made of wooden bars, with a sign reading PLEASE CLOSE GATE AFTER YOU! The gate to Ty's world.

She opened it, drove through, and latched it behind her. What was that saying from *The Wizard of Oz*? You're not in Kansas anymore? Well, she, who was at home in Hong Kong and Vancouver, with people and buildings all around, felt like she *was* in Kansas, and it was a very foreign place.

With trepidation, she drove down the road. On the side she'd come from, there were more cows. The black creatures must be the purebred Angus, Ty's dad's ranching project.

On the other side of the road, a half-dozen horses ran over to the white-railed fence and kept pace with her car, their ears pricked forward, looking curious. She'd admired the horses she saw at the rodeo. These, free and beautiful out in nature, were so much more aesthetically pleasing than the chunky, placid cows. Not that she'd say that to Ty's dad, much less anything about color streaks.

Not that she was likely to meet Ty's dad, or so she hoped.

The road led toward the foothills of the mountains. The countryside rolled gently now, and there were more trees. It was so huge and empty, but for the horses. Impressive and lovely in its own way, but a little scary for someone who'd always lived surrounded by other people.

It made her think of the book club book, which she'd tucked in her bag in case she had time on her hands while Ty was working. Marty Westerbrook had described the land she rode through as vast and awe-inspiring, and so was the scenery outside the car window. The journalist had felt that the humans in the landscape were small and insignificant. Yes, from the air, Kim's red car would look no bigger than a ladybug, and she'd be one small black spot. Marty had found the perception of vastness and insignificance comforting in an odd way.

Kim shook her head. No, it was just disconcerting.

Of course Marty could ride, and she'd been in war zones. She was brave, skilled, and versatile. Kim, on the other hand . . . Hey, wait a minute. She'd been brave enough to leave her home and parents and eagerly face a new life in Vancouver. She was skilled and versatile when it came to art, and here she was, an artist in a new world, with lots to take in and admire. This world might be foreign, but it could be a great stimulus to her creativity. Too bad she hadn't brought sketching materials.

There were buildings coming up, on the same side of the road as the cows. Ty had said she'd see the ranch headquarters, and she took in a couple of big barns, a small building labeled OFFICE, and several other buildings, all looking neat and functional. Set farther back was an attractive two-story house, painted green with white trim, bordered with colorful flowers. A couple of trucks were parked near one of the barns, and several people dressed in jeans and cowboy hats clustered around the back of one, unloading something.

As Ty had instructed, she kept driving, still accompanied by the running horses.

On the horse side of the road, she saw a fenced ring with a couple of horses in it, and a smaller barn. Up on a rise, tucked among scattered trees, sat another attractive two-story house, this one made of unpainted logs. Newish logs. Ty's house. Had to be. That was a relief. A porch ran the length of the front, with a handful of padded wooden chairs and a couple of little tables. Did Ty sit there at the end of the workday with a beer, and watch the horses run around as the sun set?

Everything he would see, and far past his line of sight, was his. He'd bought this huge piece of land with rodeo earnings. His achievement was impressive.

Her parents owned apartment buildings in Hong Kong and Vancouver, buildings where land was scarce and tiny homes nestled side by side, stacked in rows. Their property holdings were dense; Ty's were the opposite. She and he truly were from opposite worlds.

She felt a weird little pang, almost as if she wished things were different. But that was ridiculous, and she brushed the thought away.

As Kim pulled the smart car to a stop, Ty emerged from the barn, leading two horses. A quick rush of pleasure went through her. He was the perfect cowboy, fit, muscular, and totally at ease with his body in faded jeans, a straw cowboy hat, boots, and a shirt the same color as his jeans, its neck open and sleeves rolled up. Vivid memories of last night—of that fine body naked and slathered with paint—heated her blood.

Quickly he tied the reins to a rail, then came to meet her as she stepped out of the car. "You're here." He caught her up in an exuberant hug, lifting her off her feet and swinging her around. When he put her down, he said, "No problem finding the place?"

A little breathless from being swung, not to mention the flood of sensations—his outdoorsy male scent, the feel of those strong arms, the tingle that raced across her skin—she managed to say, "Not at all."

He leaned down to kiss her and she came up on her toes to meet him. The kiss dove deep and fast, and when they finally broke apart she was entirely breathless and the tingles rippled through her body.

Fifteen

see you washed off the paint," Ty said, "but you didn't get all of it." He fingered a few strands of her hair.

"That was intentional!" she protested.

His eyes danced. "Never can tell with you, painter girl. I like it."

"Thanks." She gave a mischievous grin and reminded him of his joke last night. "You don't think it will scare the horses?"

"No, they have good taste. Speaking of which, nice tee. Butterfly?"

She nodded. "Eastern Tailed Blue."

"Pretty." With a touch of hesitation, he went on. "So you've seen a bit of the spread from the road. What do you think?"

"I'm a little stunned. It's like something in a movie. I can't believe you actually own all this."

"Guess it is pretty different from what you're used to."

"Ty, it's like you own a small country. Like you could be completely self-sufficient." She paused. "Though I guess, from what you said about the ranch in Alberta, having land doesn't really make for security."

"This land and ranch are more versatile."

"I remember you saying the ranch doesn't rely just on cattle. What do you mean about the land being versatile?"

"We could grow crops if we wanted. Mom has a big vegetable

garden, and fruit as well. She's got enough chickens that we have fresh eggs and chicken."

"*Ew!* You actually kill and eat chickens?"

He chuckled. "Dad does. What's the matter, don't you eat chicken?"

"Sure. Right down to the feet. But never one I met when it was alive." She grinned. "Okay, silly distinction."

"Uh-huh. Anyhow, we could raise pigs, sheep, pretty much anything we wanted. As it is, we barter with neighbors."

"Wow. The only plants I've ever grown are in pots. And I've never even had a pet."

"No?"

"Who had time? Mom and Dad were busy building their company. And you've heard of the whole 'tiger parents' thing, where there's pressure on the kids to succeed academically? That was true in our house, with the expectation that I'd join Chang Property Management and end up running it when they retire. Or, more likely die, because I don't think either of them wants, or knows how, to stop working." A sudden chill made her shiver, and she glanced at the sky, to see if a cloud had blocked the sun. No, the only clouds in sight were the puffy ones clustered around the peaks of the mountains.

"How did you get into art?"

"Early on, a teacher told my parents I was one of the most artistically talented students she'd seen. That made them proud because art is valued in China, as it is here. They sent me to lessons and encouraged me to work hard at it, but with the idea it would be a hobby, because my future lay with the company."

"You'll show them." He rested his hand on her shoulder.

"Sure hope so." She shivered again. If she didn't come up with a brilliant plan very soon, she'd be stuck joining CPM. But Ty's hand warmed her and distracted her from her worries. No, she wouldn't panic, or let worry spoil today. If she opened her mind to ideas, the right one would come along. "Are you going to take me on a tour?"

"You bet." His arm came around her shoulders. "Let's start with the barn." He guided her across the yard as she scrutinized the ground, making sure she didn't step in anything nasty. They moved out of the blazing sun into the cool, shady building, which had an odd, but not unpleasant scent: a little musty, a little grassy, with a touch of leather and animal.

He showed her horse stalls, saddles and bridles and other horsey stuff, and a tool bench, everything neat and well maintained. In an area near the door a few jackets, shirts, and cowboy hats hung on hooks, and there were cowboy boots and gumboots lined up below.

"There should be stuff here that fits you," he said.

"I'm fine." She glanced down at her multicolored sneakers. They were supposed to be washable, but she'd just as soon not test that by stepping in horse shit. "Maybe I could use a pair of boots."

"And a long-sleeved shirt and a hat. The sun's fierce."

"I put on sunscreen."

"Humor me." He picked up a straw hat and put it on her head, adjusting the angle.

His concern was sweet, so she gave in. "Okay. But who do these clothes belong to?"

"There's some kids who live nearby whose families are having a tough time. The children don't get much chance to just be kids, and they do love to ride. They bike over when they can, and I get them what they need."

"That's nice of you."

A few minutes later, outfitted like a cowgirl, she followed him out of the barn. The boots felt stiff and clumsy; if she walked very far, she'd blister.

Ty headed over to the two horses he'd tied up. They were pretty animals, strong and sleek in the sun. One was sand-colored, with a dark face, mane, and tail; the other, smaller, was a lovely gold with a platinum mane and tail.

"The tan horse," she said. "Is that the one you rode for the roping event?"

"Yeah, that's Desert Sand." He touched the horse's nose gently with his knuckles, then stroked his neck. "And the palomino is Dawn." He gave her a pat as well.

Kim eyed the horses but didn't step closer. They might be pretty, but they were huge. And strong. Children rode them? "The kids are coming to ride?"

"Nope, they've been and gone. Reminds me, you like trout?"

"Trout?" The change of topic confused her. "You mean the fish? I've never had it, but I like fish."

"One of the kids caught a mess of trout in the river this morning and brought me a few."

"Great. So who are the horses for?"

A slow grin creased his face. "Me and you, cowgirl."

"What?" She took a hasty step backward, tripping in the unfamiliar boots. She would have gone down on her butt if he hadn't caught her arm. "I'm not going riding, Ty."

"Sure you are."

"But I've never been on a horse." Nor had the slightest desire to.

"I kinda figured. Dawn's sweet as pie and has such smooth gaits, you'll think you're in a rocking chair."

She glanced up, taking in the blond horse's powerful shoulders and hindquarters, and the leather saddle perched between them. "That doesn't look like a rocking chair to me."

"Say hi to her. Make friends."

"How?"

"Come up slowly by her shoulder, no sudden moves. Wait 'til

she turns her head and eyeballs you. You want to make sure a horse sees you, so you don't startle it."

Gingerly, she stepped toward the horse, not convinced of the wisdom of any of this.

"Don't be afraid. Some horses, horses that've been mistreated, you need to be real careful with, but not Dawn. She likes people."

The horse bobbed her head in Kim's direction as if agreeing, her ears forward and what Kim would swear was friendliness in her huge dark eyes.

"Talk to her in a soothing voice. Say hi, tell her your name, tell her she's a pretty girl. Hold your hand out nice and easy. Smell's important to horses, and she wants to get your scent. Let her sniff you."

Kim did as he said, and felt the warm puff of the horse's breath against her hand. Then Dawn nodded again, and butted her nose gently against Kim's hand.

"She likes you," Ty said. "Stroke her neck and shoulder."

She stroked, tentatively at first, then with a little more pressure, enjoying the feel of the firm, warm skin. "You really are a pretty girl," she murmured, "and your skin's so smooth."

The horse turned her head and bumped Kim's shoulder with her nose, as if she was encouraging her. This was hardly scary at all. "What a lovely name you have. Dawn. A sunshiny dawn, right, girl?"

Ty touched Kim's shoulder and nudged her away from the horse. "Here, take these." He had untied Dawn from the rail and now he pulled the reins up over her head. He offered Kim the two reins, gathered near the horn of the saddle and knotted at the ends to hold them together.

"I'm not sure," she demurred.

"You'll enjoy it. Give it a try."

She took a deep breath. Ty wouldn't let her do something dangerous. He'd look after her. Besides, she didn't want him to think she was a coward. "Okay, what do I do?" She reached for the reins with her right hand.

"Other hand. Hold the reins, and with the same hand grab ahold of the horn."

"At least you're not making me ride bareback," she tried to joke.

He chuckled. "We'll leave that for another day."

"Another day in another lifetime." She gripped the reins and horn. "Now what?"

"Right hand on the back of the saddle. Put your left foot in my hand and I'll give you a boost. Lift yourself up, swing your right leg over the saddle, then put both feet in the stirrups."

To her surprise, she managed it easily. Compared to some of her yoga poses, swinging onto a horse was a snap.

Ty studied her. "Stirrup length is right. You want the ball of your foot on the bar of the stirrup, and keep your heels down. Hold on to the horn if you want to."

"Okay." She clutched the horn.

"Good." He flashed that contagious smile of his, then untied Desert Sand and swung lightly into the saddle. "Dawn will tag along with Sand. If you tighten up on the reins and shift your weight back, she'll slow down or stop."

Kim nodded, though she was skeptical. Surely nothing she did could stop Dawn. She'd be pitting her hundred pounds against what? A thousand?

"Then let's take the grand tour." Ty gave some signal she didn't catch, and his horse began to walk across the barnyard. Desert Sand lifted his tail and deposited a pile of droppings, the earthy scent filling the air and making Kim hold her breath. It didn't faze Dawn, who followed close behind.

Kim focused on the unfamiliar saddle and the horse's motion, getting the feel of everything. She studied Ty's posture, the graceful way his body moved with the horse's rhythm like they were a single being, and tried to copy it. She might not have Marty Westerbrook's riding skill, but this wasn't a cattle drive.

They were on a trail that went past the log house. Ty turned to her. "My place, which you'll see later." He dropped a wink. "Especially the bedroom."

Oh, yes, she was looking forward to that. It would be her reward for wearing a weird hat and boots, sitting atop a giant animal, and smelling horse shit. "I like the house. It's fairly new?"

"Yeah. The spread you drove past, the house, barn, and outbuildings, were on the land when I bought it. When my folks moved out from Alberta, we all lived in the ranch house. I hadn't lived with my folks since I was seventeen, and it was pretty awkward. Built this house, the barn. Gives me a place to work with the horses away from the other stock."

"I saw the black cows when I drove in. Those are your dad's Angus?"

"Yup, but call them cattle rather than cows. Beef cattle, to be specific, as compared to dairy cattle."

"What's a cow then?"

"A female that's calved."

"Really? What are the rest?"

"The adult males are bulls or steers. Bulls haven't been castrated. Females are heifers until they calve."

"And the babies are calves, right?"

"Yup, though there are more specific terms for different ages of calves."

"That's complicated."

"Bet you artists have a dozen names for red, right?"

She nodded. "Good point."

"The one you used on me last night is my favorite."

"Mine too." They exchanged a grin. Every time she used that color, she'd remember how it looked on his naked skin. Hopefully, that would inspire rather than totally distract her.

They'd ridden into the trees and the path was dappled shade rather than brilliant sunshine. Dawn wasn't a rocking chair, but her slow, steady motion was kind of soothing. Kim let go of the horn and took a deep breath. The air smelled so fresh and, somehow, green.

They came to a fence and Ty stopped his horse, turning it to face back the way they'd come. Dawn fell in beside.

"This is the boundary of Ronan Ranch. The bulk of our land is on the other side of the road you drove in on. It's the land we use for the Angus and the specialty stock. On this side, there's a narrow strip. It's my turf for the horses."

"Narrow" meant something different to him than it did to her. Out here, everything was painted on a grand scale.

She gazed across the rolling land dotted with trees, then up toward the mountains they'd slowly been heading toward. There wasn't a soul in sight, and no sign of civilization except the fence. Yes, it was a little scary, and a lot impressive.

She'd never related to landscape painting, as the worlds she'd occupied had been urban and confined. Now she was getting a better idea of what inspired people to try to capture such natural grandeur. Sheer admiration of the beauty and scale of it, in part. But partly too it might be an attempt to . . . not own it, because no one could. To make it your own in some small way, to interpret it, to feel part of it.

Yes, she could imagine bringing watercolors and creating her own vision of this very foreign world. Ty's world, where he looked utterly at home. "I've never seen anything like this. It's spectacular."

"It's different than what we had in Alberta. I like the contours of the land, the trees. The mountains are a nuisance because they make for changeable weather, but they're damned easy on the eyes. Beats staring out at acres and acres of flat land."

She nodded. "In Vancouver, you can always see the mountains. And the ocean. It's great."

"Wouldn't have minded buying a ranch by the ocean. But I'd have had to rodeo another ten years to afford it. That would've been okay by me, but Mom and Dad were dying in those shit jobs in Alberta."

"You're a good son."

He shrugged. "Maybe I turned into a decent one."

He was a good guy, period. It was amazing no woman had snapped him up. "I don't think there's any surfing in Vancouver, but you could drive to the beach."

"Seems the only time I leave the ranch, it's to rodeo or do business."

"Not last night," she pointed out, thinking how yummy yet out of place he'd looked when she lifted her umbrella and first laid eyes on him on Davie Street.

"That was special." He shifted his horse closer, rested a hand on Kim's jean-clad thigh, and leaned over to kiss her. His lips tasted of sunshine, a hint of sweat, and sexy male.

He made her a little dizzy, and she gripped the horn again. "Mmm, a kiss on horseback. I never imagined doing anything like this."

"I never imagined having a woman paint my body, so we're even."

He guided her along another scenic trail until she heard the sound of water, and they came out beside a burbling stream. Ty swung off Desert Sand, then led the horse to the stream and tied the reins to a small tree. The horse promptly dipped his nose and drank.

Dawn ambled over and Ty stopped her, taking her reins from

Kim and tying her as well. When the horse lowered her head to drink, Ty said, "Come on down, Kim. Hold on to the horn with your left hand, take your right foot out of the stirrup, and swing your leg over."

She did so, and his hands caught her firmly at the waist. "Now take your foot out of the left stirrup and I'll let you down."

A part of her wanted to say she was capable of getting to the ground under her own steam, but his hands felt too good. So she let him lower her, and when her boots hit solid ground she realized her legs were a little trembly. From riding, or his closeness? She turned in the circle of his arms, took off her hat and plunked it on the saddle horn, then reached up to clasp her hands behind his neck.

"Enjoying yourself?" he asked.

"I am." Surprisingly, it was true. She couldn't imagine wanting to shovel manure or kill chickens, but riding in the country was pleasant.

He gave her a slow, sweet kiss, which was more than pleasant. "Take off your boots and dip your feet in the stream. It feels great on a hot day."

"Trying to get my clothes off me?" She said it teasingly, but wondered if he really was. The first time Marty and Dirk had sex in *Ride Her, Cowboy*, it was by a stream in the starlight. Kim and Ty'd had the starlight; maybe now it was time for the stream.

"Aw shucks, you're on to me." His tone was joking, though.

Just as well he didn't mean it. The idea of sex by a stream was romantic, but it wouldn't be comfortable. Besides, there were animals out here. Bears, maybe? Coyotes? Rattlesnakes? She had no idea, but she wasn't about to expose her naked body to any of them.

Sixteen

Kim found a big rock by the edge of the water, a little way from the horses. Perching on it, she tugged off boots and socks, and rolled the legs of her jeans up her calves.

Ty tossed his hat to the ground, claimed an adjoining rock, and took off his boots.

When Kim eased her feet into the stream, she shivered at the shock of cold water against overheated skin. It felt blissfully refreshing.

She took off the long-sleeved shirt she'd borrowed, and tossed it onto the rough grass at the bank of the river. Feeling more like her real self in her tee, she leaned back on her hands and lifted her face to dappled sunshine. "I'm no nature girl, but this is cool." The only sound was the burble of the stream and the occasional birdcall, the fresh scent was something she couldn't name, and not a touch of breeze disturbed the still air.

Sitting up again, she gazed into the stream, watching the way it danced around rocks and the sun glinted off it. How would she paint that? There were more shades of blues and greens, of browns and golds, than she could name. How could she capture the sense of constant motion? Generally, she didn't do representational art. While she could convey a relatively exact image of a subject, she'd rather interpret the spirit. The spirit of this stream was its cheerful burble, its dance around the rocks, the way it embodied both constancy and continual change.

Oh, yes, this was good for her creativity.

"It's one of my favorite spots." Ty's voice broke into her musings. "I come here sometimes when there's a problem I'm sorting out, or when I just want to relax."

She studied him, splashing his feet idly in the water. "You take time out to relax? Your life sounds so busy."

"Yeah, but life needs balance."

"I agree, but my parents wouldn't. They're all about work." She dipped her hand in the cool water then ran it over her warm cheeks.

"My parents were like that when they were busting their butts to make a go of it with the ranch in Alberta. But hard work wasn't enough."

"How are they doing here at Ronan Ranch number two? Still busting their butts?"

"Kind of. They say they're much happier doing this than working day jobs and going home and watching TV."

"When you find the thing you love, it's still work but it feels different," she agreed.

"You making any progress on that business plan?"

She groaned. Why did he have to remind her? Glumly she stared into the sparkling stream. "The clothing design thing just doesn't feel right. I keep hoping for a brilliant idea, but nothing comes."

"Nothing?"

A glint of sunlight sparked a memory. "Last night when we were leaving the restaurant, a thought flashed through my mind. Now what was it? You kissed me and I forgot."

"Sorry. Well, not that I drive everything else out of your mind, but sorry if I distracted you from a good idea. What were we talking about? You almost forgot your umbrella and—"

"That's it!" She stared at him, her eyes widening. "It was about umbrellas. I remembered how you'd said 'Don't fly away' earlier, and I thought that umbrellas were kind of like wings. And I have a thing for wings." She ran a hand through her hair as she remembered her train of thought. "But umbrellas are such boring wings. And I thought, do they have to be?"

He leaned forward on his rock, eyes bright with interest. "You mean you could design more fun umbrellas?"

"That are like wings. Umbrella wings, yes! Umbrellas are such boring shapes and colors." Excited, she thought it through out loud. "But if I did wing shapes, there'd have to be enough fabric to keep a person dry."

"Hey, if a cowboy hat can do it." He flicked water up with his toe, splashing her leg.

"Most of us want to be a little drier than that. I could do broad wings, or if the wings were skinny, there could be clear plastic between them." She nodded; that could work. "And parasols too, maybe painted ones. For sun protection. They're a big thing with some Asian women who don't want their skin to darken. And other women too—older ladies, or ones with delicate skin, or who've had skin cancer."

"If you had different lines"—his voice was almost as animated as her own—"women would buy an umbrella and love it, then want a parasol too."

"Ooh, and how about this? Elegant umbrellas for classy occasions, and bright playful ones for walking to work on a rainy day. Strong, masculine umbrellas like hawk and eagle wings. Kids' umbrellas like ladybugs!"

"Cute. Kids would love that."

"Women could collect fancy umbrellas the way they collect shoes."

He nodded. "Kim, I think you're on to something."

"I'd have to research fabrics. Mechanisms that work properly and don't break. Material for poles and frames. Metal would work with some designs, but it's too harsh for others. Bamboo, maybe. Oh my, I've got my work cut out for me. But Ty, it feels right!" She stared across the short distance between her rock and his, almost unable to believe this was real.

"Bet you want to dive right in and get started," he said, resignation in his voice.

Oh, yes! And yet she was here, with Ty. It would be rude to dash back to Vancouver and start work. It wouldn't hurt to let the idea gel, let her creativity have free rein, before she put her mind to the practicalities. She had to be both artist and businesswoman—and just plain *woman* woman, which was how he made her feel.

"No." She slid gingerly off the rock into the stream, the chill bite of the water creeping up her calves. One jeans leg unrolled and dragged into the water but she ignored it. She stepped carefully over to stand in front of him, between his legs. "Thank you. If it wasn't for you, I might never have thought of this."

His face softened and warmed. "Sure you would, dragonfly girl."

"Maybe. Maybe not."

"I'm glad if I helped."

"Thank you for taking me seriously as an artist."

"You're welcome." He smiled at her.

Leaning forward, she rested her hands on his shoulders and kissed those smiling lips, pouring all her gratitude and excitement and hope into that kiss.

His thighs tightened around her hips and his hands framed her head as he kissed her back. His tongue teased hers and he nipped the corner of her mouth.

Her body ignited, all the way down to her water-chilled feet.

"What say we take this some place more comfortable?" he asked.

"Back to your house?"

"No." He slid forward on his rock, nudging her back until he slipped into the stream too.

When he stepped out of the water, he didn't bother with socks and shoes, just picked up the shirt she'd cast aside and held out his hand.

She took it and followed, wincing as rough grass, tree cones, and pebbles stabbed her sensitive feet. Ty must have soles like leather. Fortunately, after a few more steps, he stopped at a relatively smooth patch of grass under a tall tree. He tossed her shirt down, pulled off his own, and spread the two out. "It's not a bed, but we only make it to a bed half the time anyway."

That was something she loved about their relationship. Before Ty, she'd only ever had sex in a bed. His way was much more erotic. Usually. As for now . . . "Aren't there bears? Rattlesnakes?"

"None that are gonna bother us here."

She pressed her lips together. Yes, she was hungry for him, but was it safe? She knew less than nothing about the great outdoors.

"Trust me," he said.

And she did. "Okay."

"Then strip for me. I want to see you naked in daylight." His voice was husky, and an erection pressed against his fly.

Strip for him? In the middle of nowhere? Did she dare? A ripple of arousal made her tremble, telling her how much she wanted to release her inner dirty girl. Ty had the kinkiest ideas, and she loved it!

She undid the button of her jeans, slid down the zipper, and eased them down her hips. Trying to imagine how a stripper might do this, she added a hip swivel and a little back arching. Her turquoise thong stayed on—for now. As her jeans cleared her butt, she rotated, still gyrating, to give Ty a view of her near-naked backside.

Gaze fixed on her, he sank down, his jean-clad butt on the rough ground, his naked back against a tree trunk. "Jesus, Kim, you're hot."

She was. Hot for him. This striptease game made her totally aware of her body, of his eyes on her, of his ripped bronzed torso, of the need he awakened in her.

She turned back, hips still grinding, and continued peeling her jeans. When they were almost at the ground, she turned to again give him her back view. Then she bent down to free first one foot from the crumpled denim, then the other. Before straightening, she separated her legs to make a vee, and looked at him upside down from between them. "So far, so good?"

"Too good. It's all I can do to keep from grabbing you."

"You could grab me."

He shook his head. "I want you to strip all the way and lie down. Like you're waiting for me. Wanting me to come to you."

If that was his fantasy, she'd make it come true. Kim straightened in a slow, catlike motion, caught the hem of her T-shirt, and lifted it to bare her back, revealing the straps of a pink bra with orange lace trim. After a couple of hip thrusts, she peeled the tee over her head. Holding it loosely folded in front of her breasts, she swiveled back to face Ty.

Shifting the shirt back and forth, with only the burble of the stream for music, she teased him before letting it drop on top of her cast-off jeans. She ran soft fingertips along the top edge of her bra, her violet-painted nails flicking sensually against her skin. Her nipples were hard, craving the touch of his callused hands, his firm lips. This bra had a front clasp. When she unfastened it, she held the bra in place with a hand over each cup.

Be careful what you wish for, Ty told himself. When he'd asked Kim to strip, he'd meant to peel off her clothes and lie down. Trust her to give the actions a sexy twist.

Here he was at a back corner of Ronan Ranch, being treated

to his own private strip show. Kim didn't seem experienced at this. It wasn't something she did for just any guy. But she was so lithe and graceful, everything she did looked erotic.

She flirted the cups of her pink bra off and on, giving him glimpses of naked flesh then covering up again.

"Take it off," he urged. He was dying to rip off his own clothes, free the hard-on that surged painfully against his fly, and make love with her. Yet watching her like this was something he'd never forget.

Never forget. The thought distracted him. He'd always assumed that one day he'd find the right woman and get married. But, hmm . . . She'd have to be something special so that, when they made love, he wouldn't think of Kim on the hood of his truck, Kim on her balcony, their paint-smeared bodies twining together, her stripping for him by the stream.

But of course his wife would be special. They'd create their own memories. Even better ones. If that was possible. . . .

Kim shrugged, freeing the bra straps to slip off her shoulders and down her arms, capturing his full attention. She held the cups in place for a few beats of the imaginary soundtrack she was stripping to. Then, finally, she let it drop.

Her perfect breasts were firm, the budded nipples a dusky pinkish brown against the paleness of skin that hadn't seen the sun. Her tan came from wearing tank tops and shorts. The rest of her skin was paler, a dramatic contrast to her black hair and the vivid colors she liked to wear.

Like that scrap of turquoise thong. Would she give him another rear view? He wasn't sure he could take it.

Tossing him a saucy smile as if she'd read his mind, she turned again and played with the center strap of her thong, tugging it away from her skin as if she intended to peel the skimpy garment off, then letting the strap fall back to hug her skin.

"Off," he said, squirming in a futile attempt to relieve the pressure against his cock. "You're driving me crazy."

"Patience isn't your middle name." She gyrated slowly as he ogled the curves of her butt.

"Patience isn't any of my names." Actually, it was. A rancher, a horse trainer, had to be patient. And with Kim, he loved the way she teased, tantalized, and tortured him. He figured she knew that without him saying so.

She turned to face him, hips grinding slowly and seductively, and finally eased down the side straps of the thong. The small triangle came away from her skin.

Ty gaped. The patch of black pubic hair was gone.

The thong dropped down to join her bra and tee. She was utterly smooth, utterly nude. He'd liked her silky feminine hair, but this was definitely provocative.

"Come over here." He pointed to the spread-out shirts.

She did her best to saunter over, but winced when a rock or twig poked her sole. She had the most feminine feet, with bright turquoise toenails. Sexy feet. Sexy woman. "Aren't you going to take your clothes off?" she asked.

"Not yet."

Her eyebrows rose. "Man of mystery."

"Not for long."

When she made to lie down on the shirt, he said, "No, on your hands and knees."

Another eyebrow lift, then she nodded like she'd figured it out. "Okay."

He stifled a grin. She thought he was going to do her from the rear. Nope. Kim Chang wasn't the only one with a surprise or two up her sleeve.

He lowered himself, and in a quick move slid his body under hers in the opposite direction. His naked back was on his shirt, his hips between her spread hands, and his face inches away from heaven: her sweet pussy. Her utterly naked pussy, rose pink and slick with the cream of her arousal.

"Oh!" She gave a surprised squeak, then another when he caught her hips and tugged her lower, those last few inches until he could swipe his tongue along her bare flesh and taste how hungry she was for him.

Her next "Ooohhh" was low and drawn-out, with a shudder of discovery and pleasure.

His cock throbbed urgently as Kim pressed her pussy against his face. He lapped her, darted his tongue between those swollen folds, then, as she panted, "Please, Ty, please," he sucked gently on her clit until she came in pulsing spasms against his lips.

When her body sagged, he caught her, lifted her, placed her gently on her back.

"Wow." She gazed up at him with stunned eyes.

"Yeah." He unsnapped his jeans. "Damn, you turn me on, Kim."

"Mutual." She dragged the word out like she had trouble pronouncing it. Or finding her voice. "Wow."

One-word sentences. He liked that he'd reduced her to that.

Standing, he tugged his jeans and underwear over his hard-on, and found a condom. Sheathed, almost bursting, he knelt between her legs. When he slipped between her thighs, she was wet and open. He thrust home in one long, smooth stroke.

Yeah, this was perfect. Her tight channel gripped him smoothly, slickly. He still found it hard to believe that a guy his size and a tiny woman like Kim could fit together so easily.

She wrapped her arms around him, one on his back, one squeezing his ass. "Oh, yes."

A two-word sentence. Sort of. That was better than he could do, though. Speech was beyond him as he stroked in and out of her, racing toward the finish his body demanded. The only sounds he could utter were groans of pleasure.

His body tightened, his orgasm shuddered through him, and she cried out as her body rippled around him.

When Ty boosted her onto Dawn's back this time, Kim was slower in swinging her leg over the saddle, and when she settled into the seat, she winced.

"Are you okay?"

"A little sensitive."

"Finding your riding muscles?"

The corner of her mouth tilted. "My sex muscles."

He squeezed her thigh. "We could go straight back rather than finish the tour."

"No, I want to see the rest of the ranch."

And he wanted to show her, though he wasn't entirely sure why. Yeah, he was proud of Ronan Ranch, but he wasn't the kind of guy who boasted about his accomplishments. It was more that he wanted to share this with Kim. So far, the self-proclaimed city girl had been surprisingly open-minded.

He mounted Sand and directed his horse along the stream, with sweet-tempered Dawn following. He was tempted to name the trees, mention that the chittering sound was a squirrel, and identify birdcalls, but figured that would be overdoing it. He did, when he spotted a doe and fawn through the trees, ease Sand to a halt. "See the deer?"

"They're beautiful," she whispered, sounding thrilled.

"Yeah, though they drive Mom crazy, getting into the garden. Easy answer's to build a tall fence, but she doesn't want to ruin the view."

"I'd like to paint them."

He reached across for her hand and they watched as the deer grazed idly. Then the doe lifted her head, twitched her long ears, and the pair bounded away.

She sighed. "Wow. I'll never forget that."

Deer, like crystal clear stars, were something he almost took for granted. Yes, he and Kim were very different.

He took her along one of his favorite trails, and stopped where they could look down at the specialty stock. "Those are my mom's critters."

She identified ostriches and llamas, and he said, "The ones that look like smaller llamas are alpacas, and the goats are angora."

"So these are for wool? Not the ostriches, though?"

"No. Ostrich meat, feather dusters, and ostrich skin shoes and bags."

"Huh. I have an ostrich skin purse. I never thought about where it came from."

"City girl," he teased. "Ranchers and farmers know all about where things come from. Like the trout waiting for us in the fridge. Getting hungry?"

"Yes, and a bit sore."

They rode back to his place, where Ty dealt with the horses as Kim returned her riding gear to its place, changed back into her running shoes, and collected her small overnight bag from the little red car.

He took her in the back way so he could leave his boots in the combined mudroom/laundry room, and toss his socks in the washer. Kim pulled off her own shoes too, and, barefoot, they went into the kitchen. Though he didn't bother with frills when it came to food, he liked to eat, and the kitchen was designed for efficiency, with high-quality appliances.

Kim glanced around. "Nice. You could fit my whole apartment in here."

Her place was tiny, but he liked how her bed was only steps away from everything else. In fact, right now he was tempted to drag her off to his own bedroom, but he was hot, thirsty, and starving, and she probably felt the same. She was staying overnight. They had time.

He opened the fridge door. "Hope you like Sleeman's lager. Or there's wine. Maybe beer now, then wine with dinner?"

"Hah," she said mildly. "You're trying to get me drunk and un-inhibited."

Seventeen

Ty grinned as he cracked the top of a Sleeman's. "You're plenty fun when you're sober. But you're not driving anywhere, so relax and enjoy." He handed her the bottle. "Want a glass?"

"No, I'll go wild and drink out of the bottle."

He chuckled, hoping she'd go wild with him, later.

She tipped the bottle up and sipped. "Mmm, that's good. Do I get a tour of the house?"

He took a long, refreshing drink from his bottle. "A quick one. I'm ready for dinner."

"I can wait for the tour."

"No, it's okay." She was polite; he'd noticed that before. It was like she wanted to please people, to put their interests ahead of her own. "Come on."

Holding hands, carrying their bottles, he showed her the big living room with the river rock fireplace, the dining room with its plain wooden furniture, and the downstairs bathroom.

"It's very attractive."

"Not your style," he guessed. The only art was a mountain landscape on one wall.

"The bones of the house and the furniture are great. But I'd add color, art, whimsy."

His lips twitched. "Whimsy? That sounds so much like me."

"I like the photos." She walked closer to a wall covered with framed photos of family and friends. "Oh, man, look at you." She shook her head over pictures of him atop bucking broncs, and winced at one where he'd been sent flying through the air.

Gesturing to a wedding photo, she said, "Your parents? They're a good-looking couple. You take after your dad."

"People say so." His dad looked happy but a little uncomfortable in a charcoal suit, and his mom, Betty, was radiant in a long dress—yellow, her favorite color, and designed simply, the way she liked.

He pointed to another photo. "That's Grandma and Grandpa's wedding picture." His grandfather wore a western-styled suit and shirt, bolo tie, cowboy hat, and boots. Ty's grandma wore an embroidered white square-dance style dress with a full skirt, beautifully tooled cowboy boots, and a matching hat.

"Look at them. How very western."

He was going to skip showing her the home gym, but when they passed the open door she stepped inside. "This is cool. Your own private fitness center."

He had weights, a rowing machine, a treadmill for when snow kept him from running outside. "Got to be in good shape to rodeo. Doesn't hurt any when it comes to ranch work either."

"You even have a yoga mat."

"I don't do yoga but I do some stretches. To loosen up, and keep on top of a couple of old rodeo injuries so I don't hobble around like an old man."

"Hard to imagine."

He took her upstairs, pointing out the couple of smallish bedrooms—for kids, one day—another bathroom, his office, and the master bedroom, with its big window facing the mountains. Lust and hunger warred, and hunger won. They'd have all night to heat up that bed.

"Let's go downstairs and I'll get dinner going." With a hand on Kim's back, he steered her toward the stairs. "I'll cook the trout on the barbecue with lemon. New potatoes with parsley, if that works for you. There's a bunch of veggies in the fridge. Pick whatever you like." He pulled out a saucepan and put water on to boil for the potatoes.

Kim squatted in front of the fridge. "Everything looks so good. Maybe a big salad?"

"Sure."

She pulled out ingredients. "Salad bowl?"

"Hey, you don't have to do that. Sit down and relax. I bet you're achy." He went to light the barbecue on the deck off the kitchen.

When he came back in, Kim had found a salad bowl, washed the vegetables and sat at the table, tearing lettuce. "A back deck and a front porch," she said. "To catch the sunlight at different times of day?"

"That's the idea. Figure we'll eat on the front porch and watch the sunset." He gave a wry laugh. "That's about as exciting as evening entertainment gets around here." What would she be doing in Vancouver? Dining with friends, going to an exhibit or the theater, dancing at a club?

"Oh, I'm betting you can provide something a bit more exciting than that, cowboy, once the sun goes down."

"Well, now that you mention it, I do have something in mind."

"Oh?" She cocked her head. Her hair looked cute, messed up from the hat. He'd expected a city girl to fuss in front of a mirror, and liked that Kim didn't.

"You're going to stiffen up, and I have a Jacuzzi."

"How decadent. As you saw, I don't even have a bathtub. But, I didn't see a Jacuzzi in either of the bathrooms."

"There's another bathroom off the master bedroom. A large bathroom with a really big Jacuzzi." He winked, his blood heating as he imagined getting her naked again.

"Really big? As in, big enough for two?"

"That's the plan."

"I like your plan."

It was kind of strange, being with her in the kitchen. She turned him on and he wanted to have sex with her, but this was fun too, chatting about whatever came to mind as they put dinner together. She sipped her lager, but when he opened a bottle of white wine from a Fraser Valley winery, she shoved the beer bottle aside, half full. "That's enough for me if I'm going to drink wine too."

He filled a couple of glasses and assembled cutlery, paper napkins, and salt and pepper shakers. "Want to take this out to the porch? I'll check the fish."

Sure enough, the skin on the three trout was crispy and brown, the filleted insides tender and moist. He dished them onto plates, two for him and one for Kim. They served themselves baby potatoes topped with butter and parsley, and sizable portions of salad.

Plates and wineglasses in hand, they headed out to the porch. The wooden Adirondack chairs had cushioned seats and broad arms, a good place to put a wineglass.

Sinking into a chair, Kim yawned, then slapped a hand over her mouth. "Sorry. That was rude."

"You're on country time already."

"Guess so. And I'm so relaxed. Coming up with that umbrella idea, I feel like a huge weight's been lifted."

"I'm kind of surprised you don't want to dive into researching it. I'm glad, though."

"There's time. Now I have the idea—thanks to you, Ty—it'll work out, I just know it." She tasted the fish. "Mmm, nice."

"Not as fancy as what we ate last night, but I like it."

"Me too. I'm not much of a cook. I eat out or get something I can microwave." She dug in with relish, taking an occasional sip of wine, smothering another yawn or two. "What time will the sun set?"

"Around eight. See the sky changing?"

"This place makes my fingers itch."

"Uh . . ." Was she saying she had allergies?

"To hold a paintbrush. Too bad I didn't bring my camera so I'd have photos to paint from."

"Why didn't you?"

She shrugged. "Asian tourist with camera? It's a stereotype."

"We don't see a lot of Asian tourists with cameras out here."

She giggled. "No, I guess not. Oh well. It would have been fun to show pictures to my parents and friends back in Hong Kong. They'd never believe where I am, what I've been seeing." She picked up her wineglass and took a swallow. "Though I don't know how I'd explain to my parents why I was here."

"Explain what? You visited a friend's ranch?"

"They're nosy. What sex is this friend? Male? You're spending time with a male friend other than Henry?"

"Henry?" A rush of something male and primal hit him. "Who's Henry? You said you weren't dating anyone."

She shook her head quickly. "I'm not. Henry's a very nice guy from Hong Kong, who's living in Vancouver. Our parents did some matchmaking. He and I were a couple until a few months ago. We haven't told our parents we've broken up."

"Why not?"

"They'll find out when we go home. Until then, let them be happy—and leave us in peace."

"Your parents have a lot of influence in your life." At twenty-four, shouldn't she be more independent when it came to her career and who she dated? And wasn't it better to tell her parents the truth than to—at least by omission—deceive them?

"Yeah. So do yours, right?"

"Not in the same way. We're business partners." He and his dad still disagreed occasionally, but—largely thanks to his mom's wisdom—they'd worked out ways of settling arguments.

"You mean they don't butt into your personal life?"

"Well," he had to admit, "Mom's been on my case to find a wife."

A grin flickered but didn't catch hold. "I wondered how a guy like you managed to stay single."

"A guy like me?"

"Good-looking, responsible, a successful businessman. Not to mention sexy." Her delicate eyebrows pulled together. "You're quite a catch for a certain kind of woman."

Not her, clearly. City girls and country boys didn't mix, not long-term. He'd known that since he was a toddler. The fact that Kim knew it too shouldn't hurt. Trying to keep his tone light, he asked, "What kind? Buckle bunnies?" Did she think he was that shallow?

"Unlike you, I don't know any buckle bunnies," she said, an edge in her voice. "But I'm guessing they're just into the glamorous side— the hottie rodeo star—not the hard work."

He nodded. "Right. To live on Ronan Ranch, a woman can't be afraid of hard work."

She tilted her head. "What's your perfect woman?"

Oddly, the answer that sprang to mind was *You*.

In some ways she was. Smart and creative, sexy and fun, unpredictable, colorful. Life would never be dull. But what was he thinking? She wouldn't make a ranch wife, and she sure as hell didn't want to be one.

Before he could answer her, a truck drove up the road and stopped. A woman climbed out.

He groaned. "Speak of the devil. You're about to meet my mom."

His mother was trim in jeans and a checked shirt, her brown hair pulled back from her face with a blue band. She looked barely forty rather than fast approaching fifty. She waved. "Ty, give me a hand."

Resignedly he climbed to his feet, set his half-finished dinner on a side table, and headed down the steps barefoot.

She handed him a basket overflowing with vegetables. Like she didn't know his fridge was already full. Then she reached into the truck again and came out with a blackberry pie. "I've been baking. Figured you and your guest might like dessert."

"How did you know I had company for dinner?"

She gave that all-knowing Mom smile. "Your dad saw the car, and it didn't come back."

"Yeah, well, thanks for the pie." He tried to take it from her but she held tight to it.

Amused and annoyed, he said, "Okay, come meet her."

"Thought you'd never ask. Didn't anyone teach you manners, son?"

By the time they reached the steps, Kim had risen and put her plate down.

"Mom, this is my friend Kim Chang. Kim, Betty Ronan."

His mother shuffled the pie plate to her left hand and held out her right one. "It's nice to meet one of Ty's friends." He was pretty sure a petite Asian woman with spiky, color-streaked hair and turquoise toenails wasn't what his mom had expected.

Kim shook her hand. "It's nice to meet you too, Mrs. Ronan."

"Mom brought pie. And veggies." He winked at Kim from behind his mother.

"I love pie. And you can never have too many vegetables." She sounded polite and a bit nervous.

"You should take some home," his mom said, "when you go." She paused. "Where's home for you? You don't live around here, do you?"

"I live in Vancouver, but my real home is Hong Kong." Kim added, pointedly, "I'll be heading back in a month and a half."

"Ah." Reluctantly, she said, "I should let you get back to your dinner." She glanced at him.

No, he wasn't going to invite her to have a glass of wine or share the pie. "Thanks for the food, Mom. See you tomorrow."

Kim said, "Yes, thanks so much. The pie looks delicious. And it was a pleasure to meet you."

"You too. Perhaps if you're here tomorrow—"

"Bye, Mom," Ty cut in.

"All right, all right." She shot one final appraising look at Kim, then headed back to the truck.

When she'd driven away, Ty and Kim sat down again and he re-filled the wineglasses. "Nah, Mom doesn't butt into my life." He took a long swallow.

Kim laughed. "It's human nature. We're lucky to have parents who care about us." She picked up her dinner plate and started eating again.

He gave a half smile. "She makes damn good pie."

"I'll save room for dessert."

"How's the trout? Sorry it got cold."

"It still tastes good. So do the potatoes. Dinner's perfect, Ty. But I shouldn't drink any more."

"Scared you'll leap my bones if you get all uninhibited?"

She chuckled. "You have excellent bones. But tonight, the fresh air's done a number on me. I'm more afraid I'll fall asleep in this chair and you'll never get me up."

Like it'd be any trouble to hoist all one hundred pounds of her and carry her off to bed. An appealing thought, but there was something else on his mind. "What did you think of her?"

"Pretty, in a natural way. Fit. Young. She must have had you in her teens."

He rarely thought about the fact that Betty Ronan wasn't his birth mom. "She's only twenty years older than me, and she looks young for her age. Hard work and healthy living, she says. My dad's almost ten years older than her, and in great shape too."

Kim nodded and put her plate aside, polished clean. "My parents are much older. They tried for almost twenty years to have a child. When I came along, they were thrilled. I got the full weight of all the hopes, dreams, and expectations they'd been saving up for all those years."

"That's a lot to put on a kid."

"It's pretty normal in the families I know." She covered her mouth to hide a yawn. "Do you have brothers or sisters?"

"I'm an only too." To his parents' regret, Betty couldn't have kids. Too bad. He wouldn't have minded a kid brother or sister. Not only to hang out with, but to maybe get his dad off his back.

"Oh look, the sky is so incredible."

He glanced up to see the colors deepening as the sun sank lower, and reached over to take Kim's hand. They watched in companionable silence as vivid rosy reds, oranges, and yellows gradually faded to more subtle shades of pink and purple. Often, Ty was too busy to notice the sunset, though sometimes he ate dinner out here and watched it. Alone. Other nights, he was down at his folks' place, talking business rather than enjoying the scenery.

Last night, when the invitation to visit the ranch had burst out of his mouth, he'd wondered if it was a mistake. If he'd regret it; if she'd be bored or sneer at him for being a hick. Now, he was glad his mouth had gotten ahead of his brain.

Sunset, a glass of wine, his fingers linked with Kim's. Life was pretty damned good. Later, if she didn't fall asleep first, they'd climb into the Jacuzzi. They'd have sex, maybe slow and gentle, maybe steaming hot. But for now, her small, warm hand in his felt exactly right.

* * *

Kim struggled to keep her eyes open. Fresh country air, terrific sex, exercise, pleasantly aching muscles, great food, more alcohol than she was used to . . . Tonight she had no urge to sing karaoke or even have sex on a truck. Her body urged her to drift into sleep.

"She's not my birth mother," Ty said.

Well, that certainly woke her up. "What? Who? Betty?"

"She and Dad met and married when I was three. She's the only mom I remember, and she's a great one. When she's not butting into my love life." They shared a smile. "She's my real mom. Just not the one who gave birth to me."

"What happened to that one?" she asked hesitantly. Had she died?

"She ran out on Dad when I was a few months old."

"Oh my God, that's horrible!" What kind of person abandoned her baby?

"It was pretty bad for him. But things worked out. Mom's perfect for him."

That was all very philosophical, and he sounded so unemotional. Trying to understand, she studied Ty's strong profile in the dimming light. "What happened between him and your birth mom? Or is that too personal?"

He glanced toward her, then back out to the shadowed land. "Miranda was from Toronto. She and a girlfriend went to Alberta on holiday, with some romantic notions about cowboys. She and Dad fell head over heels in love—or lust. Next thing they knew, they were married and having a baby."

"That doesn't sound so smart."

"Nope. It didn't take her long to figure out that ranch life's the opposite of glamorous." He gave a wry smile. "Dad, well, he can be charming, and maybe he was romantic when they were dating. But then he went back to his real self, a hardworking, commonsense guy.

My grandparents and Miranda never got along. Bottom line, she wanted the life she'd left behind in Toronto: wealthy parents, shops, restaurants, theater, friends. So she went back."

"Leaving you and your dad." She shook her head. "That's so sad. Sad for all of you." So many dreams, all blown away like dry country dust.

"Not so sad for her. She got what she wanted." There was bitterness in his voice.

She sympathized with the bitterness, but relationship stories were rarely one-sided. "Maybe. But she must have gone through a rough time for a while. All because she and your dad got carried away and made a mistake." Lust was heady; she felt that with Ty. You could mistake it for something more, and leap into a match that was totally wrong. Thank heavens she and Ty were sensible.

"Miranda probably felt miserable," she said. "The ranch wasn't what she'd dreamed of, her romantic boyfriend had turned into a hardworking rancher, her in-laws didn't like her, and her support network was back in Toronto." Quickly she said, "I'm not taking her side, okay? Just saying she and your dad both suffered from their mistake." And Ty had to feel hurt and bitter, even if he didn't show it.

"I never thought of it that way," he said slowly.

"But her answer was to bail. She sounds really immature, like she wasn't ready to be a mom or a wife, whether it was on a ranch or somewhere else. So she left and got, like, a do-over, going back to the life that suited her. It's not fair that you and your dad had to go through some rough years, but you might not have been any happier if she'd stuck around. As it was, his parents were there to help, then he met Betty. The right woman for him and the right mom for you. So it worked out in the end." Probably, that was why Ty managed to be so philosophical.

"It did."

She squeezed his hand. "But still, it must have hurt, the way Miranda abandoned you. What a shocking, horrible thing to do."

"Hurt my dad for a while, but he says Betty's the best thing that ever happened to him. As for me"—he shrugged—"I was a baby, then a toddler. What did I know? I had my dad and grandparents."

Could they make up for a mom who'd rejected him? Kim found that hard to believe. That little boy must have been deeply hurt, and the grown-up Ty had to carry some scars from that. "Did you ever hear from her again? Miranda?"

"Nope."

"And you never looked her up? Like on the Internet?"

"Why? I have a mom." Ty rose and gathered their empty plates. "Feel like some pie?"

If Miranda had hurt him, he was either in denial or didn't want to talk about it with Kim. It wasn't her business to probe. She and Ty didn't have that kind of relationship, and never would. For some reason, that thought was painful.

Eighteen

Kim shoved herself to her feet, and found another kind of pain. Riding used different muscles than walking or yoga. Hobbling after Ty with their wineglasses, she said, "Pie later, if that's okay. That Jacuzzi sounds pretty good."

He turned. "Sore? Sorry, guess I overdid it."

"No, it was wonderful. But I've stiffened up and could use a soak."

"Go on up. I'll stick the dishes in the dishwasher then come join you. If that's okay?"

She studied him, so handsome with his tousled hair, bronzed skin, a scruff of five-o'clock shadow, bare feet. It was a week since she'd first seen him: the sexy rodeo rider. Now she knew him as the best lover she'd ever had or could imagine; as a hardworking rancher who looked out for his family and even the neighborhood kids; as a guy who cooked a mean trout. As a man who had one mom who butted into his love life because she cared so much, and another who'd run out on him. *Her loss.*

Ty was so much. Yes, he was a catch for a certain kind of woman. A woman who wanted a guy who was eye candy, successful, and had an amazing work ethic and great family values—and what woman wouldn't? But Ty's woman had to be the opposite of his birth mom; she had to relish being a ranch wife.

If his dad was anything like Ty, she could understand why Miranda fell for him. But Kim wasn't Miranda. She couldn't let herself fall. Forget the Jacuzzi, the sex. She should climb in her car and drive home. Except she'd had half a beer and more than a glass of wine. Hmm. Alcohol affected her. She knew that. Maybe that was why she was feeling mushy about Ty.

The night she'd met him, she'd had too much to drink and had sex with him. Tonight, she'd again drunk too much, and now she was in danger of getting romantic.

Okay, she'd analyzed the situation, and now could control it. She and Ty knew their relationship wasn't about the future, but why not enjoy the present? Her parents wouldn't approve, but they'd never know. This was all about her and Ty.

"Kim? You asleep on your feet? I thought only horses did that," he teased.

"Sorry. Yes, please join me in the Jacuzzi." She gave a flirtatious wink. "Help me wash my back."

"Nothing against your back, but I have more fun parts in mind."

Smiling, she collected her small bag and headed up to Ty's bedroom. The décor matched the rest of the house: basic, well-made wooden furniture, everything built for comfort, the minimum of fancy touches. It was the house of a busy man who liked things simple and functional. The only art in the bedroom was an excellent oil painting of horses running across a field strewn with wildflowers.

She liked the bones of Ty's house, the choices he'd made, but the place cried out for color, more art, and, yes, whimsy.

She headed for an open door, assuming it led to the bathroom. Inside, she breathed a surprised, "Oh!"

Now this was a bathroom. There was a big window, uncovered because after all who could see in? Cinnamon-colored ceramic tile floor; light cream walls; a nice big cabinet with sink, mirror, and cupboard space below; and a shower large enough for two. But the highlight was the Jacuzzi, so big she could almost swim in there.

Every aching muscle cried, "Yes, please! Now!"

She turned the bronze tap, adjusted the temperature, then took a jar from the marble surround and tossed granules into the tub. A fresh, invigorating scent filled the steamy air, reminding her of their ride through the trees.

Candles would be nice. In the bedroom, she found plain white ones that had never been lit, alongside a souvenir ashtray from the Calgary Stampede and a package of matches. She stuck a candle to the ashtray and set it, lit, on the edge of the bath, then turned out the light.

Wincing at sore muscles, she pulled off her clothes. Reminded of her outdoor striptease, the wince turned into a grin. She slid into the warm, silky water with a moan of sheer pleasure.

Music came on in the bedroom. Not country but jazz, a female singer with a sultry voice. Norah Jones. Ty came into the bathroom and studied her. A slow smile spread over his face. "Oh yeah."

"You're not playing country music."

"Cowboys are allowed to be versatile."

"I've noticed that." She flicked a few water drops at him. "Want to be versatile in here with me?"

He shucked his clothes. The sight of his cock swelling sent a surge of neediness through her own body.

"How are your aches and pains?" He urged her forward, settling in behind her.

"Better every moment." She leaned back against him, feeling the pressure of his growing erection against her bottom.

He turned on a switch and Jacuzzi jets blasted water against her, then immediately he turned the force down. "Sorry, it was set for me. Is this okay?"

"It feels wonderful. And not just the water." She wriggled her butt against his erection.

He thrust gently against her and reached one big hand around to toy with her breast and tease the nipple.

She was sleepy, yet the tingly fresh scent energized her. Her body was tired and achy, yet Ty, naked, fondling her breast stimulated and aroused her. Then his hand dropped lower, went between her legs. He brushed her clit, making her moan, then did it again. Nice, very nice, but not what she had in mind. "I want you inside me. Slow and lazy, not fast and hard."

"I can do that."

They both rose partially so he could dry and sheathe himself. He slid into her from behind, easing her down to sit on his lap, her thighs lapping his as they settled back into the tub.

She purred with satisfaction.

One of his arms came around her waist, steadying her as he pumped slowly, so slowly, sliding in and out of her the tiniest bit.

It made the sensations more focused, more intense. She was more aware of her body, of his, not just the insistent drive to orgasm she felt when he pumped hard. She tightened her internal muscles around him, felt him pulse in response.

His free hand toyed with her nipple again, creating a sweet ache that fed the throb of arousal between her legs.

She leaned back to rest her head against Ty's strong chest. The uncovered window was black, hiding the vast, foreign world outside. The only world that counted was this intimate one where candlelight flickered and Ty moved sensually inside her. To enhance the sensations, she closed her eyes.

Now there was only the tingly scent in the air, the silky warmth of the water, the gentle swirl from the Jacuzzi jets. The tensile strength of Ty's body under and inside her, the soft rasp of his breath, her own occasional moan of pleasure. They were in a warm, wet, pulsing, golden cocoon of eroticism.

She shifted her butt ever so slightly, tightened her muscles, changed the angle.

He didn't keep up a steady rhythm. Instead, he moved, moved

again until her body quivered, then he stopped, resting inside her, until she was on the verge of begging him to please, please move again. Then, he did it.

"Your achy muscles feel better?" His voice was a husky rumble close to her ear.

"Muscles? I have muscles?" she murmured. "I'm melting. Inside and out." Except for the tight, achy need that was building.

"Touch yourself."

Her mouth opened, but no sound came out. Too tempted to resist, she slid her hand down between her legs. Her clit was swollen, and touching it was bliss.

She opened her eyes and looked down. Her body was slim, the untanned parts pale. Ty's strong legs were pale too, down to midthigh, and brown below that. Sometimes he must wear shorts rather than jeans. His cock thrust into her, thick and utterly male, brushing her hand. Her finger, so small and delicate in comparison, pressed her clit.

Inside her, tension built. "I'm going to come," she whispered. And then she did, crying, "Oh, Ty!" as waves of release throbbed through her.

He kept moving, slowly, inevitably, and that insistent slide of his cock inside her prolonged the pulsing near-ache of her climax. "Your turn." She clasped the base of his shaft in her fingers, pumping him in time with his thrusts.

His pace increased, his breathing rasped faster, then with a groan, he too exploded.

When his last spasms finally ended, Kim relaxed back against him. "I may never move again."

A kiss landed in her hair. "Can't have you turning into a prune. And speaking of fruit, are you ready for blackberry pie?"

She was ready to fall asleep on him, right here in the bath. But that pie had looked yummy. "I never turn down dessert. But didn't you say last night that you're not into dessert?"

"I make an exception for anything homemade with fruit in it."

"Good exception." Steadying herself against both edges of the tub, she managed to get to her feet. Dripping, she reached for one of the nutmeg brown towels on a rack. The thing was huge, a bath sheet not a towel.

Ty released the drain plug, and rose to follow her.

After they dried off, she chose leggings, a tee, and a thong from her overnight bag and got dressed. He pulled on sweatpants, nothing else, and hand in hand they went down to the kitchen. The lights seemed awfully bright as she plunked down at the table.

He held up the pie, its golden brown lattice top streaked with blackberry juice. "Warmed up, with vanilla ice cream?"

"Yum."

The pieces he cut were generous. After putting them in the microwave, he said, "Coffee, tea, milk?"

She shook her head. "No thanks, just water."

He poured her a glass, and one of milk for himself, then put the heated pie on the table along with a carton of ice cream. Sitting across from each other, they served themselves ice cream and dug in.

Ty's gorgeous naked torso was distracting—at least until she took her first bite of warm pie with melting ice cream. "Mmm. Your mother's a great cook. Does she grow the blackberries in her garden?"

"You don't know about blackberries, do you? They grow wild, like weeds. The kids who ride here pick pails full and bring them to us. Mom freezes them and makes jam, syrup. Gives some back to the kids."

"She's an amazing woman." Kim savored another bite, along with the view across the table. "She does all the old-fashioned female stuff plus raises animals and helps run the business. And she was a terrific mother."

"All of that."

She remembered what they'd been talking about when Betty Ronan had driven up. "You never did describe your perfect woman."

A flicker of something she couldn't read touched his eyes then was gone. "Someone who loves this kind of life, loves horses and wants to help me with them, loves kids and wants to have two or three. Someone who's, you know, not pretentious. Just natural, fun. Smart."

"Loyal," she added, thinking of his birth mother.

"For sure."

"That sounds like a good fit for you." Why should she feel a twinge of jealousy? She wanted Ty to find his perfect wife and live a wonderful life. Just like she wanted to find her own perfect husband. Her eyelids drooped from tiredness, but she was too curious to let this subject go. "What's wrong with all the women you've met?"

"I've dated some nice women. On the rodeo circuit and here. But nothing's clicked."

"What's the longest you've gone out with someone?"

He ran a hand over his stubbly jaw. "Uh, about a year, I guess. Not long after I bought this place. A woman who runs a therapeutic riding school for kids."

"What's that?"

"It's for children with disabilities. Horses and riding help them in all sorts of ways. Physical strength and coordination, confidence, communication skills, and so on."

"Like art therapy. That's terrific. What was wrong with her?"

"Not a damned thing. I really liked her, but it didn't go further than that. But I saw that for her, well . . ."

"She was falling for you," she guessed, "and you didn't want to hurt her?"

He nodded.

"It's weird how someone can look perfect on paper, but that doesn't mean the emotions will be there." And someone could look all wrong on paper, and yet you found yourself not just lusting after his sexy body, but beginning to care for him.

"Personal experience? That guy Henry?"

His words jolted her away from her silly romantic daydream. "Henry?" Perfect on paper, that was what she'd said. "Right. He's smart, successful, a good son. Considerate, nice-looking." She sighed. "I thought I loved him. Or maybe I figured I was supposed to love him. And he was a tie to home, and I was homesick."

"What happened?" He'd finished his pie and went to cut another slice, muscles rippling and flexing. This was not a man who had to worry about calorie intake.

"We got into a habit, doing and saying the same old stuff. There was no spark, no excitement." No, she wouldn't discuss their ho-hum sex life with Ty. "He's very conventional. I do believe in tradi-tional values, but I'm more experimental."

"He's too much like your parents." He sat down again with his pie.

"Maybe. He did encourage me to go into the family business."

"Was he worried you couldn't make a living from art?"

"It was more about duty and loyalty. A good Chinese kid does what their parents want."

"A person has to think for themselves."

"Tell that to my parents." She tried to capture the last smears of blackberry syrup and melted ice cream. If she'd been alone, she'd have picked up the plate and licked it. "It's a cultural difference. I know most Westerners don't get it."

"Hmm. Want more pie?"

She groaned. "It's so good, but I'm full and I'm sleepy. Maybe for breakfast?"

"Isn't that against the rules?"

"See, this is the effect you have on me," she teased back.

He rubbed his index finger gently over her top lip, held it up to reveal a smear of ice cream, then stuck his finger in his mouth and sucked it. "Do I have any other effect on you?"

Despite her exhaustion, desire rippled through her. She caught his hand and brought it down to her plate, rubbed his finger in the remaining smears, then brought his finger to her own mouth. "One or two." She sucked his finger in between her lips and swirled her tongue around it. "Take me to bed, Ty."

The next night, Sunday, Kim went to bed early, worn out in many delicious ways.

When she'd left the ranch after sex and a breakfast of blackberry pie and coffee, eager to get to work on her winged umbrella idea, Ty had asked when they'd get together again. She'd said, "I'll give you a call." She wanted to be with him but her brain said she needed to spend time away from his seductive influence, and decide whether this was a good idea.

Lust, casual sex, it was all so unlike her. She wouldn't be dumb like his birth mom and blow the whole thing out of proportion. A romance between her and Ty wasn't something either of them would consider. Besides, she had UmbrellaWings—that was the name she'd decided on—to work on, which she did all day, growing more excited every minute. Maybe the smartest move would be to concentrate on work and forget about the cowboy.

When Kim dropped into bed at nine, she stretched achy muscles and thought enviously of Ty's Jacuzzi. Of Ty in that Jacuzzi with her . . . No, she couldn't daydream. She needed to finish the second third of *Ride Her, Cowboy*.

Nineteen

Propped up on pillows, Kim studied the half-naked cowboy on the cover and remembered the waitress asking Ty if he was a cover model. Giggling, she opened the book.

Another evening on the range, sitting around a campfire. The days had a sameness. The same men were driving the same cattle across lonely, spectacular country, then gathering by the fire to eat and drink. Yet Marty's journalist brain was attuned to the details.

Len, the cowboy who turned out gourmet fare over the fire, was the oldest of the bunch. Though he never complained, he hobbled when he climbed off his horse at the end of the day. She'd asked him if he was okay and he'd said, "Old bones, Marty. We're none of us as young as we used to be. Just glad I can still be doin' this."

She also noticed when Dirk told Len to stop hogging the frying pan and let him cook them all Sloppy Joes. He hadn't said a word about the older man's frailty; he let him keep his dignity.

The food Dirk produced tasted just fine too, with a bite of spicy pepper that had them all reaching for their beer. It seemed Dirk was competent at pretty much everything.

Though he was the boss and a natural-born leader, he worked harder than any of the others—and none of them were slackers. Dirk saw everything and dealt with it: a steer with a mind of its own, a horse that developed a limp, a journalist who had fallen behind as she changed lenses on her camera. When a calf cut its legs on rocks, he roped it and brought it down, then tended to the cuts, his hands deft and gentle.

Kim smiled. Dirk sounded a lot like Ty. No wonder Marty admired him.

Dirk was finally talking to her. Last night, things had changed. In the beginning there'd been mutual lust but he'd seen her as an annoyance, maybe an adversary, and she'd been on guard. Now, there was mutual respect—as well as the lust.

Today, she'd ridden beside him off and on, asking questions about the cowboy way of life in this modern age. He talked about how ranching today differed from that of the past. She learned about types of cattle, markets, the impact of Mad Cow disease, dietary and cuisine trends, the kinds of jobs and people that made up an operation like his.

She learned other things from her own observations. His hired men were more than just employees; they were a family of sorts. Each man had strengths and weaknesses, and so long as they were loyal to Dirk, he'd support them.

Cattle ranching was more than a business, it was a way of life for these men. One that was threatened by a number of factors, and struggling to adapt and survive. Dirk told her that cattle drives like this were virtually a thing of the past, but at the Lazy Z, they liked to do some things the traditional way.

"That article of yours," he'd said, "what was that title again?"

"The Modern-Day Heroes of the West."

"That's the kind of thing gets my back up. We're not heroes. Not fools either, though some folks call us that. We're just people doin' something we love, tryin' to make a decent living and provide for our families. We're no different from anyone else."

She mused on that now as she gazed at Dirk in the dancing fire-light. Tonight, she'd deliberately not sat beside him. Her attraction to him was so strong, how could she resist touching him? But it wouldn't be good for either of them if his men knew that the boss and the journalist were having a fling.

A fling. It sounded like such a frivolous thing, out here where everything was timeless and elemental. "Frivolous" was the last word a person would apply to Dirk Zamora. What was he doing with her?

What was she doing with him? Somehow, it didn't feel like just sex anymore.

She picked thoughtfully at the label on her beer bottle. On day one, it had been sex, period. Last night, there'd been respect and liking. Now it was day three, and she felt more than liking. She was beginning to care about this man.

It was different than when she'd fallen for her soldier in Afghanistan. There, people could die any moment. It gave everything an edge, an intensity. Lust and love had come hand in hand, strong and sudden and overwhelming. Changing everything.

Out here on the range, the feelings had crept up on her over the course of the past three days as she observed Dirk, talked to him, made love with him. She shouldn't allow herself to care. He didn't feel the same way. To him, she was a passing amusement.

Except . . . that took her back to where she'd started. Dirk wasn't frivolous. Was it possible she meant something to him? And if that was true, what on earth might they do about it?

Kim shook her head. Marty wasn't a naïve kid. She knew better than to fall for a man whose lifestyle was totally different. In the Lady Emma novel the club had read, Emma had kept a practical head on her shoulders even as she'd reveled in the Comte de Vergennes's sexual attention. Kim could now relate to the allure of a cowboy, but a woman had to be ruled by her brain, not by lust or romantic notions. Unlike Ty's birth mother.

She read on, to another hot sex scene. As Dirk stimulated Marty with his fingers and tongue, Kim thought of Ty and the things they'd done together. Her body humming with need, she slipped her hand between her legs to where the flesh was tender from lovemaking. When she stroked herself, she imagined the callused pads of Ty's big fingers.

Hmm. Maybe there'd be no harm in seeing him again.

Kim spent much of Monday working on UmbrellaWings and was buzzing with excitement when she headed off to book club. Yes, she wanted to discuss the book, but she also wanted to get her friends' input on her business concept.

It was Lily's turn to pick the location. Kim enjoyed seeing what each woman came up with. They had somewhat different tastes, but were willing to experiment. Kim had discovered some great places. What a pity she'd soon be leaving this city.

This afternoon, they were meeting at the lounge at MARKET in the Shangri-La hotel on Alberni Street. Classy, as Lily's choices usually were. Walking toward the entrance, Kim saw Marielle hurrying toward her.

"Have you been making art?" she asked the other woman. Marielle's pink tee had splotches of paint on it.

"If finger painting with preschoolers counts."

Finger painting with a naked adult male was a lot more fun! She bit her tongue and instead said, "Preschoolers? Do you have a new job?" Marielle was forever changing jobs.

"I'm a substitute nanny. This girl I know's a nanny and she has to take time off to go to the Philippines and help look after her grandmother, who's having a hip replacement. I'm filling in. The dad's a lawyer and the mom's an architect with a home office. As long as she isn't disturbed between eight thirty and four, she's flexible about the rest. Like letting me come to book club or go out most evenings."

"Sounds perfect for you." Marielle was vivacious, generous, and fun; kids must love her.

"The tough part is playing the disciplinarian, but believe it or not, I'm okay at it. I just remind myself that it's in the kids' best interests to learn about structure, rules, boundaries."

"You sound like my parents," Kim complained. Then she admitted, "But yeah, I agree. I'm kind of surprised you do, though."

Marielle winked. "You need to learn the rules as a kid, so when you're a grown-up you can choose just how you want to break them."

"Like having blackberry pie for breakfast."

"Ooh, you're a bad girl, aren't you?" Marielle teased.

Laughing, they walked into the elegant, simply decorated lounge, where purple orchids graced each table. Lily and George were perusing menus. Blond Lily was dressed in her usual classy but drab tailored style, and redheaded George wore a green and white patterned blouse with her sage green suit. Both looked like they belonged here, and Kim didn't feel too out of place in leggings and one of her floaty tops. Marielle's paint-splattered tee sure wasn't standard attire, but she was so confident, nothing intimidated her.

After greeting each other, they ordered drinks. As always, Lily had a martini, George went with wine, and Marielle picked a fruity cocktail. Kim decided to change things up and not select a fancy beer. Instead, she picked a sparkling wine called Prosecco Breganze Rosa di Sera, simply because the name was so great. For snacks, they chose sushi, Thai chicken wings, and a small pizza topped with tomato, mozzarella, and basil.

Orders placed, Lily said, "Kim, you've caught up on the reading?"

"Yes. I'm sorry about last week." She glanced around. "How do you like the book?"

"It's different than Lady Emma," George said. "Emma knew she had no future with the Comte, and never developed strong feelings for him. But Marty's falling in love."

"This is the interesting thing about reading erotica," Marielle said, "rather than erotic romance."

"What?" Kim asked. "There's a difference?"

The brunette nodded vigorously. "In romance, you know they'll end up together. With erotica, there's more suspense. It's all about the woman's sexual journey—like, think of Lady Emma and the Comte. The heroine may or may not end up with the guy, or guys, who're her partners on that journey."

"I didn't know that," Lily said. "I'll get on the Internet and read more about the distinction. But for now," she went on briskly, "focusing on our book, I think it's foolish of Marty to fall for Dirk. There's no future for those two, any more than there was for Emma and the Comte."

"I agree," Kim said. "They live in different worlds, and she should be sensible enough to recognize it."

"Wow," George said. "Two cynics. Lily, who's happily married—"

"Lily," the blonde said, "who knows Marty and Dirk aren't destined for a romantic happily ever after."

"O-kay." George's brows arched. "Kim, you too? You're all about commitment and long-term relationships."

Kim's cheeks warmed. She grabbed the flute glass of bubbly pinkish-peach liquid the waiter put in front of her and took a gulp. The flavor promptly distracted her. "Oh my, that's yummy." She lifted the glass again, smelling peaches and berries and maybe roses, and took another appreciative sip. It was so summery, and she loved the bubbles.

When she put the glass down, she realized the other three women had tasted their own drinks and were waiting for her to respond to George's question. "Yes, I think love and marriage are what really count." She glanced at Marielle. "I know you like getting to know different men and don't want to settle down, but I want a life partner." A Hong Kong man who looked, and made love, like Ty Ronan.

"And because you don't think Marty'll find that with Dirk," Marielle said, "you don't think she should sleep with him?"

With Ty on her mind, Kim thought about her answer. "Maybe there are times in a woman's life when it's good to not think seriously. To have fun, enjoy the moment. Without giving your heart the way Marty's in danger of doing. Then, after, you both move on and no one gets hurt."

"Hey," Marielle said. "I didn't think you related to that, girlfriend."

"Live and learn, I guess." Speaking of which . . . "You can learn different things about yourself by doing different things and knowing different people, right? Having no-strings sex can help you figure out your own sexuality and what you ultimately want out of a relationship."

"Well said," Lily commented.

"That reminds me of the Amish book we read," George said. "Where the young people have that *rumspringa* time. They get to do things that adult members of the community aren't allowed to, and figure out who they really are."

Lily nodded. "So they can decide whether to be baptized into the community or to leave."

Marielle giggled. "Me, I've declared *rumspringa* for my whole life."

"That's not for me." Kim glanced around the table at the three women. A year ago, she hadn't met them. For the first few months of book club, they'd mostly talked about the books, then personal bits slipped in. Their discussions turned from purely literary to discussing the themes in the books, topics like male-female relationships. Yes, she now thought of these women as friends. Though it wasn't her habit to discuss intimate emotions, she would value their opinions on her and Ty. She hadn't made up her mind whether to see him again.

Besides, maybe she wanted to, for once, be the one to shock them. "I have six weeks before I go back to Hong Kong—"

"No, is it that soon?" George broke in. "Oh Kim, we'll miss you."

"You can't go," Marielle said. "We won't let you."

Kim smiled in gratitude, then leaned back as their appetizers were served.

They all dove in, then Lily asked, "Kim, what were you saying?"

She pressed her lips together, then released them in a smile. "I think I'm declaring a Chinese *rumspringa*."

"Way to go!" Marielle said. "I could hook you up with some great guys."

"No, thanks. I found my own. You're not the only one who likes hot cowboys."

Lily's pale blue eyes widened, George almost choked on a bite of sushi, and Marielle whooped. "After Blake and I left the bar, you and Ty got it on! And you didn't tell us?"

"I felt like I'd done something slutty. I mean, not that I think you hooking up with Blake was slutty, but that's not me. Or it never has been. My parents would definitely think it was slutty." She frowned, then brushed that thought away. A six-week Chinese *rumspringa* made sense to her, and her parents would never find out. "Anyhow, Ty got in touch, we had dinner Friday, then I went out to his ranch, rode a horse—"

"Rode Ty," the irrepressible Marielle broke in.

"In a Stetson," a devil made Kim say. Then, "No, sorry, it was a Resistol. Rodeo cowboys wear Resistols because that company's a big sponsor of rodeo. They wear Wrangler jeans for the same reason."

"You," Lily said, "are a big surprise."

Another flash of doubt made Kim bite her lip. "You don't think I'm slutty?"

"You couldn't be slutty if you tried," Lily said.

"It's not in your nature," George said. "Having sex with a nice guy is not slutty."

"Hear, hear!" Marielle raised her cocktail glass in a toast.

"But," George said.

"Oh-oh," Marielle teased. "Here it comes."

"It's not a criticism," the redhead said. "Just a warning. When I started out with Woody, I thought it would be casual. We're so different, I couldn't imagine him being my soul mate."

"And look how that ended up," Marielle said.

"Exactly." George's hazel eyes were serious. "My heart got involved. Fortunately, so did his, and it turned out we *were* soul mates and"—she raised her hand so that her engagement ring caught the light, sending sparkles dancing—"all's well that ends well. But you see what I'm saying, Kim?"

She nodded. "Sure. But that's not going to happen. I'll be in Hong Kong in a month and a half, and Ty will be at his big family ranch."

"You're positive about going back to Hong Kong?" George asked.

"Oh, yes. Whatever happens with my art plans—and I want to talk to you about that—there's one sure thing in my life. Hong Kong. No way are my parents going to let me live anywhere else."

"Parents don't rule your life," Marielle said.

"That's not really what I'm saying. We're a family. They've given me everything, and I love them. I love Hong Kong too; it's my home. Of course I'll go back."

Lily nodded. "I admit I don't see you living on a ranch and wearing a Stetson—excuse me, Resistol."

"Exactly." And why should those words, true as they were, give her a twinge? The country might be surprisingly nice to visit, but she wasn't into toting hay and dodging cow pies. "Ty's great, and he deserves a perfect ranch wife. Like I deserve a perfect Hong Kong husband." Her parents would try to find her one. And Ty would fall in love with some superwoman who toted hay, tended horses, grew veggies, baked pies, and raised kids. And probably didn't have a creative bone in her body, and would never dream of painting his naked body.

Feeling unsettled for no good reason, she took another drink and determinedly changed the subject. "Before we get back to the book, could I take five more minutes and get your feedback on something? How do you feel about umbrellas?"

When she got home from book club, Kim dove into Chinese *rumspringa* by e-mailing Ty to say she'd love to see him again. But when? Her fingernails tapped the table beside the keyboard. She'd like to visit the ranch again, this time with art supplies. But that was his world, and she wanted her turn. He'd made her ride a horse, which, admittedly, had been okay. Now she needed to challenge him. What would most challenge a cowboy?

Hmm . . . A group of Emily Carr grads was having an exhibit, opening Wednesday. She'd learned not to invite Henry to art events. He politely pretended interest, but was bored and restless. Why not ask Ty? How would he respond? She typed,

I've seen yours; how'd you like to see mine? World, that is.
There's an art exhibit opening Wednesday night. Want to come?

She added the link to the exhibit, then shut down her e-mail and got to work on her business research. The book club members had been enthusiastic and provided great input. Tomorrow, Kim would visit Vancouver's umbrella shop, and she wanted to have a comprehensive list of questions and ideas to discuss with the owner.

When she was done for the night, she checked her e-mail and found Ty's reply.

Bull in a china shop? But I can deal. When should I pick you up?

Grinning, she provided the details. Then she shut down her computer, stood, and did a twirly spin. She'd be seeing Ty in less than two days! Let *rumspringa* begin!

Twenty

Ty didn't have a clue what to wear to an art exhibit opening. His mother might know; she was the one who went into Vancouver for events. Tuesday morning, after he and his mom wound up a discussion of new markets for their ostrich meat, he said, "I'm going into Vancouver tomorrow night to meet Kim. There's an art exhibit she wants to go to."

His mom's strangled expression told him she was fighting to hold back a laugh.

"Yeah, fine," he said, "so I'm not exactly the arty type. But hey, if I don't have any culture, it's your fault and Dad's for raising me that way."

"I wouldn't say we don't have *any* culture, but I see your point."

"Anyhow, I wondered, since you go in to the theater and stuff, if you have any idea what I should wear."

This time, the chuckle escaped her. "How old are you? Twenty-nine? This is the first time you've asked me for clothing advice."

"Because jeans and a hat pretty much always worked, with a fancy shirt or a plain one, depending. I'm guessing that might not be the dress code for an art exhibit."

"Probably not. Why don't you ask Kim?"

Because he was trying to demonstrate that he wasn't a total bumpkin. He shrugged.

"Right," his mom said dryly. "Okay. I'm sure you'll be relieved to know, I wouldn't suggest a suit either."

"Thank God." He occasionally wore one to a business meeting, but hated every moment.

"Black pants and that black, lightweight Henley sweater. Shoes, not boots."

"Henley sweater?"

"Round neck, no collar, placket front with three or four buttons?"

"Oh yeah, right. It's comfortable."

"Leave the top button or two undone. Roll the sleeves up your forearms, the way you do with your western shirts. You'll look casually stylish."

He shook his head bemusedly. "Casually stylish. Yeah, that's me." He dropped a kiss on the top of her head. "Thanks, Mom."

"Anytime." She didn't go on but her brow had furrowed.

Knowing he shouldn't ask, he still couldn't resist saying, "What's wrong?"

"Nothing. Just . . . You're not getting serious about this girl, are you?"

"Nah. She's going back to Hong Kong." Again, he shouldn't ask, but he did. "But, out of curiosity, what do you have against her?"

"I barely met her. She's cute, polite. But son, she's not a ranch girl."

"What gave it away?" he joked. "The streaks in her hair?" Before she could answer, he went on. "No. And I'm not an arty city boy. Kim and I know that, Mom. This is a short-term thing." Though he had a feeling he'd miss the dragonfly girl, and not just for the wild and crazy sex.

"I thought you were ready to settle down."

"Haven't met anyone, so what's wrong with hanging out with Kim?"

"Nothing, I suppose. I just wonder if it's avoidance."

"Avoidance?" If he didn't see Kim, that would be avoidance, wouldn't it? What was his mom talking about? "Avoidance of what?"

She shook her head. "Nothing."

"Women baffle me."

Now, finally, she smiled. "Of course we do."

Asking his mom's wardrobe advice paid off. When Ty double-parked outside Kim's building, she climbed in and said, "Wow. Look at you."

"Recognize me without the cowboy hat and boots?"

"Barely." She kept staring at him. "You look like you belong downtown."

"It's a disguise. I really don't. Come here and kiss me."

She leaned over and her lips met his, sweet and quick. A horn honked before he could demand more.

"You look terrific," he said. She wore a short skirt made of layers of fabric that puffed it out, a bit like a ballerina's skirt—or like butterfly wings. It was patterned in several shades of orange and rust, with white and black accents. She wore it over black tights that ended midcalf. On top, she had a figure-hugging orangey red top, kind of like a dancer's leotard, and a skinny scarf wound around her neck. The scarf had a lacy black and white design. The highlights in her hair were deep orange, the paint on her fingernails white. Her shoes were platform-soled orange sandals, her toenails were black.

"Thanks," she said. "Inspired by the Red Lacewing butterfly."

He'd never known a woman who dressed like Kim. It took getting used to, but he liked it. She sure did brighten things up. And, whatever she wore, his gut-level reaction was to strip off her clothes and be naked with her. Which he was definitely going to do, as soon as the art exhibit was over.

The exhibit was at a gallery on Granville Island. Though he was no expert on driving in Vancouver, he knew the Island. Ronan Ranch supplied one of the butchers at the big market. As they drove, Kim updated him on her umbrella research.

"You base all your designs on particular butterflies?"

"Loosely. Or dragonflies or birds."

"How about attaching a card to each umbrella with the name and picture, maybe a detail or two?"

"Ty, that's brilliant!" She beamed at him, then said, "Oh, that's the turn. There, then right again."

Once parked, he went around to open the passenger door, and she slid down into his arms. "Brilliant," she repeated. "Thank you."

"You're welcome." He tightened his hold. "It's good to see you."

"You too." She fingered the open neck of his sweater. "I like this."

"The sweater or what's underneath?"

"Both."

He wondered if she had that same reaction, about wanting to get naked. He wrapped his arms around her waist and gave her a warm, lingering kiss. Not really trying to turn both of them on. That would be pointless right now. Just anticipating the end of the evening, when they'd be in bed.

She responded enthusiastically, and so much for not being turned on. "Whoa now." He eased back. "If you want to see this exhibit, we gotta stop now."

"And here I thought you were looking for an excuse to bail." She threaded her fingers through his and squeezed. "You're going to see things you hate, things you don't understand, and hopefully some stuff you like. I'm betting you won't see any western landscapes, though."

"I'll keep an open mind."

He did his best to honor that promise as she forged through the crowd inside the exhibit room. She might be half his size, but she moved with an appealing air of confidence. Glancing around, he saw sculpture, painting, photography, and things he didn't have a clue how to classify. Like that huge canvas that had not only paint but bits of metal, feathers, coins, and God knows what else.

Kim obviously had a destination in mind. *Oh good, the bar.*

"I figure this'll help with that open mind," she told him. They both chose Granville Island ales, hers honey maple and his dark.

"Let's start there." She gestured toward a selection of black-and-white photographs.

He studied them, thinking they were just a jumble of shapes, then he read the label beside one. "A lighthouse?" Hmm, now he could see it was the actual light with its many surfaces, taken from an unusual angle, with odd lighting. "Interesting. What do you think?" To him, the pictures were dramatic but chilly.

"I do like art that makes you see things differently. But you know me, I love color. I'm not a big fan of black and white."

They moved on, to the big weird thing with feathers and coins. "I don't have a clue what this is," Ty confessed.

"It's a mixed media collage using found objects."

"And I don't have a clue what you just said."

"Kind of like heifers and cows, and all those other names for cattle. To me, what really counts is the viewer's reaction. If art makes you smile, brings back a good memory, tugs at your heart-strings, or makes you think, then it's a success. It's subjective."

"So I shouldn't pretend to be an art snob?"

"You really think that would work?"

Chuckling, he squeezed her hand, enjoying the warmth and connection in this room full of strangers and unusual art. More at ease, he moved slowly around the room with Kim, sharing impressions, sometimes agreeing and often not. They joked, laughed, touched. He was actually having a good time. Maybe just the fact of being with Kim made for a good time.

She said hello to fellow students and teachers and he saw she was friendly, popular, and knowledgeable about the art. She introduced him by name, not attaching a label like "friend" or "boyfriend." He figured their clasped hands told a story.

Here, he wasn't the owner of a ranch, nor a guy with cases full of buckle belts. He was the guy holding Kim's hand. And that was a fine thing to be. When a couple of people asked whether he was an artist too, he said a simple, "No."

A few pieces of art did impress him. One, an abstract in vivid yellows and oranges with accents of green and black, made him think of sunflowers. He checked the label. Sure enough, it said "Sun Flower." "I like this."

"Me too. If a person was having a down day, this would brighten it."

When they'd covered the whole exhibit, that sunflower painting drew him back. He imagined it on the wall of the ranch office. When he was stuck at the computer, wishing he was outside, he wouldn't mind looking at that painting. He shared the office with his parents, but figured his mom would like it because it was a flower, and his dad probably wouldn't even notice. It wasn't all that expensive, and it didn't have a red dot on the label to indicate it was sold.

"I want to buy this," he told Kim.

"Seriously? Cool."

They made their way to a table where a young man with pale skin and black clothes was taking orders. He recorded Ty's information. "The exhibit lasts ten days. You'll be able to pick it up after that." He handed Ty a red dot. "Want to put that on?"

Feeling pride of ownership, Ty, with Kim at his side, returned to the painting to stick the red dot on the label.

"You bought that one?" He turned to see a chubby woman with short, curly red hair and an infectious smile.

"I did."

"I painted it. I'm so glad you like it."

"I do. It makes me feel good."

She beamed. "Thanks! That's the best compliment."

"Congratulations on the exhibit," Kim said. "I'm a student at Emily Carr, and it's great to see the grads doing so well."

"One day it'll be you," the redhead said cheerfully, then departed with a finger-wave.

As Ty headed toward the exit with Kim, he asked, "Guess you want to exhibit your work?"

"Maybe." She paused in the doorway, glanced back at the busy room, and laughed. "Yes, sure. But for me, that'd be more about play. Experimenting with different styles, seeing if people relate to my art. Mostly, I like the challenge of something like Umbrella-Wings, finding a creative way to do something practical, to create my own business niche. The other stuff, it'd just be a way of keeping fresh, artistically."

"Huh. Like for me, working with the horses is the thing I most want to do. Ranching's about family, stability, diversity. Rodeo's about fun, keeping excited and inspired."

She gazed up at him, her dark eyes sparkling under the overhead lights. "Weird how we can be so different, yet kind of the same."

It was. He mused on that as he put his arm around her and they walked to the truck. "Have you told your parents about Umbrella-Wings?"

"No. I want to present them with a complete business plan."

He opened the passenger door, she hopped in, and he walked around to the driver's side and climbed in too. "Let me know if I can help. I know you have a degree in business admin, but I do a lot of business planning with the ranch so I've got hands-on experience."

She beamed at him. "Thanks so much."

"You're coming out to the ranch this weekend, right? We can work on it then."

"Great." She touched his arm. "You can't imagine how nice it is to have someone encourage me."

He could relate to that. He started up the truck and backed out of the parking spot. "Family should do that, but I guess parents have their own issues."

"Yours too?"

"Not so much now. We're figuring out how to work together. But when I was young and wanted to rodeo? My parents hated the idea. My grandparents supported me. It made for rough times at the ranch. I was glad to take off." Though he still felt guilty for being so self-centered that he hadn't realized his family was in danger of losing Ronan Ranch.

That was the past. He couldn't change it. He glanced over at Kim. "If you come up with a great business plan, your parents will get on board, won't they?"

"Maybe." She folded her arms across her chest "I hope so. But I don't think they've ever believed I'll be able to do it. I just hope they judge my plan fairly and don't reject it out of hand." She sighed. "After all, it has to be something even my ancestors will be proud of."

"That's crazy."

She shook her head. "Let's not think about my ancestors tonight. Want to do something? Go dancing?"

It had been a long day and he wanted to be alone with Kim. Alone and naked. He stifled a yawn. "Honestly? I've been up since four and I'm beat." He reached over to squeeze her thigh. "And I've had enough of just holding your hand. If you want to dance, let's make it horizontal."

"Sounds good to me. I can't believe you've been up since four."

"Had to get up a bit earlier, so I could quit work early. Usually it's five or so." He shrugged. "Ranchers are early risers, and early to bed. How about you? Are you a night person?" Driving off the Granville Street Bridge toward Yaletown, he noted how busy the streets were.

"If I'm with friends and we get talking or go dancing, I can be up until one or two. But usually it's earlier than that. I go to bed when I feel like it. It's been nice in Vancouver, living alone and setting my own schedule rather than conforming to my parents'."

"When you go back to Hong Kong, will you get your own place?"

She shook her head. "Not only couldn't I afford it, but my parents would be shattered. I'll live with them until I get married."

"You figuring on doing that soon? Will your parents try match-making again?" He imagined her back in Hong Kong. She'd spend time with her parents, start her business, get married, have kids. She was so vibrant and fascinating; he hoped she found a guy who appreciated how special she was. Who supported and encouraged her dreams. Though he kind of hated the thought of Kim with another man.

"Inevitably. As for soon . . . Well, I don't want to marry just any guy. We have to be compatible enough and care about each other enough that I can see our marriage being happy and lasting. And I want a man who agrees we should have our own place, not live with either of our parents."

"People do that?" He couldn't imagine being married to a sexy, fun woman like Kim and sharing a home with her parents.

He pulled into the entrance to the underground parking for her building, and she clicked a fob to raise the gate. "Yes, lots," she said. "It's about finances but also about family. Extended family is a big thing, which has its pros and its cons. But for me, especially when I've lived here and been independent, I want my own apartment."

"Apartment? Not a house?"

She chuckled. "You've never been to Hong Kong. Talk about population density. My Yaletown studio would be a medium-sized place there. My parents own the building we live in there, so my husband and I could get an apartment in it. That's what a lot of families do, so everyone's close and can help each other. And," she added ruefully, "keep an eye on each other."

"I can't imagine living like that." He maneuvered into a parking spot and turned off the engine.

"But you do. Your family just does it on a whole lot of acres rather than in an apartment building."

"Those acres make a big difference."

When he went around and opened the door to help her out, she said, "But no, I don't see you being happy in an apartment, especially a small Hong Kong one. You'd get claustrophobic. People back home are used to it. And they're smaller." She hopped down, into his arms.

He closed them around her. "You're just the right size."

She wriggled her hips against him. "I like *your* size. I think I do want that dance. Vertically. And there's a benefit to being at my place."

"Lots of benefits." Like the bed being only steps away. Tonight he'd seen Kim in her natural world, the way she'd done with him when she came to the ranch. He was impressed, but it had emphasized their differences. They were overdue for concentrating on the similarities—like how compatible they were in bed.

"Slow dancing's more fun than club music," she said.

Horizontal dancing was more fun than both. He was about to lean down and kiss her, in an attempt to persuade her of that, when she spun out of his arms and headed toward the door. She sent a flirtatious glance over her shoulder. "Slow *naked* dancing's even more fun."

He was processing that when she said, "Hey cowboy, you coming?"

Oh, yeah!

Twenty-one

Ty isn't yawning anymore, Kim thought smugly, ten minutes later. Amy Winehouse's sexy contralto crooned about love and loss, candles flickered, and the window-wall was open.

She'd taken off her shoes and tights, which left her naked under her short, fluffy skirt, though Ty didn't know that yet. He'd taken off his shoes and socks and they danced barefoot, movements loose and slow, taking their time as their bodies flirted and teased and they exchanged an occasional kiss.

She fondled the soft, light fabric of his sweater. He'd surprised her tonight, in more than one way. Instead of turning up in his usual cowboy hat and boots, he looked surprisingly cosmopolitan. Still totally masculine, though, with that touch of raw male that had every straight woman at the exhibit eyeing him hungrily. His tan and sun-streaked hair, not to mention his muscular body, were set off perfectly by the sleek black clothes. More than one woman had whispered to her some variation of, "Who *is* your boyfriend?" The guesses had ranged from a soon-to-be-breakout movie star to a European billionaire.

She just smiled mysteriously, buzzed to be the girl with Ty, though the word "boyfriend" gave her a twinge. Yes, they were dating, but only short term. Still, she wasn't about to tell any other female that in a few weeks he'd be up for grabs. Not that any of the artsy women would be his type, not any more than she was.

Ty had been great company. His comments about the art were often insightful and sometimes humorous. She loved that he'd bought a painting. Maybe, when he smiled at that sunflower on a gloomy winter day, he'd think of her.

When she was back in Hong Kong, she'd think of Ty Ronan, probably more often than she should.

His voice broke into her thoughts. "Didn't I hear something about naked dancing?"

"I do recall that. Let's start with you." She lifted the bottom of his sweater.

He took over, peeling it over his head and tossing it aside. "Your turn."

Enjoying the sight of his impressive torso, she peeled off her body-hugging burnt sienna top, revealing a sexy black lace bra. She unwound her long, skinny scarf. Rather than toss it aside, she looped it around his neck, hanging on to both ends. "I've lassoed you, cowboy."

"You don't see me struggling to get away." He reached behind her to undo her bra.

Leaving the scarf draped around his neck, she slipped out of her bra, then rubbed her breasts against his firm naked body, her nipples tightening and pulses of arousal sliding through her. The fabric of his pants was so thin and fine compared to his usual jeans, straining over the thick jut of his erection, and she wriggled against it to tease both of them.

Then she reached for the waistband. This time, he didn't take over; he let her undo the button and slide down the zipper. She brushed the backs of her fingers against him, through the soft cotton of his boxer briefs. "You're wearing underwear."

"You can take it off."

"I intend to." She paused deliberately. "I'm not wearing any."

His cock jerked against her hand. "What?"

"I'm naked under my skirt." She was swollen and damp too, from wanting him, which he'd soon find out for himself.

Leaving his underwear on, she slid his pants down his long, strong legs until he stepped out of them, then she brushed her bare leg against his as they swayed in place.

He kissed her again, lips and tongue demanding now.

Her need jacked up a notch and she answered his kiss hungrily, pressing against him. The puffy layers of her skirt were a barrier, but she'd leave it to Ty to take that skirt off.

They'd stopped even pretending to dance.

His hand traced the line of her naked back to her waist in a sensual caress that made her skin tingle. He struggled with the layers of fluffy fabric until he found bare flesh. She was small enough and his hand large enough that he could cup her naked butt in his palm. One of his big fingers followed the crease between her cheeks, tracking it between her legs. Now he knew how hot and wet she was for him.

She moaned at the delicious pressure. Unable to wait any longer, she stripped off his underwear. Her hand clasped his firm shaft, so hot it almost burned her fingers.

This time, they both moaned.

She knelt, then touched her tongue to the head of his cock, licking the drop of arousal, tasting the salty musk of Ty. She swirled her tongue around him, then widened her mouth and took him in, licking and sucking, swallowing him as deep as she could. He was so big, she could barely take half his shaft. Sucking it, she pumped the base with her hand.

"Shit, that's good, Kim." He widened his stance, swaying a little. His fingers sifted through the short spikes of her hair, but other than that he kept still, giving her control. Through his heated skin, her lips felt the thick pulse of his blood. She thrummed the vein with her tongue.

His fingers tightened against her scalp, then both hands gripped her head, stopping her. "Whoa now."

She released his shaft, slackened the pressure of her mouth. When his hands eased their grip, she sat back on her heels and gazed up to his face.

He bent, pulled her to her feet, then lifted her and carried her to her futon bed, where he placed her down.

She reached for the button of her skirt, but he said, "No. Leave it on."

"Bossy." It wasn't really a complaint. Her voice trembled with need and curiosity.

"Tease." He flipped up her skirt and buried his face between her legs.

How odd, not being able to see him for the fluffy barrier of fabric. But she felt him. Oh, did she feel him. He licked her as if he was trying to lap up all the dew of her arousal, but each swipe of his tongue brought fresh moisture.

With two gentle fingers, he teased her sensitive folds, then opened her and explored. He pumped in and out, circled inside, pressed a sweet spot that made her whimper with almost unbearable pleasure. As pressure built inside her, she squirmed and twisted against his face, seeking those final touches to take her over the top.

Finally, he turned his attention to her clit, teasing it with a tiny lick, a breath-catching pause, then another lick. When she couldn't take any more, he caught it between his lips and sucked.

She arched and cried out as a sweet, intense climax ripped through her.

Ty held her until the spasms died away and her muscles loosened.

She managed to reach toward her bedside table, because this time she was prepared. "Put this on. I want to feel you inside me."

He rose from behind the barrier of her skirt. "There you are."

"Me and a condom."

"What more could a guy want?" He reached for the little package.

She held it back. "Take my skirt off first." She didn't want anything between them.

He fumbled with the fastenings, and she lifted her lower body so he could slide off the multilayered garment.

Then she handed him the condom and watched while he put it on. In the candlelight, his skin, sheened with a gloss of sweat, gleamed. Was this really her, Kim, in bed with a man who had such an incredible body?

When he kneeled between her spread legs, she eagerly lifted her lower body to meet him.

He caught her hips, steadying her, then his cock nudged her, caressed her slick, sensitive folds, and slipped inside.

She sucked in a breath. It was always a tiny shock when Ty entered her, until her body loosened and adjusted to his size. And, once it did, the sensations were pure pleasure. She lifted one leg up his body, hooking her heel over his shoulder, then did the same with the other leg, so she could take him even deeper.

Thrusting into her, he leaned forward slightly, resting more weight against her legs. "Stop me if it hurts," he panted, "but damn, this feels good."

She had a feeling that nothing they did together could hurt, at least in no more than a purely erotic border-of-pain-and-pleasure way. Right now, it was all deliciously sensual, bringing every recently satisfied cell to arousal again. "Feels good for me too. Lean down more, come into me deeper."

He bent forward slowly and cautiously, placing one hand on either side of her shoulders. Synching her movements to his, she rolled up on her back and lifted her whole lower body, putting her hands on her hips for support and spreading her legs in a vee.

"God, you're flexible. That's so sexy."

It was. She felt flexible, strong, and yes, very sexy. "All that yoga," she said breathlessly, holding her body steady to meet his thrusts. He looked so amazing, the muscles in his chest and shoulders flexing, his slick cock sliding in and out of her body.

"Only problem is, I can't kiss you."

"But you can make me come." She was on the verge as he stroked deep into her core.

Smart man, he'd figured out that her clit was the most sensitive part of her body, and he used that knowledge well. He pressed his thumb gently against it, then tapped it as his strokes grew faster and faster. It was a race to the finish line, and they crossed it together, her cry and his groan mingling in the air.

As the tension in their bodies released, he eased backward, lifting his weight off her legs. "Man, Kim, are you okay?"

She lowered her legs to the bed and stretched, relaxing pressure in her lower back while she basked in the afterglow of awesome sex. "Blissed out. Honest, I'm stronger than I look."

Ty lay down on his side facing her, and she curled toward him. He touched her cheek gently and brushed damp tendrils of hair off her face. His eyes were tawny gold in the candlelight, and looked as gentle and caring as his touch.

This, she thought. *I want this.*

Why couldn't she have Ty, long term? Life could be so unfair.

No, she quickly corrected herself. Life was great, for letting her meet this man and have this time together. She'd known all along that they had no future. This was her *rumspringa*, a time for fun, experimenting, and learning. She was learning what she wanted. A nice, smart, handsome, responsible, loyal Hong Kong man who made love to her with passion and gazed at her like she was the most special woman in the world. Who kissed her the way Ty was kissing her now, like he was cherishing her mouth.

"Do you want to stay?" she murmured. "You're tired. You shouldn't drive."

He heaved a sigh. "I'd love to, but you really don't want me climbing out of bed at four."

She couldn't suppress a grimace.

He chuckled. "Yeah, I know. I'll be okay driving. Used to drive all night when I did full-time rodeo."

It would be lovely to nestle into the curve of his body as she fell asleep, and wake in the morning to find him there. But maybe not at four.

"You're coming out for the weekend?" he asked.

How could she resist? But still, she teased, "Will I have to get up at four on Sunday?" Last weekend, she hadn't noticed the time when he woke her to make love, but the sun had definitely been up when they ate blackberry pie for breakfast.

"I'll make a special exception for you. I may even stay in bed myself, if you give me a good reason to."

"I'm sure I'll think of something."

"I'm sure you will. Now I'd better head off." He clambered to his feet, yawning.

She watched as he collected his clothes and dressed.

"Want me to close the door/window thing?" he asked. "And blow out the candles, so you don't have to get up?"

"That would be great." She stretched, luxuriating in the twinges of well-used muscles.

The window-wall creaked down. "See you Saturday, Kim."

"Night, Ty."

He puffed out the candles and she was left in darkness. The apartment door closed.

Kim grabbed his pillow and curled onto her side, hugging it. Wishing it was him. Which was dumb. Cowboy Ty was all wrong for her in so many ways—critical ways—yet in so many others he was perfect. Like, as a lover. Would she find another man who was as hot in bed?

She thrust the pillow away. Sure, she would. With him, she'd become a much better lover herself, more confident and willing to try things. He'd awakened her inner dirty girl. There was no reason that, with a future lover, her sex life—or her love life—had to be ho-hum.

As Kim headed out to Ronan Ranch Saturday morning, she found the drive almost relaxing. The last couple of days had been so busy, working on both the business plan and the assignments she needed to finish up for her program at Emily Carr. She hadn't even had a chance to read *Ride Her, Cowboy*, though she'd answered a text from Marielle, asking whether Ty kept his hat on when they had sex. Kim's reply? No, I wear it!

She'd turned down dinner with Henry, and felt bad about that. But she didn't want to tell him about UmbrellaWings for fear he would scoff and, though they'd broken up months ago, telling him about Ty would be too weird. He might be hurt, and he definitely wouldn't be supportive like her friends in book club.

Her mom had e-mailed with the date of Peter's wedding—six months down the road—and said she hoped it wouldn't be long before Kim and Henry would have an announcement of their own. Kim shook her head. So much would have changed in six months. Her parents would know about her and Henry and, who knows, she might even be engaged to someone else by then. At the moment, that was hard to imagine, but once she was back in Hong Kong, life would be different. *Rumspringa* would be over; it would be time to get serious.

If things went the way she hoped, Kim would have proved to her family that she wasn't a *flaky* artist, she was a businesslike one. She'd be starting UmbrellaWings, surely she would. The alternative, drudging away at Chang Property Management, was unthinkable.

She hadn't told her parents that she was working on a business plan. They'd raise a million objections, which might undermine her confidence. Best to present them with a finished proposal that would wow them. She hadn't told them about Henry. She certainly hadn't told them about Ty, or that she was releasing her inner dirty girl. So many secrets.

She'd always kept a few secrets from her demanding, judgmental parents, but they'd been tiny ones. Being all the way across the ocean, living independently, had turned her into . . . what? A liar? Or an adult who lived her own life and made her own decisions?

In not much more than a month, she'd be living with her parents again. What woman would she be then? Well, she'd find out, wouldn't she? For now, she was Kim in Vancouver, Kim enjoying *rumspringa*, Kim pulling her cute co-op car to a stop and getting out to unlatch the gate to Ronan Ranch. Ten o'clock. Right on time.

Last weekend, Ty had rearranged his busy schedule for her. This time she'd told him not to let her interfere. With her art supplies, she was self-sufficient.

She drove through the gate, latched it behind her, and carried on up the road. At the ranch headquarters, there were a couple of people in the yard. Ty's mom would get a report that Kim was here again. She ran her tongue over her lips. Pie would be good. As for making nice with a protective mom—well, a girl did what a girl had to do.

When she climbed out of her car at Ty's, he came out of the barn to meet her. In town, he'd looked sleek and virile dressed all in black. Here, in his element, his virility was a different sort, outdoorsy and rougher around the edges. This was the man who could ride a bucking bronc without even a saddle, who could deftly toss a calf without hurting it.

She still had trouble believing she knew a man like this, much less was his sex partner. "Hey, you," she said, smiling up at him.

"Hey, you." He smiled back, then bent to kiss her.

She came up on her toes, the kiss deepened, and she pressed her body against his, feeling his immediate response.

A cell phone rang, breaking the mood.

Ty stepped back. "Sorry, I've been waiting for a callback." He pulled a cell from his pocket, glanced at the display, then answered. "Hey, TJ, how's it going?"

Kim raised her face to enjoy the morning sun and breathed in air scented with hay, sawdust, and yes, a touch of horse manure.

From Ty's side of the conversation, she could tell he was good buddies with this guy TJ, who seemed to have a family ranch too, and also work at a resort ranch.

"Like I said in voice mail," Ty said, "the bay gelding, Rambler, is almost ready. I got another rescue horse this week, pretty Paint mare called Distant Drummer. She's in rough shape, but there's lots of potential. Think the Crazy Horse would be interested in her?"

He listened, then said, "Yeah, people do like colored horses. She's a tobiano, chestnut and white, nice markings. Okay, I'll earmark Drummer for you. As for Rambler, I'm going to the rodeo in the Chilcotin a couple weeks from now. I'll be taking Desert Sand, so I can bring a two-horse trailer and drop Rambler off at your place on the way."

Another pause, then he laughed. "Tell Robin I'm looking forward to seeing her too. She's a sweetheart."

Kim's brows rose. Hmm. Was this Robin a candidate for ranch wife? And what business was it of hers? When Ty hung up, she carefully didn't ask about Robin. Instead, she said, "You're training horses for a resort ranch?"

"Yes. The Crazy Horse in the Cariboo. Know where that is?"

"Vaguely."

"Nice country, lots of ranches. Anyhow, this woman I know, TJ, has—"

"TJ's a woman?" She shouldn't have asked, but the words burst out.

"Uh-huh. Her family has a cattle ranch, but she's a horse person like me. She works as wrangler at the Crazy Horse and takes some of the rescue horses I train. I get them healed and if their personalities are right, I send them to her and she trains them for trail rides with dudes."

"Sounds like your perfect woman." She tried to keep the snark out of her voice. "And who's Robin?"

Twenty-two

Ty grinned. "Yeah, TJ's pretty much perfect. So's her daughter. Robin's nine or ten."

"Oh, TJ's married?"

"Divorced." Another grin. "She and I get along, but more like sister and brother."

There was absolutely no reason to be glad. "I wasn't jealous or anything."

His lips twitched. "I know."

"We're not a couple. Not really. I want you to find the right woman." Her own lips curved. "Okay, I confess, I'd be happy if that didn't happen until I'd gone back home. I like being with you."

He put his arm around her shoulders and pulled her close. "Me too."

"Now do I get a proper kiss hello?"

He gave her one that curled her pink-painted toes inside her multicolored sandals, and she smiled with satisfaction. No, Ty didn't think of her as a sister.

"What's on the agenda?" she asked. "I brought art supplies so I can look after myself."

"This must seem strange to you. Me working a seven-day week."

"No. My parents usually do. And I've always kept busy. School, homework, working for my folks, doing art. I like to read, but I'm not a do-nothing person. You don't have to entertain me." She smirked. "Except in bed, later. Or out of bed, like in the Jacuzzi."

"That can be arranged." He looped his arm over her shoulders and tucked her against his side. "I've done a bunch of the regular chores. I need to practice with Sand, and I'm itching to start with Drummer, my new rescue horse. You and I could go for a ride later in the afternoon when it's cooled off a bit." He eyed her olive capris. "You brought jeans?"

"Sure. But capris are more comfy when it's hot like this."

"Look good too. Oh, Mom invited us for a meal, but we don't have to go."

So he'd told his parents she was coming. "Which meal?"

"Any meal. She figures if she words it that way, it's harder to refuse. But we still can."

"She thinks I'm going to lead her son astray. Didn't she get that I'm going back to Hong Kong?"

"Or maybe she just wants to get to know one of my friends."

She shot him a cynical glance. "You believe that?"

"Not for a moment. Well, she does, but there's a lot more going on. So, you want to say a polite 'no, thanks'?"

She twisted her lips, thinking. Parents deserved respect. Besides . . . "Will there be pie?"

He laughed. "If not, there'll be fruit cobbler or chocolate cake. Mom has a sweet tooth."

"Aha. She and I have one thing in common. Could we make it lunch, not dinner?" Lunch seemed more casual, less stressful.

"Today or tomorrow?"

"Today?" Then it would be over and she wouldn't worry about it.

He opened his cell and made a quick call, then reported back. "She's delighted."

"I bet."

"We'll head down around one. And now, I've set up some practice time with Sand. Hope that's okay."

"Sure." Watching her hot cowboy on his horse sounded like a fine way to spend a morning.

"Take your bag in, make yourself comfortable. If you want to watch, feel free."

"You bet I do." She collected another toe-curling kiss, then took her bag inside. She used the downstairs powder room to take off the wingy blouse she wore over a hot pink tank top and olive capris, and apply sunscreen. Armed with a big sketch pad and charcoals, she went back outside.

Ty was in the ring on Desert Sand, swinging a coiled rope as the horse ran in an easy long-legged stride. A dark brown horse was tied to the hitching rail and a stocky older man in western wear herded half a dozen calves into a small pen. Kim was starting to make sense of the layout of the various fenced areas. One was the paddock where the horses were turned out to run and graze. The fenced ring was Ty's practice ring, and the small pen was a holding area.

Ty called, "Hey, Kim. Say hi to Dusty, one of the best bull riders you'll ever meet."

"Probably the only one. It's nice to meet you, Dusty."

"Likewise, ma'am," he drawled, tipping his hat. "You can perch up there." He indicated the top rail of the fence.

She accepted the invitation as the two men carried on, the sparseness of their motions and speech indicating the familiarity of this routine. They were setting up to simulate what happened at the rodeo. When everything was ready, Dusty released a calf. Ty and Desert Sand shot after it, Ty roped it, then he leaped down to toss and tie it. A few seconds later he set it free, and herded it back to Dusty. Then they did it again with a different calf.

Kim balanced her sketch pad on her knees as her charcoal flew across the page, capturing action and impressions.

Ty had been compelling at the rodeo, with other cowboys around and an audience cheering, but this was fascinating. One cowboy and one horse, working with a single assistant—an assistant who, in comparison to Ty's natural grace, hobbled slowly. Though the two men did the same basic thing every time, each calf behaved differently, challenging Ty. The constant was the teamwork and communication between rider and horse. It was a thing of beauty in its way.

It was also sexy as hell: the horse's powerful muscles, Ty's agile body, his curse when something went wrong, the white flash of smile at a perfect run. No other man she'd ever met would be capable of doing something like this.

If that was all Ty had been, just a handsome, skilled cowboy, that would be sexy enough. The fact that he also ran a successful, diverse enterprise like Ronan Ranch, that in his own way he was as successful a businessperson as her parents, made him even more impressive. A responsible guy who set a course and succeeded was sexy. Top that off with the knowledge that he was a skilled, inventive lover—her lover . . . Oh, let's face it, sitting on that top rail watching him, sketching him, thinking about his many charms, was a delicious torture.

It also made her seriously crave the chance to draw him nude. After they'd had sex. Otherwise, she'd never be able to concentrate. If seeing him practicing in the ring made her squirm with desire, she could only imagine how turned on she'd be if she drew him naked.

After ten or twelve runs, Ty called a halt to the practice. "Thanks, Dusty, that was great."

"You and Sand are looking good," the older man said. "Oh, Ty, Marge says don't forget you're coming for dinner Monday."

"I'm looking forward to it."

Ty went into the barn with his horse, and Kim smiled at the stocky assistant. "That was fascinating, Dusty. I'm a total newbie when it comes to rodeo. You were a bull rider?"

"Yes ma'am. Damn fool thing to do." One corner of his mouth tilted. "But I wouldn't trade one day. Except that last one. Bull rolled on me, broke my back. They said I was damned lucky to live, much less ever walk again."

Now she understood why he hobbled so slowly and awkwardly. "Oh my gosh, I'm so sorry." And so glad Ty didn't ride bulls. Not that one of those bucking broncs couldn't do the same thing to a man.

He shrugged. "The risk is part of the life. Anyhow, I did get on my feet again, enough to work in a feed store. Then three years ago I saw Ty's ad about needing folks to work at Ronan Ranch."

"And he hired you." A happy ending to a sad tale.

This time both corners of his mouth tilted, and his denim blue eyes lit. "Damn fool thing to do," he said for the second time. "But rodeo cowboys are family. We look out for each other."

"Looks as if you're pulling your weight," she pointed out.

"Took a while. And only thanks to him and his parents giving me the time, the help." He paused, swallowed. "The hope."

She remembered what Ty'd said that first night. A ranch on the way to Hope. When she commented about the name being symbolic, he said it was a second chance for Ronan Ranch and for his family. For Dusty too, it seemed, and his wife, who no doubt preferred seeing her man active and happy. Also for those disadvantaged kids Ty helped. Unexpectedly, she, who wasn't the emotional type, found her eyes misting. "I'm glad for you. And I can see how much you're helping Ty."

"Hope so. They're good people, the Ronans."

"I believe you."

With painful slowness, he clambered onto his dark brown horse. Then he herded the calves out of the holding pen and down the road. Kim did a quick sketch, thinking that the man would fit just fine on Dirk Zamora's cattle drive in *Ride Her, Cowboy*. Dirk, like Ty, would give Dusty a chance.

"Kim," Ty called, and she turned to see him at the barn door. "I need to shower off the dust and sweat before lunch. Care to join me?"

Oh, yes! She clambered off the fence. "Is there time?"

As she joined him, he looped an arm around her shoulders. "I shower fast."

"I hope you don't do everything fast."

Laughing together, they hurried inside and upstairs, where they stripped off their clothes in a messy trail on the way to the bathroom.

"Shower cap?" she thought to ask. "If I get my hair wet, it'll mess up the color."

"Might have one." Naked and supremely hot, he opened a cupboard and pulled out a plastic bag with hotel-size toiletries. He also tossed a condom on the counter by the shower.

Kim rummaged in the bag and triumphantly pulled out a small package of her own. "Don't laugh," she warned as she slipped the plastic hood over her spiky hair.

The corners of his mouth pulled and his eyes danced, but he shook his head solemnly. "You look cute."

"Just what every woman wants to hear when she's about to shower naked with a man," she said ruefully.

"And sexy," he added. "Very sexy."

The man clearly wanted sex, and knew that laughing at her wasn't the best method of getting it.

"In fact," he said, "they should put you in an ad. It'd sell a lot of shower caps."

She gave an amused snort. "Don't push it, Ty."

"I'll just shut up now." His eyes still sparkling, he turned away to get the shower going, then he stepped under the spray. The shower was large enough that there was no need to pull the curtain.

He didn't, and nor did she.

His back was to her, and Kim took a moment to enjoy the view. Water sluiced over his head, darkening his hair, molding it to the strong shape of his head. Streams ran down his muscled back and broad shoulders, to the hollow at the base of his spine, over the taut curves and pale skin of his butt. She'd read that women didn't get aroused by looking, but her body disagreed. Watching hot water course over Ty's body was enough to send warm pulses of arousal darting through her veins to pool between her legs.

He turned to face her. "Waiting for an invitation?"

She stepped in to join him, his body taking the brunt of the shower water so that only a fine mist sprayed over his shoulders to touch her face and chest. His own chest was soaked, droplets gleaming on his brown skin and catching in soft curls of hair. She spread her hands over his pecs, tested their muscled perfection. One day, she really did want to draw this man.

Now, though, arousing him was her goal. She leaned forward to lick water from his nipple, then she sucked the small bud, teasing it to hardness. Glancing down, she saw his cock swell and lift.

He turned and did something with the shower control, and suddenly it was raining. Rather than water from a showerhead pounding against his back, now a gentle rain came from the ceiling, sprinkling both of them. Shielding her eyes with a hand, she gazed up and realized he'd installed a rainfall shower. She'd never been in one before and, entranced, said, "This is wonderful!" It was like standing outside in a warm spring shower. Naked. With a shower cap on her head. And with Ty.

"You could design a line of shower umbrellas," he joked.

She chuckled. "Kind of defeats the purpose."

"Which some of us would say about shower caps," he pointed out, green sparkles dancing in his eyes.

She really didn't want him thinking about the unsexy shower cap. And she knew the perfect way to distract him. Enjoying the soft patter of drops on her shoulders, she wrapped one arm around Ty's body and slid down until she was kneeling, hugging him with her hands cupping his butt and her face pressed against his waist. She licked his navel as his cock rose to bump her chin. It had been her ultimate goal anyhow, so why delay any longer? She tongued the crown, tasting mostly shower water but also a seductive hint of musky, aroused male that grew stronger as she opened her mouth and took him in.

He was so big, and her mouth was small. She couldn't encompass much of him, but she sucked and licked him like he was a Popsicle, melting faster than her tongue could keep up with. The full, dusky head of his cock, the sensitive ring beneath the crown, the thick shaft with that throbbing vein—all so erotic. Her pussy craved that organ, and she squeezed her thighs together, feeling a deliciously frustrating ache of desire.

Ty groaned, shifted, braced himself with a hand against the wall. He widened his legs.

She dipped her head, working down his shaft with her tongue, caressing his balls gently with her fingers, then with her tongue. Her own body tightened and vibrated with arousal. She thrummed the sensitive spot between cock and balls.

He thrust convulsively. "Jesus, Kim."

Then he bent and caught her under the armpits, hauling her up roughly, needily. He grabbed the condom and sheathed himself, then he hoisted her as if she were weightless.

Under the rain shower, she wrapped her legs around him tightly, anchored herself with an arm around his neck, and reached down to guide him into her more than ready body. *Oh, yes!* That was exactly what she needed.

There was little more she could do than cling to Ty as he held her hips steady and plunged into her, deep and hard, over and over. The rain was gentle and steady, a counterpoint to his jerky, forceful thrusts. Inside her, there was friction, her muscles gripping and releasing, his shaft stroking, bringing every cell alive. Tension, delicious tension, building, building until she couldn't bear it.

And then Ty found a spot, a magic spot inside her, a bright, sweet, blazing spot, and she lifted her face to the rain and cried out as her body broke and convulsed in bliss.

Dimly, she was aware of Ty giving a wrenching groan, climaxing inside her, almost losing his balance but somehow managing to stay on his feet. To keep her safe in his arms.

Then, slowly, he let her down.

Breathless, legs trembling, she managed to step out of the shower. She peeled off the shower cap, reached for a towel, and then—yes, she was definitely shaky—leaned against the counter.

Ty switched off the rain and stepped out, grabbing a towel of his own. "Wow. Some shower."

She smiled. "Gotta love the rain."

He wrapped the towel around his waist and leaned down to kiss her.

Shoving away from the counter, she came up on her toes and pressed her wet body against him, enjoying the easy sensuality of a kiss after sex. A kiss that wasn't about need or arousal, just about sharing, giving thanks, saying "I think you're special."

Then she sighed. "We should dry off and get dressed or we'll be late."

"Mom will hold lunch."

She separated their bodies and toweled herself vigorously. "Or come see what's keeping us." The afterglow of sex hadn't even worn off, and she was starting to get nervous. With Chinese parents, she knew the proper way to behave, the polite things to say, the correct answers to give to questions. But Ty's parents were an unknown quantity.

It didn't really matter if she impressed them, but it was ingrained to want people, especially of the parental generation, to like her. She didn't want to embarrass herself or Ty.

When Ty dressed in shorts and a tee, Kim said, "You're not wearing jeans. So it's okay that I'm in capris, not jeans?"

"Jeans aren't a uniform," he teased. "They're just practical for a lot of ranch work. You look great, all pretty and summery."

"But not like I belong on a ranch."

"You look like you. Works for me." He studied her, saw tension crease her forehead. "What are you worried about?"

She shook her head. "Nothing. Let's go. And by the way, you have nice legs."

"You have nice everything."

As they went down the stairs, he asked, "You okay with walking down to their place?"

"Ty"—she rolled her eyes—"I walk four or five kilometers a day."

Maybe it was her petite size or her artistic style, but he kept forgetting how fit she was. "Okay, good." They went out the front door. "If my mom gets too pushy, change the subject."

"You figure she'll get too pushy." She said it resignedly, not as a question.

He sighed and threaded his fingers through hers. "You've met her."

"Right. She'll get pushy. Okay"—her tone brightened—"let's

make a list of things I could say to change the subject." She slanted a gleaming gaze at him. "I could ask to see your baby pictures."

"Oh Lord, don't do that."

She swung their clasped hands as they headed down the road. "What'll you give me if I ask about ostriches rather than baby pictures?"

He laughed. "What do you want, Kim?"

"Darn, I was hoping you'd say, 'anything.' "

She had something in mind. He could see it in her eyes as she went on. "I'm seriously thinking I'll have to ask about baby pictures. I bet you were the cutest baby."

"Nope. Ugly as sin."

"Really? Now I have to see."

He groaned. This was blackmail. What did the woman want? Sex, hopefully. Not that she had to blackmail him to get that.

"Did you have hair or were you bald?" She slipped her slim hand free of his, thrust it into his back pocket, and squeezed his ass. "Were you a chubby baby with a cute little round butt?"

"Stop, stop, I give in. Anything. I'll give you anything." *Sex, please.*

"I know what I want."

"Dare I ask?"

"To paint you naked."

"You already did." And they'd had great sex. "Sure, we can do that again. But maybe with food, and I get to paint you too."

"Ooh, I like that. But that's not what I meant." She released his ass and went back to holding his hand.

He scratched his head. Sometimes, he and Kim were in sync. Other times, he didn't have a clue what she was talking about. "What, then?"

"In art school, there are life classes."

"Life classes?" Another art term that made no sense.

They turned onto the side road to Ronan Ranch headquarters and his parents' house. The area around the barn was clear; the ranch hands would all be on lunch break.

"Life drawing," Kim said. "As in, drawing from life."

"Beats drawing from death," he joked, still not understanding. "Oh, you mean still lifes? Like, uh, pears in bowls?" Nothing against pears, but he liked outdoorsy subjects.

"Mmm. But life drawing's also called figure drawing because our subjects are humans."

"You sketched me for the last hour or two."

"I'm talking about human still lifes. Not moving." She tugged on his hand, pulling him to a stop so they faced each other. Staring up at him, a wicked gleam in her eyes, she said. "And nude. You take your clothes off and pose for me, and I sketch you."

His jaw dropped.

"Or," she went on, "if you don't want to, I'd love to see those baby pictures."

"Ty! Kim!" It was his mother's voice.

He turned and saw her standing by the open front door of the house, wearing a yellow tee and a denim wraparound skirt, waving.

Kim waved back and called, "Hello, Mrs. Ronan." Then, quietly, to Ty, "Posing nude, or photos of baby butt cheeks?"

"This is blackmail."

"It's your choice, cowboy. But posing nude would be sexier."

Sexy? He'd have said embarrassing. *Hmm. Maybe it could be sexy.* Stretching out to showcase the muscles she liked to ogle, watching her sketch every line of his body. It'd be a turn-on. For him. How about for Kim? Would she be able to stay in artist mode, or could he get her all hot and bothered? Which one of them could hold out the longest? Whatever happened, it'd end in sex. That, he'd guarantee.

"Ty?" It was his mother again.

"You said the S word," he told Kim. "Posing nude. Definitely." Then he called, "Coming, Mom," and, hand in hand, he and Kim walked toward the house and up the steps.

"It's so nice of you to invite me over, Mrs. Ronan," Kim said.

"We always love to meet Ty's friends. And please," his mother said as she led the way into the house, "call me Betty. I've got the table set on the back patio and lunch is in the fridge, all ready to go." They were in the kitchen now and she pointed out the open back door. "You and Ty go on out and I'll just bring everything along."

"No, please, let me help." Kim pulled her hand free from Ty's. "What can I do?"

"That's sweet of you. The two of you could take out the salad, deviled eggs, and lemonade."

Ty opened the fridge door and began pulling things out. "Where's Dad?"

"Changing out of his work clothes. He'll be down in a sec."

The aroma of fresh bread filled the kitchen as she took an Italian loaf from the oven.

"That smells delicious," Kim said.

Ty gave Kim a big bowl of pasta salad dotted with chunks of cheese and brightly colored vegetables, hefted a platter of deviled eggs and a pitcher of lemonade, and led her to the patio.

"Oh, wow." She put the bowl on a table laid with bright place mats and napkins, cutlery, and glasses. "This is lovely."

The patio was a simple wooden one, like at his house, but his mom's planters and hanging baskets overflowed with late-summer blossoms in every shade imaginable. Kim stepped to the railing and gazed out at the garden, her eyes wide. "I've never seen anything like this."

Close to the house were more flowers, the herb garden, and some fruit trees. Past them, covering more than an acre, were rows of vegetables ranging from radishes to corn, and also strawberry, raspberry, and blueberry plants.

"You can't possibly eat all of this," she said. "And it must take so much work."

"Some of our staff who don't have gardens help with the work and take what they want in exchange. And we trade with our neighbors. One has a dairy, and from others we get pork, bacon, lamb."

"You really are self-sufficient."

A voice from behind them—his dad's—said, "It's a good feeling. You must be Kim."

They both turned, and Kim stepped forward. "Mr. Ronan, thanks for having me over."

His dad, a silver-haired version of Ty, was dressed in shorts and a short-sleeved shirt. "Call me Brand." He shook her hand.

"Brand? Really? I mean, like on cattle?"

He grinned. "My parents had a sense of humor. Actually, it's Brandon, but I'm always called Brand." He studied Kim. "Well now, aren't you as pretty as one of the butterflies on Betty's flowers?"

Kim beamed. "You look like Ty, but you're far more charming."

Ty groaned, but his dad chuckled. "Comes with age."

"What's this I hear about charm?" Ty's mother came out the kitchen door with a basket of freshly sliced bread and a butter dish. She put them on the table and slipped her arm around her husband's waist. "You? Charming? How come I never see that side of you?"

He hugged her back. "Are you saying I take you for granted, sweetheart?"

"Yes," she said promptly, and they all laughed.

Twenty-three

They sat around the table, eating with gusto as Kim complimented the food and asked about the garden, the ranch, and the community. Ty liked watching her, her pretty face animated. He tried not to remember the steamy shower they'd shared, for fear his mother would somehow read his mind.

His mom began some not-so-subtle probing, asking Kim about her background. When Kim talked about having lived in Vancouver as a child, his mother said, "It must have been hard on your family, being separated for four years when you were little."

"Yes, but Mom and Dad are very practical and business-oriented. Mom researched the Vancouver housing market and business laws. Dad came over, and they decided on a couple of buildings in Yaletown. They brought over property managers from our company in Hong Kong and Mom trained them."

"If they worked for your parents already, weren't they trained?" his mom asked.

"But there are different laws, business practices, markets, customs."

"Of course," his father murmured. "We found that, just coming from Alberta to BC."

"If your parents had bought property and turned it over to a Vancouver property management firm," his mother mused, "it would have been easier. But they wouldn't do that, would they?"

"No. They're hands-on. No one does things as well as they do."

His mom gave a firm nod. "I'm sure that's true."

It struck Ty that his parents and Kim's might get along. They had some core values in common: family, hard work, being your own boss.

"You're in Vancouver to study art," his mother said, "but you already have a business degree. That's an unusual combination. What career are you aiming at?"

Kim's chin lifted. "I hope to start my own business." She took a breath. "An umbrella company."

"Umbrella company?" His dad, who hadn't said much, broke in, scratching his head like the phrase made no sense to him.

"Yeah, Dad, umbrellas," Ty put in. "They're the things those city folk who don't wear cowboy hats have to carry when it's raining." When he said the last word, he winked at Kim.

Color brushed her cheeks, telling him that she too was remembering their steamy rain shower.

"And someone has to make them," his mom said. "But it's a rather unusual business."

"Kim's an unusual woman," Ty said. "She has a great concept. It combines her artistic talent and her business sense."

Kim gave him a quick, appreciative smile. "I'm working on a business plan now, so if you have any suggestions I'd love to hear them. It's called UmbrellaWings and . . ." She went on, quickly and effectively outlining the basic concept.

Ty loved to see her excitement when she discussed her ideas. On his parents' faces, skepticism turned to interest and then enthusiasm. He couldn't resist putting his arm around Kim's shoulders and giving her a squeeze, getting a quick flash of smile in return.

"You'd base the business in Hong Kong?" his mom asked.

"Yes, of course."

Ty had known that, so why did he feel a bit of his own pleasure fade?

"Well," his dad said, "I think you've got a notion there that just might work."

"I hope my parents agree. I've kind of been groomed to join the family company."

His parents exchanged glances. "A family business is a good thing," his mom said. "It's meaningful."

"I know." Kim toyed with the last scraps of bread on her plate.

"What's for dessert?" Ty asked. Okay, maybe it was a clumsy segue, but he didn't want his folks pressuring Kim, siding with her parents.

"Plum cobbler," his mother answered.

Kim moaned, then her hand flew up to cover her mouth. "Sorry. That sounds so good."

His mom rose. "With ice cream?"

"Oh yes, please." Kim leaped to her feet too and started collecting dishes.

"No, you relax, Kim," his mom said. "You're our guest. Brand will help me."

His father gave a start, then rose. "Right. Of course I will."

When his parents had gone into the kitchen, Kim said, "They're talking about me."

He squeezed her shoulders again. "Kim, you're great. Like Mom said, relax."

"I know. I just want them to like me. I don't want them to think you're crazy for liking me." She put her hands to her face and shook her head. "Can you imagine what I'd be like if I was actually someone's girlfriend, trying to win his parents' approval?"

He didn't want her being someone else's girlfriend. But of course she would be. Some Hong Kong guy's girlfriend, then his wife.

They'd have kids. Cute little black-haired kids. Would she color streak their hair? He sure hoped she married a man who was okay with that.

Whimsy. She'd used that word, and he'd said it didn't sound like him. No, he wasn't the whimsical sort. But she was, and she'd shown him that whimsy brightened life up.

He reached for one of her hands, tugged it down from her face, and intertwined his large fingers with her small ones. "That lucky guy's parents would be nuts if they didn't like you."

She lowered her other hand. "You're nice. Have I mentioned that?"

"I thought I was hot," he teased.

Her lips curved, finally. "Nice and hot. Definitely."

His parents returned then, each carrying two bowls with plum cobbler.

As soon as Kim had taken a bite and complimented the dessert profusely, Ty's mom asked, "How did you two meet?"

Kim's eyes widened and met Ty's. Then her lips twitched the tiniest bit and she said, "My book club was on a research trip. We were reading about ranching. Cattle ranching. Now, Ronan Ranch is so interesting, with the specialty stock too."

"Yes, it's quite a mix," his mom said. "So this research—"

"Like ostriches," Kim, who rarely interrupted, broke in, shooting Ty a sly look. "They're so odd-looking and it's hard to believe you get meat from them. I'm really curious about that."

His mother stared at Kim.

Ty not so subtly kicked his mom's foot under the table. If he didn't rescue Kim, she might ask about baby pictures. "Mom, you're the ostrich expert. Fill Kim in."

She shot him a narrow-eyed look, then complied. For the rest of the meal, they talked about Ronan Ranch, and Kim spooned up every bite of her cobbler.

He watched that spoon going into her mouth, the way her pink lips parted and she sucked every morsel in with an expression of pleasure. Watching Kim eat dessert was one of the sexiest things he'd ever seen. When he kissed her, she'd taste like the tartness of plums and the sweetness of ice cream. And he intended to kiss her, long and hard. "Time to go," he said abruptly. "Thanks for lunch, Mom."

As he rose and urged Kim to her feet, his mother said, "What do you have planned for this afternoon?"

She couldn't really read minds. Could she? He tried not to flush. "Thought I'd work with the new rescue horse, the Paint mare." After he and Kim got some alone time.

As he and Kim walked away from the house, he clasped her hand. There was so much more he wanted to do, but he felt his mom's eyes on their backs. And then there were ranch hands bustling around the barnyard. Eyes everywhere. No damned privacy.

Kim had expected to relax once she got away from Ty's parents' scrutiny, but there were people working around the barn. Ty raised a hand to them, exchanged a few words of banter, and Kim knew they were all noting the way he clasped her hand. They were thinking "girlfriend," assessing her, realizing that she didn't belong here. She wanted to yell, "It's just temporary!"

Which it was. So why did she feel depressed and disgruntled?

Ty bumped her shoulder gently with his and said quietly, so none of the workers around them could hear, "Congratulations, you survived lunch with my parents. What did you think?"

She took a breath, trying to focus on the simple pleasure of his shoulder against hers, their fingers linked together. "Delicious food, but that's not what you're asking." Her sense of humor returning, she went on. "I have to admit, I was happiest when we were talking about ostriches."

"Me too. Beats baby pictures."

They shared a grin. "I'm not letting you off the hook on the life drawing," she teased.

"We'll see about that." He broke off to answer a question from a ranch hand, then said to Kim, "I'm sorry Mom pushed so much."

"I wish your parents wouldn't worry. They're scared I'm another Miranda, but you and I know we're casual, short term." Much as Kim might, in her secret heart, yearn for things to be different, they weren't. Reality was reality, and she and Ty were both realists. In not much more than a month, she'd be gone. Feeling out of sorts again, she said, "Why don't they believe us?"

"Beats me."

"Parents always think they know better than us," she complained. If her parents knew about Ty, they'd be even worse than his. She could hear her mom ranting that the ancestors would roll over in their graves, out there in the countryside where her parents had come from.

"Yeah, and they rarely do." He put his arm around her shoulder.

Warmth rippled through her and her spirits lifted. Why was she feeling negative? It was a beautiful day and she was with an amazing man. "Anyhow, aside from that, I like your parents. I like how they are with each other, and how all three of you are together. People tease each other, but it's relaxed and easy. You're like a team."

"We are a team."

They were on the main road now, walking up to his part of the ranch. But they still weren't alone. They had to move over to the shoulder to let some piece of farm equipment rattle slowly by.

"Your mom may nag you about getting married," Kim said, "but she doesn't treat you like a child. My parents still do."

"Remember that I've been away from home, supporting myself, since I was seventeen."

"My parents would never have let me."

"Mine weren't happy about it."

He'd mentioned this before. "Because they wanted you to ranch rather than rodeo."

"Yeah, and with my grandparents taking my side . . ." He shook his head. "Things weren't good. I couldn't wait to get out of there."

Kim couldn't imagine defying her parents that way. "You succeeded, though. And it was your success that let you buy Ronan Ranch number two. They have to treat you as an equal."

They moved off the main road and walked toward Ty's barn, where a horse whinnied as if sensing their presence.

"Once you get UmbrellaWings going," Ty said, "your parents should do that too. Right?"

"I hope." They didn't want her to succeed at anything other than CPM. If she did, would she win their respect? Would they even appraise her business plan with an objective eye? All she could do was hope, prepare the best damned plan she could, and try not to worry.

"Hey," Ty said. "Alone at last."

His words, and the shock of dim light after bright sunshine, drew her attention back from her troubling thoughts. They now stood just inside the barn door.

"Alone if you don't count a couple of horses," she said, smiling as she guessed what was on his mind.

"They won't mind."

"Mind what?" she teased.

"Everything I've wanted to do for the past hour, but couldn't. Woman, d'you realize the way you eat dessert should be illegal?"

She let out a surprised chuckle. All she'd done was spoon up delicious cobbler; it hadn't occurred to her to try to be sexy. She'd been too nervous, too focused on his parents, particularly his mom, to even think about sex. Now, though . . .

She stretched her body, wriggled her shoulders, moved her head back and forth to ease out the tension. "Whew. You're right, I survived. And we're alone, cowboy. Tell me about all the things you wanted to do for the past hour."

"Huh-uh."

"No?"

"I'm not much of a one for words." Even in the dim light of the barn, she could see the gleam in his eyes. "I'm a man of action."

"They do say that actions speak—"

Before she could finish the phrase, his big hands cupped her shoulders, urging her upward as he bent down.

She rose up eagerly, letting everything else slide away except the pure sensuality of the moment, the sheer pleasure of being with Ty. His breath smelled of plums, his lips were warm and firm as they met hers, his tongue licked into her mouth as if he was tasting her. And then more urgently, as if that first taste was addictive.

Talk about addictive. She could never get enough of kissing this man. Or of the press of his solidly muscled chest against her soft breasts, the hard ridge of his erection calling forth a needy feminine ache.

She palmed him through the soft cotton of his shorts, but it wasn't enough. She needed to see him, caress him, then take him inside her, to stoke that ache until it coiled tighter, higher, then finally broke in waves of satisfaction. "I want you," she whispered against his lips.

"Hell, yeah. Me too."

He fumbled with the fastenings of her capris as she slid down his zipper. How convenient that he wore shorts and sandals. So much easier to get out of than jeans and boots.

Reaching inside his underwear, she grasped his shaft greedily, his hot flesh almost searing her palm.

"Shit," he breathed, "that feels good."

A horse whinnied from a nearby stall.

"Shit!" Ty said again, this time in a completely different tone.

"Someone's coming." He pulled away, hurriedly tucking himself back inside his shorts, zipping up, yanking his tee down so it hid the evidence of his arousal.

Meanwhile, Kim, annoyed, did up her capris. She supposed she should thank the horse for its warning, but she was too frustrated to feel grateful.

"You in the barn, Ty?" a voice called. It was his father.

"Yeah," Ty called back, exchanging a rueful glance with Kim.

She remembered how he'd been dismayed about the way extended families in Hong Kong often lived on top of each other, and she'd commented that Ronan Ranch wasn't all that different. His parents were proving her point.

A moment later, Brand stepped through the door. "Thought I'd come watch you work with Distant Drummer."

"Sure, Dad." Ty's tone was neutral. He turned to Kim. "Want to watch, or go sketch somewhere else?"

So much for having sex any time soon. Resigned, she said, "I'll watch, if I'm not in the way."

Under his breath, he muttered to her, "It's not you who's in the way." Then, more loudly, "Won't likely be very exciting, but you're welcome to hang out."

She went into the house to gather up her charcoals and sketch pad, then joined Ty's dad, who was perched on the top rail where she'd sat earlier.

"Ty's getting the horse," he said.

Brand Ronan, brown and fit in khaki shorts and a casual shirt, was an attractive man. The resemblance between father and son was pronounced. Ty's more sensual mouth appeared to be the only thing he'd inherited from his birth mom. Looking at Brand gave Kim a good idea of how great Ty would look as he aged.

Man and horse emerged from the barn. Ty must keep spare jeans and boots there, because he'd changed out of shorts. He walked slowly, leading the horse by a rope attached to her halter. Distant Drummer danced skittishly, tossing her head and rolling her eyes so the whites showed. To Kim's inexperienced eyes, she looked scared. "She was abused?" she asked Brand quietly. "She's pretty, but she's skin and bones." The horse's sweat-covered coat had a beautiful abstract pattern of white and brown splotches, and her tail and mane had both colors as well. But the hair was dull and sparse, her bones stretched the skin, and she had several nasty wounds.

"Starved and beaten," he confirmed. "She's a young horse and has probably never been treated right by humans. This is going to be a tough one."

"Ty's earmarked her for his friend TJ at the Crazy Horse resort ranch. So he thinks Distant Drummer will be good for trail rides. That seems like a stretch."

He nodded. "Yeah, but Ty has a way with him. When it comes to horses, he sees beyond the surface. Somehow, it's like he can see their soul." He gave an awkward chuckle. "Sounds a little weird, but it's true. He can read a horse's potential, and he'll get them to realize it, no matter how long it takes."

"He really is a horse whisperer? I'm not even sure what that means."

Another laugh, this one more comfortable. "It's become this fancy Hollywood-type term. Really, it's just a person who can connect with horses, especially when it comes to training them and helping them recover from abuse or trauma. Ty's always had a bond with horses. When he was less than a year old—couldn't even walk, just crawl—he used to disappear from the house and we'd always find him with a horse. He'd curl up at a horse's feet and go to sleep, and that horse would protect him like he was its own foal."

The image made her grin.

In the ring, Ty unclipped the lead rope from the horse's halter.

She skittered away, eyeing him, then started to run around the outside of the ring, her movements stiff and jerky.

He stood in the center of the ring and didn't move toward her. In a soothing voice, loud enough to carry across the ring, he said, "It's okay, Drummer, there's nothing to worry about here. No one's gonna hurt you, not ever again."

Kim opened her pad and began sketching the horse. "What does Ty need to do to heal and train her?"

"There's two kinds of health, right? Physical and emotional. Physical's the easier one. Our vet checked the mare, and she has some wounds from being beaten, she's dehydrated and malnourished, and she had an infection. But she's basically sound. Meds, nourishing food, exercise, and time will fix the physical problems."

Head bent over her pad, she nodded. "Emotional has to be harder. Like with kids who've been abused. I don't know how a person can ever really get over something like that. Maybe it's the same for a horse?"

"A horse can learn to trust and move on. Humans are pretty darned resilient too."

His words reminded her of how shattered he must have been when his wife abandoned him and Ty. To throw his heart in the ring again, after an experience like that, would be tough. But he'd done it with Betty. "Having the right person helping makes a big difference."

"Yeah. And Ty'll give a horse all the time it needs. He'll push, but gently, and he's got all the patience in the world."

"What does he actually do?"

"Gets to know the horse and lets it get to know him. Shows the horse that it can trust him. Once he figures out a horse's personality, then he really starts working with it."

She nodded. Even in her limited experience, she'd seen that horses had personalities.

"Right now, he's letting her run off some energy, nerves, and fear. He wants her to get used to him being there, to learn that his voice and presence are reassuring, not a threat. Then he needs to show her that he's the leader, because horses are natural followers."

"So he just . . . waits?" Kim glanced from her sketch pad to Brand.

"Waits and goes about his business." He gave her a wry grin. "She's a female. She'll get curious. Maybe not today, maybe not the next day. Once she gets comfortable with him being around, she'll come over to him. If I was a betting man, I'd say he'll be brushing her in a couple weeks, and a month or two after that he'll be up on her back."

She thought about the time involved. "This is a rescue horse. Ty's sending her to his friend. Will TJ pay for her?"

"A little. Might cover the cost of the horse's food and meds, but not Ty's time." He tilted his head and gazed into her eyes. "Ty trains other horses too, for good money. But the rescue animals . . ." He shrugged. "He can't stand to see a horse suffer. Not when it can heal and go to a good home."

No, of course Ty couldn't. If it meant getting up at four, he'd look after that horse. Kim had never even had a pet, but her heart gave a mushy throb.

Distant Drummer had stopped running and stood with her head down, like she was tired. But when Ty shifted position, she jerked to alertness.

Ty kept talking to her. "Figure you might be getting hungry, Drummer girl. Feel like some sweet alfalfa?" He moved across the ring, walking away from her, while she watched warily. Kim realized he'd placed some hay outside the ring, and he reached between the bars to grab a large handful. He tossed it down. "Try that out and see how it tastes."

When he walked back to the center of the ring, a path that took him toward the horse, she pranced away. But when all he did was take up his same old spot, she calmed down. Gradually, keeping an eye on him, she inched toward the hay. She lowered her head, sniffed it suspiciously, and then, still watching Ty, snatched up mouthfuls hastily as if she was afraid someone would take it away or chase her off.

Kim sketched away and after a few minutes, Brand said, "Ever drawn horses before?"

"Just this morning, when Ty was practicing with Desert Sand."

"Mind if I take a look?" he asked diffidently.

Twenty-four

Nervously, Kim handed Ty's dad the pad. "They're just rough sketches."

Turning the pages carefully, he looked through her drawings. His face didn't show a lot: a raised eyebrow, a quick grin. He went through all the ones she'd done today, then came back to one of Ty atop Desert Sand, racing toward a calf as he swung his rope. "You're good."

Did he mean it, or was he being polite? "Thanks."

"Just a few strokes, and you catch what's going on. This is Ty."

The compliment from his dad meant a lot. "Thank you."

"You willing to sell this one?"

"Oh! Oh, really?" She flushed with embarrassment and pleasure. "No, please, it's yours. A small thank-you for your hospitality." Gently, she separated the page from the pad and handed it to him.

He took it carefully. "Well, now, that's awfully nice of you. Betty's going to love this."

"You're both very welcome."

He nodded. His eyes—a more weathered version of Ty's hazel ones—gazed solemnly into hers. "He's a good man."

"I know." Maybe the best man she'd ever met. But why was his father telling her this?

"This is what he's about. The ranch. Horses. The life has its own beauty, but it's about hard work and patience, day after day."

Ah, now she got it. He'd probably come here because his wife sent him, and he was warning her off. "I know that too."

In the ring, the horse, still eating hay, cocked its tail and deposited a pile of droppings, scenting the air.

"Hay and manure," Brand said wryly, "it's never-ending. The novelty wears off damned quick. It's not a life for a city girl."

She wanted to point out that she wasn't Miranda, his ex-wife, but he might be offended that Ty had told her about his birth mom. Instead, she said, "I know that too, Brand. I'm going back to Hong Kong." Much as she'd enjoyed her time in Vancouver, she'd always looked forward to the day she returned home. And yet, now . . . No, what was she thinking? Quickly, she went on, speaking as much to herself as to him. "It's my home, just like Ronan Ranch is Ty's."

His eyes softened. "I like you, Kim. Sorry if I'm, uh, being heavy-handed. But Betty and I, we love our son. We don't want him getting hurt."

"Nor do I." She frowned at him. "You should give him some credit. He knows what he's looking for in a woman. Betty's set the . . . what's the term? . . . gold standard? He's not going to settle for less." Even if Kim hadn't been returning home, Ty would never, not in the long term, want a woman like her, one who'd be more hindrance on a ranch than helpmate.

His lips, thinner than Ty's, pressed together. "I'm not saying you're less. Just different."

"Oh!" He'd managed to surprise her. "Well, thanks."

Ty strolled slowly to their end of the ring. Speaking in the reassuring tone he used with the horse, he said, "Drummer and I are wondering what's going on over here."

"Just heading back to work," his dad said. He held up the sketch. "Look what Kim gave your mom and me."

It was the first time Ty'd seen what she'd been working on that morning, and Kim was delighted by the way his face lit. "Would you look at that?" He glanced from the sketch to her. "That's damned good. How in hell did you manage that, with everything going so fast?"

"Lots of practice."

"Do I get one too?"

"Anything I draw at Ronan Ranch," she promised, thinking about the nudes she intended to make him pose for, "you're entitled to keep one."

"I'll leave you to it," Brand said, heading toward the road.

When he was out of earshot, Ty touched her shoulder. "He give you a rough time?"

She smiled at her handsome cowboy. "No. He told me what you're doing with Distant Drummer." She glanced across the ring and said, "Well, how about that? Your dad said females get curious, and I'd say your horse is wondering what we're doing." The horse had stopped eating and was staring at them with her ears cocked forward. "Either that or she's jealous that you're paying attention to me, not her."

Ty turned slowly, so he half faced Kim and half faced the horse. "Hey now, Drummer. Why don't you come over and join us?"

The horse snorted, tossed her head, then returned to eating hay.

Ty planted his hands on either side of Kim's hips, as she perched on the rail. "I like seeing you sitting here, all colorful and pretty, sketching away like crazy." He leaned forward over her big sketch pad and gave her a slow, teasing kiss.

"I like watching you. Sketching you. Speaking of which, when are you going to pose nude for me?"

He chuckled. "You still on about that?" He shoved himself back to a standing position. "I'd best get back to Drummer. Don't want her to feel neglected."

"Coward."

He wandered across the ring, even his slow, steady gait startling the horse, then left the ring and went to the barn. Puzzled, Kim saw the horse's ears twitch nervously as if she too wondered what was going on. Ty came back with a stool, a couple of bridles, and a box. Kim learned, from what he said to Drummer, that he was cleaning tack.

She opened her sketch pad again. With neither the man nor the horse moving much, she could do more detailed drawings than she had this morning.

Head down, she was engrossed in shading Drummer's coat, when a *whuffling* sound made her look up. She managed to restrain herself from giving a start. The horse had snuck up on her and was standing close by, her posture wary as she stretched her head out to snuffle at the sketch pad.

Softly, keeping her voice steady though her heart raced, she said, "Yes, I'm drawing you. You're such a pretty girl, and you're going to be gorgeous when you're healthy." When would that be? Hopefully, before Kim went home to Hong Kong. She wanted to see Drummer healed, her coat glossy, her spirit restored.

"I'm not sure what I should do." She spoke as much to Ty as to the horse.

"Keep sketching, Kim. Talk to Drummer but don't pay her too much attention or you'll make her nervous. Keep your movements slow and steady, nothing sudden. You're doing great."

She obeyed, glancing slowly up at the horse now and then to confirm a detail as she worked, and keeping up a stream of low-voiced chatter. Getting used to the one-sided conversation, she told the horse all about UmbrellaWings.

Ty didn't move closer, and the horse didn't move away. She just watched Kim, almost as if she found her presence calming.

"I think you like hanging out with me, Drummer girl," Kim said.

"I like it too. Do you know, until last week, I'd never been on a horse? I was a little scared, to tell you the truth. Maybe like you are now. But Ty gave me a wonderful horse and she was so nice to me."

Huge, limpid chocolate brown eyes focused on her and she sensed a question in them.

"Ty's good about looking out for you and making sure you don't get hurt. He'll be good to you. You can trust him."

The horse took a step closer. Her head bobbed. Her nose brushed Kim's drawing hand.

Kim froze, not wanting to frighten her, and somehow managed to keep talking. "You have such a warm, soft nose, like velvet." Unable to resist, she moved her hand the tiniest bit so her knuckles brushed the horse's skin.

Drummer let her do it, then, apparently thinking enough was enough, backed away and headed over to the hay she'd been munching on earlier.

Ty strolled slowly over to Kim, beaming. "That was great."

She beamed back, elated. "It was."

He dropped a quick kiss on her smiling lips. "She likes you."

"Maybe she relates better to females?"

"Or she just likes you." His eyes danced. "I like you."

"I know that. Maybe she likes being a model. See, it's not such a painful experience, Ty. Now that she's set the example," she teased, "you'll be more relaxed when it's your turn."

"Posing nude? You just won't let that go, will you?" But the gleam in his eye suggested he was getting into the idea. Tell a guy something was sexy, and you had him hooked. "Nah," he said, "I don't think 'relaxed' is the right word. And, while we're talking about sex—"

She stifled a laugh and said innocently, "Were we?"

"I think that's enough horse time for now. I want to get you alone and take up where we left off when Dad interrupted. I can't wait to get those clothes off of you."

"Hey, you'll be the one stripping, cowboy." She couldn't wait.

"It's definitely time to put Drummer back in the barn." He touched Kim's bare arm. "Normally, I'd go and attach the rope to the halter and lead her back into the barn, but that'll stress her. What would you think of trying to get the rope on her, since she likes you better?"

Her? Work with an abused horse? The idea thrilled and scared her. "What would I do?"

"Pick up the rope, walk slowly toward her, making sure she can see you and has time to adjust to you being there. Talk to her; don't stare her directly in the eye. If she lets you, clip the rope onto the halter ring and walk slowly toward the gate. I'll open it and take over from there."

She bit her lip. "She won't attack me?"

His hand still warm and reassuring on her arm, he gazed into her eyes. "Can't say for a hundred percent positive, but I'm pretty sure not. She shouldn't feel threatened, and she doesn't have a reputation for being dangerous. If anything does happen, I'll be here."

She gazed into his clear hazel eyes and saw his sincerity.

"Kim, I wouldn't suggest it if I thought you might get hurt. But if you're at all worried, we won't do it."

She gazed away from Ty to study the poor damaged horse that some brute had traumatized. The horse that had come up to *her*, touched her with that velvety nose. "I want to."

He squeezed her arm, approval in his eyes. "Thank you."

She handed him her drawing supplies and eased down from the rail to stand inside the ring. Restraining her usual lively pace to a slow saunter, she made her way over to the discarded rope and picked it up, then continued inching her way toward Distant Drummer, talking as soothingly as she could. Whatever she was doing worked, because she successfully reached the horse's shoulder. She was tempted to try to stroke her, but Ty hadn't said to, so she didn't. Instead, making sure the horse could see what she was doing, she raised the rope.

Drummer snorted and shifted restlessly, moved a step away, then stopped.

"Don't be scared. I'm not going to hurt you." Kim moved toward her again, and this time clipped the rope to the halter. "Now, how about going back into the barn for a rest? I bet Ty will find a nice snack for you, like, uh"—what did horses enjoy?—"an apple or carrot?"

When she pulled gently on the rope and headed toward the gate, the horse went with her. "Maybe I should keep leading her?" Kim offered as Ty opened the gate.

Frowning slightly, he studied her and the horse for a long moment.

She shouldn't feel hurt that he didn't trust her. After all, what did she know about horses?

But he said, "Why not? You're doing so well. Into the barn, the big box stall on the right," and gratification filled her. Trying to convey confidence and reassurance to Drummer, she walked slowly onward. The horse followed docilely all the way into the stall. Kim stepped out the door, flicked the latch closed, and unclipped the rope from the halter.

The horse studied her, ears forward, eyes intent. It seemed to Kim that she was saying, "Come back and visit me again."

"I will," Kim murmured. "I'll see you again, Distant Drummer. Maybe next time I'll stroke you."

Slowly, she moved away from the stall door, then turned to Ty. Heady with her success, knowing she'd had a small taste of that sense of connection between horse and human Ty's dad had spoken about, she said, "I did it. She let me."

"You were terrific." There was something in his eyes—approval, the same excitement she felt, and something more, like he was seeing her differently. He put down her art supplies and bent to kiss her.

She reached up to loop her hands around his neck. Mmm, talk about connection. A zing shot through her at the touch of his lips, heating her blood in a flash.

When they came up for air, she leaned back in the circle of his arms. "You weren't sure I could get her from the ring to the barn."

"If it hadn't worked, she'd have been free, with that rope dangling. It could have been dangerous, and it would've been hell to catch her."

Her eyes widened. "Oh gosh, I never thought of that. Why did you let me do it?"

His shoulders lifted in a shrug. "Instinct. I trusted you, trusted her. Sometimes, you have to trust."

"I guess so." She did trust him, unquestioningly. It was gratifying to know he trusted her, especially with something as precious to him as a traumatized horse. She felt like she was glowing with pure happiness.

"And I was right." Again, that odd look was in his eyes, as if the connection between the two of them went much deeper than liking and sex.

Out of the blue, a lightning bolt of pain pierced her glow. Oh God, why was life so unfair? Why was the deck stacked against her and Ty, so that a future together was impossible?

She sucked in a deep breath. No, she couldn't think that way. She was a realist. Hadn't she disparaged Marty Westerbrook for getting all romantic over Dirk Zamora? No way would she make the same mistake. Ty was a great guy and a fantastic lover. Period.

Oblivious to her mental turmoil, he said, "Before we get carried away, we promised her a treat."

"Right." She stepped away, glad to break contact for a moment, to regain her composure.

He handed her an apple. "Hold this on your palm, not cupping it, just with your hand flat. See if she'll take it."

She moved back to the stall door. "Drummer girl, I have a yummy apple for you."

The horse studied her for a long moment, then cautiously stretched out her neck and snatched the apple in a quick, darting movement.

Kim watched her eat it, and imagined the future. Ty would heal this horse, they'd develop a special bond, then Drummer would be sent away. His friend TJ might be great, but Drummer would lose Ty. Under her breath, so Ty couldn't overhear, she told the horse, "You have to be a realist too. You have to be strong, Drummer."

Then she turned back to her sexy lover, determined to enjoy the moment. "What were we talking about? You stripping, wasn't it?"

Twenty-five

No, it was you, stripping," he teased back, capturing her hand. "But first . . ."

"What?" She rolled her eyes. "You have to feed a horse or something?"

"I thought I'd show you the hayloft."

Now? He wanted to show her some dusty hayloft *now*?

"Don't frown," he said. "It's a nice hayloft. With sweet, new hay. It's one of the best smells in the world. Spread a clean horse blanket on it, and you couldn't have a better bed."

"Oh! I get it." She gave a flirtatious grin. "Yes, cowboy, please show me your hayloft."

Clasping her hand, he led her through the barn, passing several other stalls, all empty, and racks of saddles, bridles, and halters. Along the way, Ty collected a plaid blanket. They arrived at a wooden ladder and she climbed it.

Emerging through the hole in the loft's floor, she gazed around. "What a great place." Under a slanted roof, bales of pale golden hay sat in neat stacks. Windows at each of the short ends gave dim light, and the temperature was cool compared to the blazing heat outside. Kim inhaled deeply. Yes, the scent was wonderful, kind of like newly cut grass but with a tang that reminded her of lemongrass.

He came up the ladder to stand beside her. "We use the big barn for most of our storage, but it's handy to keep some hay here too.

Besides, when I designed this place, I figured it wouldn't be a barn without an old-fashioned hayloft. Memories of childhood."

"Yeah?" She turned to him.

"In what little spare time I had, I'd go up in the loft, lie down on a pile of hay by a window, and dream."

"About horses and riding in rodeos?"

"Uh-huh." He gave a wicked grin. "And when I hit adolescence, about girls too."

"Then," she guessed, "there came a time when you stopped just dreaming and started bringing girls to the loft."

He chuckled. "Yeah, that happened a time or two before I finished high school. But with Mom and Dad and my grandparents always around, it was tricky."

"Speaking of which, your mom isn't likely to drop by, is she?"

"No, she'll be out with her critters."

Ty went to one end of the loft, where an old recliner chair sat by the window, suggesting he still came to the loft to dream. He dragged it aside, then pulled some hay from a broken-open bale and spread it where the chair had been.

Kim gathered an armful and went to help, but paused when she saw the view. The other window must look out at Ty's house, but this view was of open land, where a few horses stood under a cluster of trees, looking sleepy, and— "Oh my God!" She dropped the hay and turned to Ty. "Look! That horse is—" No, she couldn't say it, but the horse looked dead, spread flat on the ground on its side, unmoving.

He straightened from spreading hay and looked out. "Sleeping."

"Really?" She put a hand over her racing heart. "I thought they'd curl up, or something."

"They sleep in different positions. Standing up, most often. And no, they don't fall down. They're built to do it."

"Strange." Reassured, she turned from the window. "I have a lot to learn." There was no long-term purpose to understanding Ty's world, yet she wanted to.

He spread the plaid blanket on the bed of hay. "First lesson: making love in a hayloft."

"An excellent place to start." She reached for his belt. "I think I've mastered unbuckling belts. Though if you wore one of those fancy rodeo buckle belts, I could be in trouble." Today his belt was plain brown leather, masculine and well worn.

"Which proves you aren't a buckle bunny."

She undid his jeans, peeled them down his hips. He sat to pull off his boots, then stood again, quickly getting rid of his socks and jeans then pulling his shirt over his head. While he undressed, she took off her own clothes. They stood in front of the window, naked, with no one to see but the horses outside. She felt free, brazen, glorious.

Ty drew her down on the blanket. Hay rustled beneath it, releasing more of that tangy lemongrass scent.

"Mmm," she said. "If I was a horse, I'd eat that."

"I'd rather eat you."

"That could be arranged." She lay back, raised her arms above her head, and stretched sensually, displaying her body for him. "Have your way with me, cowboy."

"Close your eyes."

Smiling in anticipation, she did.

She'd expected him to head between her legs or to kiss her, but instead she felt something small and a little rough brush against her throat. "What are you doing?"

"Keep your eyes closed."

The thing moved across her breast, flicking her nipple to alertness. It was sensual, pricking her body to awareness wherever it touched. She'd guess it was a small china bristle artist's brush, but Ty wouldn't have something like that. It kind of tickled, but in a way that made her moan and arch her body, not giggle.

He ringed her navel with it, then dipped lower until the thing flicked her clit. Back and forth, round and round, back and forth again. It was tantalizing, enough to make her damp and needy, to make her clench and twist with arousal, but not firm enough to make her come.

Tired of being obedient, she opened her eyes and discovered he'd been driving her crazy with a stem of dried grass with a feathery end. "Ty, enough teasing. I need you to get serious."

"This serious enough for you?" He tossed the grass down and in a moment had covered his erection with a condom.

"Come here."

"Bossy," he teased, but he obeyed, dropping to his knees.

Aching with the need he'd built in her, she bent her knees and raised her lower body in clear invitation.

He accepted, easing slowly inside as his lips met hers. His tongue mated with hers as, filling her completely now, he pumped back and forth.

Good old basic sex, sweet and simple. Really, was there anything more satisfying? Especially when the man in question was so strong and beautifully muscled, when she'd spent hours longing to be with him like this, and when the scent of fresh hay perfumed the air?

Kim sighed with sheer bliss, matched the insistent rhythm of his body, and let him take her up, up, and . . . "Oh, Ty!"

Ty, drained and satisfied, summoned the energy to separate his sweaty body from Kim's. He sprawled beside her on the blanket, hay rustling beneath him.

She inhaled deeply and blew out a puff of air. "I think the scent of hay is an aphrodisiac."

"You're the aphrodisiac, Kim."

She turned her head to look at him, and smiled. Her gaze made a slow perusal of his naked body. "I know what you mean." Then her expression sharpened and suddenly, she was scrambling to her feet and pulling on her capris and tank top. "Stay there, don't move."

"Kim?"

"Just wait. Please?"

"O-kay," he said slowly. No, he'd never understand women.

But a few minutes later, her actions spoke louder than words. She came back up the ladder with sketch pad and charcoals.

"You're not really going to do that." She'd made the idea sound sexy, he reminded himself. But at this moment, having enjoyed a spine-cracking orgasm, he felt more self-conscious than turned on.

"You promised to pose."

"You blackmailed me."

She waved a dismissive hand. "Whatever."

"Blackmail's a crime," he pointed out.

"So report me. Maybe to your parents. Then we'll look at your baby pictures." Her dark eyes twinkled. "Personally, I'd rather draw your naked adult butt, but if I'm forced to look at photos of your baby butt cheeks, I'll do it."

She was so damned cute, he figured she could make him do pretty much anything she wanted. Earlier today, she'd drawn him clothed, and that hadn't bothered him one bit. His body was fine. Strong, well muscled. He had no reason to be embarrassed. She'd drawn nude men before. Which reminded him of that idea he'd had, about trying to make her squirm. Okay, maybe he could get into this.

"I need a . . ." she muttered, frowning.

"What?" He started to rise.

"No, don't move."

She dragged over his old leather recliner and settled onto it with her pad and a charcoal.

"What do you want me to do?" he asked.

"Don't move."

"Jesus, that's the third time you've said that."

"And this time I mean it literally. Don't move a muscle."

"Can I breathe?" he joked.

"If you must."

He lay sprawled on his back, arms and legs flung out, head turned to the side watching her. The position was comfortable. He could stay like this for a while and see what happened.

Kim was busy with her charcoal, gazing up at him, down at the pad, back at him. She looked like an artist, not a lover, and he felt self-conscious being studied like this. His nose itched and he wanted to scratch it, but Kim had given him his orders. "How long?" he asked, trying not to move his lips.

"It's only been five minutes. Models hold a pose for twenty minutes or half an hour."

"Did I mention I'm a cowboy? A rancher?"

"Rumor has it that being a rancher and horse trainer calls for some patience."

He was second-guessing his plan to try and turn her on—not that she'd let him flex a muscle anyhow. Though he figured it'd be a sexy game, she might think he was disrespecting her as an artist—and he did respect her talent. Maybe he should focus on viewing her as an artist, appreciating the chance to see her at work. If only it wasn't him she was drawing nude.

No, wait a minute. He didn't want her drawing some other naked guy, especially not one she'd just had hot late summer sex with.

"Okay, Ty," she said, "you can stretch, then we'll do another pose."

Relieved, he sat up, rotated his shoulders, then hugged his knees while she kept the charcoal moving. "You sketch a lot of naked men?"

"Naked men and women. All ages, all body types. Life drawing isn't about making a pretty picture, it's about capturing reality. Developing your skills."

"Huh. So I guess it's kind of like a doctor or massage therapist, and you get used to seeing naked bodies as, uh . . ."

"Subjects." She nodded and glanced up. "Like a bowl of fruit, a vase of flowers. But the fruit and flowers are inanimate. Human subjects are more fascinating. Each is a unique person with so much going on inside them. All the amazing physical stuff, but also all their thoughts, feelings. Worries and hopes, fears and dreams." She shifted the charcoal to her left hand and shook out her right one.

"If you're doing portraits," she went on, "you want to capture the essence of the person. With figure drawing, you may focus more on the physical aspects, or even draw just one thing, like a hand. Depends what you want to get out of it."

"Why do you want to draw me?"

A gentle smile touched her lips. "Because you're beautiful, in such a masculine way. I've drawn men with perfect bodies, but they're more . . . Well, like they'll be hairless. Maybe gay. Likely ego-involved. They don't exactly seem masculine to me. You, Ty, you're all male."

"Uh, thanks."

"Break's over. Find another position you can hold for ten minutes."

He liked watching her, so he reclined on his side, head pillowed on one folded arm.

After she'd been sketching for a couple of minutes, he asked, "Will you kill me if I talk?"

"A guy who wants to talk. How rare," she kidded. "No, it's okay."

"Are you sketching my whole body or just a hand or something?"

She glanced up from the pad, grinning. "If I was going to sketch one part, it wouldn't be your hands, nice as they are."

"There's one part of me that couldn't hold still if it was the subject of your attention."

"That's the one I had in mind."

And that one, obviously recovering from lovemaking, responded with a twitch and began to harden. Now that they were talking, this was personal. He didn't feel like an inanimate object being studied objectively. "See what I mean? Does that often happen with male models?"

Her cheeks, already sun-kissed, went pinker. "No. It's such a, uh, structured thing, posing in front of an art class. It's not at all sexy."

He shuddered at the thought of posing for a class. "A hayloft's sexy. And you're sexy, all businesslike with that pad and charcoal. I'm trying not to move, but my body has a mind of its own." His cock was swollen now, ready for action again.

"I'm not so businesslike." She shifted, squirming. "When you get turned on, it turns me on too."

"So we can quit now," he asked hopefully, "and fool around?"

"Just another one or two sketches," she begged. "Think of it as foreplay."

"Foreplay works better when we touch each other."

"You're so conventional."

What was more conventional than an old-fashioned cowboy? Yeah, Kim was good for him, doing unexpected things, challenging him, teasing him.

When she said, "Okay, you can stretch and change position," he decided to give her an artistic challenge. In a quick, easy roll, he came up on his knees. Then he grasped his erect cock.

"Oh!" Her eyes widened.

"You can draw action. You did it this morning."

"I, uh, I can draw action," she repeated, her gaze locked on his hand as he began to stroke up and down.

His body tightened, as much from her attention as from the firm slide of his warm hand against sensitive flesh. "Then go for it. You wanted artistic foreplay, right?" Would she actually sketch him masturbating? And if she did, which one of them could hold out longer?

She swallowed. "Uh, right." When she got going with her charcoal, her hand moved more quickly, with longer, less controlled strokes.

As for him, he had to restrain his strokes as beads of come seeped out the tip of his cock. He didn't want to climax without her, just to turn them both on. It was sure as hell working for him. He'd jacked off more times in his life than he could remember, but it had never felt so sexy. Breath rasping in his throat, he managed to say, "How's the artistic foreplay working for you?"

"It's too good," she whispered. "I can't stand it. I'm too hot for you." She cast her art stuff aside and took the couple of steps to the blanket, where she dropped down beside him.

He lay back, hand still grasping his erection. "No. Clothes off first."

She made a frustrated sound, then whipped off her clothes. And then, like a kid reaching out for a special treat, she leaned over and stretched both hands toward his cock.

He started to take his hand away, to let her take over.

She surprised him by capturing his hand and holding it there, with both her own hands cupped around it. "Let's do it together. Show me what feels good."

"Being inside you would feel good."

"But I want to see you come like this."

Arousal shuddered through him, the fierce need to pump faster and faster until he climaxed, hard and hot. Unable to resist, he stroked his hand up and down, hers going with it, holding his fingers tight against his slick, swollen shaft.

Kim's face was flushed, her gaze focused intently on what they were doing.

Ty's balls tightened, the ache of needing to come a fierce pressure. Everything in him focused on the surge of climax, then he let go. His come spurted out in jets across his belly. He groaned with pleasure and relief, riding those sensual highs.

Finally, his muscles began to relax. He studied Kim's face as she released her clasp on his hand, then he let go of his cock.

Her eyes glittered. "That's the sexiest thing I've ever seen," she breathed.

"It felt pretty damned sexy too."

He forced strength into his muscles and rose partially, enough to tumble her. Quickly, he swiped an edge of the blanket across his damp chest before leaning over her. "And when it comes to sexy, nothing beats this pretty body."

Then he bent down, committed to giving her the same pleasure she'd just given him. Her pussy was soaking wet, and when he licked her cream she whimpered and ground against him, letting him know how turned on she was. He thrust two fingers inside her, plunging them in and out with a spiraling motion, reaching every intimate, hidden part of her.

"Come for me, Kim." He closed his lips on her clit, flicked his tongue across it, and sucked.

She cried out, high and shrill as a bird, and climaxed in powerful, shuddering spasms.

Lying naked on the blanket, Kim's slim body in his arms and the scent of hay in the air, Ty noted the quality of light outside the barn window. The afternoon was fading. He wondered if Kim was up for a ride. Sharing his favorite parts of Ronan Ranch with her made him feel . . . He wasn't sure how to describe it. Proud? No, not exactly. Contented? That came closer.

But when he rolled on his side to face her and asked, "Feel like going for a short ride before dinner?" a quick frown crossed her face before she banished it.

She sat up, naked and beautiful, a slant of sun through the window glinting across her black hair with its purple and orange streaks. "Sure."

"Hey, if you don't feel like it, it's okay."

"No, I do. I really enjoyed it last week."

"But?"

Twenty-six

Kim gave a quick toss of her spiky hair. "Nothing. It was just, you'd mentioned maybe helping me with my business plan."

"I thought we could put the morning aside tomorrow, do it when we're fresh."

Her face lit. "Really?"

"Sure."

Her smile widened. "A whole morning? Ty, that's generous. And yes, I'd love to go for a ride with you."

He did a quick cleanup in the small toilet-sink bathroom in the barn while she went into the house to change into jeans.

Dressed in riding gear, Kim joined him as he tied the horses to the hitching rail.

"Hi, Dawn, it's good to see you again." She approached the palomino the way he'd instructed her last week, and stroked her, crooning something close to her ear. Then she looked up and nodded toward the bay gelding. "Who's her friend?"

"He's Rambler, the horse that's going to TJ at the Crazy Horse."

"The rescue horse. Can I touch him?"

"Sure."

She approached the bay more slowly than with Dawn, murmuring sweet nothings to him. The horse's ears perked forward with interest, and Ty smiled when Kim stroked him and he arched his neck happily.

While she talked to the horses, he saddled and bridled them, then they headed out on a different trail from last weekend's. Not that there was a lot of variety to the scenery, unless your eye was fine-tuned to nature.

Rambler did well. Ty had ridden him on these trails before, always alone, but the horse had no problem being with Dawn and Kim.

As for Kim, after the first few minutes, she looked relaxed, moving fluidly with Dawn. If she was staying in Vancouver, he'd make a rider of her.

But she wasn't.

She'd only been to Ronan Ranch twice, and he knew she didn't belong here—and didn't want to belong here. He also knew that his days were lighter for having her here.

She lifted her face to the late afternoon sun, gazed about alertly, and seemed content to ride in silence.

What was she thinking? When she was back home in that crowded, bustling Asian city she loved, would she remember this? Would she find moments of peace in the middle of her busy life, thinking about being here with him? And how often would he think of her? Miss her?

Figuring she'd enjoy watching the sunset at dinner, he headed them back to the ranch and made quick work of dealing with the horses.

"Hungry?" he asked as he and Kim walked up the back steps of his house, arms around each other's waists.

"Starving."

"Country air and exercise have that effect." They took off their footwear in the mudroom, then went into the kitchen. "You eat beef, right?"

"Absolutely."

"Thought you might like to try our Black Angus." He opened the fridge and lifted out a long rectangular pan wrapped in plastic. "I got these marinating." He peeled off the wrap to reveal skewers with cubes of beef interspersed with pearl onions and chunks of green and orange bell peppers. "We could cook up rice or potatoes, or I have half a loaf of Mom's bread."

"The bread would be great. Especially when I can relax and really enjoy it."

"Yeah. Sorry about my folks." He headed out to light the barbecue.

She followed. "My parents would be worse, if they met you."

An unusual emotion—anger—nipped at him. "Am I that bad?" he asked, unable to keep a trace of bitterness from his voice.

"Of course not! You're fantastic." With a hint of wistfulness, she said, "If you were Chinese, living in Hong Kong, running a company rather than a ranch, they'd adore you."

And so would Kim. He snorted. "Then I wouldn't be me."

"You'd still be strong and smart, handsome, responsible, successful, caring, loyal to your family, kind to the neighborhood kids and to broken-backed rodeo cowboys."

"Dusty told you about that?" With mixed emotions, Ty scraped the barbecue grill. Kim thought he was all those nice things? Yet he wasn't good enough for her to consider as more than a fling, or to take home to her parents. Not, of course, that he wanted to be taken home, to move to Hong Kong and adopt her way of life.

What the hell was going on with him? He'd never felt so confused over a woman.

"Dusty said there's some kind of code among rodeo cowboys," Kim said. "But it's more than that. You'd have given him a chance anyhow, because you're that kind of guy." She said it with certainty, and of course she was right.

He put the skewers on the grill, where they sizzled, a bit like his own volatile emotions. After closing the lid, he turned to Kim. "Your parents still think you're with Henry?"

She nodded.

"Have you even told them you and I are friends?"

"No."

He frowned. On that list of attributes about him, she hadn't included honesty. But that was a big one for him. It was how he'd been raised. Kids should respect their parents, and Kim seemed to, but to him respect and deceit didn't sit well together.

"What's the point?" she defended herself. "It would just upset them."

His jaw clenched. "You're saying I'm not important to you." Even as he spoke the words, he felt like a whiny teenage girl.

"That's not true!" Her vehement denial sounded sincere.

But how could he judge? Clearly, she was an expert at deception.

"Look," she said, "I know it's hard for someone from the West to understand."

"Right. Only Henry really understands you." It was probably true, damn it. Everything about Kim confused Ty.

"Ty, don't be mad. Where's this coming from?"

He shook his head. "I don't know. I mean, I know we're just casual, until you go back *home*." He couldn't stop himself from putting a snarky emphasis on that last word.

"Your parents are right that I'm not the woman for you." Her eyes narrowed with an emotion he couldn't read. "My parents, if they knew, would feel exactly the same, and they'd be right too. You and I both know that. Right? So I don't get why you're upset."

She looked so earnest, so pretty, so colorful, so . . . Kim, he couldn't stay mad. "Yeah, you're right. Except sometimes, you and me, it feels like . . . more. Like it could be more."

Her dark eyes went kind of melty. "Oh, Ty, I feel that way too."

She did? Really? They stared at each other. If Kim had feelings for him, then—

She blinked and said firmly, "But it can't be. We both know that. We're realists. We can be lovers, we can be good friends, but we can't let it get any deeper than that."

The cold, hard truth. Recognizing it, he sighed. "Hell, yeah, I know. This isn't some sappy romance novel where people from different worlds somehow, magically, get a solution that makes everything turn out."

One corner of her mouth kinked up, but without a hint of humor. "That's for sure." She squared her slender shoulders. "But it's up to us to enjoy the time we spend together and create our own happy ending. Like, maybe we'll stay in touch after I go home."

Did he want to? A sizzling sound made him remember the barbecue. He opened it and turned the skewers. "Almost done. Want to grab plates and pour some wine?"

"Sure." She went into the kitchen.

Alone, he mused about staying in touch. How would he feel, getting wedding pictures? Would she wear white, or was red traditional for Chinese women—or would she go for something less conventional? Maybe paint butterflies on her dress? Streak her hair? He thought about his parents' and grandparents' wedding photos, where each bride's personal style was reflected. He hoped Kim married a man who wanted her to do that.

Except, he didn't want to know who that man was. The man she would let herself love, the one her parents would approve of, the one she'd build her future with.

"Ty?" she called. "Want me to bring you a glass of wine?"

Damn, he'd forgotten the kebobs again. "No, just the plates, thanks." Hurriedly, he opened the grill and removed the skewers, as Kim arrived with plates to put them on.

In the kitchen they sliced chunks of bread and buttered it, picked up glasses of red wine, then headed out to the front porch. The sun was halfway down, the blue sky streaked with orange. They settled side by side in padded Adirondack chairs.

Ty hoped Kim didn't say anything more about staying in touch. Maybe he'd change his mind, but at the moment he figured that when she left, that should be that. Out of sight, out of . . . Would he ever get her out of his mind?

"This is so good," she said.

He glanced over, saw that she'd tasted her kebob. "Glad you like it." He ate a bite, pairing meat with a tender, sweet pearl onion. Yeah, it tasted fine. But his mind drifted back to something his mother had said. "Mom made a strange remark the other day."

"Let me guess. About me?"

"More about me, I think." He took a sip of wine. "She was on at me about finding a wife and settling down. I said I hadn't met anyone yet, so why not hang around with you? Then she said maybe it was avoidance, but she wouldn't tell me what she meant."

"Seeing me is avoidance? Like, if you spend time with me, it keeps you from looking for someone . . . more suitable." Her mouth twisted. "I could see my parents thinking that."

"Maybe that was it."

"Or maybe," she said reflectively, then stopped. "No, I'm no amateur shrink." She sipped her wine and gazed out at the sunset.

"Tell me what you're thinking."

She shrugged, still staring at the sky. "Your birth mother walked out on you and Brand. Your dad went through a rough time, but Betty came along. He had the guts to fall for her and risk his heart again, which couldn't be easy." She glanced toward him, then away. "Your birth mom abandoned you too."

Was she saying he was a coward, afraid to fall for a woman for fear she'd leave? "I was a kid," he scoffed. "I got over that long ago."

"Have you ever fallen in love?"

"Uh, not really."

"Why not?"

"Jeez, Kim, it's an emotion. You feel it or you don't."

"Do you even know what it feels like?"

Did he? Was it like when you looked at a woman being gentle with a damaged horse, and you wanted to pick her up and hold on to her forever? But no, he wasn't in love with Kim, and he wouldn't let himself be. Besides, she picked on him. "Do you?" he parried.

"I thought I did, with Henry. And with a boy when I was eighteen. But in both cases, it just kind of . . . fizzled. I guess I'm a little confused."

There was a lot of that going around. "So, what are you avoiding?" He tossed out the challenge.

It took her a moment to answer. "Fair comment. I don't think I'm avoiding anything. I want to love and be loved, to build a life with someone. But Ty, I'm twenty-four and I've thought I was in love twice. You're five years older, and you've never felt that way."

"I've been with loads of women."

"Buckle bunnies. Maybe that's avoidance too."

Damn, she could be annoying. "It's hot sex."

By rights, her temper should be rising too, but Kim surprised him as she often did. "And hot sex can be great. But Ty, you're a special guy. You have a huge heart. You give it to your parents, to broken-down cowboys, to disadvantaged kids, to damaged horses. Why have you never given it to a woman?"

He opened his mouth to respond, but had no idea what to say. Instead, he used his mom's bread to mop up some kebob juice from his plate, then took longer than he needed to chew.

Kim went back to her own meal and they ate in silence. A truce, he figured, and was glad she'd dropped the troubling subject.

Out of the corner of his eye, he saw her stifle yawns. Finally, she put her empty plate aside, finished the last of her wine, and relaxed back in her chair. "The stars are coming out," she said drowsily.

The sun was down, the sky a dark blue against which the first stars gleamed. There was nothing like an evening sky to mellow his mood. He turned to ask Kim if she wanted more wine.

She was asleep, curled in the chair with her legs tucked up and her head resting on the cushion tied to the back. She looked small, delicate, almost vulnerable. She looked . . . The word his mom used to describe baby animals flashed into his mind. *Adorable*.

If he woke her, she'd flip a switch and be on. She'd help with dishes, be happy to have sex with him. She liked to please people. Even when she challenged him, she did it nicely and backed down when she saw he was uncomfortable.

The dragonfly girl was normally so animated. Seeing her like this sent a soft wave of tenderness rippling through him. He wanted to look after her. She was worn-out from the fresh air, the unaccustomed setting, and a couple of rounds of sex.

He rose and eased her into his arms where she nestled against him with a sleepy sound of contentment. Being careful not to jostle her, he went inside and up to his bedroom. He bent to pull back the duvet then laid her gently on the sheet. Knowing she wouldn't want to sleep in jeans, he managed to get them off her. She stirred, but didn't wake. He decided to leave well enough alone and not take off her top or panties.

After tucking the duvet around her shoulders, he studied her head as it rested on his pillow. Normally so vibrant and expressive, her face was equally beautiful when it was relaxed in sleep.

Down he went to tidy up the dishes, smiling at the thought of returning to bed and sliding in beside her.

* * *

Kim woke to pale light, air that smelled green and fresh, and birdsong coming through the screened open window. Stretching contentedly, remembering some very hot middle-of-the-night sex and hoping for another round, she rolled over.

And found herself alone in Ty's big bed. The bedside clock said five thirty. Ty had promised they'd work on her business plan, so probably he was trying to do some chores first.

Awake now, and never much of a one for lazing in bed, she rose and pulled on the first thing that came to hand, Ty's discarded shirt. Curling up in the chair by the window, she checked her cell.

There was a text from Marielle and—no surprise—e-mail from Kim's mom.

Marielle's message read, Having fun riding cowboy Ty? Bet he's hotter than Dirk Zamora!

Chuckling, Kim texted back, Hot, hotter, hottest!

Then she read her mom's e-mail.

Kim, you'll be home soon and we need to decide on your role at
CPM. You have worked for the company since you were a child,
and it's time you stepped into a management position. Yang Hong
is perhaps ready for promotion. You could take his current position.

Yang Hong was property manager for one of CPM's smaller apartment buildings. Kim had the knowledge to do the job. And she'd hate it. Slowly, she typed her response.

Mom, please don't do anything hasty like promote Yang Hong
until we've had a chance to discuss this. I have another idea,
which I'll share with you this week.

She hoped to finish up the business plan and send it to her parents in two or three days. They just had to like it, and release her from her obligations at CPM.

Trying not to worry, she took a quick shower. Toweling her hair afterward, she realized she'd forgotten to bring the artist's chalk and flat iron that she used to streak her hair. She made a face at her reflection with the plain black hair, and wondered fancifully if Ty would recognize her without streaks.

She slipped into stretchy, skintight purple shorts and a bubblegum pink workout bra and headed downstairs to Ty's home gym. Ignoring all the fancy equipment, she unrolled a black yoga mat to face the window and eased into her routine.

As always, she started with Sun Salutation. Her body flowed easily from one position to another, stretched out, held, then shifted fluidly to another. She inhaled, exhaled, and cleared her mind of CPM, her parents, Ty's parents, the strange conversation she and Ty'd had last night, that almost turned into an argument. She refused to even think about UmbrellaWings, or how long she and Ty would keep seeing each other.

By the time she stretched into Downward Facing Dog, she was in the zone. When she finished Sun Salutation, she moved on to some of her favorite, more complicated positions.

Five or ten minutes later, she was sitting on the mat feeling the stretch of Monkey Pose, her legs in forward/backward splits, her back straight, her arms lifted to the sky, palms together as she gazed out the window. A small sound made her glance over her shoulder toward the door.

Ty lounged against the frame, casual and delicious in old jeans and a short-sleeved plaid shirt hanging loose over them.

"How long have you been watching?" she asked, coming out of Monkey Pose to sit cross-legged, facing him.

A corner of his mouth tilted up. "Awhile."

"I thought you were doing chores."

"I was, then picked up fresh eggs for breakfast. I figured you'd be asleep." He moved toward her. "That's sexy, that yoga stuff."

"It is?"

Twenty-seven

N ow Ty was close enough she could see the gleam in his eyes. Yes, apparently he did find it sexy. How about that?

She grinned up at him. "You could help me stretch. For example—" She lay back, then lifted her legs up and over her body so her butt faced him and her feet touched the floor behind her head.

"Jesus, you're a contortionist."

"You can't imagine all the ways my body can move." She spread her legs in a vee so she could peer up at him from between them.

"You're giving me some great ideas."

"You really should learn yoga, Ty," she teased. "Just think of all the possibilities." But then she remembered: What was the point? She wouldn't be around long enough to explore those possibilities with him. As for Ty, he'd marry a woman who didn't start her morning on a yoga mat; she'd be out doing chores. A partner, working shoulder to shoulder with him.

So much for clearing her mind, and for the mellowness yoga had brought to her. Staring up at him from between her legs, so tall and handsome in the early morning light, his hair tousled, his skin tanned from being outdoors, a day's worth of beard stubble on his face, Kim realized something. She truly was jealous of the woman he would marry. Not that she wanted to be a rancher herself, but she wanted Ty.

She'd felt twinges before, jealous ones and mushy romantic

ones, but she'd brushed them off. Now, in the clear light of dawn, she faced the truth: she was falling, seriously, for Ty Ronan.

"Kim? Are you all right? Do you have a muscle cramp?"

"Huh?" Had she been grimacing? "No, I'm fine." *Just stupid*. And she was not a stupid woman. She was realistic, focused, future-oriented. She shook her head. She would *not* fall for Ty. She was not Marty Westerbrook. Nor was this George and Woody's romance—where, though they'd been opposites in many ways, there was no big barrier to the two of them being together. Or at least, no barrier as big as the distance between Hong Kong and Ronan Ranch, where her and Ty's separate futures lay.

He was her friend and sex partner. She wouldn't allow herself to consider any other possibility because there was none.

She curled her legs back over her body and rolled fluidly to her feet. "Hey cowboy, what do you say? Want your first lesson in yoga sex?"

"How about we start with you taking your clothes off? Then do that thing where you're standing up, legs spread, and you stretch down to the floor. I can take it from there."

She peeled the exercise bra off. "You mean Downward Facing Dog?"

He yanked his shirt over his head, not even bothering to undo the buttons. "You made that up."

"No, seriously, that's what it's called." She stripped off her yoga shorts and thong and stood, proud of her toned body, aroused at the thought of playing sexy yoga games with Ty.

He'd taken off his jeans and underwear. His cock was swelling, rising. After he took a condom from his pocket, he tossed the clothes aside and sheathed himself. "Show it to me again."

Totally aware of his hungry gaze, she moved slowly and deliberately as she got down on the yoga mat on her hands and knees, then slowly lifted her knees away from the floor, lengthening and straightening as she went, firming and stretching every part of her body into the final position. Feet on the floor, legs in a straight line, back and arms in another straight line down to her spread hands on the floor. From the side, the way Ty would see her now, she knew her body formed a perfect right angle, an upside down vee.

He moved to stand behind her and she was very aware of her naked butt pressed up in the air—of the view Ty had of her butt cheeks, the crease between, and her damp, swollen pussy, denuded of hair. She felt exposed and kind of vulnerable, but at the same time conscious of her female power.

"Wow," he said. "You blow my mind, Kim." He cupped her butt in his two big hands, squeezed her taut muscles, then traced the line between them with a callused finger. He did it slowly, and by the time he arrived at her clit, moisture trickled down the inside of her thighs.

She tilted her head so she could look back, between her legs. Ty's much bigger, well-muscled legs were behind hers and he'd bent down to tease her pussy. She saw his fingers reaching from behind and watched as they stroked and toyed with her. His touch felt so good, but she wanted more. She wanted all he had to give her.

"Do me like that," she murmured, her voice husky with arousal, a little flustered at her own boldness. "I want to watch you come into me."

"For a dragonfly girl"—his voice was rough-edged too—"you have one hell of a dirty mind."

A shudder ran through her as he tapped her clit. "Is that a complaint?"

"Not for one moment. But you're sure this won't hurt?"

"I can hold this position forever." Still, she widened her stance and softened her knees, giving her body more flex.

As she watched, he nudged the head of his sheathed cock against her, probing between her pussy lips. Her body loosened, took him in, clung to his fullness. Her thighs glistened with her juices as he slid in, deeper and deeper.

Gripping her hips, he began slowly, carefully, to pump back and forth. He pulled out, swollen and slick, eased back in, went a little farther each time. Seeing his impressive length, she marveled that her body could handle all of him. But wow, did he feel fantastic.

The blood had rushed to her head and she felt tingles through her upper body, which somehow intensified the whole experience. Was she light-headed, or just incredibly turned on?

Though she hated to stop watching, she tilted forward to rest her forehead against the yoga mat. She tilted her pelvis, flexing back and forth to meet his thrusts, pressing against him each time he lodged himself fully inside her. A slight shift in angle, and she made sure each thrust rubbed against her sensitive clit. Her whole body tingled with erotic pleasure, and the need to climax built into a tight coil that centered all her attention as she reached, twisted . . .

Ty leaned forward, the pressure on her clit heightened almost, but not quite, to the point of pain. And then one more thrust, and sweet, blissful, crying out loud with it, release.

His body shuddered with his own orgasm, but he didn't let his weight collapse on her. His hands steadied her hips, kept her on her feet even as her overtaxed muscles began to soften and tremble.

His cock pulsed inside her a final time, then he eased back and away from her, still holding her firmly. "Man," he gasped. "Are you okay?"

Somehow, she forced strength into her arms and legs and gingerly managed to lower herself to the mat. She slumped on her hands and knees, then gradually stretched out each limb. "I'm fine. That was incredible, Ty." She sat cross-legged and smiled up at him. "You definitely bring out the dirty girl in me."

He grinned widely. "Glad to oblige. I sure like reaping the benefits." He stretched his hand down. "Feel like a shower?"

"I think we could both use one." She put her hand in his and let him pull her to her feet.

"And then breakfast. I'm starving."

They gathered their discarded clothing and headed up to the bedroom. This time the shower was a quick, functional one. Dressed again, they went to the kitchen and put together a huge veggie and cheese omelet. They teamed it with sliced peaches, Ty's mom's bran muffins from his freezer, and strong black coffee. Then, second cups of coffee in hand, they went to his home office. Kim stuck her flash drive in his computer and shared the draft of her business plan, plus her research notes.

He was brilliant, helping without trying to take over the way her parents always had when she discussed school assignments with them. He asked questions and made suggestions, and together they pumped up the plan, plus identified a few points she needed to check out. She hoped to finish off those details tonight and Monday and e-mail the plan to her mom and dad.

"Your parents have to be impressed," Ty said, apparently with total confidence.

"It takes a lot to impress them." It would take a *whole* lot to persuade them to give up the career goal they'd committed her to even before she was born. But they had to judge UmbrellaWings fairly. They couldn't just impose their own dream and ignore hers. Could they?

"Worrying doesn't help," he said. "Concentrate on the stuff you can control."

"You're right. I know you're right."

"I should head down to ranch headquarters to handle some orders and correspondence. You want to use this computer to work on UmbrellaWings?"

She glanced out the window at the sunshine and beautiful scenery. "I'll have time later. My fingers are itching to draw."

"Make yourself at home."

Last month, she'd have snapped off a sassy retort about how a city girl could never be at home surrounded by cow pies. Now, even though his world was so different from hers, she didn't feel as much like a fish out of water. "Thanks. I think I'll take my watercolor pencils up to the loft, and work on the view out the window."

They shared a kiss, then went their separate ways.

In the loft, Kim at first simply drew what she saw. Then, as she got a feel for the shapes, colors, and textures of the ranchland, she let loose her imagination and went more abstract, playing with different kinds of designs. She was engrossed, so engrossed that she didn't realize Ty had joined her until his shadow fell across her pad.

"Interesting," he said. "Guess I was expecting a landscape."

"I did a couple of those too." She flipped back to show him.

He studied everything she'd drawn, then returned to one of the abstracts. "The first ones are good; they're what I see. But this, it's like what I feel when I look out that window."

"Thanks."

He rested a hand on her shoulder. "You're good, Kim."

Tentatively, she offered, "Would you like to have that one?"

When he didn't leap to say yes, she quickly said, "No problem if you don't."

He shook his head. "It's not that. Just, after you're gone, will I want memories?"

Stunned, hurt, she stared up at him. "You want to forget me? Like I never existed?" Was she so . . . trivial to him, like another damned buckle bunny?

Something shadowed his hazel eyes, turning them forest green. "No, I don't guess that's gonna happen. So yes, I'd like that drawing. Can I have one of the roping ones too?"

Reassured, she said, "Of course. Would you like one of Distant Drummer?"

He shook his head. "Not the way she is now. Once they're healed, I don't want to think about how they used to be."

"I can see that." And the mood was far too solemn. What was going on with the two of them? To lighten things up, she asked, "What about one of the nudes?"

He looked horrified. "Oh Jesus, no."

She laughed, then he did too.

And then he took the art supplies away from her, pulled her to her feet, and they undressed each other in front of the open window. He sat down in that battered old chair and she sat on his lap, facing him. When he was inside her and she started to ride him, he reached down for his cowboy hat and plunked it on her head. "Hang on cowgirl," he said. "Here we go."

When he pumped his hips upward, meeting her halfway, thrusting deep and fast, she teasingly warned him, with what breath she could summon, "This ride had better last more than eight seconds."

And it did. Fast then slow, passionate then tender, through it all she clung to him. They kissed, then she arched back so he could bend his head to suck her nipples, and that sweet pressure brought her first orgasm. Her second came when his callused finger gently rubbed her clit. And her third was in perfect harmony with his own forceful climax.

No, Downward Facing Dog would never be the same for her, and she'd bet the same was true for Ty, with his old chair.

Driving home, Kim's body throbbed as she remembered all the ways she and Ty'd had sex. He was the most incredible lover. Wherever they were—her apartment, a hayloft, or a Jacuzzi—he was inventive and considerate, strong and gentle, and he gave her such pleasure.

This coming weekend, he was going to a rodeo in the interior.

They'd talked about her going with him. It would be a wonderful experience—a scenic tour; cheering him on when he rode; spending the nights in some cute motel.

As long as she kept her head and remembered that this was just her *rumspringa*, not her future, her heart should be safe. But could she really do that? Each time she was with Ty, it got harder to control her emotions.

Back in Vancouver, she drove her iCar to the drop-off spot half a block from her condo.

Her studio was stuffy, so she flipped up the window-wall before getting to work on UmbrellaWings. When she felt hunger pangs, she nuked some noodles with shrimp and veggies, and ate while she worked. Finally, around ten, she ran out of steam.

As usual, she checked Facebook and e-mail before bed. There was an e-mail from Lily, to the other club members.

Just a reminder that the final discussion of Ride Her, Cowboy is tomorrow. Kim, it's your turn to choose location. Let us know.

Oops. She'd forgotten it was her turn. She picked a place where they could sit outside or in, weather permitting.

Mahony's at Burrard Landing on Coal Harbour. I'm looking forward to hearing what everyone thinks of the ending.

Whatever that ending might be. She still had to read the last chapter.

Five minutes later, she was settled in bed with the book.

Flipping back a few pages, she refreshed her memory. Right, the cattle drive was finished and, back at the Lazy Z Ranch, the cowboys had dealt with the horses and headed off to their homes. Marty, who'd had only sponge baths and quick dips in streams, was dying for a long, hot shower, so when Dirk invited her to his house, she accepted the invitation. Kim turned the page.

Marty was in the shower, alone, crying at the thought of leaving Dirk. Would they ever see each other again?

Kim bit her lip. Yes, the idea of saying good-bye to Ty was sad. Really sad. But, as he'd said, it was a waste of time worrying about things over which she had no control. Surely, once she was back in Hong Kong, moving ahead with her life, she'd be fine. She'd have fond memories—sexy memories—and that'd be it. Maybe she and Ty would keep in touch and, as with Henry, they'd come to be friends and nothing more. Could she think of Ty as just a friend?

Frowning, she read on.

Even had there been a hair dryer in Dirk's guest bathroom, Marty wouldn't have taken the time to use it. She had to get out of there— onto the road, off to the airport in hopes she could get a flight today. She needed to focus on the story, turn it in, start on a new assignment. Keep busy, get on with her life, travel to the next interesting place where she'd meet fascinating people who . . . who, she feared, could never drive memories of Dirk from her mind or her heart.

She applied a little makeup to hide the signs of tears, dressed in cotton pants and a blouse, and squared her shoulders before heading downstairs to say good-bye.

He was in the kitchen, sifting through a stack of mail. His hair was damp too, and he was in fresh jeans and a white tee, his feet bare on the tiled floor.

She filed one more image in her memory photo bank, then cleared her throat. "I should hit the road."

He spun. "What? No, don't go."

"You don't need to feed me another dinner. If I leave now, I should be able to get a flight out tonight."

He walked toward her, biting his lip and looking nervous for the first time since she'd met him. He reached for her hands and, stupidly, she let him take them. "No," he repeated. "Don't go. Not tonight, not tomorrow. Not at all."

Something leapt in her heart. "What do you mean?"

"Sorry, I know you have a job. Of course you have to go."

The something that had flickered to life fizzled. "Yes, I do."

"But I wondered . . ." His indigo eyes gazed intently into hers and his face looked taut and strained. "You have to have a home base. How about making it here?"

"Here?" Hope flamed to life again. "With you? What are you saying, Dirk?"

His hands tightened on hers, squeezing painfully. "I love you, Marty."

"Me? Really?" No, she couldn't believe him. "But we're so different." Not that that fact had stopped her from loving him.

"We are. I'd always expected to fall for a woman who loved my way of life. But then you came along, and you're . . . everything, Marty. Smart, pretty, brave, strong, fun and the sexiest woman I've ever met. Yeah, I'd rather have a woman who lived here with me all the time, but your job means a lot of travel and I know you love your job, so—"

"I don't." The words burst out. Quickly followed by, "And I do love you, Dirk."

His strained expression faded slowly, and a wondering look of joy replaced it. "You love me?"

"I tried to stop myself, but I couldn't. Because you're everything too. Everything I could ever imagine wanting in a man. And this country is stunning. Inspiring. And the guys you work with are like a family and—"

"You'll stay?" He broke in, sounding like he didn't dare believe it was true. "Make this the base for your travels?"

Thoughts and feelings that had been building for the last two years flowed together, weaving seamlessly, forming a picture that felt absolutely right. "How about if I just stay, period? I used to love roaming the world, from story to story. But lately it's lost its luster. I started longing for a real home, but the idea of settling down by myself felt lonely. Being here with you—"

He was beaming. "Maybe having a kid or two?"

"Oh, yes. I love kids."

"But your work. What would you do?"

"I love writing. I'm guessing you have a local paper." Ideas flowed faster than she could speak. "I could do articles, maybe a column. I might start a blog about the ranch way of life, through a stranger's eyes. And I've always had the idea of one day writing a book about my travels. You know, the story behind the stories you read."

"About the person who writes those stories, and what she goes through to do it." He nodded. "When you sat by the fire telling us about your travels, you had us guys spellbound."

There were a few more paragraphs, which Kim skimmed out of a sense of duty. Then she closed the book and rolled her eyes. "Blah, blah, blah, and they all lived happily ever after."

Wasn't that just so unbelievably neat and tidy? Of course Marty'd been just dying to give up her successful career, exactly at the moment she and Dirk fell for each other. And of course she had a brilliant idea for writing a memoir, and she could do it living on the ranch. For sure, her book would sell to the first publisher who saw it, and they'd pay a million dollars for it. Because, as Kim had just been reminded, this was *fiction* and bore little resemblance to reality.

She remembered what Ty had said about their relationship. How it wasn't some sappy romance novel where people from different worlds got some magical solution. *Yeah, exactly!*

Disgruntled, she whacked the stupid book down on the bedside table and flicked off the light.

* * *

Monday afternoon, Kim hurried into Mahony's, an Irish-style pub on Coal Harbour. George sat alone at a window table. Her red hair and amber suit almost glowed against a backdrop of sullen clouds that threatened rain.

The pub had a great selection of beers, but tonight Kim decided on a split of Henkell Trocken sparkling wine.

George, who had her usual glass of white wine, raised her eyebrows. "Celebrating?"

"I finished my UmbrellaWings business plan and sent it to my parents. Fingers crossed!"

"You're fast! Yes, I'm crossing my fingers for you."

"What are we crossing fingers for?" Marielle asked as she and Lily joined them, the brunette vivid in a yellow top, the blonde looking drab in shades of gray.

Kim told them, and Lily said, "You pulled it together in a week? Kim, are you sure it's thorough? Your parents may only give you one shot at this."

"It's thorough; it really is. I've worked all my life in business, and I have a degree. Besides, Ty helped me with it and he's—"

"Ty helped you?" George broke in.

"The hot cowboy's good for something other than sex?" Marielle teased.

"He has a ranch. He's a businessman."

The perky young waitress came to take drink orders: a martini for Lily and something called an Irish Rose for Marielle. They ordered snacks too, agreeing on steamed shrimp dumplings, spicy cayenne chicken wings, and smoked salmon on herbed rye bread with caper dill cream cheese.

"All right," Lily said. "We'll all cross fingers that Kim's parents are wowed by her proposal. Now, let's talk about the book. What did everyone think of the ending?"

"I wanted to throw the book against the wall," Kim said. "I don't buy that Marty, a woman with a successful globe-trotting career, would suddenly give it up to go live on a ranch and write a memoir."

Marielle nodded. "Marty has the world to choose from, all those amazing men, and she's going to turn into a hermit on a ranch? She's crazy."

"The things women will do for love," Lily said dryly.

"You didn't like the ending either?" Kim asked her.

The blonde sipped her martini, looking thoughtful. "Well, I did buy that they'd fallen in love and had good intentions about making things work. I'd like to think that's enough for the long term, but I'm not sure. They're such different people. George, what about you?"

"I think it will work. Sure, in some ways they're different, but what's wrong with that? It's stimulating."

"Yeah, you don't want a clone of yourself," Marielle put in.

Kind of like her and Henry, Kim thought. But still . . . "She's giving up her career."

George shook her head, wavy red hair tossing around her striking face. "Changing to a new one. And she was ready for that change. There were signs all through the book."

"There were?" Kim asked.

"George is right," Lily said. "I saw that her lifestyle had worn thin, the nomadic thing of going from one assignment to another, never having real friends because she wasn't in one place long enough. Once, the only thing that mattered was the next story, but now she wanted something more meaningful."

"She'd fallen in love before," George said, "and I bet she'd have settled down and been happy. But when her soldier was killed, she shut that side of herself away and focused on work. It's what I did when my husband died. Then Woody came along, and I couldn't help loving him."

"But you didn't have to give up your career for him," Kim protested.

"Marty wanted to change her life," George said. "To have a home and family. She'd been considering writing a memoir, and I think she's excited about diving into it. Kim? Marielle?"

Marielle ran her hands through her long, curly black hair, pulling it away from her face. "Okay, I hear you. If it was me, it'd be a crazy thing to do. Cowboys may be hot, but I'd go nuts on a ranch with one man. But maybe it is the right thing for Marty."

"Maybe," Kim admitted. "I guess I was seeing her through my eyes too." And not paying enough attention to the book, because she was distracted by Ty and UmbrellaWings.

The waitress served their drinks and Marielle raised her glass. "To Kim's UmbrellaWings. May it take off and fly!"

Kim raised her glass, hoping with all her heart that her parents would like her plan.

Twenty-eight

Their waitress set down platters of appetizers, and for a few minutes the four women dished out bites of this and that, tasting and sharing opinions.

Then George said, "Kim, you said you'd been seeing Marty through your own eyes. You're talking about you and Ty?"

Kim swallowed a bite of shrimp dumpling. "Um, yes." She took a breath, deciding how much to share. Though she had lots of friends, she'd been brought up not to share too many details of her personal life. Yet, she wanted to, and it felt safe. "Globe-trotter Marty, Hong Kong city girl Kim, each meeting a cowboy who's rooted to his ranch. Having a short-term fling. I didn't pay enough attention to the differences."

"Such as?" Lily asked quietly.

"Marty was a nomad with no home. I have parents I love dearly, and a wonderful home in Hong Kong. Maybe she'd grown jaded with her career, but mine's just beginning and I'm so excited about it."

"You could base UmbrellaWings in Vancouver," George said. "We'd all like that."

Kim smiled at her. "Thanks. But there's never been any question that I'd return home."

"If you cared enough for Ty, wouldn't that give rise to the question?" the redhead asked.

Kim bit her lip. "You don't know my parents. Staying here isn't an option. Besides, it would be stupid to let myself care that much for a man who's not available."

"Seems to me he's pretty available," Marielle said. "You've been out there every weekend."

"Two weekends." So far. "This is just a fling. It's my Chinese *rumspringa*, right? He wants a ranch wife."

"That's what Dirk thought he wanted," George pointed out. "Before he met Marty."

True. Even though Marty wasn't the kind of woman he'd been looking for, he loved her and wanted her. He wanted her even when he thought she'd keep roaming the world. But Ty wasn't like that.

"Look," Kim said, "this is a total secret, okay?" After collecting curious nods, she went on. "Ty's birth mom ran out on him and his dad. She was a city girl, and she hated ranch life."

"Are you saying you hate ranch life?" George asked.

"Aside from the hot sex?" Marielle added.

"I couldn't imagine living there. The city's an adrenaline charge: bustle, color, vibrancy. Galleries, restaurants, I couldn't live without them."

"So you do hate the ranch?" Lily asked.

Slowly, Kim shook her head. "It's kind of nice. It's a bunch of contrasts. Hard work, but peaceful too. Huge and stark, like Marty found on the cattle drive, and yet it's seductive in how it draws you in. When I sketched it, I felt like I was coming to understand it."

"Sounds like you could see yourself living there," George said softly.

"No, of course not. The only place I'm going to live is Hong Kong."

"Which isn't peaceful," Lily said dryly.

"No, but . . . it's home. Anyhow, Ty's dead set on finding a woman like the mom he grew up with. The opposite of his birth mother. A country girl who'll do all the ranch stuff with him. Not an artist who wants to make umbrellas."

"If he loved you—" George started before Kim cut her off.

"He doesn't. And I don't love him." Her voice rose. "We're not you and Woody, okay?" Nor Marty and Dirk. It was *not* okay for Kim to fall for Ty, and she wouldn't do it.

"And even if you did love each other," Lily said, "it's hard maintaining a relationship when your careers are on such different courses."

Something about her voice, a note that might have been pain, made Kim focus on the blonde. There was a sad, reflective look in her clear blue eyes. While Lily participated fully in discussions about books and the other women's lives, she never said much about her own life. She was older, a family practice doctor, and had been married a long time. That was all Kim knew. Except that, more than once, she'd seen signs of tiredness and worry on Lily's face.

There wasn't much more than a month left before Kim would return to Hong Kong. She might never know Lily's problems, might not have time to fly back for George and Woody's wedding, might not find out if variety-loving Marielle ever found a man—or a drink or a job—that won her heart.

As for Ty, maybe it would be best not to keep in touch. Kim wanted to hear how Distant Drummer made out, but did she really want to know about the woman Ty fell in love with and married? The one who was everything she was not?

Kim was walking home from Emily Carr across the Granville Street Bridge Tuesday afternoon when her cell phone rang. Call display showed her parents' number.

She froze, a surge of nausea almost bringing her to her knees. They could only be calling about her business plan. This was it. The moment she'd anticipated since she was a child with a passion for art. They would give her a thumbs-up or a thumbs-down, and her future would be decided.

She stood at the bridge railing and forced herself to press the screen to accept the call.

Her mother's voice spoke, loud enough to be heard over the traffic. "Your father is here with me and we have been over your plan with a fine-tooth comb."

Not even a hello. Was that a good or a bad sign? Kim gripped the railing. "And?"

"We want you to join Chang Property Management, as we've always intended."

The nausea churned and she took shallow breaths, trying to quell it. "Call you back," she managed to get out, then she ended the call.

This was it. The worst had happened. Every dream she'd ever had, crushed. She was a butterfly who wanted to fly, and they'd torn off her wings. She wanted to scream, wail, throw herself over the rail of the damned bridge. But she didn't have breath in her body to do any of it. She hung on to the railing, the only thing that kept her on her feet.

And then—oh hell, who cared what passersby thought?—she sank down on the sidewalk, knees up, arms wrapped around them, face buried. When she'd worked summers and part time for CPM, she'd been bored and frustrated, but she had always kept the dream alive that she'd escape one day. Now . . . How could she even contemplate the future?

Betrayed by her parents, knowing Henry would take their side, she lifted her cell again and called the one person she could talk to.

"Hey, Kim," Ty answered. "How's it going?"

Tears slid down her cheeks. "Crappy. My parents rejected my business plan." Last night, she'd e-mailed him a copy of the final product, and he'd said it was a winner.

"Shit! Shit, Kim, that sucks."

His vehemence almost made her smile through her tears. "To put it mildly."

"They're crazy. It was a terrific plan."

"I thought so too." She huddled, looking out at the water so the strangers walking the bridge's sidewalk wouldn't see her tear-stained face.

"They never gave you a fair chance."

She'd always believed that they would, despite their own strong desire that she join CPM. "No. I feel"—she hated to disrespect her parents, but all the same—"betrayed. Maybe they never believed I'd come up with a plan, but they never said they'd flat-out reject it if I did."

"Aw, honey, I'm so sorry."

Honey? Even in the depths of misery, she noticed that he'd called her honey. He'd never done that before.

"What are you going to do?" Ty asked.

"Do? They didn't give me a choice."

Silence. Long enough that she asked, "Are you still there?"

"Yeah. And Kim, I don't want to beat up on you when you're down, but this isn't your parents' decision to make."

"Ty, I told you—"

"Yeah, yeah." He cut her off. "I'm not Chinese and I don't get it. But I know that parents and kids often have issues about control as the child grows up. We sure as hell did in my family. Dad and I would've come to blows a time or two, if Mom or one of my grandparents hadn't stepped in."

He so didn't understand her family. Wryly, she said, "I don't think punching out my father's going to fix this."

"Wouldn't have fixed my problems either. What I did was leave home and go my own way."

"I can't believe that solved everything."

"It didn't. Because I was a hothead, and my grandparents weren't exactly diplomatic about supporting me rather than my parents. We all could've handled it better. I've always felt bad about that."

"You have?"

"Kim, while I was proving my independence and being a rodeo star, my family lost Ronan Ranch. I didn't pay attention to what was going on back home. I was selfish, and didn't help them."

Her head ached from sorrow and tears, which made it hard to think, but all the same . . . "So you're saying I should join CPM and support my parents?"

"No, I'm saying you should do things better than I did. Their company's not in trouble, is it?"

"No, it's doing very well."

"Does the company need you?"

She brushed tears from her cheeks and rose. The world was still turning: traffic on the bridge, boats heading in and out of False Creek, the late afternoon crowd gathering on the deck of Bridges' restaurant. "No. But Mom and Dad want to keep it in the family. There are several other relatives working there, but I'm their only child."

"They're proud of their company, like my folks with Ronan Ranch. Here's something my grandma told me, not long before she died. My dad wasn't just mad at me when I wanted to rodeo full-time, he was hurt. I was rejecting the ranch he'd worked so hard to build and took such pride in."

She bit her lip. "I can see that." As she walked toward home, she imagined Brand Ronan facing a headstrong young Ty. "I bet he was worried too."

"Worried?"

"He'd lost your birth mom. Now there you were, wanting to leave the ranch too, and to do something dangerous."

"Huh. He never said any of that."

"Do men ever say things like that to each other?"

"I guess not."

"And I didn't realize how badly it must hurt my parents that I never embraced the business they built." So, she was doomed. Doomed to be the good, respectful daughter rather than build her own dream.

"Then do it better than I did. Go after what you want, but consider their feelings."

"Go after UmbrellaWings? But they said no."

"You don't need their permission. You're a grown-up."

And the only child in a Hong Kong family with traditional values. If it had been tough for Ty to defy his parents, and it had caused bad relations for years, how much worse would it be for Kim? Her parents might be so hurt and embarrassed that they'd cut her out of their lives.

"Why did they reject it, anyhow?" he asked. "I thought it was a solid plan."

"I don't know."

"They didn't tell you?" he said disbelievingly. "You let them get away with that?"

"I was too shattered to ask questions. I said I'd call back."

"Then ask, and defend your decisions. Or, if they have objections that make sense to you, go back and do more research, more analysis. They're successful businesspeople; they might have useful input."

Hope fluttered tiny wings in her chest. "Maybe." She took a deep breath. "You're right, I'll do it."

"Good for you. Don't let them bully you, dragonfly girl."

The expression brought both a smile and a fresh mist of tears. She was so glad she'd called Ty—but what was life going to be like when he was no longer in it? "I'll let you know what happens."

Squaring her shoulders, she marched into her building. In her apartment, she opened the window-wall, washed her face with cold water, took a couple of deep breaths, then made the call.

When her mother answered, Kim said, "What didn't you like about my business plan?"

A pause, then, "It's not a plan to join CPM."

"Yes, I got that." And she wasn't going to let them get away with it. Pacing across the small apartment, she asked, "But the plan itself, what's wrong with it?"

"I didn't say there's anything wrong with it."

Kim's jaw dropped. "You think it's good? But you're still insisting I join CPM? Mom, that's not fair." Remembering her conversation with Ty, she said, "I mean no disrespect to CPM. You and Dad left your homes to go to Hong Kong and you built an amazing, successful company. Your relatives and ancestors are so proud of you. But it's something the two of you built together. It's your thing, not mine. I want a chance to build something that's mine."

"CPM is established. Secure. You'd have a good future there."

"I know. But it's not what I love." She'd always hated arguing with her parents, and usually backed down. Now, there was too much at stake.

"You can still do your art. You're talented, and we've always encouraged you."

"Yes, and thanks for that. Mom, I'll do art as a hobby, but I want to incorporate my artistic talent in my own business as well. I know that starting a new company isn't a secure thing, but I'm willing to take the risks." Remembering something else Ty had said, she went on. "You and Dad are so business savvy, if you have input as to how to improve my plan and reduce the risks, I'd love to hear it."

Besides, the stronger her proposal, the more likely she'd find financing to start her company.

After a long pause, her mother said, "As you know, there are no guarantees in business, but your father and I think this could work."

"Then . . . what are you saying?"

She heard murmurs between her mother and father. Then her mom said, "Your father and I thought you wanted to paint all day, exhibit, try to sell paintings."

If that was true, they'd never truly listened to her.

"We knew you had a good business brain," her mother went on, "but until now we didn't understand that you were capable of combining it with your art. If this is what you truly want, Kim, and you're prepared to work hard for it, then you should have it."

"I . . . wow." Really? Had she won? Was it possible?

"We want you to think very, very carefully about this. But if you're determined, then we'll provide start-up financing."

For the second time in an hour, Kim sank to her knees. "What?" Had she heard correctly? She'd designed the plan not just for her parents' approval, but to convince a financial institution to provide a business loan. It had never occurred to her that her parents might provide financial support. "Seriously?"

"Seriously. If you're absolutely sure." Up until now, her mom's tone had been subdued, but now, sounding more emotional, she said, "But if you joined CPM, it would stay in the family, and that's important to us."

Kim heard a murmur of agreement from her father.

"It will always be in the family," Kim pointed out. "You've hired so many relatives." But she knew that wasn't the same as having their only child in management. She'd won, and in the process she'd hurt her parents. An idea occurred to her. "Mom, I really don't want to eventually run CPM, but maybe I could still be involved. I wouldn't have a lot of hours to give, but perhaps there's something I could do."

Her mother must have put her hand partway over the phone. Kim heard a babble of Cantonese as her mother spoke to her dad in quick, excited bursts, and her father responded in his slower, deeper voice. She couldn't catch what they were saying. Then her mom spoke into the phone again. "The Board of Directors. Would you serve on it?"

"I'm honored that you'd ask. Yes, of course." Kim realized that, thanks to seeing Ty with his parents and hearing about their struggles, she'd finally grasped what a family business truly meant. "Mom, I would love to be part of what you and Dad have built together."

"Good. Very good." She was silent for a moment, then said, "It's a pity Henry is so involved in his own family's business."

"Henry?" Kim blinked, and rose to her feet again. "How does he come into this? And I thought you liked that he worked in his family's company."

"That was when we thought you'd slowly take over running CPM. The next best option would be for your husband to come into the company."

Kim's mouth fell open. Clearly, the time for half-truths was past. "I need to tell you, Henry and I are friends, but we're no longer dating."

"Aiya!" When her mom was really upset, she reacted first in Cantonese.

Kim walked onto the tiny balcony. "He hasn't told his parents, so please don't say anything."

"I'm sorry about this, Kim."

"Me too." Once, she'd thought she and Henry were so compatible. Now she knew their compatibility was more about their common background and culture, not similar interests and dreams.

"Hmm . . . Have you met Jim Lau?"

"Who? No, I don't think so."

"He is a young lawyer at CPM. He has great potential. If you married him, perhaps he might eventually take over and we would still keep the company in the family."

Oh my God. Trust her mother. "Mom, I—"

"When you come home, you'll meet Jim. You'll like him."

Was that an order? she wondered ruefully.

A lawyer with CPM, not a cowboy. Who knew, Jim Lau might be her perfect match, and that would make her parents so happy. Trying to ignore a ridiculous ache in her heart that protested against dating any man who wasn't Ty, she said, "I'd be happy to meet him."

"Ah, that is very good. I will arrange it. Now, your father wishes to talk to you."

He said, in his choppier, more accented English, "Kim. A lot happening."

"You and Mom are being wonderful about UmbrellaWings. Thank you, Dad."

"You are only child. You will make family proud."

"I'll try my best."

"We check flights. Send ticket."

Yes, her time in Vancouver was nearly at an end, but she wasn't ready to set an actual date to leave. "We can deal with that in a few weeks."

"No. Now. You come home now. Tomorrow or next day."

Twenty-nine

Kim's brain had processed so much in the last hour that it now stalled. "What are you talking about? My two years aren't up."

"No reason stay."

"But my studies at Emily Carr . . ."

He huffed, then switched to Cantonese. "Your classes are over and you're just finishing assignments. Do that here. You want to start your own business and we have offered to help. Why wait?"

Because she wanted to spend more time with classmates and friends, to have a few more get-togethers with book club. To revisit her favorite spots in Vancouver and see the ones she'd never gotten around to.

She wanted to spend more time with Ty.

Vancouver wasn't Hong Kong. It wasn't home, but it was a wonderful second home. A city that was cleaner, fresher, and prettier than Hong Kong. A city where she'd made friends and had developed UmbrellaWings with their help. George had even suggested she build her business here.

Was that crazy? "What if—?" Words crammed her throat. She swallowed, then forced them out. "What if I started up the company in Vancouver? Umbrellas are a huge thing here. I think Vancouverites would love my ideas. They like beauty, nature, and a touch of whimsy." What was she thinking? She belonged in Hong Kong with her parents. She was too young to start a business all on her own. As for Ty, even if they did spend more time together, she'd never somehow morph into a ranch wife.

Her father had covered the phone. She heard that dim gabble of Cantonese again.

Then he spoke to her in that language, his voice firm. "Don't be foolish, daughter. You belong here with us. You will start your company here."

Tentatively, she said, "I could start it here, then expand internationally and set up an operation in Hong Kong."

"No. If you want our approval, assistance, and financing, you will start it here."

"Give me that phone," her mother said to him in Cantonese. Then, in English, "Kim, this is very disappointing. What is wrong with you? We give you what you want, and you fling it back in our faces?"

"Oh, Mom, I don't mean it that way. I'm so grateful. But I do think Vancouver might be the perfect location to launch Umbrella-Wings."

"*Perfect* is here, with your parents' guidance. We will send an e-ticket, and you will come home."

Kim walked inside and glanced around the studio apartment she so loved. She breathed in, then out. All right, she'd leave. In a way, her parents' decisiveness was a relief. The idea of staying in Vancouver and starting a business all by herself really was crazy. Besides, she couldn't bear to disappoint and hurt her parents any more than she'd already done. "Yes, Mom. But please, could I have a little time to wind things up here and to pack?"

"Movers will pack your small place in two hours." A pause, then a huff. "Fine. We will give you one week." Her mother ended the call.

Dazed, Kim flopped down in her reading chair. She'd been given the one thing she most wanted in life, the thing she'd dreamed about since she was a child. She should be ecstatic. She should be jumping up and down, buying champagne, calling her friends to go out and celebrate.

What was wrong with her?

She gazed around the studio, the place where she'd experimented with her art. Where she'd experimented with sex, with Ty. She'd have to give notice to her parents' building manager. Next month, this would be someone else's home. She'd be living with her parents.

Which was good. Really it was.

She pulled up e-mail, sent her notice, then studied a message from Henry suggesting they have dinner on Thursday.

E-mail wouldn't do for this, so she phoned him. "Henry, I'm sorry but I told my parents about us not being together any longer."

"I thought we agreed to wait until we went home."

"It turns out, I'm going home in a week." Those words didn't seem real. She filled him in on the details.

"I knew you wished to pursue art, but I did not believe you'd come up with a realistic plan. I am sorry that I doubted you." He sounded formal and truly apologetic.

"It's okay." He was a product of his upbringing, just as she was. "There's a part of me that wishes I could stay in Vancouver and start the business here," she confessed. "To be independent. But I know I'm too young and inexperienced."

"I have the same wish to be independent sometimes. But this is disloyal to our parents, who gave us everything."

"I suppose."

"Perhaps when we are both home, your and my relationship will be different. You—we—will be less, uh, distracted by things that are not relevant in the long term."

Like her Chinese *rumspringa*, her passionate dirty girl fling with Ty Ronan? Was Henry right? Would things look different once they were back in Hong Kong?

"We get along, Kim. We care for each other."

"We do, but that's not enough." Even if Ty wasn't the right mate for her, she wanted passion. A person deserved that. She hoped both she and Henry would find it, but she didn't believe it would ever flame between the two of them.

He sighed. "If you are sure."

"I am. But thanks for helping make my time in Vancouver so great. Every time I felt homesick, you were like a touch of home and you made me feel better."

As she ended the call, her e-mail pinged. Her mother had sent an e-ticket for a flight Wednesday morning, next week.

Biting her lip, Kim called Ty again.

"You talked to your parents?" he asked, without even a "hi."

"They tried to talk me into working for CPM, but I didn't back down and they finally said yes."

"That's wonderful. Way to go." He sounded genuinely happy for her, happier than she felt right now.

"Thanks. Yes, it's great."

"You don't sound as excited as I thought you'd be."

"I am. It's taking time to sink in. And, well, there's more good news and, uh, some surprising news."

"Go on."

"My parents said they'd provide start-up funding."

"Man, you really must have impressed them. Congratulations, honey."

Honey. There it was again. And he sounded so thrilled and proud that she could barely force the next words out. "But I have to go home next week. I'm flying out Wednesday morning on Cathay Pacific."

"What?" he exclaimed. "Next Wednesday? Damn, I thought you had a month left."

"They said if I'm going to start a business, I should come home and do it."

"But . . . Well, huh." The happy excitement had disappeared from his voice too.

"Yeah. I wasn't expecting that."

They were both quiet, then he said, "The rodeo this weekend? I guess that's not going to work out?"

"I have so much to tidy up here." It was a half-truth. Mostly, she'd feel too sad, traveling with Ty all weekend and knowing she'd never see him again.

"This isn't good-bye," he said firmly. "Not like this, on the phone."

Tears filled her eyes again. It would be painful to see Ty. But no, they couldn't end it this way. Struggling to keep her voice even, she said, "I could drive out tomorrow afternoon."

"I'll get some champagne and we'll toast UmbrellaWings." But he didn't sound in any more celebratory a mood than she did.

She held it together to say, "That sounds good," before she ended the call and surrendered to tears.

Wednesday morning, Ty and his parents met to discuss changing feed suppliers. When, for the third time, he asked his dad to repeat what he'd said, Brand Ronan grumped, "Where's your mind this morning, son?"

"Kim called last night. Her parents like her business plan, and she's going back to Hong Kong next week."

"It's probably for the best," his mom said. "Before the two of you got in too deep."

The ache in his heart told him she might be right. Or that he might already be in too deep. He hated the thought of never seeing Kim again. But was that just because she was a sexy, vivacious woman, or were his feelings more serious? He'd never felt this kind of ache before.

"You knew she wasn't going to stay." There was a touch of sympathy in his dad's voice. "City folks will always be drawn to big city life. She told you that."

"She did." He'd seen the way she enjoyed Ronan Ranch, but she'd always made it clear she loved Hong Kong. So why did he feel closer to her than to any other woman he'd ever dated?

"I like Kim," his mom said briskly, "and I wish her well. Now you need to move on. You know Bill and Kay Field at Dairy in the Field?"

"Of course."

"Their niece Sandy got her degree in agribusiness and has come to work at the dairy. She's mid-twenties, pretty, real down to earth. Why don't I ask them all over for dinner?"

"Mom, I don't need you matchmaking." He looked to his dad for backup but got only a shrug.

"You're not doing so well on your own," she said. "Dating women like Kim, who you'd never settle down with."

Ouch. "The right woman will come along." Ty knew his tone was less than convincing. Right now, it was hard to imagine caring for anyone other than Kim.

"The right woman might come along to the dinner table," his mother said tartly, "if you let me invite Sandy. What have you got against a girl you've never met?"

"Nothing. It's the principle of the thing."

She rolled her eyes. "It's avoidance."

"You said that before," he snapped. "What the hell—heck—are you talking about?"

She pressed her lips together, then released them. "You're scared of being abandoned. Miranda left, and you never got over it."

"Oh Jeez." He raked his hands through his hair. "I was a baby. I don't even remember her. Besides, Dad got over it just fine."

"Your dad was a man, with a man's brain to make sense of things."

"And Betty to help me do it," his father put in quietly.

His mom sent him a loving glance, then turned back to Ty. "You were a child. Childhood experiences have a powerful influence."

"You snuck off and got a psychology degree in your spare time, did you?" he taunted.

"Don't sass me. You're not too old to have your ears boxed."

"Sorry, Mom."

"The one person in the world who was supposed to love and protect you instead walked out on you. That had to leave a scar."

He barely resisted groaning.

"A scar that makes you afraid of loving, of committing to a relationship, for fear of being abandoned again."

Kim had hinted at the same thing, but backed off. Could these two women possibly be right? "Feed suppliers," Ty said firmly. "Are we gonna give the new guys a try?"

By the time Kim's red car turned into his road, Ty had done a lot of thinking. Analyzing emotions and relationships was not his strong point, and he'd gotten himself all confused.

She climbed out of the car and started toward him. Today she wore a copper tank top painted with green and black stylized wings, and a long, floaty skirt with a similar pattern in greens, coppery-orange, and black. Her hair was streaked with bronze and green.

Kim was so out of place here, and yet she looked exactly right. Suddenly all the confusion stilled and something settled in his heart, deep and true: a certainty that said, "Her. This is the one."

She'd asked him if he knew what love felt like. He hadn't. Now, he did.

This. This powerful surge that was ecstasy, fear, and nausea all in the same moment, like the one time he'd been damn fool enough to try bull riding. The nausea, he figured, wasn't caused by love, but the fear he might lose her.

Might. That was the operative word. His dragonfly girl couldn't really intend to go back to Hong Kong. If he felt like this, she had to feel it too. Sure, their two worlds were very different, but somehow there had to be a way they'd mesh. Just the way he and she did, as if they'd been made for each other.

He strode to meet her and, without even a hello, swept her up in his arms and swung her around. She was light as a bird, graceful as a dragonfly, pretty as a butterfly. The woman had wings, and she'd flown away with his heart. Hell, she'd even made him whimsical.

He could have spun her forever—and would have, if it could keep her with him. But reality had to be dealt with. Putting her down, he said, "Congratulations on UmbrellaWings, honey." Inside, his heart was chanting, "You can't go, you can't go, you can't go."

"Thanks." She smiled, not beaming with joy but tentatively. "It's pretty amazing. I couldn't have done it without you."

She didn't have to do anything without him. Not ever again.

He had to have her. Right now. Had to merge with her, knowing that he loved her. "The hayloft. Come up to the hayloft." Where better than his special spot for planning and dreaming?

She studied him. "I like the hayloft." Again, he sensed reserve. Kim thought this was their last time together, while he was determined it wouldn't be. He had to break through her reserve, find the passionate woman, make her feel what he did. Taking her hand, he guided her into the barn and up the steps to the loft.

His battered old leather recliner was in its spot by the window. He sat down. "Come here."

With a questioning look, she sat across his lap, looping her arms around his neck. "Ty?"

Why did he used to think long blond hair was pretty? This, right here in his lap, was perfection. "Oh man, Kim, you're something." He flicked one of those sassy green strands of hair. "Dragonfly or butterfly?" He knew she'd have the name.

"Downy Emerald dragonfly."

"Pretty." He ran his finger down the straight line of her small nose. Traced the slight bow of her upper lip, the subtle curve of her lower one. Her lips parted and her tongue touched his finger. When his finger stilled, she drew the tip of it into his mouth and sucked.

Beneath his fly, his cock filled, imagining the suction of that small, warm, talented mouth. He shifted, letting her feel his hard-on under her butt. He slid his finger from between her lips and kissed her, not invading her mouth but toying with her lips, using his tongue and teeth to caress and nibble and tease.

She sighed, wriggled her butt against the hard ridge of his erection.

Slowly, he took the kiss deeper, trying to tell her everything he felt. That there was tenderness as well as passion, respect as well as lust. That there was love.

When their lips finally parted again, her dark eyes looked huge and dazed. Shiny, almost as if she was going to cry. No, God no, he didn't want to make her unhappy. "Kim, I—" He didn't know what he was going to say, and she stopped him before he could figure it out.

"Don't talk," she said.

He was going to ask why, but she distracted him by slipping off his lap and reaching for his belt buckle. She undid the belt, the jeans, and he helped her slide his jeans and underwear down his hips. He started to stand, to take off his boots and tangled clothing, but she said, "No. Like that." And when he reached up to take his hat off, she said, "Leave it on."

She reached under her skirt, and a skimpy purple thong flipped into the air.

He barely had time to grab a condom from his pocket before she sat down again, this time facing him, straddling his knees. The flock of green and copper dragonflies on her skirt fluttered between them.

She took the condom and sheathed him.

He'd have kissed her again, touched her pussy and made sure she was ready, but she took control. She lifted up, guided him between her legs, shuddered slightly as he slid in.

"Kim, are you okay?"

Thirty

on't talk," Kim repeated, husky-voiced. She looped her arms around his neck and began to move, sliding up and down his shaft, slow inches at a time, each move seating him more deeply inside her.

Ty remembered that first night, when he'd plunked his hat on her head and she'd ridden him with one hand waving triumphantly in the air. He'd only just met her; she was sexy and intrigued him. Now he knew her. He loved her.

He hugged her and leaned forward to kiss her, but she was arching back, away, so that her breasts thrust toward his mouth. Hard nipples poked against the thin cotton of her copper tank top and the bra—green, he knew from the straps—beneath it. No man in his right mind could resist an offer like that. He moistened the cotton with firm swipes of his tongue, pressing it against a tight nipple, and she shuddered again. His hat tilted, tumbled off his head. She gripped his head in both hands, pressing his face against her breast while he sucked.

He switched to the other breast, and she whimpered, her body clutched, then the spasms of her climax pulsed against his cock.

Those pulses urged him to join in, to surrender, to pump hard and climax too, but he managed to resist. He wanted this to last.

But it seemed Kim had other ideas. Still pressing his head against her chest, she flexed internal muscles around him—clutch and release, clutch and release—in an irresistible rhythm.

He groaned, trying to hold on, but then she lifted up and down on his shaft, added a hip swivel, ground herself against him. Her body gave one clear signal. Come now, and come hard.

And he did, crying out hoarsely as he emptied himself inside her.

He heard her cry too. A sound, maybe a word. His name? The blood roared too fiercely in his ears for him to make it out.

He knew what *he* wanted to say. But was this the moment to tell her he loved her? The sex had been great, but she hadn't even kissed him. Or let him talk.

Maybe she was thinking about leaving. Hopefully, she was thinking that she'd miss him. Enough that he could talk her into staying. Should he ask her now?

No, she freed her death grip on his head and climbed off his lap, turning away, looking for the thong she'd tossed aside. With her back to him, she pulled it on under her skirt, not even flashing him a look at her pretty legs.

Biting his lip, he got himself pulled together too.

Champagne. Alcohol, bubbles, a celebration of her success. That would get her in the right mood.

"I have champagne," he said to her still-turned back. "Let's drink it on the porch." They'd toast her business and then he'd ask her to stay. To build UmbrellaWings here, to give him a chance.

"Sure. That sounds nice." Her voice was light, a little artificial.

She went down the wooden steps ahead of him, and through the barn. "How's Distant Drummer doing?" Her words floated over her shoulder.

"Looking healthier and settling in. Go say hi."

Slowly, she approached the box stall, crooning sweet nothings.

Ty held back, crossing his fingers and sending a mental message to the horse: *Help me, Drummer girl. This is Kim. You like her. Let's persuade her to stay.*

He heard a snort, the *whuffle* of soft breath, then the horse came from the back of the stall, her ears pricked forward. She bobbed her head a couple of times. Kim held out one small, orange-tipped hand, and Drummer nuzzled it.

The horse hadn't done that yet with Ty, and he wasn't one bit jealous. This was another sign that Kim—just the way she was, whimsical, creative, and soft-hearted—belonged here.

"Oh, you do look good, Drummer," Kim said as she gently stroked the horse's face. "You're gaining weight already. Most of us females think that's a bad thing, but on you it looks terrific. Soon you'll be all sleek and healthy. And oh I wish"—she broke off, took a quavering breath, bowed her head—"wish I could see you like that. I'll m-miss you, girl." Her drooping head slowly lifted and she said, more firmly, "You're going to have the best, happiest life with Ty's friend. I hope you're being nice to Ty, girl. You can trust him, you really can."

After several long minutes, the horse moved away and Kim came to join Ty. Drummer must have worked some magic, because this time Kim did look him in the eyes, and she reached out to link her fingers with his. "I'll miss seeing her heal. And I'll miss you, Ty."

It was on the tip of his tongue to say, "You don't have to." Was this good timing, or bad? "Let's drink some champagne and talk."

"Sure. We'll toast UmbrellaWings." The cheer in her voice sounded forced. "That is, if a guy who chooses cowboy hats over umbrellas can bring himself to do that."

Yes, they'd toast her success, and before the evening was through, he hoped they'd be toasting a lot more than that. Like their future.

As they walked toward his house, a drowsy summer breeze fluttered her skirt.

"You look pretty, honey." Had he told her that before? "You always look so pretty. Like a dragonfly lit down in my yard."

She gave a surprised smile. "What a wonderful thing to say. I figured you'd think I look frivolous and out of place."

"How can a dragonfly be out of place?" Jesus, not only whimsical, but almost poetic. He really must be in love.

She studied him curiously, but didn't say anything else as they went up the steps. Then she smiled again when she saw the table he'd covered with a checked cloth and topped with a bunch of mixed blossoms he'd filched from his mom's garden. "This looks so nice."

"Relax on the porch and I'll get the wine."

He went to the kitchen and returned with an ice bucket and two champagne flutes—chilled, because he wasn't a hick. He'd driven to the liquor store and studied the selection of champagnes. Over the years, he'd drunk his share of the beverage, celebrating rodeo wins and ranch successes. He figured Kim had too, as her parents were wealthy.

Dom Pérignon was classic, but the label didn't say "Kim" to him. The bottle that leaped into his hand was the one with pink apple blossoms etched on it: Perrier-Jouët Belle Epoque Rosé. Pink champagne. Girly stuff, and he sure hoped she liked it.

When he took the bottle from the ice bucket, she clapped her hands together. "Oh Ty!"

"It kind of looked like you," he said, voice a little gruff.

He eased out the cork on a sigh and wisp of vapor. When he poured, the color was a delicate pink, like the engraved blossoms. He raised his glass. "To UmbrellaWings, Kim. May it be a great success, a terrific outlet for your creativity, and bring you fun every workday."

"Thank you, Ty." She clicked her glass against his. "To Umbrella-Wings."

They both drank, then she said, "Mmm, delicious."

"It's not bad." In fact, he was too nervous to taste it. He pulled his chair around to face hers. "I was wondering . . ." Rather than leap in, he'd edge his way there. "Have you thought of basing the business here, rather than Hong Kong?"

A shadow crossed her face. "I told my parents Vancouver could be a great place to launch the company."

He liked that she'd had that idea, but he didn't like that shadow. "What did they say?"

"A flat-out no." Her mouth twisted. "I'm only twenty-four. How could I start up a business here, all by myself, without their help? Besides, they said they'd only provide financing if I went home."

He frowned. "Your business plan was designed to get institutional financing."

"I know, but now I won't have to."

And he'd bet her parents' financing would come with strings. Pointing that out probably wasn't the way to win her. "As for being alone here, I'd be happy to help you."

"Oh, Ty." Her dark eyes had a soft, vulnerable look. "I'm going to miss you so much."

His heart throbbed painfully. Whether or not it was the right time, he had to tell her. "You don't have to. You could stay. I want you to stay."

Her eyes widened for a long moment, then she gave a wry smile. "Marielle said the same thing. Ty, I value my friends here—I value you—but my family, my life, is in Hong Kong."

Damn it, he wasn't like Marielle, and he wasn't doing this right. "We're more than friends. I think we could be a lot more, if we gave ourselves a chance."

"But . . . I don't know what you mean. What kind of chance? You want a ranch wife who's like your mom, and I want—" She broke off.

"What? What do you want?"

She worried her lower lip. "The life I've always hoped for?" It came out as a question rather than a statement.

"And what's that?"

Now she sounded more certain. "To live in a big city, be close to my parents, be financially independent, pursue my art, marry a man I love, and have kids."

"Vancouver's a big city, and you're only a day from Hong Kong."

"But us dating, that would have to end, right? You want a ranch wife and—"

"Stop saying that," he snapped. Then he took a deep breath. "Sorry. Yeah, that's what I thought I wanted. But then I met you, dragonfly girl. You're not the perfect fit for the ranch, but I think you just might be the perfect fit for me."

"Wow," she breathed, her dark eyes dreamy. Then she frowned. "No, wait. How can you say that? We barely know each other."

"That's why I want you to stay in Vancouver. Let's spend more time together and see where things go. Life with you . . . well, it sure wouldn't be the life I'd imagined, but it'd be way more interesting."

Her lips twitched. "That's true." Then they straightened. "But you need an equal partner, someone who'll shovel manure and tote hay bales, and all that stuff."

That was what he'd always imagined, but now he shook his head. "I do that stuff perfectly well myself. What I need is someone who cares about the things I do. Who'll be patient with a damaged horse, who'll brighten every day just by being in my life. Someone fun and smart and sexy."

"You brighten my life too." Her eyes were as soft as her voice. "But asking me to change my life just because we have fun together . . ."

"It's more than that." Wasn't it more for her as well as for him? But he heard what she was saying, and knew he hadn't been totally honest. "Honey, you're the only woman I can imagine being with."

"Ty," she said wonderingly, her eyes huge and, he thought, vulnerable. "That's . . . amazing. I'm honored. You're an incredible man, but we do barely know each other."

"I know you well enough to love you." The words burst out and his heart jerked. He'd done it. Taken the leap; risked everything. Laid his heart on the line and given her the power to break it. To reject him, to abandon him.

In that moment, he realized his mom and Kim had been right. Yeah, he'd been scarred by what his birth mom did, and it had taken him until now—it had taken Kim—for him to have the guts to risk the same kind of pain.

Her eyes had gone even wider and her skin was pale.

He forged ahead. "I've never felt this way about anyone before. I know it's too early for promises about the future. I know it's a lot to ask, that you change your life for someone you've just met. But Kim, if you feel anywhere near the way I do, then give us a chance to know each other better. I think we do have a future, and it's going to be something very special."

"I, uh . . ." Now she was so pale, he was afraid she'd faint.

His own heart thudded so fast he might damned well hyperventilate and pass out too. Still, he managed to force out more words, a challenge that scared him more than lowering himself onto the back of the rankest bronc he'd ever ridden. "Tell me you don't think you could ever love me, and I'll back off."

He loved her. Kim stared at that strong, striking face, saw the affection and the fear in his hazel eyes. It was the fear that convinced her he really meant it.

Ty Ronan loved her. The rodeo hero, the man who'd given his

parents a second Ronan Ranch, the guy who had endless patience with wounded horses, loved her. For the first time in his life, he was in love, and it was with her.

Her heart was full to bursting with sweetness and pain. He wanted her to stay. Yes, of course she'd played with that idea, but she'd never considered it seriously. She couldn't. It wasn't possible. It would shatter her parents. Turn her life upside down.

He said he'd back off. All she had to do was tell him she couldn't love him.

She didn't love him. She'd always told herself she absolutely wouldn't love him.

His hands held hers, so strong, so warm. Like a lifeline, even as he'd tossed her into a turbulent sea of emotion.

"Kim? Are you okay?"

Okay? A hysterical giggle rose in her throat and she choked it back. She'd never been less okay. He loved her? How dare he say that? How dare he make her examine her own feelings more closely than she wanted to? How dare he make her realize that . . .

Oh damn it, she did love him.

No, that wasn't supposed to happen. She was supposed to be in control of her emotions. "Damn you." The words slipped out, barely audible. "Damn you, Ty Ronan."

Shock tightened his features. "Kim?"

"I love you too." This time her voice was decibels louder, almost a yell. "I didn't want to—I don't want to—but I do." She knew her expression was belligerent as she stared at him, but really, how dare he do this to her?

"I knew it," he said, which would have been kind of arrogant and obnoxious if the joy on his face hadn't been so clear.

Oh God, he was so adorable, and she did adore him. "I love you, Ty Ronan," she said wonderingly.

"I love you, Kim Chang." He grabbed her hand and surged to his feet. "And I want to make love to you, knowing how we feel about each other." With his other hand, he picked up the champagne bottle. "Come to bed with me, honey."

She remained seated, staring at their joined hands. She shouldn't do this. When she'd driven out, she'd told herself she wouldn't have sex with him, then she hadn't been able to resist. But she'd tried to tell herself it was just great sex, one final orgasm before she resigned herself to celibacy for a while. Pretending hadn't worked very well, and now it would be impossible. Now, she'd know they were truly making love.

And damn it, she wanted that. She couldn't stay in Vancouver; he was crazy to think things could work between the two of them. But to be with him one final time . . . To make love with Ty, knowing they loved each other. How could she not do that? In a way, the act—and the memory later—would break her heart, but in another way they'd fill her heart with a love she'd never experienced before.

She tightened her grip on his hand and rose. "Yes, let's go to bed."

He handed her the bottle, and she assumed he was going to pick up the flute glasses, but instead he scooped her up in his arms.

"What?" She gave a surprised laugh and wrapped her free arm around his neck. "Seriously? You're going to carry me all the way upstairs?"

He laughed too, sounding almost giddy. Could a tough cowboy really sound giddy? "Kim, you're light as a bird, graceful as a dragonfly, pretty as a butterfly."

Her eyes widened. Giddy *and* poetic? He really must be in love. A surge of intoxicating joy rushed through her. "I'm also a woman in love, who can't wait to get naked with you." She craned her head up to steal a kiss.

With his strong arms cradling her, he made short work of the stairs. He let her down beside the bed and, with eager, fumbling fingers, they undressed each other. He was erect already, and she was moist and needy.

Ty pulled the covers back. "Lie down, honey. I want to kiss every sweet inch of you."

And he did. He thrummed the sensitive spot where her neck met her shoulder, an erogenous zone no one had ever discovered before. He licked round and round her areola, then finally sucked her achingly tight nipple until the sweet pleasure shooting straight down to her sex made her climax. Startling her, he poured pink champagne into her navel, then lapped until it was gone, and kept on lapping until need built again. She shuddered, her hips twisted, and she begged, "Ty, I need to come. Make me come."

Then he moved down to her clit, swirling his tongue around it until her body clutched and spasmed in release. But he didn't stay at her pussy, he moved down her legs, trailing kisses across the tender skin of her inner thighs, exploring the creases at the backs of her knees, even lightly massaging and kissing her feet.

Every inch of her, he'd said, and he was making good on that promise.

And in the process, his tongue and lips claimed her, marked her. Branded her with sweet kisses that, invisible though they might be, she couldn't imagine ever forgetting.

He ended up back between her legs, his deft fingers and mouth exploring her with familiar intimacy, wringing another orgasm from her and leaving her limp with satisfaction.

Ty rose above her, so strong and handsome, her cowboy with his streaky hair tousled, his tanned cheeks flushed from giving her great sex. His erect cock brushed her thigh as he reached toward the bedside table for a condom.

"My turn," she said. "I get to kiss you all over." Yes, she wanted to. In a minute, when she managed to get some strength back into her body.

"Next time," he said. "I can't wait to be inside you."

He took a pillow and eased it under her lower back and butt, raising her lower body. Then, as she smiled at him and spread her legs in welcome, he slid inside. She took him easily, her body slick and primed from all those orgasms.

Almost, she'd have thought she was too blissed out to possibly get aroused again, but when Ty began to pump, her body quickly responded to those sensual strokes. Or was it to the sight of his perfect body, the glow of love in his hazel eyes, the mushy fullness in her heart? She reached up to loop her arms around his neck, to pull his head down to hers. "I love you, Ty." It felt so good, and so scary, to say those words.

"I love you, Kim." He kissed her, his tongue thrusting in time with his body's movements.

Her body pulsed around his cock, urging him on as he stroked that sweet spot inside her.

He angled his movements so that, when he was all the way in and their bodies met, his cock pressed against her clit.

They broke the kiss and just stared into each other's eyes as both their bodies tightened, tension built, the achy need to climax peaked. This felt more intimate than anything Kim had ever experienced. And when they crested, when climax rocked their bodies, they did it together, crying out in a male-female duet.

The aftershocks rippled for a long time as she clung to Ty, then finally he relaxed down to rest atop her, taking most of his weight on his legs and elbows. He smiled at her, said, "Yes. That's what it's like to make love with the person you love."

"Yes." It was wonderful, amazing, earth-shaking, and already she was starting to feel sad.

Ty rolled away, disposed of the condom, and reached for the champagne bottle. He hoisted it, said, "To us," took a swig then handed it to her.

Slowly, she sat up, reaching down to pull up the sheet and tucking it under her arms so it covered her breasts. Propped with pillows behind her back, she took the bottle. "To us." Her voice came out flat. The wine, when she took a sip, was still bubbly and delicious, and somehow that seemed wrong.

She handed the bottle back and wrapped her arms around herself as if, at this too-late date, she could protect her heart.

Ty sat on the side of the bed, facing her. "Is something wrong?"

"Wrong?" Tears threatened. The most wonderful, intimate, loving sex of her life, and she'd had it with a man she'd never see again. A man who didn't even seem to realize something was wrong. Annoyance mingled with pain. "Well, how about us? Like, we're all wrong for each other."

"What?" He shook his head, looking baffled. "We're right for each other. This was great, wasn't it? Making love like this?"

"Yes, of course. It was"—she swallowed hard—"incredible."

"Then what are you saying?"

"That it was, well, I guess I'd call it good-bye sex."

His jaw dropped. "Good-bye? What the hell are you talking about? I thought you'd decided to stay."

He'd thought that? Had she been unclear? "Ty, this couldn't possibly work out between us."

His jaw tightened. "Like hell it couldn't."

Seriously? He thought they were somehow going to ride off into the sunset together? Frustrated, but trying to sound reasonable, she pointed out, "If we were right for each other, it'd be easy. Everything would fit the way it's supposed to. Like it did for my parents, and for your dad and Betty."

He took a hearty slug of champagne. Sounding a little annoyed, he said, "Everything fit for you and Henry."

"Exactly! If things didn't work for Henry and me, how could they possibly work for us? Besides, I thought I was in love with him too. I mean, I *was* in love, and it fizzled out. That could happen with us."

Scowling, he asked, "You feel the same way for me as you did for Henry?"

That stopped her. "No," she admitted. "With you and me, it's more passionate. And stronger and deeper. And more exciting. With him, it was comfortable." Not that she didn't feel comfortable with Ty too, but it was—there was that word again—"different." "Henry and I didn't need to explain things. It was like he was already family." Right down to him agreeing with her parents about her career.

"But where's the fun, the stimulation, the challenge?"

Feeling disloyal to her good friend, she said, "I don't think Henry's into that kind of thing. Like, he's enjoyed living an independent life here, but there's no question in his mind that he'll go back to Hong Kong and take up the life his parents have always planned for him."

"That's okay if it's the life he wants."

"I don't think he's let himself consider any other possibility."

"Then you're not alike, you and him. You fought for the chance to follow your passion and create your own life."

He was right. Henry had thought she was disloyal to even contemplate it, yet Ty had helped her make that dream a reality.

Ty sighed, then handed the champagne bottle back to her. "Have a drink and relax, Kim."

Relax? Impossible. But she did unwind one arm from around her body and take a slug of wine.

"Think about the life you want to create," Ty said. "Imagine it. Can you see yourself basing UmbrellaWings at the ranch? Going into Vancouver for business. Traveling to Hong Kong whenever you want, and going other places too as the company expands. But living here, with me. Helping me with Drummer and the rescue horses that come after her."

Yes. No. She bit her lip.

"Going for rides," he continued. "Dipping your feet in the stream, having dinner on the porch in summer while we watch the sunset, or in front of the fireplace in winter. Catching up on each other's days, sharing ideas."

Yes, she could imagine it. But . . .

"Working as partners. Helping each other build our own businesses." A twinkle lit his eyes. "Hanging your art in the house. Making love wherever and whenever we want."

"As long as your parents don't drop in," she murmured. But yes, the picture he painted was a seductive one.

"You and me, curling up in bed together at night, and waking up together in the morning."

"At four o'clock?" she had to say. "Sorry, cowboy. Wake me up when you come in for breakfast."

"You bet. Unless you're already up doing yoga, or phoning New York or Hong Kong."

Damn him, she could imagine it. What an amazing life. It could work. She took another sip from the bottle, and bubbles sparkled and fizzed on her tongue. A romantic wine, and a romantic image. Her romantic side wanted to buy into this future, the rosy one he'd created in her mind. But she'd always been a realist . . .

She remembered the book club debating whether Marty and Dirk's relationship would last. The others had persuaded her it might—because she and Marty were very different women.

"Talk to me," Ty said.

Thirty-one

K im wasn't used to sharing her deepest emotions, her doubts, her hopes. Conversation with her parents was pragmatic, and even with her friends she didn't share her intimate feelings. She'd bet her cowboy wasn't big on talking about emotions either. But in a relationship—and she could no longer pretend this was just a *rumspringa* fling—you had to share.

Slowly, she started. "I love my parents. Hong Kong's always been my home. Vancouver's my second home and I love it, but I feel a strong tie to Hong Kong. And to my parents. I'm their only child, and it's a tight bond."

He leaned forward to rest a hand on her sheet-covered knee. "I know."

She appreciated that he didn't say that it was a short flight to Hong Kong. They both knew that, and knew that making flying visits now and then was very different from living with her parents. "Security is a big thing in my family. Financial and emotional. I've never been financially independent, and now I'm starting a business. My parents would help, with financing and by sharing their knowledge and experience."

"Your parents would help." His tone was noncommittal. "Would UmbrellaWings be your company, or theirs?"

"Mine."

"If you had a different opinion on something than they did, whose would rule?"

She frowned slightly. "Uh, I'm not sure."

"Two against one. And they have all that knowledge and experience."

"Yes, I'd listen seriously to their opinions."

"You listened to mine when we were working on the business plan. But you're the one who made the decisions. Would it be like that with your parents?"

It never had been, yet UmbrellaWings was her idea, her vision, her plan. She shrugged, unsure.

"Has it ever been like that, with them?"

"With the business plan. They didn't challenge anything I proposed."

"Except your idea of launching it in Vancouver."

"Well, yes, but for personal reasons. Because they want me home." She tossed her head. "Just like you're trying to influence me for personal reasons."

The corner of his mouth twisted ruefully. "I'm just saying, listen to us with your mind and your heart, and decide what *you* really want to do. That's what counts, honey."

A nice sentiment. A Western one. Where she came from, duty and family loyalty were what counted. His comment made her think of how strongly her parents would disapprove of him. If she said she'd fallen for a cowboy/rancher and was staying in Vancouver so she and Ty could decide if they had a future, her parents would be shattered. The ancestors would be shattered.

She sighed. "My parents have always loved and cherished me. I've never had to wonder if that love was real or would last." How could she jeopardize it on the fragile hope that things would work out between her and Ty?

"Then they should love you, whatever you do." His mouth twisted ruefully. "Even if they get pissed off for a while."

She knew he was thinking about his parents' reaction when he'd chosen rodeo over ranching.

He went on. "With parents and kids, you don't get to pick 'em. But you do pick the person you want to spend your life with. You meet someone, get to know them, feelings develop, you get married."

Or, in an arranged marriage, you got married then those other things were supposed to follow. Neither situation offered a guarantee of happily ever after. "That's a lovely idea. And if I'd met you when I moved here, we could have dated and seen where things went." If the relationship had become serious, she'd have told her parents and . . . She shook her head. No, she still couldn't imagine it working.

"Anyhow," she went on, "if I stayed now, with us barely knowing each other, we have no idea if things will work out." Anxiety ratcheted up inside her. Why couldn't he see what a huge, crazy thing he was proposing? "What if I'm not happy? I'd have shattered my family, risked my career, and where would I be? Stuck on a ranch in the middle of nowhere."

His shoulders straightened and his jaw tensed. "Being on Ronan Ranch isn't being *stuck*. And it's not in the middle of nowhere, it's in beautiful country, an hour from Vancouver, halfway to Hope. A day from Hong Kong, damn it."

"That's not what I mean!"

"I haven't a clue what you mean," he said coolly.

She wasn't entirely sure she did either, at this point. Gripping the sheet tightly to her chest, she said, "It's all too much. Every little bit of it—starting a new business, my relationship with my parents, you and me having such different homes and loyalties. Our relationship being so new, the fact that your parents really don't approve of me and that'd go double for mine, with you. If you made me stay here rather than—"

"Made you?" He looked outraged.

"I didn't mean it that way!" Did he have to misinterpret everything she said? It just proved they could never be a good match. "I meant," she explained, "my parents would hate it if I stayed here. There's absolutely no way they'd approve of us being together."

"Jesus, Kim, grow up!" He jerked to his feet and paced a couple of steps away, dragging his hands through his hair.

She glared at his naked back, so broad, strong, and forceful. "What's that supposed to mean?"

He spun and faced her. "Start thinking for yourself. Stop letting your parents rule your life."

Feeling vulnerable being naked in bed, she climbed out and started to dress. "Stop telling me what to do."

"Fuck."

Hurriedly, she pulled on the rest of her clothes. She hated raised voices, hated fighting. Her heart raced painfully and she tried to calm down. It was in her nature to want to please people, but she couldn't make both her parents and Ty happy. The best she could hope for, with him, was to make him understand. "Look, you of all people should understand family loyalty. You bought this ranch partly because of your parents. You felt guilty for running out on them when the first ranch was in trouble and—"

"I didn't run out on them, damn it!"

He kind of had, but rather than point that out, she kept quiet.

Apparently, he didn't feel the least bit vulnerable, being naked. He paced away, came back. "Okay," he said more calmly, "so I felt guilty. And I knew they hated their town jobs. But I wanted this ranch too, Kim. I didn't want to rodeo full-time forever. I wanted a home, land, the country. Horses and cattle. Down the road, a wife and kids. It's a way of life, a way I've always known and one I choose. Don't you get that?"

Though he loomed over her, she stood her ground, hands on her hips, and stared up at him. "Yes. My way of life's in Hong Kong." But even as she said the words, she knew that, in the midst of Hong Kong's color, bustle, noise, and pollution, she'd miss Ronan Ranch.

He stared back as if he was seeing her afresh. "Damn it. You said it before, more than once. I should have listened. Thank God we didn't take this relationship any further. You're just like Miranda."

"I am not!" How dare he say that? "I'd never run out on my child."

"How about on your husband? Or your boyfriend? What happens when the excitement wears off? When the stuff that seemed different and fascinating turns out to just be dust and chores?"

Dust and chores? She knew that wasn't how he saw Ronan Ranch. Nor would she ever see it that way. Not with the grandeur of the mountains, the graceful deer, wounded horses to heal, flowers and fresh fruit and crisp streams and the freshest air she'd ever breathed. Still, it wasn't her home, and would never be. She wouldn't run out on it, because she'd never choose it in the first place.

"Run home, Kim," he said tiredly, as if he'd read her mind. "Run back to Hong Kong and your parents. You say it's about loyalty to them. Seems to me it's cowardice. You don't have the guts to figure out what you want and go for it, when the going's hard."

"I do." She gazed at him, the man she'd finally admitted she loved. "The going's hard now, Ty. I love you and I don't want to hurt you. But I believe that what I'm doing is right."

"Then maybe it is. For both of us. But when you're back home, think about the symbolism of those wings you love so much."

"The symbolism?"

"Wings are about flight. About soaring high and free, wherever you want to go. Can you do that when you're with your parents? Can you take UmbrellaWings wherever you want it to go? Can you fall in love and marry the man you choose? Or will they clip your wings? Will you forever be painting wings, and never taking flight yourself?"

Ooh! He would never, ever understand. He didn't even want to try. He said he loved her, but all he wanted was to slot her neatly into his comfy little life. "You have a lot of nerve, saying that," she snapped. "If I stayed here, all the risk would be on me. You wouldn't be risking one thing! If you and I broke up, you'd still have your home, your business, your family."

He was impossible. What had she been thinking, even starting up with him? That idiotic book had bewitched her, had made her abandon her normal common sense. Now, her heart ached and tears burned behind her eyes.

"This is crazy," he said, glaring at her. "What were we thinking?"

"Exactly!" She spun on her heel. "Have a nice life," she tossed bitterly over her shoulder.

"Count on it." She'd never heard a man snarl before, but that was definitely what he did.

Fierce energy carried her down the stairs and out to her car, but once inside her hand trembled as she tried to fit the key into the ignition. Tears blurred her vision, but she blinked them away. If this was love, then love sucked. She was never going to fall in love again.

She made it down the ranch road, unlatched the gate, drove through, then got out and latched it again. Resting her arms on the weathered wooden top rail, she stared back at Ronan Ranch, with black cattle grazing in one field and horses frolicking in another.

Then she put her face down on her crossed hands and let the tears flow.

* * *

Monday afternoon, Kim trudged to book club. Her eyes burned from tears, shed and unshed.

Marielle had chosen The Black Frog, near the steam clock in Gastown. Arriving late, Kim found the others wrangling over appetizers. Consulted, she said, "Whatever." It wasn't like she had an appetite.

Redheaded George was vibrant in a silk jersey blouse patterned in shades of copper. Would Kim have time to fly back for her and Woody's wedding? Would she be invited? Out of sight, out of mind. She was just a member of a book club, only starting to become a friend.

Marielle, in a figure-hugging purple tee over black leggings, looked gorgeous as always with her smooth coffee-colored skin, mass of curly dark hair, and flashing eyes. The woman who lived life as an ongoing *rumspringa*. Kim loved her generous spirit and joie de vivre. Would Marielle ever settle on one drink, one job, one man, or would she always be happy to keep sampling?

Lily, wearing a dove gray jacket and pants with an elegantly simple white top, had a light tan which set off her fair hair. But rather than appearing relaxed and end-of-summery, she looked tired. These days, she always looked tired. Would Kim ever find out what was going on with Lily? Did it have to do with her marriage?

"Lily, what does your husband do?" she found herself asking.

Three faces turned toward her with surprised expressions.

She flushed, feeling pushy. But if she didn't find out now, she never would.

"Dax is a helicopter pilot," Lily said slowly. "A bush pilot." At last week's book club, she'd said it could be hard to maintain a relationship when the partners had really different careers. Was that from personal experience?

"Wow," Marielle said. "I'd never have guessed. A family practice doctor and a bush pilot. That's another attraction of opposites, like Woody and George."

And me and Ty. "You've been married how long?"

"Ten years. I was twenty-two."

"Younger than I am now," Kim said.

Lily pressed her lips together, then released them. "This is a book club. We should decide on the next book."

Kim was still curious, but couldn't be pushy enough to persist.

Their drinks arrived, and as the waitress served them, Kim reached under the table for the large bag she'd brought with her. From it, she took three carefully wrapped cylinders. Silently, she handed one to each woman.

Thirty-two

These are either paintings or umbrellas," George guessed.

As a foretaste of what UmbrellaWings might do, Kim had bought parasols made of rice paper and bamboo, and painted them.

Marielle was already ripping the paper off hers. She pulled out the parasol and promptly slid it open and squealed with pleasure. Hers was vivid yellow, decorated with a cloud of bright butterflies in all shades of orange, accented with black and a touch of purple. "This is gorgeous!" She glanced at the tag Kim had made. "Based on the Common Buckeye butterfly."

George went next. "Oh my!" On a pale peach background, dragonflies with iridescent green wings took flight. "Kim, it's beautiful." She read the tag. "Downy Emerald dragonfly."

Lily opened her gift. On a creamy yellow background, Kim had painted fanciful butterflies with wings in delicate shades of blue and green, veined in gold. She'd wanted to compliment Lily's delicate coloring, with her pale wheat-colored hair and striking light blue eyes, but was afraid the effect might be too feminine and romantic for Lily's taste. Still, the pleasure on the doctor's face appeared genuine. "Thanks so much, Kim." She studied the tag. "Queen Alexandra's Birdwing butterfly. Kim, these tags are a terrific idea."

"Ty thought of it."

"Smart man," George said. "What did we do to deserve the gifts?"

Kim swallowed hard. "I'm going home on Wednesday."

A mingled chorus of moans and questions greeted her announcement.

"Long story short, my parents approved my business plan and they've offered financing. I'm going home to get things started."

"Congratulations, Kim," Lily said. "But we're sorry you're leaving so soon. Or at all, actually." The other two nodded agreement.

"Me too." For a woman who didn't cry, tears were rising to Kim's eyes surprisingly often these days. She took a slug of ale. "But I'm excited to get going with UmbrellaWings."

"You don't sound excited," George said softly.

"I am, but it's hard leaving Vancouver, the friends I've made. I'll miss you all."

"You can't go," Marielle said. "We'll kidnap you and keep you here."

Kim managed to smile. "Thanks. I wish there were two of me, so one could stay."

"What about Ty?" George asked.

She shrugged and tried to sound offhand. "Easy come, easy go. My Chinese *rumspringa*'s over. In Hong Kong, my parents will keep an eagle eye on my dating life."

"You can't give in to all that old-fashioned crap," Marielle said.

"I love my parents, and respect them."

"And clearly they love you," Lily said. "But they should respect you too. I know different cultures have different customs and values, but in today's world, you should have free choice, Kim."

"Oh, they won't force me into an arranged marriage. We already had that discussion. But they want me to marry someone I'm compatible with, someone who'll fit into the family. That gives the marriage the best chance of success, doesn't it?"

"Yes." George glanced up from the green onion cake she was cutting. "But true compatibility, not just superficial things. Like, in the beginning, Woody and I thought we had nothing in common except lust. But when we got to know each other, we realized we're perfect together. Our core values are the same, but we're different enough to challenge each other and keep life interesting."

"And you have to keep life interesting," the irrepressible Marielle tossed out.

"I think you made a wise decision, Kim," Lily said. "Are you sure you're all right with it?"

Kim squeezed her eyes shut against another hot burn of tears. She wasn't the kind of woman to air her angst in public. In fact, until now, she'd never had any serious angst.

A warm hand touched hers and George said, "You're not, are you?"

Eyes still shut, Kim shook her head. Whether it was the illusion of privacy given by hiding behind her closed eyelids, or the warmth in George's voice and touch, she found herself revealing the truth. "I'm not. I love him. And he l-loves m-me." Her voice broke and tears escaped to slide down her cheeks.

Georgia squeezed her hand. "I'm sorry, but I don't understand. If you love each other, what's the problem?"

Kim took a deep breath then opened her eyes and flicked at the tears on her cheeks. "It couldn't work. It's all too much." She stared into George's concerned golden brown eyes. "Imagine if you and Woody had just met, and suddenly he was traded to a team in Florida. Your career's here, your mom's here, your friends are here. Would you go with him?"

"No, but I wouldn't break up with him. We could try a long-distance relationship."

"What if your mom hated him and—"

"Your mother's met Ty?" George broke in.

"No, of course not. She's never even heard of him. But she and

Dad would hate him. He's not Chinese and he doesn't live in Hong Kong. They'd think he's totally wrong for me."

Marielle, who'd been flipping through her cell phone, lifted her head. "What do *you* think, Kim? It's your life. I could say you'd be crazy to settle down with any guy, but that's me. That's how I am. You, you've always said you want the long-term thing. I just hunted back through e-mails from when we were reading Lady Emma. This is what you said."

She read from her screen. "'I'm happy to read about Emma's raunchy adventures. LOL. But for me, I want the whole package: sex, caring, and commitment.'" She looked up. "Is Ty the kind of guy who believes in that stuff?"

Kim nodded. "Yes, but—"

"You didn't say Chinese," Marielle interrupted, "or that he had to live in Hong Kong. You said sex, caring, commitment."

"The rest went without saying."

"Does Ty feel the way you do," George asked. "That your relationship could never work?"

"If he had any brains, he would," Kim groused. "No, he had to go and make things harder by asking me to stay."

"Stay?" Marielle asked. "As in, like, a proposal?"

"God, no, he's not that stupid. Just a 'why don't you stay and let's see where things go' kind of thing. Which," she said grimly, "involves absolutely no risk to him, but it could mess up Umbrella-Wings for me, not to mention the effect on my parents. They'd be shattered. I can't even imagine what they'd do."

"Cut you out of their lives?" George asked. "Surely not. You're their only child."

"Okay, I don't think they'd disown me. But they'd be devastated. I couldn't do that to them."

"You'd rather have them control your life?" Marielle asked.

Kim wanted to say that it wasn't like that. Yet it kind of was. Ty had said her parents would clip her wings. That she'd end up always painting wings, never flying herself. She'd accused him of trying to control her too, but really, she'd been unfair.

He was right about her parents. Their love led them to try to control her life, to protect her. They'd guilt her into not flying at all, or only doing it on a short, safe tether, in a direction they approved of. But Ty wasn't like that. Yes, he wanted to be with her, but he encouraged her to be independent. He liked that they were different and didn't always agree. He'd support and help her, but he'd encourage her to fly high and free.

Ty believed she was—or at least could be—a strong woman. To her parents, she'd always be the child they wanted to shelter and guide.

Yet she loved her parents. She owed them so much. Slowly, she said, "My parents have already done something huge for me, not making me join Chang Property Management." And the offer to stay involved with CPM had been Kim's, not something forced on her by her parents. "And in helping me with UmbrellaWings."

"Neither of which gives them the right to own the rest of your life," George said quietly.

Why did no one understand? If she told Henry about her situation, he'd get it immediately. Of course, he'd say she should never have gone out with Ty in the first place, and he'd be right.

Or would he? Hadn't she broken up with Henry because he was so conventional?

Could she honestly wish she'd never met Ty Ronan?

"Ask yourself this," George said. "Can you imagine your life without Ty?"

"Yes, of course." And she could. It would be the life she'd always dreamed of. But when she'd lain in bed in her tiny room in Hong Kong, dreaming those dreams, she'd imagined not only having her own artistic business but finding the perfect man. Now, how could she possibly meet a man, Chinese or not, who could measure up to Ty? A man she could love more than she loved Ty?

Lily put down her martini glass so hard it clacked against the wooden table. "Kim may well be right. Sex, caring, and commitment are great, but you have to be practical. If two people are very different, and if there are factors working against them—like parental disapproval or whatever—it can be hard to make things work."

Kim gazed at her, the doctor who dressed in classy clothes and drank in classy lounges, who'd been married for ten years to a helicopter pilot. Were they having trouble making things work?

"But not impossible," George said. "If people are flexible and willing to work hard at it, why shouldn't it work? Kim, I'm not saying your life wouldn't be complicated, but it could be rewarding too."

Kim had been raised to believe it took hard work, every day, to achieve what you wanted. Hard work had never scared her. As for flexible . . . Well, she was when it came to yoga. Did that count?

She thought of Ty, the man who often rose at four so he could do everything that needed to be done. How did he feel about hard work when it came to relationships? And could he, the guy who'd admitted to butting heads with his dad, be flexible?

She valued security; she'd never been a risk-taker. Ever since she met Ty, he'd basically dared her to take one risk after another. Sex under the stars had been fun. But now, he was asking so much more.

If she stayed, she'd be taking huge risks. Her parents might never forgive her. Her business might fail. She and Ty might not work out, and she'd be heartbroken and alone. How could she fly, if her heart was broken?

Thirty-three

It had been a long weekend, the rodeo running through Monday. Ty spent the whole time trying not to remember that Kim should have been there with him. That Kim had chosen Hong Kong and her parents over him. He arrived home around midnight, tended to Sand, and then fell into bed, where sheer exhaustion sent him to sleep.

Tuesday morning, he rose at five, glad he never needed much sleep, and went down to ranch headquarters to catch up. When he stepped through the door, he stopped dead. He'd asked his mom to drop by the gallery in Vancouver and pick up the Sun Flower painting the next time she went into town. There it hung now, across from the desk. One day, when he looked at it, maybe it would make him feel happy. Today wasn't that day. He put his head down and got to work.

It must've been an hour or two later when the sound of boots on the floor and the smell of coffee had him lifting his head. "Mornin'," he greeted his father, gratefully taking the insulated coffee mug he handed over. "Thanks."

"Saw the light on." His dad settled into a chair, his own mug in hand, and gestured toward the painting. "See your mom picked that up? I like it."

"Yeah."

"She took that sketch Kim gave us in for framing. Wants to hang it in the living room."

Great. He'd have reminders of Kim in the ranch office and his parents' place. Not to mention his own house, where he couldn't even work out in the gym without thinking of her.

"Have bad luck at the rodeo this weekend?" his dad asked.

"Mixed. I got a rotten draw in the bronc riding, but Sand and I won tie-down roping."

"Good stuff, son. And you got Rambler up to TJ Cousins okay?"

"Yeah. Had a good visit with her and her family."

They drank coffee in silence. Then his father said, "So this has to do with Kim."

"What? What are you talking about?"

"Your mood."

"I don't have a freaking *mood*."

His dad nodded. "Yeah, you do. What happened? You know it'll go easier if you tell me first. I can ask Betty to lay off."

"Like that ever works." Ty almost smiled. Then he shrugged. "No big deal. I'm just not happy about Kim going back to Hong Kong."

"Sorry, but better to find out before you got in too deep the way I did."

"I guess." He wasn't about to admit that he'd gone and fallen in love with Kim. But he did ask, "When she left—Miranda—did you try to stop her?"

"Hell, yeah. I wasn't gonna let your mother walk out on you if I could stop her."

"Or on you either, right?"

Brand Ronan said gruffly, "Felt like she walked away with my heart and I'd never get it back."

Yeah, that was the feeling.

"Miranda was immature," his dad went on. "I didn't see it at the time. Hell, we both were. She was so glamorous and exciting compared to the girls I'd grown up with. I was stupid. It's not the surface that counts, it's the substance." A complacent smile curved his lips. "If a man's lucky, he can find substance in a pretty package, though. Best thing that ever happened to you and me was when Betty came into our lives."

Ty nodded. "In the end, Miranda did us a favor."

"Guess so." He took another long swallow of coffee. "Like Kim's done you a favor, leaving before things went any further."

Ty drank coffee too, hoping the caffeine would help him make sense of things. His dragonfly girl was glamorous and exciting all right, but she was substance, through and through. Even Distant Drummer recognized that. "A part of me wishes things would've worked out."

"If wishes were horses." The sentiment had been repeated many times in their household.

"I hear you."

His dad rose. "Come over to the house for breakfast?"

"Not today."

"See you later then." He rested his hand on Ty's shoulder for a moment before leaving.

After he'd gone, that expression repeated itself in Ty's head. *If wishes were horses, beggars would ride.* And Kim would want exactly what Ty did: to live with him here at Ronan Ranch while she built up her business and explored her art.

What the saying meant was that you didn't get what you wanted unless you busted your butt to make it happen. He'd grown up with that philosophy, and following it almost always worked. And if he didn't bust his butt, he generally didn't get much of anything. The only thing that had come easy for him was the buckle bunnies. Surface, not substance.

Kim had accused him of trying to control her. He didn't think he'd done that. He wanted her to be free, to have whatever kind of life she wanted. Was it pride and stubbornness that made him think that, if she was honest with herself, she'd choose a life with him? That she could fly when she was with him?

He'd laid his heart on the line for Kim and she'd trampled it. He'd told her he loved her, he'd asked her to stay, and she'd rejected him. She said she loved him, but he didn't believe her. She'd abandoned him just the way his birth mother had.

She'd accused him of asking her to take all the risks. Didn't she know he'd risked his heart? What higher risk was there?

Maybe none, but he'd asked her to risk other things too. Her career, which might flourish better with her parents' support in Hong Kong. If UmbrellaWings was anywhere near as important to her as Ronan Ranch was to him . . .

For him, it wasn't just the ranch, his horses, it was also his parents, even his staff like Dusty, the battered old bull rider, and those neighborhood kids who'd been dealt a rough hand. Ronan Ranch was family and a way of life for him.

Kim's parents and her life in Hong Kong were all of that for her.

For the first time, he truly glimpsed what he'd asked her to risk. All on the gamble that their fresh new love would grow into what he imagined it could be: something strong and fine and everlasting.

Thirty-four

Wednesday morning, in a taxi on the way to Vancouver airport, Kim wanted the next eighteen hours to be over. The airport rituals and waiting time, the fourteen-hour flight, the taxi to Chang Property Management, and the talk—THE TALK—with her parents.

She was tired, nervous, excited, determined. Today, her parents would have to recognize she was an independent adult. Mentally, she reviewed and refined the points she would make.

First and foremost, she loved her parents dearly and always would. She appreciated everything they'd done for her, and she admired and respected them. She wanted to see them as often as possible and she hoped they would do her the honor of allowing her to be on the board of CPM. Perhaps she could even have a role in the Vancouver operation. Because she hoped—no, she *intended*—to return to Vancouver to live. Perhaps, even, to Ronan Ranch.

Yes, she would tell them about Ty. She would tell them she'd fallen in love with a man any parents should be thrilled with: hardworking, responsible, successful, loyal, and very close to his own parents. She would dare them—no, challenge them—no, she would *humbly submit* that they could not find a better man for her among their friends and colleagues in Hong Kong. Even if they believed they could, it was her heart that would make the decision.

She would start UmbrellaWings in Vancouver. If they withdrew their offer of financial support, she would understand completely and seek financing, as outlined in her business plan. She hoped that she could ask their advice, as she respected their knowledge, but all business decisions would be hers.

Kim was young, but thanks in large part to the way they raised her and the responsibilities they'd given her, she was an adult. It was time they stopped sheltering her. They had been young too, when they came to Hong Kong to begin a new life together and start their own business.

She would invest her brain, her heart, and her soul in her new relationship and her new business. Yes, both ventures were full of risk and insecurity, but she was strong and flexible enough to embrace insecurity and believe in her own abilities. She would make mistakes, but they'd be her mistakes and she'd learn from them.

"Which airline?" The taxi driver's voice broke into her rehearsal.

"Cathay Pacific."

She'd exchanged the one-way ticket for a return flight coming back on Saturday.

It was too much to hope that her parents would see her side of things in the beginning, but she would persist. Water against stone; she hoped to wear them down. She'd show love, patience, and determination until, even if they didn't approve, they at least said they wouldn't disown her. If worst came to worst and they issued an ultimatum, she would hate it, but she would still leave Hong Kong, and persist from a distance.

As the driver parked, she pulled out money to pay him. Whatever happened with her parents, she would be back in this airport on Saturday.

Then she'd drive out to Ronan Ranch—the ranch halfway to Hope—and tell Ty that she chose him. That she loved him and she wanted to take their relationship to all the wonderful places it might go.

The driver took her carry-on from the trunk. She wheeled it into the airport and, familiar with the layout, headed automatically for the Cathay Pacific counter.

"Kim." A male voice spoke from behind her.

Startled, she turned. "Ty!"

The tall, rangy cowboy peeled himself away from the wall he'd been leaning against and walked toward her. He looked heartbreakingly handsome in his boots and Resistol hat, black jeans, and white, western-style shirt.

Her skin tingled with sensual awareness, a visceral surge of lust heated her blood, and her heart filled so full with love she was surprised its rapid beat wasn't audible. Ty was here. But why? Was this good? Bad?

Had he come to say good-bye? What if he'd changed his mind about loving her, and was happy she was leaving? Should she tell him that she planned to come back? Her brain was so jumbled with questions she could barely manage to ask, "What are you doing here?"

"You told me what flight you were on. Remember?"

"No! That's not what I mean." Did he have to be so exasperating? "Why? Why did you come?"

"Ah. Well, I came to tell you I'm a hardheaded arrogant bastard."

That was good, wasn't it? "Uh . . . That's not exactly the way I see you," she said cautiously.

Ty peeled her hand off the grip of the carry-on and took both her hands in his. Why did everything always seem to settle when he did that, like nothing could go too horribly wrong?

"I love you, Kim, and I don't want to lose you."

Breath whooshed out of her with relief. She hadn't known she was holding it. "I feel the same way. That's why—"

"Shh. Let me say my piece, honey."

It was going to be okay. Surely it was going to be okay. And come to think of it, she very much wanted to hear his piece. "Okay."

"You were right. I was asking you to take all the risks. That's not fair. That's not how I want this relationship to be. We're equals, you and me. All the way. We need to talk about what we both want, and work things out together."

He looked so serious and totally earnest. "Like, maybe I need to look at business opportunities in Hong Kong. Dad and Mom, Dusty and the gang, they can run Ronan Ranch for the most part, with me flying back now and then, consulting by phone and e-mail, and—"

"No, Ty," she broke in, heart melting, eyes tearing. "You belong at the ranch."

He shook his head. "I belong with you. Don't fly out of my life, dragonfly girl."

Misty-eyed, she smiled. "Take a look." She took the e-ticket from the side pocket of her shoulder bag and handed it over. "It's a return ticket. I'm going to tell my parents I love them, but it's time for me to live my own life."

Finally, a smile touched Ty's lips. "Does that life include me?"

"You're the best part. I'm going to tell my parents about us. They'll take it hard, but I'll persist. They've always said what they want most is for me to be happy. You, Ty, make me happy."

She'd barely said the last word when he let go of her hands, pulled her close, and kissed her.

Happy. Oh, yes, this was what happy felt like. Their lips and tongues spoke messages of passion, sharing, and love. Heat rippled through her and she felt both boneless and strong in his embrace. Their bodies were so different, his so big and muscular, hers so petite and lithe, yet they fit together perfectly. It was, she thought dazedly as they surfaced from the kiss, the way their personalities and lifestyles were too. Very different, and yet they really could fit perfectly.

"Time to check in," Ty said, taking her hand and reaching for the handle of her carry-on.

"I hate to leave you. But I'll be back soon. I'll e-mail you my flight information. Oh, there's one small wrinkle. I'd given notice on my apartment, and they've already rented it. But I'm sure I'll find another. My family does, after all, own that building and another one, so—"

"Come stay at the ranch."

Her heart said yes, but she wondered aloud, "Are we moving too fast?"

He shook his head. "Nope."

Nope. One little word. And he was right. Exhilaration made her want to laugh, to have him spin her, to make an utter spectacle of themselves right here in the middle of Vancouver airport. But of course a well-brought-up Chinese woman like her would never do that.

Coming back to her senses, she realized Ty had bypassed the automated check-in machine. She tugged his hand. "I already checked in online. I can use the machine."

"But I can't. I need to buy a ticket."

She stopped dead and stared up at him. "What?"

"I'm coming with you."

Wow. Just wow. Except . . . "Ty, that's sweet, but this is about me being independent. I have to do it on my own."

He gazed deep into her eyes. "I get that. You and your parents need time alone when you tell them. But then I want to meet them. I know I'm not their first choice of what they want for you, but I'm a decent, hardworking guy, and I love you. I want them to know that. Then maybe they won't worry quite so much."

Her heart turned to mush, knowing that he understood how important her parents were to her. "I like that idea. And just so you know, you're my first choice of what I want for me."

He started to kiss her again, but reality sank in and she said, "No, wait, you can't come. You need your passport."

She spoke the last words just as a woman behind them said dryly, "Your turn, lovebirds, if you're really going."

Ty flashed her his charming smile. "We are."

He stepped forward to a check-in agent, hauling his passport out of his pocket. To Kim, he said, "If you said you still loved me, even after I'd been such a jerk, no way was I going to let you get away again." Then, to the agent, "Tell me there's a seat on the flight to Hong Kong."

Kim handed over her e-ticket. "This flight," she said, just in case there was another.

The attractive middle-aged Chinese woman in her red uniform smiled as she clicked keys. "You're in luck, sir."

"Believe me, I know that." He put his arm around Kim's shoulders, then favored the agent with that sexy, charming grin. "Bet you can fix things so Kim and I are sitting together."

She laughed. "How did you know I'm a romantic at heart? I've already done it." Then she said, "Ms. Chang, your automated check-in said no bags to check?"

"That's right."

"How about you, sir?"

"Not a one." He raised his Resistol. "I travel light."

Kim teased, "Are you planning to wear that when you meet my parents?"

"Nah." Eyes gleaming with mischief, he plunked the hat on her head. "I was kind of figuring you might."

She smiled up at him from under the brim. "I love you, cowboy."

"And I love you, dragonfly girl." Then he bent to kiss her again.

Deep in her heart, she felt the certainty that, through hard work, determination, and the power of love, everything was going to work out perfectly.

ABOUT THE AUTHOR

Savanna Fox is the new pen name for Susan Lyons, who also writes as Susan Fox. *Publishers Weekly* refers to her writing as "emotionally compelling, sexy contemporary romance."

Writing as Susan Lyons and Susan Fox, her books have won the Gayle Wilson Award of Excellence, the Book Buyers Best, the Booksellers Best, the Aspen Gold, the Golden Quill, the Write Touch, the More Than Magic, the Lories, the Beacon, and the Laurel Wreath, and she has been nominated for the RT Reviewers Choice Award. Her book *Sex Drive* was a *Cosmopolitan* Red-Hot Read.

Savanna/Susan is a Pacific Northwester with homes in Vancouver and Victoria, British Columbia. She has degrees in law and psychology, and has had a variety of careers, including perennial student, computer consultant, and legal editor. Fiction writer is by far her favorite, giving her an outlet to demonstrate her belief in the power of love, friendship, and a sense of humor.

Visit her website at www.savannafox.com for excerpts, discussion guides, behind-the-scenes notes, recipes, giveaways, and more. She loves to hear from readers and can be contacted through her website.